Changeling Press LLC
ChangelingPress.com

And Call Me (Duet)
Friends to Lovers Medical Romance
Will Okati

And Call Me (Duet)
Friends to Lovers Medical Romance
Will Okati

ISBN: 978-1-60521-959-2
Second Edition

Publisher:
Changeling Press LLC
315 N. Centre St.
Martinsburg, WV 25404
ChangelingPress.com

Printed in the U.S.A.

Anthology Editor: Karen Williams
Cover Artist: Bryan Keller

The individual stories in this anthology have been previously released in E-Book format.

Table of Contents

And Call Me in the Morning.................................4

    Chapter One 5

    Chapter Two..17

    Chapter Three 35

    Chapter Four 48

    Chapter Five 63

    Chapter Six 79

    Chapter Seven 99

    Chapter Eight 117

    Chapter Nine...131

    Chapter Ten..147

    Chapter Eleven..158

    Chapter Twelve...179

    Chapter Thirteen...191

    Chapter Fourteen..204

    Epilogue 224

And Call Me in the Evening................................229

    Chapter One 230

    Chapter Two..246

    Chapter Three 263

    Chapter Four 277

    Chapter Five 291

    Chapter Six 306

    Chapter Seven 320

    Chapter Eight 335

    Chapter Nine...349

    Chapter Ten..359

    Chapter Eleven..374

    Epilogue 386

Will Okati...399

Changeling Press E-Books.................................400

And Call Me in the Morning
A Friends to Lovers Medical Romance
Will Okati

Take two, and call me in the morning.

Eli and Zane. Colleagues at work and close friends, though on the surface it's an unexpected friendship between an odd couple. While Zane took the "high school to college to med school" track, medicine is Eli's second career and the best choice he ever made. He has work that he loves, an extended second family of colleagues and friends, and Zane.

So why does everyone make such a big deal about the pair of them?

Yes, they spend a lot of time together. It doesn't mean they're a real couple. When teased about it one too many times by their colleagues, Zane challenges Eli to set the record straight with a kiss to prove there's absolutely no chemistry between them.

Neither expected a spark to ignite between them. More than a spark. Desire. Passion.

Zane wants to try getting up close and personal again to see if it was a one-time fluke or something more. Eli thinks he's too old to jump the fence now, but he can't say no to Zane and he doesn't want to.

Truth be told, Eli's not so sure they can set the record straight after all.

Chapter One

Falling in love with his closest friend had never been something Eli planned to do with his life. Wasn't as if he could have stopped it, though.

Sometimes love just happened.

Even if it took him a while to figure that out.

* * *

"There you are." Zane laid down the heavy, ivory-colored menu he'd been idly flipping through as Eli approached, making his way through the maze of tables at their regular bistro. "I almost thought you weren't going to make it."

Eli sat with a *thump*, running his hand through his dark brown hair, cut short but still quite capable of standing on end. He grimaced when he discovered he'd forgotten his stethoscope, still wound around his neck.

"Long night?" Zane asked, already waving their server over with the universal "coffee here" gesture.

Eli relaxed and let Zane take care of him. Some days, a man truly appreciated a friend who'd have his back when he needed a rock to shore up against. "Long, long night. Three-car pileup at an intersection. I didn't want to leave before everyone was stable."

"That's my boy." Zane shifted out of the way to let their server pour Eli's cup. She was a pretty thing, well packed into her curves -- curves that she offered not so subtly for display.

Zane ignored them. He'd taken Eli's face in his hands and begun to assess him for signs of exhaustion. The guy had good hands, firm and dry and dexterous. They felt nice and cool against Eli's skin. He let Eli go with a light slap to the cheek. "Your eyes look like burned holes in a blanket. You should go home and get some rest."

"Like I'd miss a chance at a fine, elegant brunch?" Eli rolled his eyes.

"Heaven forbid." Zane gave good deadpan. "Jeez. This is the kind of place I fear running into my family." Just how moneyed Zane's family was, Eli didn't know. Coming from an ivory tower was a sore spot for Zane, who much preferred the life he'd chosen in a grittier world.

Eli segued to spare Zane any discomfort. What were friends for, right? "You were on last night too. How'd you manage to get away in time for a shower and a sharp morning suit?"

"Questions, questions." The corners of Zane's eyes crinkled when he smiled. "Unlike some of us, I leave when my shift's done."

"Since when? You're as much of a workaholic as I am, if not more. A hospitalist's work is never done, especially at Immaculate Grace. What was I thinking when I chose that as a career, anyway?"

"That you're a glutton for punishment?"

"True enough." Eli drank deeply of his coffee, almost moaning in appreciation. The influx of better-than-decent caffeine stimulated his brain. "Before I forget, I got those concert tickets you begged me for. Two, even." He patted his dark brown shirt pocket. Plain clothes for a plain man, built tough to last, Chicago born and bred for forty-three years.

Unlike Zane, who looked as fresh as a daisy in a casual white linen jacket, pale violet button-down, and pressed slacks. Pretty as a picture, coming across as maybe five years younger than his forty-one. Zane brightened and made a grab. "Good seats?"

"I'm told they're the best. Ah-ah-ah." Eli tapped his pocket again. "I also got advance tickets for a Cubs game when the season starts. Fair is fair. I try not to fall asleep during the chorale or chamber music or whatever you want to call it, and you endure beer, umpire heckling, and giant foam fingers."

"Done and done. You drive a hard bargain." Zane clinked coffee cups with Eli. He hadn't looked away once, but Eli liked that about Zane. When he gave you his full attention, nothing else seemed to matter to him. All part of the Zane package, and it made him the best doctor Eli had known. "I --" He stopped, interrupted by the chiming of his pager. When he checked the number, he grimaced. "Damn. Sorry, I've got to take this. Keep that warm for me."

"What did I tell you? Workaholic. Hey! Do not let them talk you into coming back to the hospital today."

Zane waved backward at Eli as he walked off. Eli watched him go, amused.

A different server, young and male, approached with the coffeepot. Eli suspected the waitress had gotten fed up with flirting and traded off. Fine by him. This kid had a good eye for refills. He held his cup up. "Keep it coming, but we're not ordering yet. Still waiting for two."

And they'd better hurry, if they know what's good for them.

Eli wasn't a huge fan of this bistro. Without Zane there to provide a buffer, the place was too rich for his blood. Made him feel like any second someone with a pedigree was going to jump out from behind a column and ask him what a working-class stiff like him thought he was doing here.

"Of course, sir. I'm sorry if I'm being rude," the waiter said, deftly pouring. "If I could ask -- you two make such a handsome couple. How long have you been together?"

Not this again. Eli didn't even have to ask what the kid meant. Wasn't the first time he and Zane had been mistaken for a couple, and he'd bet his hard-earned MD it wouldn't be the last. "Sorry to burst your bubble, but we're not."

The waiter's coffeepot slipped. "You're not -- oh. Oh my God, I'm so sorry."

"No problem." Eli waved him off before the kid could apologize again. He'd almost gotten used to the assumption. Whatever people saw in Zane and him, he had no idea. Felt like being on the shooting range sometimes, as many assumptions made about them as they had to dodge. Once corrected, strangers were mostly good about apologizing and moving on.

Friends of theirs, on the other hand, were not so accommodating.

"We made it!" Diana and Holly -- also doctors, both familiar faces at Immaculate Heart -- swarmed the table in a cloud of perfume and joie de vivre. With them, more hesitantly, came a fresh-faced kid Eli vaguely recognized as an intern. The ladies dove into the fresh baguettes and cherry jam their new waiter discreetly slid onto the table before exiting at speed, stage left.

Eli stayed well back from the carnage. Friends they might be, but Holly and Diana -- well, it was best to stay on your toes around them. "Who's the boy toy?"

Holly, a pale, Nordic-type blonde, swatted Eli's arm. "Be nice. Taye's been at work for almost twenty-four hours. He deserved a break, so we brought him along to give him a treat."

Eli didn't doubt she spoke the truth. The intern was gray with exhaustion and had bags under his eyes big enough to carry the US mail. For all that, he wasn't bad-looking. If you noticed male attributes, that was. A well-shaped face and a kind mouth, reddish gold hair cut short and sleek. Eli could tell he was probably handsome given the way Diana eyed him with impressively dirty intent.

"Really?" Eli nudged Diana under the table.

Diana, forty-two and unashamed, attractive in a gamine sort of way, wrinkled her nose at Eli. A damned fine cardiologist and an innovator in her field, she had the sense of humor of a collegiate and saw no point in growing old gracefully. She nudged back, and *ouch*, she was wearing pointy-toed shoes. "Bah humbug."

Taye watched them with big eyes. "Is there something going on here that I should know about?"

"Not a thing," Diana said. Butter wouldn't have melted between her cherry red lips. She stole Eli's coffee and sipped demurely.

Holly petted Taye's hair. "It's all right, Taye. No one here's going to bite."

Taye cracked a grin. "Right. It's just -- three doctors and me. All of you have been in medicine since I was in grade school. I'm a little nervous."

"Shows what you know," Eli said, jumping back into the conversation. "I just finished my residency last year." He shrugged. "My midlife crisis came early. What can I say?"

"Seriously? But you seem so... I mean, you're... The way you take charge, I'd thought you were an old pro."

"Thank you. It's never too late to teach an old dog new tricks. And before you ask, I'm forty-three." Eli took his cup back from Diana, only to find it empty. "Wench."

She smirked at Eli. "And don't you forget it. So

where's your wife?"

"Right now, specifically?" Eli checked his watch, a gift from Zane when he'd been hired on as an attending. "Hell if I know. Either in Nepal with Paolo or in Paris with Neo. I lost track." Either way, she was doing adventurous things with a man who isn't married to his job. He couldn't blame Marybeth. Cops made terrible husbands. When he'd decided to switch to medicine, that'd been the last straw, and he wished her well with... whoever was on the menu this week. "Enough about me." They knew damn well he didn't like to talk about personal business in public.

Holly and Diana exchanged glances, the secretly amused and utterly female method of communication Eli had never learned to interpret, God help him.

"Good for her. I was talking about your other wife," Diana said around a bite of ruby jam and baguette.

"Beg pardon?"

"She means Zane," Holly said.

That, in Eli's opinion, was taking it too far, especially in front of a colleague Eli didn't know. "Enough, the both of you."

Holly ignored him serenely and put her chin in her hands. "Come to think of it, this might be the first time I've seen you without him in weeks."

Eli could feel Taye watching them, fascinated. "My private life is not up for scrutiny, but for the last time, Zane and I are not together. How many times do I have to say this, and to how many people?"

"Wait, what?" Looked like Taye had forgotten his nerves. He turned to Diana instead of Eli. "Zane is Dr. Novia, right? They're not..."

"*No*," Eli said, annoyed. A flicker of motion in his peripheral vision filled him with relief. "Zane, for the love of God, would you get behind me on this?"

Diana and Holly dissolved into giggles. Zane shrugged, untroubled as ever, and took his seat. He tucked his pager away. "What are we being ridiculed for today?"

"Same old, same old," Eli said. He passed Zane the bread and jam. "Apparently we want to jump each other's bones."

"An oldie, but a goodie." Zane lifted his chin at Taye. "What are you looking at, junior?"

Taye coughed. "Nothing. Sorry." He retreated behind a mouthful of fresh-from-the-oven baguette.

Eli had to admire Zane at work. They could have used a laser stare like Zane's on the force back in the day. He'd have had perps pissing their pants with nothing more than a look.

Zane turned it on Diana. "Look at you, Mrs. Robinson."

Diana possessed not the smallest trace of shame. "You wish you had my cojones."

"True."

Their byplay didn't stop Holly. Nothing did, as far as Eli could tell. Hell, her husband egged her on; Eli held it in private opinion that the pair of them enjoyed more kink than a Slinky. She folded her hands beneath her chin and gave Zane her best you-can-trust-me psychotherapist face. "It just seems obvious to everyone but the pair of you."

"It's true," Diana said. She started to pick through the packages of fake and real sugar, searching for Splenda. "You go to the symphony together. Ball games. *Brunch*, for God's sake. And when was the last time you went out with a woman, the pair of us aside?"

Eli opened his mouth, closed it, and rubbed the

bridge of his nose. "So it's been a while. I don't have time for playing the field when I'm trying to get ahead with my career."

"But you have time to spend with Zane," Holly said sweetly.

Eli gave up. For the moment.

Diana didn't. "Take, for example, the way you two are sitting. Shoulder to shoulder."

"The table is crowded," Eli protested. "Four-person table, five people jammed in. You're plastered against Taye."

Diana smiled like a cat who'd just gotten her first taste of the cream and said nothing.

Fine, that hadn't helped. Frustrated, Eli looked to Zane for support. No luck; Zane was busy waving for more coffee all around.

Eli wasn't an idiot. When he examined Zane through objective eyes, he could see the appeal. Zane looked closer to thirty than forty, excepting the smile lines and small sprinkling of silver in his hair, and it was a trim, fit thirty with a body he kept in tip-top shape with rigorous exercise.

Not that Eli had anything to be ashamed of on that count, either. Zane's enthusiasm for biking and boxing had chivied Eli out of the threat of middle-aged spread and back into better shape than he'd been on the force. Handsome, fit, successful.

So yes, he noticed these things. Didn't everybody? And so they spent most of their time together. Mankind wasn't made to be alone. Big deal.

Zane's beeper shrilled. He rolled his eyes to the heavens. "I'm going to take this in my car. If the waiter comes around, order for me, but no meat. As soon as we're done here I'm going back to Immaculate Grace and carving myself a filet of intern. Not you," he said as an aside to Taye. "You're doing great. Keep up the good work. Eli, tell them I want the usual, okay?"

Eli didn't let Diana or Holly ask. "Yes, I know his usual. Belgian waffle with cinnamon sugar and whipped cream, the real stuff, and a fruit salad. *No* strawberries." He swatted Zane's hip as Zane scooted behind him and away. "Don't worry; I've got it covered."

"No strawberries?" Taye asked.

"He's allergic," Eli said. Medicine fell outside the personal-business umbrella, and Zane considered nothing taboo anyway. Still grated Eli's nerves a bit to answer. "I've never seen how allergic, but he carries an EpiPen. No sense taking chances."

Hoping the subject would be dropped, knowing there was no way he'd get that lucky, Eli studied the menu until he could no longer ignore the women clicking their tongues at him. Approximately thirty seconds. "What?"

The women exchanged Highly Significant Looks. "Doth the gentleman protest too much?" Diana asked.

"He doth," Holly agreed. "Let me ask you a question, Eli."

"Since I'm well aware that I can't stop you, please, proceed." Eli crossed his arms and waited for it.

"How much time did you spend with your ex-wife before she took off for -- where was it again?" She shushed him before he could answer. "It's Austria with Pieter, by the way. I actually know this, and you don't. Now tell me: how much time do you spend with Zane?"

Eli scowled and said nothing.

Holly pounced. "You see? I'll bet you can even tell me where Zane was night before last."

There was no way he would win here, was there?

"My place," Eli admitted. "Takeout and *Die Hard*. What's your point?"

"I think their point is that you're all but married," Taye said. Apparently he'd chosen sides. Good to know. For that, he would pay. "Look, I know a few things about what it's like to love your own gender. It's strange as hell at first."

Diana's face fell in a way that would have been heartbreaking if it hadn't been ever so satisfying instead. "You're --"

Taye blushed but kept his chin up. "Yes."

"No disrespect to you personally intended, Taye, but can I just say *ha*?" Eli pointed at Holly and Diana in turn. "Your gaydar needs a tune-up."

Diana didn't take defeat graciously. She narrowed her eyes at Taye. "Prove it."

"Hey." Eli straightened. "Nobody around here has to prove anything. Diana, leave him alone."

Taye's color heightened. "I can fight my own battles, thanks."

Eli held up his hands in mock surrender. "Suit yourself, tough guy."

Maybe it was the lack of sleep followed by the powerful coffee, or maybe Taye was one of those fortunate fools who didn't hesitate to jump in where mortals feared to tread. "Excuse me." Taye touched the waiter's arm as he approached, coming in on the third round of coffee refills. "Would it be all right with you if I kissed you?"

The waiter stared at him. Eli waited for the "No!"

Instead, their waiter did a quick check to make sure no managerial eyes were on him, slid his carafe onto the table, and pressed in close to Taye. "I thought you'd never ask, handsome." He stood on tiptoe and --

Eli sighed. Holly made cooing noises that

unfortunately didn't cover up the noises of a highly enthusiastic kiss. A darker mood still shadowed Eli's thoughts when the sound of the smacking prompted a stir in his groin.

He tapped his foot thoughtfully. *All right, so maybe it's been a longer dry spell than I'll admit to this crowd. I'm a busy man. That doesn't mean listening to two pretty boys make out turns me on. Or Zane. It just means I need to get laid, or at least spend a quality afternoon with my right hand.*

"Is that what we're leaving instead of a tip?" Zane made his reappearance without fanfare or notice from anyone except Eli. "If that's the case, we should take Taye out with us more often."

Eli chuckled. "I was just enjoying the sight of Diana proved wrong."

Diana scowled at Taye. "He's your boyfriend, isn't he? No wonder you were willing to brunch instead of crash."

"Can you blame me?" Taye kissed the waiter again, this time on the tip of his nose. "See you later, handsome."

Was he? Eli couldn't see the appeal, himself. Waiter-boy was shorter than Taye by at least half a foot, wiry, curly dark hair, a button nose... Okay, maybe he could see it a little. Discomfort at PDA aside, Eli was man enough to admit the pair of them were almost cute. He knew he'd be just as fidgety with a hetero couple. The last time Holly's computer-something-or-another-engineer husband, Keith, had come along to brunch, he'd almost wanted to crawl under the table.

Not even Diana could stand up against that. She sighed and shifted fully from tigress on the hunt to full-fledged fan club member. "Worth it."

A faint touch at his elbow drew Eli's attention to Holly. "You see?" she asked, quiet as a mouse. A far-too-knowing mouse. "That's the way you and Zane look at each other. You're the only two who can't see it."

"Be that as it may. We're not interested. Not homophobic, Taye, so no offense to you. You two ladies, stop going there. This is the last time I'm going to ask. We're friends. That's all. Leave it alone."

Diana clicked her tongue against her teeth. Eli didn't like the look on her face. Too suspicious by half. "Let me ask you this. How do you know there's nothing more to it? Have you ever tried?"

Even Holly tried to shush her at that, but the damage was done. "I think we're done here." Eli dropped his napkin on the table and stood. "My private life is just that: private. I've had about enough of defending myself."

"Like I said. Protesting too much," Diana said. She wasn't one to back down. Normally Eli liked that about her. Normally. Not so much now. "Look it up."

Chapter Two

Zane caught him up before Eli had reached the parking lot. He might have expected it. Did, to tell the truth. Eli stopped midreach for his keys and waited.

Zane fell into step beside Eli, pretending to busy himself with reaching for the pack of smokes and lighter he kept on him at all times. A doctor who smoked. Eli had never quite gotten the sense in that, but everyone had at least one vice to keep 'em human.

Didn't mean he'd silently suffer secondhand. "Light that around me and die."

"Nice." Zane wrinkled his nose. He slid the Zippo back into his pocket and tapped the cigarette filter against his wrist instead. "I'm still hungry. Want to take one car and swing by a drive-through?"

"You don't have to leave. This is my issue."

"No? Hate to break it to you, pal, but you're not the only one they had in the hot seat." Zane shaded his eyes to look up at the sun. "Speaking of which, it's going to be strangely warm today."

"Zane."

"What? I'm just saying." Zane stopped at last but in front of Eli, effectively halting his progress as well.

"We've got to do something about them. You realize that."

"Calm down. They'll get tired of heckling us sooner or later."

"Really? How long have they not gotten tired of it so far? Two years and counting?"

"Two years' worth of overpriced bread and jam," Zane agreed. "Maybe you should cut them a break."

Eli flicked his ear. "Come again? I couldn't have heard you right."

"They just want us to be happy. What's so bad about that?" Zane scruffed his hair. He wouldn't quite look at Eli, but then again, that wasn't so unusual. The man had a strange and, in his own special way, brilliant mind. In Eli's experience, Zane saw life as one giant chess game, and he tended to keep an eye on three or four possible moves in the future.

Huh. On second consideration, Eli wasn't too sure he liked the possible applications here. "Spill it. Whatever you're thinking, it can't be good."

"Suspicious, aren't you? It's almost like you know me." Zane snapped back to the here and now, all casual joie de vivre again. "Promise you'll hear me out first."

"This should be good." Eli glanced behind himself and propped his hip on a behemoth of an SUV that would hide them nicely from the bistro. Unintentional cover, but he'd take what he could get. "Fine. Lay it on me."

"Interesting choice of words." Zane's lips quirked. "Here's the skinny. They keep nagging at us. We keep saying no. They're not hearing the 'no.'"

"I'm with you so far."

"Ask yourself: why are they not hearing the denial?"

"They're stubborn deviants who don't have the sense to come in out of the rain?"

Zane laughed. "That too. But they're scientists, like us. For a given value of science. I think Holly's got some kind of voodoo going for her instead."

"Can't argue with you there. Where were you going with this?"

Eli watched the sunlight play off Zane's hair in glints as Zane visibly sorted through what he wanted to say next. He'd moved past the overdue-for-a-haircut stage and into the length that only a guy with the kind of presence Zane had could make work. There were a couple of pictures of Zane floating around in his apartment, college-era vintage, where he had hair down to his ass and a goatee that went surprisingly well with his tie-dyed T-shirts and stonewashed jeans.

Eli could wish he'd known Zane back then, except that if they'd met, he'd have probably been there to arrest him. Zane had known how to sow his wild oats. He wondered how long that stage had lasted.

Zane rubbed his chin, the fine layer of stubble, just dark enough to be visible, rasping against his palm. "Remember you said you'd hear me out. I'm holding you to that."

"Now I really don't like the sound of this. But yes, I promised." Zane didn't make a habit out of leading Eli astray. Might be an interesting ride, but they got where they were headed in the end. Usually.

"Here's what I figure. We're science brained." Zane twirled his finger by his temple. "A good doctor is also a cynic. We require proof before conclusions. Shouldn't be too hard."

"And exactly how do we get this proof?" Eli crossed his arms, and his legs at the ankle.

"Let me kiss you."

"I beg your pardon?"

"Eli, hear me out." Zane came closer. Not that they didn't invade one another's personal space as a matter of course, but there was a certain intent to his moves now that made Eli go very still. "It makes sense."

"From an unbiased perspective? Yes. Doesn't mean I want to kiss you."

"What if I want to kiss you?" Zane laughed at Eli when he gaped. "For proof, you big dumb ox. We try it. It's terrible. A sloppy mess. Then we can present them with the evidence and that ought to do the trick."

"This is Diana and Holly we're talking about here. They'd want photographs. Video."

"Diana might. Holly will take us at our word, and she'll work Diana over if she's convinced. Besides, do you really want pictures floating around?"

"Good point."

Zane, Eli couldn't help but notice, hadn't stopped his slow but steady forward progress, way past even a friend's boundaries of personal space. They were a hairbreadth away from touching chest to chest now, and Eli could smell the light crispness of Zane's cologne. Maybe that was what made him slightly breathless.

"Details are important." Eli kept his hands tucked firmly under his arms. They twitched, wanting to -- what? Reach out and touch someone? This wasn't him. SUV or not, they were in public, for Christ's sake. He'd had a hard enough time kissing his wife. Just wasn't anyone's business but his own.

Then again, this was Zane, who let it all hang out, so much so that Eli sometimes wondered if he had anything left inside.

Nevertheless, Zane was a guy, and this wasn't ground Eli had trod before. Understandable that it'd put a man on edge, right? Maybe. Maybe not quite as much an excuse for making him light-headed and torn between *yes* and *no*.

Zane seemed to know exactly what Eli was thinking. He had a way of doing that. Mind reading, or he just knew Eli that well. No telling which, sometimes. "It's me, Eli. You trust me, right?"

Only one answer for that. "I do."

"Then let me take over here. I've got it under control. One kiss and we're done with this nonsense for good. Do it for me, okay?" Zane was suddenly touching Eli's face again, a different experience this time. Though his hands were still cool and soothing, they lingered instead of briskly checked, and the feel of them made a knot thicken in Eli's throat.

"I still don't think it's a good idea."

"Noted. Now shut up," Zane said and kissed him.

Eli kept his eyes open, stunned into immobility. He'd thought a *peck*, not -- whatever this was. Zane's lips were soft and insistent, and dear God, was that a flicker of tongue tickling at the closed seam of Eli's lips?

At first, the kiss was every bit as bad as Eli had predicted. Both he and Zane were used to being the dominant, the one who called the shots. They both zigged when one should have zagged, both pushed forward when one should have given way, and the sensation of rasping stubble made the experience surreal.

But then... then Zane sighed, a whisper of breath, and the kiss grew slower, softer, deeper. Zane tilted his head just -- *so* -- and then it was the most natural thing in the world for Eli to thread his fingers through Zane's hair and pull him closer. For Eli to rest his hand at the small of Zane's back and anchor him there. To slide his tongue between Zane's lips and stroke. He tasted of coffee and cherry jam and something different, something completely unlike kissing a woman and maddeningly enticing.

The cigarette dropped unlit, forgotten, to the pristine gravel beneath their feet.

Eli had never kissed anyone who kept their eyes open too, and once he and Zane had locked stares, Eli couldn't look away. He was drowning in clear, shocked gray and didn't surface when they parted, breathing shallowly through their mouths. Zane stayed otherwise put. So did Eli. More than his lips had reacted to that kiss, and if Zane moved one fraction of an inch closer, he'd know more than Eli wanted him to.

My God. This was supposed to put an end to the whole question. Not raise a hundred more.

Guess he never was too old to be surprised by life, was he?

* * *

Men were not the greatest of communicators. Eli would be the first to own up to that. Especially him. Sometimes men didn't talk because they didn't want to. Sometimes because they had no idea which words they could possibly use after what he'd just done. They'd done. Jesus.

"So… that happened," he said and immediately wanted to kick himself. *Smooth, Eli. Smooth like glass.*

Zane's breath was warm on Eli's lips, his gaze stunned, and his fingertips trailing over Eli's jaw. "My God."

"Yeah. Him. Allah, Buddha, Vishnu, and Ganesha too." Eli stepped back, out of immediate reach. Funny how it didn't seem to help ease the tightening panic in his chest. "I should go."

"What?" Zane switched to fingering his own lips. The movement drew Eli's eye to kiss-swollen firmness and the faint strawberry hue of light beard burn.

Right. That, Eli couldn't take. He made himself turn his back. "I'll see you later."

He'd hoped Zane would linger in his daze for a while. Often happened that way when something had his attention by the short hairs. As luck would have it, not so much now. "Do you really think walking away is the way we should go here? Give me a break, Eli.

We're friends. It'll be fine."

"What else should we do?" Eli couldn't keep his back to Zane. Honor demanded he at least face the guy. "What the hell are you smirking at?"

Ungenerous. Zane wasn't smirking but smiling. Grinning. Amused. "It bothers you that much, kissing me and liking it? Because in case you missed it, you weren't alone there."

"It doesn't bother you?"

"That, I didn't say."

"And there you have it." Eli made himself stay put. He wasn't a coward, for fuck's sake; the last thing he needed to do was prove that wrong by running. Pressing his point, that was different. "All those in favor of pretending this never happened, raise your hands."

Zane didn't. "Don't run away, would you? Something like this, you can't play ostrich over."

"Yeah? I've got no problem with that."

"You should." Zane approached Eli with a sort of definite intent that Eli recognized now.

"What do you think you're doing?"

"Kissing you again. Once could be a fluke. Twice? Maybe we'll know we've got something. Hold still."

"You sound like you're about to wipe a smudge off my cheek."

"More like lay one on."

Maybe if he hadn't said that, Eli would have gone for it. Who was he kidding? No maybe about it. He wanted that, and to be frank, it scared the hell out of him.

"No." He pointed at Zane. "I've got to go."

"You don't *have* to go anywhere. We're both off for the day. Eli, would you just stay put and let's figure this out?"

"Nothing to figure out. I told you it was a bad idea. Move it already, would you?" Eli's temper was on the rise.

Zane looked aside, but not off into space. More with his laser stare directed to the left, as if should he look at Eli, he'd say more than he wanted to.

"What?"

Zane shook his head. He didn't look back at Eli. "Okay. If you need to go, then go. But you know where I'll be."

Yeah, Eli did. He also knew that right now, Zane's mind would be working sixty miles to the gallon, coming up with God only knew what. Zane could work that way, process that fast. Not Eli. So help him, it took him a while.

"I know," Eli said, and made himself walk away. Not that it helped. He could feel Zane watching him all the way to his car.

If he still felt Zane's presence afterward, driving away, Eli told himself that was his imagination keeping Zane lingering with him and the pressure of Zane's lips still making his tingle. Imagination and nothing more.

* * *

Could he stop thinking about that kiss? No. Or, sort of. Eli was too tired for rational processing. He was over his hours and too tired to risk any kind of patient care, but as a bolt-hole, the doctor's lounge at Immaculate Grace worked. With the background noise of the hospital, he could let himself tune out and nurse cup after cup of the worst coffee in the city. Thick as tar and just about as tasty, exactly like your crazy great-uncle used to make. It'd put hair on your chest. Eli didn't need help in that area, but what the hell. Gave him something to focus on besides…

Zane's lips, soft and sweet. Parting to let him in, tasting of bitterness and sugar.

His cell phone chimed, volume set to low. Incoming text. Eli automatically checked, the response ingrained after years when paying attention to what people had to say literally meant the difference between life and death. Funny how he hadn't been able to do that with Zane, huh?

So, I'm a twat. Nothing you didn't already know. But I'm apologizing.

From Diana. Eli thumbed Delete and pushed the phone into his shirt pocket, where it hung heavy against his chest. He scowled and tossed back another draught of ink masquerading as Columbian freeze-dried. The message joined the mental bank where Holly's e-mail from earlier already lived. Not so short but as directly to the point.

We pushed you too far. Please accept my apology, and let's talk about this.

Psychotherapists. Talking was what they did best. What had he been thinking to start spending time with one of them?

Zane had liked them. Where Zane went, Eli followed. That was the odd thing about Zane and had been from the start. Eli wasn't the easiest person in the world to get to know. That, he'd own. Took people time to get past his walls, and few ever made it beyond the perimeter. Zane? He'd blown through as if they weren't even there. Effortless conqueror.

Maybe because he knew where to give when he needed to. Some might call that weakness. Eli chose to see it as masterminding.

Had Zane planned that kiss? Was what Eli had felt a normal reaction to your straight friend laying one on you? Eli didn't know. Couldn't tell. Wasn't sure he wanted to. With Zane, anything was possible.

Christ, but Zane's lips had been soft.

"Fuck," Eli muttered. He couldn't stop tapping his foot. Too much coffee. He stood and paced to the window.

So there was no denying it to himself, was there? He'd enjoyed that kiss. More than enjoyed, God help him. Every time he remembered a detail, it made him want to do what Zane asked and try it again. But c'mon. This wasn't him. Never had been. And fucking a friend? Bad idea. Bad to the infinite power of bad.

Fucking? Jesus. Eli flinched away from the word choice. But what else was he supposed to think of? Love? Somehow he couldn't see hearts and flowers here.

Okay. He didn't want to, but he was. That kiss had him all turned around.

If at all possible, Eli liked having a game plan. A road map, as it were. Granted, it was usually more of a grand scheme sort of thing. Cops and doctors, both had to think on their feet, right? Still, as long as Eli knew where he was going and how he wanted to get there, he'd damn well see it through or die trying.

This thing with Zane? No clue. Well. None except for what he'd been trying to avoid even more than the kiss: the growing, uneasy certainty that this was what they'd been heading for all along. Whatever "this" was.

Wondering gave way to a brief flash of fantasy:

Zane, pliant and willing and giving. Zane, curled warm and tight in his arms as if he belonged there.

Eli glanced out the window and snorted a laugh. "Speak of the devil, hmm?" he murmured. When he looked down, he had a great view into the skylight of the free clinic attached to Immaculate Grace. And what did he see? Zane, running on even less sleep than Eli but back in scrubs and his coat, a chart in one hand and a terrified intern hanging on to his every word. Laser stare activated. Getting the job done, making his word law.

Everywhere Eli turned, all roads led to Zane. A sense of inevitability had already seeped beneath Eli's skin, and to be perfectly honest? It scared the fuck out of him, but despite all his protests, it didn't scare him as *much* as he thought it should have, and that scared him most of all.

Eli lingered at the window, uncomfortably aware that he was spying but not so much able to make himself look away. How often did he have a chance to observe Zane in the wild without knowing Zane had his location, reactions, and probable actions charted on a mental map? How rare was it to just look without being looked at in turn?

Okay, so that was bullshit. Eli wanted to look, and so he did.

In his element, Zane was the finest doctor Eli had been privileged to know, and he'd met more than his share. First the idiots who'd poked and prodded the hell out of him after he'd been shot in the line of duty. A cop's worst nightmare, right? Some idiot pops you with a bullet, and before you know it, the higher-ups are talking desk duty and disability. Be reduced to an old man without a purpose in life before he was forty? Not going to happen. Eli'd gone to that very free clinic looking for the only second opinion he could afford.

That'd been where he'd met Zane, who'd taken his case and his cause without hesitation. Even then Eli had been struck by the passion in him, his sense of purpose, and his common sense.

Zane. He left a permanent impression, no doubt about that. A handshake, a smile, a frank opinion with no bullshit. Hard pill to swallow. It'd gone down surprisingly easy when Eli watched Zane move around the room with brisk, economical movements and the banter that already came easy between them and thought, Maybe I can't wear a badge any longer. I wonder if I could do this instead.

He'd never looked back since. Never had a chance to, not once Zane had found out. Cheering section, enabler, and, pretty soon, closest of all friends, striding in where no one else went with his head held high. They'd kept in touch during Eli's long years at Duke University, and Zane had pulled some strings to get Eli back at Immaculate Heart for his residency.

Zane. All roads led back to Zane, didn't they?

Eli drifted, so slowly he wasn't aware of the transition, in the way he watched Zane. Noticing things he never had before. How Zane's scrubs top pulled tight over his chest, packed with lean muscle. The corded strength in his forearms when he leaned over a counter and gestured wildly with a pen. Forearms Eli knew were corded with firm veins.

And as he looked, he began to think of other things. Slow, so slow, pictures filtering into his mind.

Desires.

If he were to do this -- if -- maybe it would go something like...

* * *

Eli stopped Zane with a hand to the shoulder. All the lights were out in the free clinic, everyone gone home for the night. Zane and Eli left behind, workaholics to the last, but somehow that was different when you had each other's backs and counted on one another. Zane, exhausted but still crackling with life, his gray eyes tired but his wicked smile ready.

"Something on your mind?" Zane asked, as if Eli wasn't certain Zane knew damn well what kind of bee he had in his bonnet.

"Don't ask questions if you already know the answers." Eli let his fingers trail down to the neckline of Zane's scrubs. Strange how Zane's sleek chest held as much appeal in its way as the firm swell of a woman's breasts. Maybe more so. How long had it been that way?

"Maybe I want to hear what you've got to say. Ever think about that?" A planner he might be, but Zane's impatience got the best of him four out of five times. He draped his arm over Eli's shoulder and tugged him in. More, he nudged Eli's foot with his and guided him closer.

Eli came. No reason not to. This was easy, natural, the way it should be. He slid his arm casually around the small of Zane's back and rested his palm on Zane's hip, taut and flat instead of rounded, and liked it. His leg was pressed to the join of Zane's. "Nah. I know you. You're easy."

"Guilty." Zane relaxed his pose, letting Eli push his leg between, and shifted his weight so that Eli held him up. "What are you going to do about it?"

* * *

Eli snapped out of the fantasy.

What was he going to do about it? That was the million-dollar question, wasn't it? And the biggest irony of all? If he'd had a problem like this before, who would he have taken it to?

Zane.

Zane, who glanced up at the skylight as if he could sense himself being watched. Eli jerked back, heart thudding in his throat.

Someone caught him. For a breathless second, Eli thought it'd be Zane. Instead, it was the last person he would have expected.

"Taye?" Eli pulled away from Taye's tap on his shoulder. "No one ever taught you not to sneak up on an ex-cop, did they?" He had a sensation of spiders crawling over his skin. "It is Taye, right?"

"It is." Taye shook Eli's hand, surprising and impressing him. Manners. Nice. "Sorry. My brother's on the force. NYPD. I know these things."

"Not much you don't know, is there?"

Taye held his ground. Ballsy, wasn't he? Eli could respect that. "I wouldn't have intruded, but I called your name three or four times and you didn't hear me. I thought you might be asleep on your feet." A glint of humor broke up his seriousness. "I'm new, but I've been around long enough to know *that* happens too."

"True." Eli sat on the windowsill, welcoming the cold bite of slate through his clothes against his too-warm skin. "What can I do for you?" he asked, figuring Taye had seen a fellow doctor and come to get a consult on something. The usual from an intern.

He was wrong. "I wanted to apologize," Taye said, meeting Eli's eyes the way so few people did. "We don't know each other. My being in on that brunch wasn't right. Neither was my ganging up on you. I was out of line."

"Damn right you were." Still... "Takes balls to own up to that. Thanks." Eli offered Taye his hand. "We done here?"

Taye nodded, no comment, and turned to go. Maybe it was because he didn't pry. Didn't ask. Either way, sometimes a man -- even one like Eli -- had to make snap decisions without checking the grand scheme. Not as if that hadn't gone a hundred percent out the window already today.

Bad choice of words.

"Wait up." Eli didn't say it loudly, but Taye halted just the same and looked back at him. "C'mere."

Brows slightly furrowed in curiosity, Taye did as he'd been told. Eli could tell he was still his own man, doing this because he chose to and not because he was intimidated. Tough kid indeed.

Trouble was, once Eli had him there, he had no idea where to start. Helped that Taye waited and let him find the words. Eli pinched the bridge of his nose and sighed. "Okay, this goes no further than the two of us, right?"

"Of course," Taye said, and nothing more. Eli could really grow fond of this one. Go figure. He was no Zane, but then again, who was?

Eli started once, twice, and stopped both times. This wasn't something he did, even if he needed to. The times, they were a-changin', but still a work in progress. "Christ. Help a guy out, would you?"

"I don't know what this is about."

"Please." Eli aimed a narrow look at Taye. "You're an intern, so I know you're not stupid. Take a wild guess."

"Oh." Comprehension dawned. "Huh." Taye parked his ass on the back edge of a couch. "Exactly what do you want me to say?"

"Hell if I know." Eli's shoulders slumped. Just a little. "Pick something. We can play hot and cold."

Taye chuckled. "Or I can tell you how I think it is."

"So we're still doing hot and cold. I can work with that."

"Right." Taye studied Eli, taking his measure. "Something happened after you left. Dr. Novia left too, so whatever it was, it involved him."

"Way too hot there, kid. Were you watching us?"

"Nope. I've just been there, is all. I'm not asking for details. If you want me to help, you have to let me help."

Advice given to every patient. It rankled, but the truth of it couldn't be denied. "Sorry. Proceed."

"Here's what I think you want to ask," Taye said slowly, visibly picking and choosing his words. "What was it like for me the first time I realized a guy hit my buttons?"

Eli licked the tip of his finger and pressed it to his chest with a small, mock sizzle. "Except I'm not into guys. Never even crossed my mind, and I'm forty-fucking-three. That's pretty late in the game to experience this particular epiphany."

"No, it's not."

"Excuse me?"

Taye shrugged. He popped off the couch and headed for the coffeepot, almost drained dry but with half a Dixie cup's worth in the bottom. He wrinkled his nose at the mess and switched off the pot to make some fresh. "I've known older who still didn't have a clue."

"I was married."

"And? There's guys who've been married for thirty years. Twenty. Fifteen. Never at all. You're not exactly unusual."

Oddly enough, that was good to know.

"But I do get that this is out of the norm for you. Right?"

"Spot on."

Taye nodded. "So you're not into men. But

you're thinking maybe you're into Dr. Novia." Taye kept it down, which earned him more of Eli's appreciation. "That is what you're getting at, isn't it?"

"Frank little bastard, aren't you?"

"Playing coy is a delaying tactic. You're not the first bi-curious guy I've counseled." At Eli's puzzled look, Taye explained, "Gay-Straight Alliance in college and then in med school. Trust me, this is old hat."

"Maybe for you. Not for me."

"It's not the first time I've heard that, either."

Fine. Eli cut to the chase. God help him, he was asking to be schooled in romance by a guy half his age. "What should I do? And don't tell me, I already know. You've heard that before too."

"I have." Taye reached for the stethoscope hanging around his neck and hung on to both ends. "The answer's usually different each time, though."

"Great. And in this case?"

Taye shook his head. "It's not my answer. You're the only one who can figure it out."

Eli let his hands slap down on his thighs. "Well, thank you, Yoda."

"I wasn't done, asshole. Oh shit. I mean Dr. Jameson."

"Kid, I think we're way past being polite. Call me Eli."

"As long as you stop calling me 'kid.'"

"Fair enough."

Taye tipped him a cockeyed grimace. "Eli. What I can tell you is this: don't let being afraid scare you away from a good friend. You'll regret that more than anything."

"Is that what you tell all the guys questioning their sexuality?"

"Nope. It's what I tell everyone." Taye let go of

his stethoscope. "Look. I heard what Dr. Holly said to you. Couldn't exactly avoid it, you know? You and Dr. Novia, you do look at each other the way Richie looks at me, and me at him. If I *was* going to tell you what to do --"

"Which you're not."

"Which I'm not," Taye agreed. "It'd be not to make any snap decisions either way. Take your time and think. Because make no mistake, Dr. -- Eli. This is huge."

"Yeah," Eli said. "I know."

Taye gestured to indicate he was done. Good enough. "Want some coffee?"

Eli had had enough that he doubted he'd be sleeping that night, but what the hell. The batch Taye had made actually smelled good. "Sure thing." He wasn't sure what made him ask. "Richie, that's the waiter? He teach you how to make decent coffee?"

"That he did." Taye offered Eli a cup. God. Tasted as good as it smelled. "For what it's worth... Richie and I were friends first."

"And now you..."

"I love him," Taye said, simple and unashamed. "It was only afterward that I understood I always had. Think about that too."

Right. Like Eli would be able to *stop*. He lifted his cup to Taye and drank deeply.

Chapter Three

Eli tugged on his second glove and stamped his boots in the fresh layer of snow still falling from the sky in slow, lazy drifts. A Chicago boy, snow didn't bother him. It'd be a hell of a thing to slip and fall on his ass when he was on his way to proposition his best friend.

He made a face to himself. *Proposition. Nice word choice there, Eli.* More like… face the music. That'd do. And in this case, as with all others when the music promised to be rough going, a smart man went bearing gifts.

Eli chuckled under his breath. Not so different from Marybeth, was it? If he'd pissed her off, he'd bring home a single rose or a bouquet of irises, or on the occasion of one spectacular fuckup, he'd managed to scrape together the cash for a tennis bracelet. Lucky him, Zane was a little easier to please. Eli pointed himself in the direction of the Starbucks on the corner facing the hospital and started walking.

As he walked, absently watching the puffs of steam that wisped around his face with each breath, Eli applied his mind to the status quo. After Taye had left, he'd fallen asleep. Hadn't meant to and sure as hell hadn't thought it possible, but either good coffee miraculously wrought from stale beans and a drip pot was a soporific, or Taye had slipped a Valium or three into the pot. Eli wasn't sure which and frankly didn't think he wanted to know. The pot *had* been suspiciously clean when Eli woke. Either way, the quick nap helped. Gave him a brain reset, as it were. A fresh perspective.

And when he'd glanced out the window and seen Zane working at the station beneath the free clinic's skylight, slumped in a chair and hunched over a stack of charts, Eli had known: reset or not, the new way in which he saw Zane hadn't changed.

More important, neither had the old. The nap had let that surface. No matter what else, Zane was the closest friend of Eli's life. So maybe it was a little weird to lean on the guy who'd thrown you into a tailspin. So what? He could count on Zane through the worst of anything else.

Only made sense to do that now.

Granted, the coffee wasn't just a peace offering. Zane wasn't the only one who could play mad scientist and work up experiments. As one last test before diving right into the lion's den, Eli wanted to get a good look at the world and make sure he knew where he stood. Zane deserved no less.

Comparison and contrasts. Go.

Could I be attracted to Diana? he asked himself, waiting for the light. Several idiots decided they'd scramble across the walk during a lull in traffic. Great. They'd probably be scraping the bastards off the pavement later on. *Diana. Hmm.*

No, he decided. Diana might be pretty with her pixy haircut and her tight little curves and her sassy smile, but she was one hell of a firecracker and she liked 'em young. High maintenance and quick to fly off the handle. Not like Zane, who'd sit calm and quiet and think his way through the situation at hand. He might come up with something as explosive as Diana, but hey, at least his fuse was on a sensible rigging.

Am I attracted to Holly? Eli asked himself once he was across the street, the fragrance of Pike Place already rich in his nose as the Starbucks door opened and shut on a stream of foot traffic. Jesus, why didn't they just install revolving doors already and be done with it?

Holly… no. That one didn't take too much thought. He'd have to take Keith out of the picture, and frankly Keith was the one guy around who could probably take Eli in a fight. Also, he'd overheard far too many details about Keith and Holly's sex life to know that woman might be serene and sweet on the surface, but she liked her whips and chains at home. Nothing against it, just very much not his style.

Eli smirked. Hell of a world when considering a gay hookup with his straight friend was the lesser of two kinks, wasn't it?

What about Taye? Less surety there. Eli guessed Taye was a cute little twerp, but he was taken, and it didn't feel right considering even he had been able to see how nauseatingly in love Taye and Richie were. Even so… *no.* Taye didn't do it for Eli. *Interesting.*

Eli pulled open the Starbucks' door and stepped into a world of steam, java saturation, and consumer-conscious appeal. Worked too. Like others around him, Eli stopped and sighed with satisfaction and appreciation.

"Can I help you?" The barista behind the register managed to stay chirpy after who knew how many customers in a given hour. Cute little thing, her red ponytail pulled through her hat and her shape svelte without being stick-figure skinny. She had a great smile.

Beyond that, she only brought one word to Eli's mind: *jailbait.* "Caramel frappuccino," he said, naming Zane's favorite. Crazy bastard. Even in the dead of winter, he loved his sweet, creamy-cold drinks. "Venti."

The barista called his order to the man working the bar. Older, with a little more age and experience worn into his face, he was maybe thirty, and he'd seen some life. Eli thought he spotted a tattoo mostly hidden by the guy's dark hair. He had a crooked smile, friendly brown eyes, and strong hands.

Nice guy, but in this case he did less for Eli than Taye did. *Interesting-er and interesting-er.* He tipped the guy outrageously in silent apology for eyeballing him and headed back out with gift in hand. On his way back to the clinic, he considered stopping at a news kiosk to pick up a pack of Zane's favorite cigarettes, but on second thought, he didn't want to make peace that badly. Heh! Maybe this would be a way to finally coax Zane off the smokes. Who wanted to kiss an ashtray?

Eli slowed in front of the door to the free clinic, midreach for the handle. He could see Zane inside, almost done with his stack of charts. Mostly alone, the clinic briefly quiet. Great timing, then. He rapped on the door and waved the plastic cup.

Zane sat back, his grin bright and broad, and waved Eli in. And Eli felt it again, same as before, only maybe stronger now. Something he couldn't so much define as he could break down into its component elements: warmth. Eagerness. Relief. A feeling like opening your eyes on the first day of summer vacation. Sinking into a soft bed at the end of a long day. The anticipation of waiting for your prom date to come down the stairs.

Eli appreciated that Zane kept his seat as he approached, letting Eli take the lead. Zane did know him well. And with each step, the anticipation and eagerness that both scared the hell out of Eli and spurred him on grew. Might be a short trek from the door to where Zane sat, but by the time Eli reached Zane he was equal parts wreck and as calm as the eye of a storm.

"That for me?" Zane reached for the frappuccino. He kept his calm gaze on Eli, weighing him in the balance but not with judgment. Eli knew he could go either way and Zane would accept that.

Gave him a boost of courage. "Yours." Eli held onto the cup just long enough to give him a reason for his fingers to brush Zane's. The slight inhale told him Zane knew exactly what he was doing and what he was really saying. All of it. "Just so you know, I have no idea what I'm doing here."

"Idiot," Zane said around the lip of the cup. His eyes sparkled with gentle mischief. "That's the whole point to doing this with me. We figure it out together."

For that, Eli almost wanted to kiss him again. Not yet. But soon.

* * *

Funny thing was, the aftermath of their big emotional moment seemed somehow... anticlimactic. Needed at the forever-understaffed clinic, Zane had stayed on for the duration. Dead on his feet, Eli had gone home.

He remembered sitting on the edge of a lounger to take off his shoes, and that was about it. Sleep tended to overtake a doctor off duty, the body taking command over a brain kept over-busy and over-stressed.

Funny thing about a mind overcharged with stimuli during the day: the dreams were completely out of this world. As in, from Mars. Eli couldn't think of any other way to explain them. Normally, they were your usual fare -- giant IV poles chasing him around the Immaculate Grace's parking garage, suture kits doing the cha-cha around a gurney, decent food in the cafeteria. Par for the course.

Today, his brain had treated him to picking up

right where his idle fantasy had stopped earlier. Sort of.

* * *

Zane sat on Eli's lap. Didn't seem strange in the dream. More... comfortable. His weight was familiar and easy, his hands loosely knotted behind Eli's neck, and their foreheads pressed casually together. "You're kind of an idiot sometimes," Zane said.

"Takes one to know one," Eli said. "Kiss me."

"Since you ask so nicely." Their lips met. Familiar now but no less exciting when Zane let Eli take the lead and opened for him. The sleek glide of his tongue teasing Eli's kindled the sparks of wanting that moved Eli to pull Zane closer and hold him with one fist in Zane's hair and one hand spread over a tight ass cheek, amazed at the firmness of the flesh and chuckling in satisfaction at the groan he coaxed from Zane when he kneaded the taut muscle.

Right about then, Holly tapped Eli on the shoulder.

"Kinda busy here," Eli said between kisses. Zane had his shirt open and began a most pleasant stroking beneath. "Mind coming back later?"

"I don't have to go anywhere for you to know I'm right," Holly said. "I just wanted to tell you not to fight this."

Zane had his lips on Eli's neck, sucking a love mark beneath his jaw. "Does it look like I'm fighting?" Eli asked, incredulous.

"Don't mind me," Diana said. She tossed popcorn kernels into her mouth from the bucket she carried. "I'm just here for the show."

"The point is," Holly said, laying gentle hands on Eli's arm, "you can't change what you are, or will become. You both want this, even if you didn't know it. All you can do is accept who you're becoming."

"Accept this," Zane said. He snapped his fingers. Holly, Diana, and Taye -- who'd appeared to dance the hula in drag behind them -- all disappeared.

"What took you so long?" Eli asked, getting back to the good stuff.

"Like I said," Zane told him, loosening Eli's belt. "Sometimes you're an idiot. Then again, so am I. Kiss me."

"All you've got to do is ask," Eli said. He reached for Zane's belt and --

* * *

Woke up, blinking at the darkness of the room, striped with the red of stoplights and the wavering beams from cars outside. Chicago at night sounded about as lively, or more so, than Chicago by day, a hum of excited life outside easing Eli back into wakefulness.

"The hell," he said to himself, unfolding gingerly from the awkward position he'd curled up in on the couch. "My neck is never going to forgive me. Ugh."

Sheer habit moved him to check his phone for messages. He had one text. From Zane. Once again, reflex took over, and he read it.

Shake a leg, old man. Hey. We're okay, I promise.

"We're okay," Eli muttered, dry washing his face with his palm. "Says you. You weren't the one who dreamed about --" He stopped, blushing. "Forty-three years old and I'm turning red over a sex dream. Christ."

Eli hit Reply and sent back a three-word message. *On my way.* Come what may, he'd be a sorry friend if he left Zane to deal with this on his own. That wasn't how they worked. He might need tequila to get through whatever conversation followed, but that was what friends did. And no matter what, Zane was his best friend first and last.

Even if Eli did now wonder -- all too vividly -- if Zane's lips would be as soft or his kiss as sweet as memory promised.

So maybe he'd stick his head under the faucet before he left. A good dousing of cold water might cure what ailed him. Then again, it might not, and he wasn't too sure he wanted it to.

* * *

Eli let himself into Zane's apartment with the key that lived on his own chain. Stopped when the significance registered. Sighed. At the time, his having gotten his own key made sense. He and Zane were always running in and out of one another's apartments. Eli had forgotten his lunch? No problem, Zane would pick it up for him. Zane needed a clean shirt? Eli would swing by before work.

Now Eli found himself wondering if there was more to keys and easy familiarity than he'd previously thought, and hated the new uncertainty. Life had been simpler before he'd kissed Zane.

Then again, Eli supposed anyone who'd ever kissed a friend probably felt the same way.

Zane's apartment door swung open smoothly on well-maintained hinges. Though he had a comfortably middle-class apartment in a middle-class neighborhood and God knew he didn't fling his cash around, certain things gave hints about Zane's more than middle-class upbringing. For one, the leather living room set, buttery soft and welcoming, and for another, the soft rugs that cushioned a tired man's aching feet.

No lights on. For a moment, Eli wondered if he'd missed a text from Zane telling him to meet up at a bar.

Somewhere a little more neutral than a suddenly portentous home. Then he caught the sound of water pattering down on tile, followed by Zane's slightly off-key tenor cheerfully massacring its way through an a capella rendition of something Mozart.

Habit. Eli had done this a hundred times, if not more. He toed off his shoes and padded toward the bathroom to knock on the door, always left slightly ajar to let steam out. This time, he hesitated before applying knuckles to wood. If he wanted to, he could sneak a peek through the slight gap in the door.

Before he could properly think about it, he did. He couldn't see much, not through the frosted glass of the shower door, but he got a glimpse of bare skin pinkened by the heat of the water and a shadow of dark hair sleek at both head and below the waist. Looked and, for a still moment, couldn't look away.

The water shut off abruptly. "Eli?"

Eli blinked and snapped out of it. "Yeah, I'm here." He coughed. "I mean, I'll be out there. In the den. Waiting for you."

Was it just him, or did Zane hesitate, as if he thought about turning around one way or the other? Half-exposed, he could go either way, and dear God, Eli didn't think he could cope with the choice.

He wasn't sure what to feel when Zane opted for discretion and whipped the draped towel off the top of the shower door. "Give me a minute."

Eli rested his forehead on the cool wood paneling and tried to ignore the temptation to let himself look again. Despite it all, or maybe because of it, he couldn't help but chuckle quietly to himself. "Take your time. I'm not going anywhere."

"So you say," Zane muttered.

How to respond to that, Eli didn't know. He

settled for tucking his hands in his pockets and turning to prop himself on the wall instead. "You feel up to going out to get a drink? I'm in the mood for McClosky's."

"I have beer here." The shower door rattled. "Give me ten. Wait. I'm decent. Look at me."

Eli didn't generally refuse Zane. He did as he'd been asked, simultaneously relieved and disappointed to see Zane cloaked in huge, soft blue towels. With his wet hair plastered over his forehead and his grin both shy and cheeky, he looked at once about half his age and exactly like the friend he'd always been. "I just need to know that we're good, you and me."

"Of course we are." That didn't even need considering. "I'm not letting that change."

"Good." Zane took on a slightly brighter glow. Uh-oh. That was his "considering mischief" expression. "Fix yourself a drink. Me too. I think we're both going to need one."

"Do I want to know why?"

"Want to? Probably not. Need to? Probably yes. Let me get dressed and settled, and I'll explain myself."

"Zane --" Eli stopped himself. "Okay. I'll be on the couch. But if I fall asleep again waiting for you to make yourself pretty, it's on your head."

Zane's quiet laughter followed Eli back to the den. The warm sound wrapped around Eli like a blanket, same as it always had, and for the second time in less than ten minutes Eli wanted to turn around and trace sound back to source.

He made himself finish the outward-bound trek instead.

* * *

Zane emerged from his bedroom dressed in a

soft oatmeal-colored sweater with dark flecks that reminded Eli of cinnamon sugar. He'd paired it with comfortable, broken-in jeans that hung low on his hips.

Really low. He'd worn those jeans around Eli more times than Eli could count, but Eli had never before noticed how low they dipped, hanging off the sharp definition of Zane's hip bones and displaying the smallest hint of happy trail.

He didn't realize he was staring until he saw that Zane had come to a stop. When he looked up, embarrassed, he saw Zane grinning at him with the same old saucy flair.

"Quit gawking at me," Eli grumbled. "Fair warning, pal. That hundred-year-old scotch you have is going down tonight."

"Oh really?" Zane arched an eyebrow.

And right back to embarrassment. Jesus. If this was the way they always talked, no wonder people got the wrong idea about them. Or was that Eli's brain working overtime, seeing innuendo where none existed?

"We're fine," Eli had said, and by damn if he wouldn't make it so. Somehow.

Zane seemed willing to help with that goal. Once he had a drink in hand, he hopped into his accustomed place perched on the arm of the couch and stretched, yawning. "Ended up staying all day," he said as casually as if this were any other evening. Good. "Interns, I swear. The kid who interrupted us twice earlier? He paged to apologize for apologizing."

Eli snorted. "Tell me I was never that bad."

"No. God, no. You actually know the difference between your ass and your elbow. After that, I spent the rest of the day at the clinic. Which you knew." Zane rubbed his eyes. "They're going under, Eli. It's only a matter of time."

Damn. Zane couldn't have loved a baby more than that clinic or been more loyal to its mission than a faithful hound. "You're a good doctor," Eli said abruptly and without prompting.

"You're not so bad yourself. Which brings us back to interns." Zane propped his elbows on his knees. One of those who sometimes talked with his hands, he gestured as he spoke. "The second I laid eyes on you, I thought, There's someone who knows what he's doing. I figure it's because you came to the field when you were old enough to understand the difference between your ass and your elbow."

Eli laughed.

So did Zane. "I speak the truth. Sometimes I wonder if sending eighteen-year-olds off to college to decide their futures isn't the dumbest idea ever. Maybe a couple hundred years ago when eighteen was actually an adult instead of an overgrown adolescent."

Eli nodded, rubbing his chin with his thumb. What he knew, but didn't bring up, was the fact that Zane had been on the fast track for medicine long before he was eighteen. Groomed for it since elementary school, the youngest of a family of doctors that wanted nothing more than to produce yet another MD.

Zane finger combed still-damp hair out of his face. He hadn't shaved, leaving a shadow's worth of fine stubble on his cheeks. The man would look good with a beard, Eli thought. Unlike himself. Eli looked like a horse with a mold problem when he tried facial hair. Then again, Zane made almost everything look good.

Yeah, Eli had noticed these things before. He'd thought everyone had. Now he guessed not.

"Sometimes," Zane said, choosing his words with obvious care, "the way I see it, a person needs to get out and live some. Try new things. Find out who they are and what they really want."

"I recognize a segue when I hear one." Eli sat forward on the couch and mirrored Zane's pose. "So we're going to do this, huh?"

"I think we might," Zane replied. He watched Eli with the same curious intensity of focus as he had in the bistro. This time, Eli recognized it. This time, the shudder of sensation wasn't fear. Well. Not all fear. Something Eli couldn't quite put a name to. "I think we have to."

Chapter Four

Eli waited.

Zane waited.

Eli kept his lips zipped.

"I can outlast you, you know," Zane said.

Eli sighed. "Fine, I give."

"About time." Zane's posture eased. His drying hair fell over his face again. "So I was thinking, uh… Damn." He bit his lip. "Okay, having a little trouble with the words, now of all times."

"You, speechless? I should have brought my camera to get a picture." Eli took a second look at Zane. The man had a tremendous sense of self-presence. Handsome and he knew it, and a sharp dresser within the limits he set himself. Even his lounging-around clothes were chosen to fit and present his best side.

Soft, touchable sweater. Come-hither-and-tap-this jeans. Stubble. Hair in disarray that invited smoothing. Bare feet. Nothing anyone could truly point to as a come-on, but only an idiot wouldn't be able to read between the lines.

Looked like Eli wasn't the only one seeing things in a new light after the kiss at the bistro. Or maybe…

"Can't hide anything from you, can I?" Zane asked with the wry twist of his lips that indicated he knew he'd been made.

"Subtlety is not your middle name."

"Where'd I lose you?"

Eli waved at the general area of Zane's neckline. "Right around the part when you flashed your tits." Over Zane's laughter, Eli sighed and made himself lean back on the couch. "I'd just like to go on the record as saying this is nuts."

"You're not telling me anything I don't already

know." Zane stretched his arms over his head. "Anyway, the outfit. Consider it an experiment on my part. Worked too."

"How so?"

"You looked."

"That I did." And he wanted to look again.

"Shows you have good taste, if you ask me." Zane eased down next to Eli. He almost seemed to crackle with the kind of energy that meant he was cooking up something interesting. "Here's what I figure. We try it again."

Eli froze.

Zane jostled Eli. "Hey. This is me here. Stay with me. It's just a kiss. Maybe it *will* be awful this time. Too much saliva, too much tongue, too much stubble, whatever. We'll know it was a fluke. We write it off to outside influence and get on with our lives."

"Or..."

Zane shrugged. Eli envied him his casual acceptance. Or was that a facade? Maybe so. Interesting. The man had balls. Now more of a consideration than ever. "Or we'll have a hell of a lot more to figure out. Are you with me?"

"Zane..." Eli hesitated, one foot off the ledge. "I don't think this is me."

Zane laid one hand on Eli's knee. "Hey. Don't go and start thinking you're in this by yourself. I've got the other oar, and I'm rowing, brother. I'm rowing hard because these are fucking deep waters."

"But..."

Zane slid his hand higher, slowly enough to be stopped. "You're not into guys. But I'm starting to think you're into me."

"Zane --"

"I wasn't finished. I'm starting to think I'm into

you too. So." Zane stopped moving. "What do we do with that?"

"We could panic."

"True. Or I could take you by surprise," Zane said and kissed him.

It went slower than that, of course, but only later would Eli be able to track how it'd happened. Zane slid down to lie on the couch, on his side, and at that range it was easiness itself to roll over him and take Zane by the chin, tilt his face up, and fit them together.

Zane's lips were as soft as Eli remembered. They tasted of the scent of leather and a hint of peppermint and underneath that the baseline Zane that Eli was already growing accustomed to. It all registered, then dissipated because when a man was being kissed the way Zane kissed Eli, there wasn't room for anything else.

He found himself with his fingers in Zane's hair, sifting the strands, as silky as they'd been before. More so, freshly washed and dried and left to fall as they wished. Warm. So was the nape of Zane's neck, and that was the perfect place to rest his hand to guide Zane.

Zane drew back, only far enough to sit upright. "Angle," he said. "Up or down?"

Eli wanted to say up. The couch was better. But something in him wanted more. "Down," he said roughly, kicking his legs out and making room between coffee table and couch. "Room to move."

"You think I'm putting out on the first date? I'm not that kind of girl, you tramp." Zane grinned when he succeeded in making Eli laugh and, in the wash of good humor, slipped down to join Eli on the floor, stretching out beside him, taking up all the available space, too close for comfort, just close enough to entice.

In for a penny and all that. Eli took half a second to adjust to the sensation of firm legs pressed to his and the rise and fall of Zane's chest with each breath, and then the nearness of his mouth commanded all Eli's attention.

This time, Eli was the one to kiss first. He knew his place now, a firm grip to guide Zane where he wanted the man -- *man*; was this ever going to get less strange? Then again, he wondered that every time, and so far, as soon as Zane's lips were pressed to his, he forgot that it mattered.

Zane sighed, a wisp of breath that tickled Eli's cheeks. He slid his arm around Eli's waist and began to pull him over, Zane more on his back, Eli draped halfway on top of him. Legs separated, Eli propped on his hip.

Curiosity killed the cat, but as Eli recalled, the other half of that old saw was, "But satisfaction brought it back." He rubbed his cheek against Zane's and turned his head to take a hazy-eyed glance down Zane's body. As he'd thought, Zane liked this kissing stuff plenty. He was hard in his jeans, solid, but gentleman enough not to push the issue.

Eli might have loved him a little for that. One step at a time, right? Yet somehow... somehow he couldn't look away. Not out of horrified fascination, but something different. Intrigue? Maybe.

"Hey. Back up here." Zane nudged Eli into place. "We're not done."

Eli took a moment to trace the sharp angles of Zane's cheekbones and the cleft in his chin, marveling at the differences between man and woman. "Not by a long shot," he agreed, coming back in.

They'd kept it chaste so far. PG-13. This time, Zane reached for Eli and kept him closer, tighter, his hand firm on Eli's back, with the heat of his palm pressing a brand through Eli's sweater to his skin. As he did, he let his lips part, just the way he had before, only better now that Eli didn't want to hesitate to slide inside and taste him.

Jesus. That first slick stroke went to his head. Eli stopped, hissing.

"No, you don't." Zane prevented him from retreating. "It's just me. It's okay. Like that. Just like that." He helped and guided Eli back into action. Smoothed over the bump in the road until it was forgotten.

Eli rolled more firmly into place, draped over Zane's chest. One thigh pressed to Zane's hip, his own burgeoning hard-on kept considerately away from contact. Scary as hell. Amazing. He drew Zane's lower lip between his teeth and sucked, nibbled lightly.

"Can I..." he asked, not sure what he was asking but confident Zane would probably have a better idea. The guy knew him so well, after all.

"Anything." For once in his life, Zane's gray eyes were hazy, out of focus. He returned the bite, sharper, with interest. "You don't even have to ask."

"I know." Eli took a deep breath and let his hand drift downward. Not too far -- nowhere near ready for *that* yet -- and plucked at the loose hem of Zane's soft, touchable sweater.

Zane watched him, curiosity cutting some of the daze, and a wicked grin rising when Eli slid his hand beneath to rest on Zane's bare stomach. That grin disappeared when Eli stroked him, unconsciously, not wanting to stop once he'd started. "Oh God."

"You're telling me."

"More," Zane said, dragging Eli down to him. Turnabout being fair play, and Zane being Zane, it was only natural -- and welcome, surprisingly so -- when Zane skimmed a caress up beneath Eli's sweater and found a place to rest on Eli's back. His skin was so warm, hot, Eli wondered if Zane would leave a print there long after they were done.

Zane being Zane, it also figured that Zane would follow through and up the ante. He drew a line up and down Eli's back. "Hairy chest, I can deal with," he said between kisses. "If you'd had a hairy back, I'm afraid I'd have kicked you out."

"No, you wouldn't have," Eli said, emboldened by the turn-on of the touch and the ripe softness of Zane's mouth yielding to his. Zane tasted so good and gave way so sweetly, better than any woman Eli could remember. Better than Marybeth, bless her thin-lipped soul, and that was enough thinking about his ex-wife. He cupped Zane's cheek and held him in place, kissing deep and wet and -- *oh*. Eli grunted into Zane's mouth at the sudden, rough pressure.

"Are you groping my ass?"

"Is that a problem?"

"Not sure." Eli swallowed around a knot in his throat. "I don't think so."

"Good," Zane said happily before returning to the business at -- well, at hand. Eli sensed that Zane was discovering the same bonus as Eli: doing this with a man, you could be just about as rough as you wanted. They knew they weren't going to break.

Eli wanted a little of that action himself. He found Zane's upper arm and pulled. "Like this. This. Roll over."

Zane chuckled, soft and low and knowing. He didn't let go of Eli; matter of fact, he tickled at Eli's belt and slipped the tips of his fingers beneath. Just feeling him up, not going any further. Still making Eli abruptly nuts, crazy enough to grab a solid handful of tight ass and knead. The sound Zane made, fed between his lips, took care of the rest of Eli's online brain and left him with nothing but feeling.

Strong hands sweeping up his back and down to his ass, the flex and give driving heat deeper and harder. Zane would leave bruises; Eli found he welcomed the thought of them. Wanted to give Zane a mark of his own.

Action followed impulse. He left Zane's lips to let himself do what he wanted and travel down, following stubbled cheek to the underside of his jaw and beneath the ear, then down the throat until he could feel Zane's pulse hammering beneath his lips.

There? Yes, there. He kissed once, twice, hard, drew a bit of the flesh between his teeth and bit. Just enough pressure to raise a welt.

Zane tugged Eli's hair, not hard enough to hurt or really make him want to move. "You want me in turtlenecks for a week? I'll look like a fruity poet."

Eli chuffed a quiet laugh. "Don't like it?"

"Didn't say that."

This was intoxicating. Eli let go and let himself travel. Down, farther down, to the neckline of the sweater that'd tormented him before. He hesitated, wanting it off. Too much? He shifted forward, wondering if he had the balls -- and his thigh came into contact with something hard that wasn't knee or hip.

Zane flinched, shuddered -- whimpered, a tiny noise that drove out all questions, at least for the moment. Christ, that was his dick, and he was hard enough to drill through a wall. I did that, Eli thought, stunned. It's because of me.

He challenged anyone not to be turned on by that. "Off," he said, jerking at the edge of Zane's sweater. "Off, right the fuck now."

"On the first date?" Zane nipped the corner of Eli's jaw.

"I think we're beyond -- oh, God. *Oh.*" Leave it to Zane not to be shy or to be a slow learner. He'd begun to rock forward, slow and easy did it, but not mistakable, nudging Eli with his dick. Giving him room to back off if he wanted.

Eli did want. Didn't. So confused. Only not confused at all, not when Zane took it that one step further and molded his hand over Eli's dick and pressed down. Eli grunted and bowed inward. Too good. He didn't know how long it'd been since someone else's hand was on him, and Zane --

Too good. Eli caught Zane by the wrist and held him away. "Stop," he said, feeling the heat of his own breath on Zane's skin. "I don't think --"

"Exactly. Don't think." Zane cupped Eli more firmly, not going anywhere anytime soon, and massaged.

"Oh, *fuck.*"

"Looking like that might happen someday," Zane said. He drew a teasing stripe up Eli's cock and, thank God, let go. Last thing Eli wanted -- at this point -- was to go off like a teenager, and he'd been dangerously close to that happening.

Back to the kissing and the slower sweeps of hand and the drawing closer of bodies. Slower, and slower still, until they were almost at a standstill, mouths together but not moving. Zane's eyes were nearly closed, glints of gray all Eli could see. "If you don't want this to get a lot more serious, better stop now," he warned Eli.

"I don't know," Eli said. "Yes. No. Hell, I don't know what I'm saying." He reluctantly let Zane go.

Sure, he wanted to grab and rut and fuck. He was a guy. But now they'd stopped kissing, and the cooler air had begun to make itself felt around them, the urgent rush had eased up. His brain struggled with the disconnect between *friend* and *lover* -- not as strong as before, no, but once again there in his head.

"Hey." Zane rubbed his thumb under Eli's jaw. "Do not lose your cool. It's me."

"Trust me, if I didn't know that, we wouldn't be here right now." Eli let himself indulge and kissed Zane's forehead. Girly, but Zane didn't mind. In fact, he smiled, loose and easy as if he'd come. Eli wondered, then realized it'd be a hell of a lot harder -- so to speak -- to tell if a guy had faked it.

So they were both strung out, on edge, yet full up. "So," Eli said. He found Zane's hand and played idly with Zane's fingers, looking at them so that he wouldn't slip into the "what have I done?" panic that he kept at bay with an effort. He hadn't lied. Anyone but Zane and they'd have been eating his dust long ago. Zane was different. Zane was... Zane. A law unto himself. Terrifying. Fantastic.

"So," Zane echoed. He sighed and pressed his head to Eli's chest briefly before propping himself on his elbow to face Eli. "Not a fluke, huh?"

"I think we can rule that out, yes."

Zane chuckled. He reached out to smooth down Eli's rumpled hair. "Good. Not that I'd mind further testing."

"I bet you wouldn't." Eli let himself look at Zane, drinking in all the details from flushed cheeks, the pinkness spreading down to his chest beneath the sweater, and back up to the cockeyed grin and sleepy, content gaze. "I still have no idea what I'm doing."

"Give yourself some credit. You're doing fine."

Zane pressed his forehead to Eli's and rolled them together. "Besides, it's the both of us. We figure it out together. One for all."

"And two for the price of one." Eli fidgeted, the nearness fast making him more interested in going on than stopping, though he knew he'd regret it if he did push the issue. Fuck in haste, kick yourself in leisure. "So," he said again, rolling strands of Zane's hair between thumb and forefinger. "We're both in the game. Help me figure out where we go from here."

* * *

"Okay. Give me a minute. I've got to catch my breath." Zane lay on his back, hands laced together beneath his head. Eyes closed, breathing quick, he presented a picture of deliciously debauched man. Eli hadn't ever imagined a guy this way. Never had reason to. But should he ever have gone there, he wouldn't have thought a man could look like this: rumpled hair, lips reddened and plump from kissing, and clothes in disarray.

The clothes. Those drew Eli's eye and kept it there. Zane's sweater had ridden up just far enough in his exploration that it bared a tempting strip of suntanned skin and muscle, with a trail of hair that arrowed down from his navel to disappear beneath his jeans. Eli knew, in theory, why it was called a happy trail, and he'd always been plenty happy with his own trail and the good times it led to.

Strange, in a good way, to look at another's and comprehend all over again why that stripe of hair earned its name. To know that he wanted to follow it down.

And Zane knew what he was thinking. Always did. He nudged Eli with his knee. "You wanted to discuss?"

"Suddenly, not so much," Eli said, voice rough in his throat, and bent his head again to fit his lips to Zane's. He thought Zane might have said, "Thank God," but he wasn't paying much attention.

Keeping to his word, Eli didn't ask out loud. He wanted, he directed, he took. Slipped a hand beneath Zane to guide him up, sitting, and pulled sharply on the hem of Zane's sweater. *Off.*

"Yeah?" Zane whispered, lips at Eli's ear. "You're sure you want to see me?"

Eli jerked more firmly on the sweater.

"Careful of the threads," Zane objected.

Eli kissed him quiet, then pliant, amazed at the thrill of satisfaction when Zane moaned and went loose in his arms. When he let Eli do what he wanted and guide the sweater up and over his head. Zane's hair stood out like a dandelion, crackling with static electricity. Eli took half a second to chortle at the sight -- what else were friends for? -- before Zane took control again and dropped back to lie on his elbows, baring all that skin in invitation.

Sneaky bastard. Not half bad-looking, either. Eli gazed, fascinated, at Zane's chest. He'd seen it before, sure. They'd changed in front of each other, washed Zane's car back before he'd had a fit of environmental consciousness and sold the monster, had worked out until their shirts were molded to their bodies with sweat.

Those experiences didn't so much compare. For one thing, Eli could reach out and touch now, and he did. One palm to Zane's stomach, his fingers splayed wide, feeling the jerk and shudder of Zane's reaction.

He let that hand slide up, over muscles and ribs and between Zane's pecs. He had less hair than Eli, and his skin was smoother. Eli wondered how they would look together, side by side, and there was no good reason why he couldn't find out.

And so he did. He let go of Zane reluctantly, only long enough to sit up and yank his thermal shirt over his head. Shorter hair, no crazed dandelion look, not that he gave that more than a second's worth of thought because as soon as he'd seen, he wanted to see closer. He lay down beside, then on Zane.

Christ. The first touch of skin to skin made Eli jerk, a full-body shudder that Zane echoed. He'd have compared more, looked harder, if Zane hadn't speared his fingers into Eli's hair and hauled him in for a kiss that might have lasted hours. Eli lost track. All he knew was that somewhere in the middle, he needed to touch more. Arms, chest, stomach, none were quite enough until he was back at Zane's hip again.

Until he found himself toying with the button and zip of Zane's jeans, the heat of his solid erection radiating against the side of his hand, and Zane's breathing quick and shallow against his lips.

Terrifying. Almost too much so. Almost --

Zane knew exactly what Eli was thinking. Always did. Never let anyone say Zane wasn't a quick study or that he didn't understand what made Eli tick. He was at the perfect angle to slide his hand down the back of Eli's jeans and squeeze his ass.

"Fuck!" Eli hissed between his teeth and bowed his back, wanting both to draw back and to grind forward.

"Play your cards right," Zane said. He kneaded muscle and nudged Eli closer, closer, closer still. "Do it. Give me your hand."

How was Eli supposed to say no to that, especially when he wanted it enough to make him crazy? So strange. Yet not at all. Fuck, he'd never make sense of this. All he could do was act. He took a deep breath, exhaled it into Zane's mouth and undid the fastenings of Zane's jeans in a rush. Zane's cock filled the gap he'd made, rubbing up firm and scorching against Eli's palm. It jerked when they made contact, as Zane drew in a shocked gasp and then groaned.

"More," he demanded. Begged. "Eli, please. More."

"I've got you," Eli said. In for a penny. In for a fuck. This was Zane falling apart beneath him, and he was the one who'd made it happen. Eli didn't have the words.

It still took courage to nudge Zane's snug-fitting boxer briefs down, to uncover sleek hips and, though he couldn't quite make himself look, to wrap his hand around hard flesh and squeeze. Zane swore, butted his head hard to Eli's chest, and, before Eli could process what was happening, came, spilling sticky heat over Eli's fingers that dripped back down over his belly.

No man could stand up to that. Eli let go to fumble at his jeans, realizing when he made contact that his fingers were wet with Zane's cum. The slick glide of that on his cock undid him too. He didn't have the presence of mind to guide the jets over Zane, but God almighty, he wished he had, and the thought of it made him grind his teeth together until his jaws creaked, made him come hard, wringing himself out.

He collapsed then, head thumping down on Zane's chest where he could smell sweat and cum and soap. "Christ," he said, out of breath. Embarrassment hovered just beyond the horizon, barely staved off. For now.

"Third base on the first date," Zane said, sounding stoned, lazily brushing at Eli's hair. "I guess I am that kind of girl after all."

It made Eli laugh, exactly what Zane had no doubt intended. He found himself pressing a kiss over Zane's sternum. "You, my friend, are a strange man."

"Guilty," Zane said, satisfaction and afterglow drawing the word out into one long sigh. "Hypothesis confirmed, proved, rubber-stamped, and Viagra not needed. Not a fluke."

Eli had sobered. He rubbed his thumb over Zane's stomach, smearing it in the last of the drying cum, rubbing it into Zane's skin. Zane grunted but let him do as he liked. "Not what I'd pictured," he said, knowing Zane would understand him.

Zane chuckled lazily. "And what did you have in mind?"

"I honestly don't know."

"Regrets?"

"No," Eli said. It was only partially a lie. Okay, mostly a lie, but not for reasons he could or wanted to explain. It'd been... clumsy. Rushed. Heat and need and wham, bam, over. Not that that was a bad thing. Hot and heavy suited him fine.

Now, if he just had a practical clue about how to take it further...

Zane tweaked Eli's ear. "Quit thinking so hard. You're giving me a headache. C'mon. I have a decent bed. We should use it. I don't even mind being the little spoon."

Eli snorted. "Now why doesn't that surprise me?" he asked, already doing as he'd been told. "Topping from the bottom. I can see how this is going to go already."

"It's like you know me or something." Zane took Eli by the hand and began to lead him from the room. Stopped, squeezing Eli's fingers startlingly tight. "Glad it was you," he said. He pressed his forehead to Eli's.

"Don't think it could have been anyone else."

"Zane --"

"Shh." Zane bit Eli's lip, a tiny, tantalizing nibble. "For once in your life, just take the compliment, would you?"

Chapter Five

"So what did you get up to last night?" Diana slapped a stack of charts on the counter by Eli's elbow to get his attention. The gambit worked and then some, startling Eli into nearly -- nearly -- knocking his morning coffee over the edge and into the bank of computers at the nurse's station.

"Nice, Diana." Eli made sure his java was safe. "Give a guy some warning, would you?"

"Not my style."

"Granted. Did you want something?" Eli couldn't quite remember what she'd asked. He was in a fog this morning, head crammed with thoughts and memories and phantom touches.

Diana leaned over the counter, elbows on her charts. "I asked where you were last night."

Eli's pulse sped up. "Excuse me?"

"Holly and I went for tapas, and we decided to play some pool afterwards. We must have called you half a dozen times to see if you wanted to come along. We could have used your unique talents."

"You mean you wanted me to help you fleece the locals."

"And?" Diana shrugged, unperturbed. "A girl's got to get her kicks somehow."

An awful thought occurred to Eli. "Please don't tell me you went to some side-street dive without me."

"Hey! Have some Chicago pride."

"Bullshit. I grew up here. You didn't. If you two princesses headed off the beaten track, they'd have wiped the floor with your perky asses."

"If you'd come, we might have gone somewhere a little more exciting, but no, we played it safe. Wound up in a café eating half our body weight in cheesecake. Then Happy Holly got to go home and jump her husband with the sugar buzz."

"If that's code for something, I really don't want to know about it."

Diana relented. "I was worried about you. Sue me."

"Must have switched my phone off. My mistake; won't happen again."

Diana's lips thinned out. "Eli, you know better. What if you'd been on call?"

"I wasn't, and I said it won't happen again, Diana." Eli scooped up his coffee. "Christ. I'm not here even five minutes, and I'm getting harassed. Lay off, would you?"

"Eli?" Diana asked, exuding great, white-knuckled patience. "You really need to get laid." And with that she was gone in an offended rustling of starched lab coat and White Linen perfume. At least Eli thought it was White Linen. What the hell did he know about perfume, anyway?

Odds were, just about as much as he knew regarding schtupping his closest friend. Which was to say, he didn't have a fucking clue, pardon the expression.

"I'm officially in over my head," Eli muttered, sipping his coffee. "Fuck me!" He jumped.

"Maybe later." Zane slipped around Eli and leaned on the counter. Thank God, no nurses or orderlies or candy stripers around to see. He cocked his head. "You look like a thunderhead."

"You think? You just goosed my ass."

"You didn't seem to mind last night." Zane clicked his tongue at Eli and winked at him before reaching for the charts. He flipped the top one open and, reading it, asked, "You're staring at me as if I've committed some unspeakable sin. What?"

Eli rubbed the back of his neck. He couldn't help noticing Zane had worn a turtleneck today, and he could see all too clearly in his mind's eye the strawberry of a love bite he'd left over Zane's pulse. Zane fingered it even as Eli watched. Unconsciously? Perhaps so. Made him want to relent, but some things he couldn't do. Not even for Zane.

Christ, he hadn't thought this far. Should have. Last night, the in-versus-out question hadn't even entered his mind.

Mistake.

Zane turned to Eli, laser stare out in force. Eli found he appreciated it far less than usual at this moment. "Either you tell me or face the consequences. Like maybe I don't come over tonight."

There. That'd give any man impetus to spit it out. "Not at work." Eli put a sideways step's worth of distance between them. There. He felt better already.

Not so much when he registered the quick flash of hurt on Zane's face. "Not at work?" Zane echoed, taking back that step.

"I'm not joking."

Zane frowned. "Didn't think you were." He sighed and stopped. "Okay, okay, I get it."

"Do you?"

"Trust me." Zane fingered the side of his neck. Contrary prick. "It's not as big a deal as you're making it out to be. We're all over each other all the time. It's going to look stranger if we suddenly start playing keep-away."

At least he understood. Eli relaxed a fraction. "I am what I am, Zane."

"You and Popeye."

"Regardless." Eli wished he could rewind and restart this conversation from the beginning. Maybe not let it unravel on him this time. "I'm not sorry," he said, lowering his voice to barely above a whisper. "Not about what happened. But it's my business. Not anyone else's."

"Hmm," Zane said, without elaborating.

Eli waited. No way Zane could hold anything in for long. He'd suddenly started to get a nasty suspicion that that particular aspect of Zane's character might prove problematic. But they were friends above all. Zane would respect that, wouldn't he? Always had before.

Then again, things were changing, weren't they?

Eli closed the distance between them, as he would have two days ago. "Don't get pissed. You knew how I feel about broadcasting my business."

"Sure I do." Zane flipped the chart shut. "Here's the thing, Eli. It's not just your business. It's mine too."

Eli's words escaped him. Damn. The truth of that couldn't be denied. He should have thought about this. Really, really should have. "Zane --"

Zane had already moved on, the clouds past the sun they overshadowed, leaving blue skies behind. Somehow Eli didn't buy it. "Relax, don't worry. We'll work it out together. That's the deal, right?"

Eli's breath escaped him in a sigh of relief. "Thank you."

"Don't thank me," Zane said, proving Eli's suspicion that this wasn't over yet. "Working it out doesn't mean sweeping it under the rug. I've got a theory, and you're going to listen to it because I am your friend as much as you are mine and you know how *I* am too."

Eli couldn't say no to that. Fair was fair. He closed his mouth and gestured for Zane to have out with it.

"Here's what I think," Zane said, slowly and thoughtfully, gazing off into space at his dozen different options and selecting what he wanted. "You've always been private because, frankly, the stuff you keep to yourself isn't that great. Teasing, harassment, all that joyful material. You've never had anything particularly good to keep to yourself before."

Damn him.

"So just think about it," Zane said. He clapped Eli on the shoulder, same as he always would have. Friends and nothing more. Well, if you didn't count the quick rub of his thumb in a less than platonic way. "Until then, I'll be here." His grin emerged, impish and playful, making Eli feel better about himself.

Eli covered Zane's hand with his own, roughly, fast, but enough. He didn't see this changing anytime soon. Or could he? He didn't know. Seemed like confusion was fast becoming the status quo. "I'm not going anywhere either," he said, not sure if he meant it as a warning of how things would always be or a promise of how they could alter. He couldn't change who he was.

Or could he? Hadn't he already?

"Dr. Novia? Oh God, there you are." An intern, spattered with the effluvia one inevitably got spattered with working the ER, clattered down the hall in a beeline toward them, her eyes too wide and the classic new-kid panic etching white lines on her face. "There's a situation --"

"Calm down. Breathe. I'm on it." Zane took her by the shoulder to steady her. "Right behind you. Okay?"

Eli had noticed before how Zane was hands-on with everyone. The reminder at this present time helped and allowed him to give Zane a gentle push, just like he would have -- before. "I think that's your cue."

"Duty calls," Zane agreed. He hesitated only long enough to give Eli a look that felt oddly just like a kiss, and a grin. "It's funny, you know?"

"What is?"

Zane shrugged. "Things keep slipping out of my hands. Never mind. Rain check for now. We'll get back to this later. Deal?"

Eli couldn't say no to him. "Deal."

The kiss in Zane's gaze grew hotter, almost making Eli blush. "I'm counting on it."

Zane made good his escape, his easy lope keeping pace with the frantic intern. Eli stayed put and watched him go. He propped his elbow on the counter, scrubbed his hand over his face, and shook his head. If he didn't want this so much, he'd reconsider. What was done, was done. And he didn't regret it.

He didn't have a clue how to handle it, but he guessed that was part of the journey.

Eli looped his stethoscope around his neck, secured his coffee, and started walking. He'd come in early as per his usual when he had a lot on his mind. Time still before he started his rounds, time he'd planned on using in the hospital library. A doctor, especially someone barely newer to the field than that poor intern, couldn't research enough if he wanted to keep up with the pack.

Thing was, at this juncture Eli had the feeling there were other things he needed to concentrate on more. Like last night.

Eli wanted to stop, close his eyes, and remember. He didn't, though that didn't stop his memories from playing themselves out in Technicolor flashes deep in his head. Who knew it could be that good? Holding a cock wasn't what he'd ever figured would flip his switch. Hammer on his switch.

Normally, coming before the game had even started would put a damper on things. No pun intended. This time Eli couldn't say he was too sorry. Any further and -- hell. Who knew how bad it could have been?

Handjobs, those might not be too hard to figure out. Blowjobs? Christ. Eli didn't have a fucking clue except for vague notions about not using teeth.

But how did you manage not to do that? Teeth were there, right next to a man's lips, and from what he'd gauged, Zane wasn't exactly small. Eli doubted he could fit that into his mouth, period -- and whoa, that thought made Eli stumble half a step.

Give a blowjob? This was never going to stop being bizarre. Maybe even more so because, despite the rush of alarm, the rush of desire was equally strong.

Eli waited for the momentary wave of shock to pass before he walked on, reasonably proud of how he wasn't letting any of this maelstrom show on the surface. He hoped.

What he could use right now, really use, was someone's advice, and wasn't that a hell of a kicker? Eli considered reading up on it. He'd gotten damn good at cracking the books in recent years. Somehow, though, that didn't seem quite right. He knew from experience that he could memorize the procedure for, say, setting femoral swans, but when a doctor had his hands on living flesh and someone was counting on him... whole different ballgame.

Who could he talk to, though? Diana? Eli snorted. Diana would never let him hear the end of it, and by the end of the day, everyone *else* would know too. Not going to happen. Same with Holly. She'd psychoanalyze him to death, and he'd end up trying to convince her that a cigar really was just a cigar when actually, it wasn't. Made Eli's head hurt just thinking about it.

Wait. There was one person he could talk to. Not just about technique. Maybe about the rest of it too.

Eli hesitated, not totally on board with his forming plan. It chafed at his nerves to think about going to anyone, but when it came down to brass tacks, there was *one* for whom the barn door had long been left open, the bag had been emptied of cats, and the ship had sailed away. Plus, this person did have a way of pouring oil on troubled waters. Not something to be sneered at.

Still bugged him.

Bite the bullet, Eli. Fine. Needs must when the devil drove. Eli tossed back the last of his coffee, crumpled the cup into a ball to squeeze out the last of his tension -- *ha* -- straightened his shoulders, and went in search of his apparent new confidante.

Maybe, if he could get their ear, they might have some insight into what Eli suspected was going to be a real problem. Zane was right. Wasn't just Eli's business any longer.

He just hoped like hell that Taye was working today.

* * *

Eli sat on the edge of the nurse's station, paging through the schedule. Interns, interns everywhere, but nary a Taye to be found. Someone had drawn a line through his name. Strange. Not a little worrying.

"Drat it." Out of the corner of his eye, Eli saw a woman standing on tiptoe, trying to reach the highest shelf of charts behind the station. She clicked her tongue at the inaccessible heights.

"Holly," Eli greeted her, nodding. "Problems?"

"Someone's absconded with the stepladder, I think." She pressed her hand to her forehead. "Not that I enjoy playing the helpless female card, but could you give me a hand?" She pointed at the one she wanted, the edges hanging off the shelf but still out of her reach.

"Strawberry shortcake." Eli tipped it off without effort.

"We can't all be giants and Amazons, Eli," Holly rebuked mildly, already paging through the chart. She paused long enough to give him an arch sideways look. "Besides, I've been told by reliable sources that I'm much more of a Very Berry Surprise."

"Somehow, that fails to shock me." Eli took his seat again. Huh. Now that he could put a name to the face and Taye had become recognizable, Eli realized he usually followed Holly around like a lost puppy. Perfect opportunity. "Where's the boy toy?"

"If you mean Taye, say so. He called in," Holly said, on the surface appearing to be lost in her chart. Eli saw the slight worry lines on her face and knew differently.

Mild concern arose. "He okay?"

Holly stopped pretending to read her patient's history. "I'm not sure."

Eli didn't like the sound of that. "He knows it's not a smooth move for an intern to duck out for the sniffles, right?"

"Eli, don't be an ass." Holly sighed. "I'm worried. If you happen to hear from him, would you update me?"

"Sure," Eli agreed reflexively. Then --"Wait. Why would I hear from him before you?"

"I'd thought the two of you were hitting it off."

"Uh-huh."

Holly dimpled at him. Mischief. Great. "Did you know that the two of you are very much alike?"

"What?" Of that Eli had his doubts, and they must have shown because Holly's amusement at his expense grew exponentially. "Not so."

"Quite so." Holly held the chart close to her chest. "The difference being that he's what you could have been if you'd learned how to access your emotions more than your machismo."

"Funny lady. See if I help you reach the high shelves next time."

"I'm serious, Eli." Holly laid her hand on his arm. Some women were born to stay calm under any stress. Eli doubted you could ruffle Holly's composure with a wood chipper. Add a doctorate in psychology on top of that, and *bam*. Powerhouse. She studied him, observing something -- who knew what. "Look for yourself the next chance you get."

"I'd have thought Zane and I were the Doublemint Twins around here."

She didn't tease him when Zane's name came up. Points for her. "Not so," she said, mimicking his lower bass. Okay, she didn't tease him in a way he *objected* to. Yet. "You're opposites in almost every way."

Unexpected, that. "Seriously?"

"Without a doubt."

Huh. Eli shifted and made room for Holly to pass. An impulse struck him, acted upon without thought. "Do you have Taye's cell number?" He growled and went red at her knowing look. "I just want to check on the kid."

Holly rotated her hip at Eli. He could see her day planner in the pocket. Old-fashioned, she kept one on paper. "Help yourself. And Eli?" She winked. "It'll be our little secret. Although I do think it's sweet."

"Sweet?" Eli raised an eyebrow at her as he retrieved the book.

"You're a wonderful doctor. Smart, insightful, skilled. But you never reach out to people. Usually. This gives me hope, Eli." Holly patted him on the knee and was gone, calling over her shoulder, "I'll need that back by the end of the day!"

Eli waved her on, already in the T's and running his finger down the page. So he was worried. Sue him.

* * *

No answer. Eli tapped his cell phone against his leg, beating out a quiet *rat-a-tat* syncopation of concern. Troubling. Who else could he ask? Technically not allowed but he'd bet it could happen. Gossip flew as thick and fast around here as rice at a wedding. Doctors, nurses, interns -- everyone used the station as a perch, a watering hole, and an oasis for breather-or-breakdown moments.

As such, Eli found himself perfectly placed to overhear his name mentioned in conversation.

"Dr. Jameson?" An internal medicine specialist Eli didn't know leaned on her elbow and spoke to another woman, somebody Eli only vaguely recognized. "Taken, I think."

"I didn't see a wedding ring."

"He's not married. Divorced, maybe? But he's not the social type. Either he's involved, gay, or wed to his job. Not the best kind of guy to set your sights on."

Amen to that, sister. She had savvy. Eli listened more closely, despite knowing full well that eavesdroppers never heard anything good about themselves.

"He *is* a cutie," the internist allowed. "For a guy

his age."

Ouch. Eli revised his opinion of her.

"He's a great doctor. And he's not that old," the second woman said. A nurse practitioner, Eli thought. Pretty enough, with soft brown hair that curled around her face and smooth pale skin. Her eyes were brown, though, not gray like Zane's.

Huh. Eli smiled a private smile. Interesting, that. Zane was his go-to standard now. He thought he might like that.

"Dr. Jameson's old enough that he's off my radar," said the internist. "You want someone young, hung, who knows how to work it, and can go all night." She patted the nurse practitioner's shoulder. The way they interacted reminded Eli of himself and Zane. "Are we still on for going through that stack of journals tonight? I'm so far behind on my reading it's pitiful, and I need to get back in mental shape."

Maybe the nurse practitioner was still smarting under the sting of aspersions cast. "The competition for that position at Duke is going to be tough. Are you sure you want to apply?"

Meow. Eli hid his broadening smile. Also, his curiosity. What position was up for competition at his alma mater?

The internist shrugged, transparently pretending to be supremely unconcerned. "I could have a snowflake's chance in hell for all I care. For a shot at Duke, even a teaching position, losing a few nights' worth of sleep to work on my pitch isn't even a blip on the radar." Her touch gentled. "Don't get pissy over Dr. Jameson, okay? Men aren't worth it."

And back to *ouch.* With it came the customary sense of annoyance that went hand in hand with people who didn't know Eli chattering on about him.

Eli slid off the counter, still unnoticed, and eased down the hall. A small comfort to have other things to occupy his mind.

An opportunity to get on the faculty at Duke. Be damned. Eli tugged at the ends of his stethoscope. Talk about the opportunity of a lifetime. Not that he'd actually ever leave Chicago and head back south. The four years he'd spent away at med school in North Carolina had been enough to make him want to put down roots when he came back home.

Still, what an opportunity. Only the best of the best dared hope for a prayer. Eli wondered for a second, just wondered -- would he have a shot if he tried?

Something to think about, anyway.

* * *

"You'll notice that I'm not talking about Zane." Diana tossed her coat on the lounge table across from Eli and sat heavily, thumping her head on her arms. "Mostly because I've had the day from hell. You?"

"Hello to you too, Diana." Eli flipped over his stack of printed articles on the position recently opened at Duke Medical School. On paper, he made a good candidate. Tempting, if only just to see if he could do it.

"Is there any coffee in the pot?" Diana asked, muffled by her arms.

"There's something in the decanter. I wouldn't call it coffee, per se."

"I don't even care. I need a jolt." Diana popped up but didn't make it so far as her feet, rubbing the bridge of her nose instead. Looked like she had a headache.

"Allow me." Eli made quick work of fetching her a cup, though he didn't think she'd thank him for it after she'd tried a sip. Still, what were friends for?

"You're an angel. Or a devil." Diana sniffed the coffee and made a wry face. "Possibly both. Please take note that I'm still not talking about Zane."

Eli had to laugh. "And yet you've mentioned his name twice."

"Fine. I'm not talking about the doc with the crazy eyes. Better?"

At least she was smiling now. Eli decided that was a fair trade. "Noted, and thank you."

Though... come to think of it, he wouldn't have minded a mention of Zane. The day had passed in a blur of patients and bleating pagers. Eli would never regret choosing the path of a hospitalist, but when the pace heated up, whew. He'd barely had a chance to breathe today, much less catch up with the man in question.

"I'm sure I'll regret asking this, but why aren't you talking about Zane?"

Diana snorted over her coffee. Indelicate, but that was Diana. "Don't give me the innocent act. I'd bet my sex drive you've got a certain apology text from me saved on your phone with no plans of deleting it while I'm still alive. I'm on my best behavior."

Eli had more pressing concerns. "You honestly don't look good, Diana."

She shrugged and swirled the coffee in her cup. No zinger of a comeback about how much prettier she was than him? All was not well. "Told you, rough day. Most of it spent dealing with all the shit that rained downwards after some administrative bitch-slaps."

"Not again." Eli frowned. "They aren't going after the cardiology department, are they? I can't imagine they'd be so stupid."

"Us? Hell no. But would you care to take three

guesses what they're firing at in the hole?"

A sinking feeling began to coalesce in Eli's stomach. "Not the free clinic."

"Got it in one."

Not good. The free clinic was Zane's baby, or close enough. It consumed all his passion and energy not spent otherwise -- on Eli. Huh. Eli took care to hide his abrupt worry. "Do you know specifics?"

"I know generalities." Diana pushed the vile coffee aside and sat back, sighing. "Budgets are tight, corners need to be cut, the free clinic gets it in the ass without lube. Again."

"Christ. Does that leave them with any operating capital at all?"

"Not enough to stay open for much longer. The death of a thousand cuts. You know how it goes. They'll last a week, maybe two on band-aids and aspirin and ingenuity, and then?" Diana drew her hand across her throat. "Sometimes I hate modern medicine. It's all about the Benjamins."

"Mmm." Not that he could deny the truth of that, but Eli wasn't listening as closely as he might have. He pulled Diana's rejected coffee to him and sipped, lost in thought. Zane wasn't going to take this well.

Ah. The light dawned. "This would be why you brought up but specifically weren't mentioning Crazy Eyes," Eli said, piecing it together. "Because you know he's going to be either wrecked or on the warpath and wanted to give me the heads-up."

Diana looked slightly embarrassed, not a familiar expression for her. "See earlier mention of text. I went too far. Still, I'm looking out for you. And him. You're both dear to me, no matter how it might seem sometimes."

Eli was strangely touched. "Thank you."

"Don't thank me." She jerked her head to one side, indicating the hallway. "Go catch up with Crazy Eyes before he explodes. You think I look rough? Should have seen him when he stalked into administration like a grizzly bear on a mission."

Not, *not* good. Eli scrambled to his feet. "You couldn't have told me this before?"

"I had to work my way up to it. Who knew if you weren't going to give me the cold shoulder?"

"Diana." Eli made himself pause long enough to take up and squeeze her hand. "I'm not great with feelings. But that won't happen. Okay?"

The surprise in her reaction stung, but her dawning relief eased the bite. "Good. Now go get him, would you?"

Still Eli hesitated. "What about you? You'll be all right?"

"I've got a hot date tonight. After that, I'll be super or know the reason why."

Impulsively Eli kissed the top of Diana's head.

"What the hell was that for?"

"For being a good friend," Eli said. He would have added more if he hadn't heard the slam of a door being opened far more forcefully that the hinges' design allowed and, immediately following that, the particular staccato stomp that he knew as well as his own footfalls. Zane. "And I think that's my cue."

"Yeah," Diana said with a chuckle, taking the coffee back once more. "That's what he said. Work it, baby."

Dear God. So much for Diana behaving herself. Eli shook it off and went after Zane to see how bad it was, though to be honest, he had a pretty good idea.

Chapter Six

Eli reached Zane just in time to see him draw back his fist and aim it at a perfectly innocent wall. He caught Zane by the arm and wrestled him back. "Calm down. What did the sheetrock ever do to you?"

Zane snarled and shook Eli off. Damn. Nowhere near explaining himself yet. It was a rare occasion when Zane's sangfroid reached the end of its tether, but when it did, look out. Earthquake time. *Boom, crash,* and don't forget about the aftershocks.

"Zane, talk to me." Eli kept guard on his friend -- his lover, now -- like a basketball player defending the goal. He wasn't exaggerating. Punching a wall and destroying his hand was the least of what Zane could get up to when truly overwrought.

Zane had run his hands through his hair so many times it stood nearly upright in disheveled clumps, his tie was mostly undone and his shirt half-untucked, and he'd taken off his lab coat to roll his sleeves up to the elbow. The muscles in his arms flexed as he bunched his fists, and the muscles in his legs jerked with irritation as he began to -- not pace. Stalk. To and fro, reminding Eli of a caged tiger. His gray eyes were almost black. He looked dangerous.

Eli wondered exactly how bad a person it made him to be slightly turned on by Zane in a tempest. More than slightly.

He reined in his newly awakened libido and, though he didn't make a grab for Zane, stood firmly in his path. "Zane. Talk to me," he repeated with firmer emphasis. "I heard what happened."

"Then what the fuck do I need to talk about it for?" Zane swerved past Eli and made to roll on by like a thunderstorm.

"Uh-uh. I know you, friend." The time for

delicacy was past. Eli took Zane by the biceps and gave him a push. "Roof. If you're going to blow your stack, you do it in relative privacy."

* * *

Everyone needed a place to go and scream at the heavens sometimes. On busy days, it might be choked with frustrated doctors and nurses come to rage against the universal machine.

Lucky them, no one else was to be seen on the expanse of gravelly roof tar and assorted city flotsam that coated the roof of Immaculate Grace. Eli made sure the stairwell door was shut behind them and that he stood between Zane and the edge before letting go. "Let it out. I've got you. Shout, scream, whatever you need. Take a swing at me if you want."

"Pass." Zane's wrath had cooled during the forced march up the stairs. He scrubbed at his eyes and kicked the wall behind them, but nowhere near as forcefully as he might. "What I'd do without you, I don't know."

"Probably make an ass out of yourself in front of millions." Eli guided Zane down to a seat beside him on a concrete extrusion of the roof. Possibly a long-capped-over chimney. The hospital had age on it. Too bad wisdom didn't go hand in hand.

Zane propped his elbows on his knees and kept his face in his hands. Funny how familiar a pose despair was when one worked in health care. "You know," he said, "you're the only person I've ever been able to do this with. Lose my cool, let off some fucking steam, punch things, you name it."

Eli blinked, nonplussed. He didn't ask about Zane's family. He'd met the ice-cold remnants of the old-money crew, and they wouldn't show an emotion if threatened at gunpoint. But... "Not even with Diana?

Or Holly?" They'd been Zane's friends first.

"Those two? As if. They're... women. Dainty."

"Don't let Diana hear you say that. She'd rip your nuts off. Holly too. Either that or she'd smile ever so sweetly at her husband and get him to do it for her. Weaker sex, my ass."

Zane half laughed, not as if he found it funny, but it was a start, and Eli would take what he could get. "You asked me to talk; I'm talking. Quit flapping your gums and listen."

Eli spread his hands wide to indicate Zane should bring it on. He had asked, after all. Even if he had a feeling this would make him uncomfortable -- compliments, truly not his thing -- he was obligated to listen. Besides, what was he doing that no one else with a heart wouldn't?

Zane collected himself before he went on. "I've always been someone I was expected to be," he said, slowly choosing his words. "The son of doctors, successful doctors, game players. My wheels were greased, and I was set on the lickety-split track before I knew how to walk. You knew this."

"And? It paid off. You're the best doctor I know."

"Not the best. Look in the mirror sometime." Zane handwaved Eli's protestations. "That's not the point. I'm good. Sure. I know I am. But was it who I was supposed to be?" He rubbed his eyes. "And now, with what the system's become even since I started working..." He shook his head and sighed, the look on his face so woebegone and lost that Eli's heart would have gone out to him even if he'd been a total stranger.

Eli squeezed Zane's leg. "Still here. Still listening."

Zane covered Eli's hand with his own. His shook just a little. "You know... more and more I think we're not here to treat patients any longer. Not to heal. We're here to turn a buck and milk the insurance companies, and the one who dies with the most prescription drug T-shirts wins."

"It's a hell of a thing. I know. But without us -- without you -- it'd be a fuck of a lot worse for those we can help."

"Yeah." Zane's laugh lacked even the small trace of humor it'd contained before. "True. But you would see it that way. You love what you do."

"And you don't?" Eli asked without thinking.

Zane was quiet for too long. "On days like today, when I'm told that everything I promised when I took my MD is on its way out the window, sometimes I wonder if I ever loved it at all, or just the ideal. Sometimes I have no fucking clue who I am."

"Zane…"

"Forget it." Zane stood with an abrupt push and tried to smooth his hair. "I'll be all right. Mr. Bounce-Back-from-Disappointment, that's me, and fuck knows I've had plenty of practice. I have a few resources I can try to tap to help the free clinic."

It was like poking a stick in a lion's cage, but Eli had to. "And if they don't come through?"

"Fuck me if I know," Zane said. He exhaled deeply. "You busy tonight? I really don't feel like going home alone."

Not an unfamiliar question, but the subtext, that was new. Strangely enough, Eli wasn't bothered. More relieved. Talking was great. He often thought it didn't accomplish much, especially when emotions ran this deep. Normally he'd have suggested a good hard run or a session at the gym where they could beat holy hell out of punching bags or spar with one another.

He had the distinct feeling that if he went home

with Zane tonight, none of the above would be on the menu. And with that came a warming sense of liberation. Stress relief. That he could do. He thought. He was willing to give it a shot, inexperience be damned for now. And hell, if it was bad, then maybe it'd get Zane to laugh and mean it. His pride could take the hit.

Besides. Eli wanted nothing more than to follow Zane home, come what may. Wanted to take care of him.

"Can't say I feel like going home to an empty apartment myself," he said. "Your place or mine?"

Zane bit his lip. "Your place. It's nicer."

"It's a West Side shithole."

"It's real," Zane shot back. "It's lived-in and comfortable, and it's a home. Eli. Please."

He didn't need to say anything more. "I've got you," Eli said, tossing his arm over Zane's shoulders. "Always. C'mon. Half an hour on the El and we're there." He rubbed Zane's back through the sigh of relief he gave and led his friend away from the hospital toward something they both wanted.

Maybe even something they both needed.

* * *

"I was married once."

"Beg pardon?"

"Who said stop?" Zane nudged his toe into Eli's ribs.

Eli had been in the process of sliding Zane's left shoe off his foot. Both were propped in his lap, Zane sitting perpendicular to him on the far end of the couch. He'd done this before, the technique learned to impress girls a long time ago, but Zane was an absolute, shameless whore when it came to massages of any sort. He'd hoped to rub away the last lingering traces of Zane's inner turbulence over the clinic, at least for the night. Should have known that with Zane, once you oiled his joints, anything could happen.

Slowly Eli picked up Zane's foot and dug the pads of his thumbs into the sole. "I trust there's more to this story. You know about Marybeth, and I don't know about -- what was her name?"

"Mmm." Zane closed his eyes and arched his back, almost wriggling like a cat with the pleasure of being touched. He laughed and pressed his half-full tumbler of brandy to his cheek. "I actually don't remember."

"Oh, now see, now I don't feel quite as bad about never hearing this story before." Eli tweaked Zane's big toe. "So tell me about her."

"Paris," Zane said, gazing at the ceiling and lost in memory. "I think I was twenty-two. Just graduated from college and on a temporary AWOL from the family before med school."

Eli listened and worked at the same time. Zane looked wistful somehow, nostalgic and strangely small. "She must have been pretty," he said.

"That's the thing. She really wasn't. Except, she was. No. She had something compelling about her. If you saw her on the street and she didn't say a word, you'd walk right on by." Zane sipped his brandy. "Once she looked at you and spoke to you, *bam*. You were hooked."

Eli chuckled to himself. "Sounds like someone I know."

"I'll take that as a compliment." When Eli looked to him, curious as to whether or not Zane was being sarcastic, Zane was as serious as a judge.

To that, Eli didn't know what to say.

"We were together three nights. No, four. If you

count the first one, when I was drunk, stoned, who knew what." Zane began to grin, looking backward at the wild child he'd been. "I don't remember how we met, just that suddenly she was there, laughing at me, calling me on my 'stupid American bullshit' in that adorable accent. She had her hair in two loose braids, as black as soot. Her eyes, those were pretty. Pale green."

He fell silent. Eli waited.

"She took me home. I never knew why. Fed me leftover coq au vin and bread and some amazingly bad wine. She was training to be a chef. I'd forgotten that part."

"What happened?"

Zane's growing warmth in the memory abruptly evaporated. "Three days later, I was on a plane headed for Boston. She wanted me to stay. I had to go. Really don't want to talk about that part of it. The point is I never saw her again, and now I don't remember her name." He snorted softly. "Pathetic, huh? It wasn't even legal, really, just something one of her friends did. Said a few words and told us we could kiss."

Eli massaged Zane's tense foot, searching for something to say. "It's still better than most people ever have."

That brought Zane out of his brown study. "True." He lifted his glass to Eli. "Then again, sometimes some of us get second time lucky."

"Dr. Novia, are you trying to charm me?"

"Alas. He's seen through my clever scheme." Zane leaned his head back. "Maybe? I don't know. I wanted to share something with you, and that was what I had. Felt good to get it out too."

"Why didn't you ever before?"

"Because I've never told anyone about her."

Zane regarded Eli through slitted eyes. "You're the first. Strawberries," he said, shifting focus to the lights of the brandy in his glass. "I miss strawberries. Drop a perfect red berry into a flute of pale gold champagne, and you've never seen anything prettier. Sometimes I wish I could nibble on just one. Just to know that taste again, even for a second."

Eli reached for the glass and took it away, putting it safely out of reach. "If you've had enough to start thinking nostalgia trumps anaphylaxis, you've had too much. I'm cutting you off."

"Probably right." Zane stretched his arms over his head and yawned. "I -- oh. *Ow.*"

Eli winced at the note of pain Zane reached. He knew the likely cause. "What have I told you before? You get this worked up, your body pays for it. Your back's probably knotted like a bead mat."

Action followed impulse. Maybe not impulse. As soon as Zane had started talking about this Parisienne who'd stolen his heart, Eli had felt the prickling of something he'd be tempted to call jealousy. If that wasn't completely idiotic.

Not that he cared to analyze too closely. He spread his legs, noticing only now how immediately intimate the position seemed, and pointed at the floor. "Shirt off. I'm already playing massage parlor tonight. I can do your back too."

Zane's eyes closed in relief and thankfulness. "Best. Friend. Ever." He scooted in and lowered himself awkwardly. Eli had to help with the shirt. Not that he minded.

Zane's skin was smooth and warm and softer than Eli would have thought. Far less hair on his sleeker chest than Eli's. Funny how everything was slightly different now. Seen through new eyes. He'd meant the massage to be all business. Wasn't quite how it worked out. Instead of hard, fast, and firm, a good pounding to break down the tight spots... instead, Eli couldn't seem to make himself move quickly. He wanted to linger, to trace the graceful sweep from shoulder blades to small, and press his lips to the nape of Zane's neck.

"Hey." Zane dropped his head against Eli's inner thigh. "It's just me. No one to be scared of. Stay with me, okay?"

Eli huffed out an amused breath. He should have known. Of all the people he could keep secrets from, Zane never had been one of them. "Scared, no. Uncertain, yes. I'm a forty-three-year-old virgin to this, friend."

"I wouldn't say that." Zane rolled his head lazily, no doubt not incidentally teasing Eli's interested dick. "You've gone boldly forth, at least a little."

"I wouldn't call that little." Eli cupped the top of Zane's head to hold him still. "A man has his pride."

"Yes, and this specific man is an idiot." Zane craned around despite the strange angle to twinkle up at Eli, all good humor restored. Eli decided instantly that the price tag of his dignity was worth it. "Besides, how much experience do you think *I* have? Come down here, or I'll come up there."

Eli's heart rate picked up. He rubbed strands of Zane's hair through thumb and forefinger and stroked over his temples. "And what then?"

"Then we do what we do best. Figure it out together. Or," Zane said, clumsily climbing to his feet. He offered Eli his hand. "Or we could do this somewhere more comfortable. If you're up for that."

Eli considered demurring and thought there was absolutely no point in pretending that didn't light his fire. He took Zane's hand and squeezed it wordlessly.

Zane's smile was brilliant.

* * *

Zane turned on one bedroom light, just one, the lamp on Eli's bedside table. With its dark shade, it produced only a soft, buttery glow that warmed the room. Eli knew this room like the back of his hand. A place to sleep, and ever since he'd lived here, pretty much nothing more than that.

Not so now.

All of Zane's attention was fixed on Eli, drinking him in slowly with long sweeps from head to toe. A curious fascination and concentration made Eli feel -- he wasn't sure how to describe it.

"You have me at a disadvantage," Zane finally said, the suddenness of his voice making Eli jump. He fingered the buttons on Eli's shirt. "May I?"

What? Oh. Eli backed up until the backs of his knees hit the bed and he could sit, needing the support. Zane followed him and went down on one knee in the spread vee of Eli's legs.

Zane drew Eli's shirttails out of his belt and began to work his way up the buttons, pausing between each to feather touches over the bare skin beneath. "Eli? Let me take the wheel." When Eli began to demur, male pride protesting being treated -- well, like a woman -- Zane shook his head almost firmly, almost vulnerable. "Please. I need this."

Eli never could say no to Zane. He didn't start now. He swallowed down the last of his trepidations, or tried to, and deliberately ignored the rest until they melted into anticipation that brought butterflies instead of knots to his stomach. He nodded, not trusting his voice, but it was enough.

"Thank you." Zane pressed a kiss to Eli's chest

and stood to push Eli's shirt off his shoulders. Eli shook his arms to let the shirt slide down and off.

A thought occurred to him. Zane could take the reins, but that didn't mean much if the horse didn't want to run. He slid his arm around Zane's waist and tugged lightly. "Down here?"

"Thought you'd never ask."

They were of a size, he and Zane, Zane perhaps a little smaller and less broad in the shoulders, but he had strength where it counted and he was able to push Eli down on his back in the bed. The comforter smelled familiar to Eli. Soothing. Adding Zane's scent to the mix made it exciting. Cinnamon to coffee, spicier, warmer, slightly exotic but comforting at the same time.

Zane lay half on, half off Eli, one leg thrown over him and the rest of his body weight propped on his elbow. "Come here," he said, drawing Eli to him.

Eli knew how to kiss Zane now, but it was no less exciting for being familiar. Maybe even more so. Couches and floors, those were great. Beds made everything somehow more real. He found the place he liked best to hold Zane, the flat of his hip and the tight curve of his ass, and kneaded him through the slow, deep kiss.

That wasn't all he did. Somewhere in the middle, when Zane's breath grew tight and Eli could tell he wanted to shift forward, Eli let go of Zane's hip and teased his way around front. He was getting used to finding and feeling the rigidness of a cock instead of the warm softness between a woman's legs. Maybe even liking it better.

No. No maybe about it. Curious to see if it would have the same effect on Zane as it had on him, Eli palmed Zane's dick and pressed in, giving him something to push against.

"*Oh*" tasted sweet from Zane's lips to his, as did his tiny, broken whimper. "Don't stop."

"Not planning on it." Eli found the tab of Zane's zipper and drew it down. He drew the edge of his thumb up and down the side of Zane's dick. Curiosity overcame the last of the shyness. "Let me see you."

"Oh, fuck." Zane abruptly pulled away and braced himself on his arms over Eli.

"Christ. What?" Eli tried to rise to his elbows. "You okay?"

Zane laughed, choppy and a little too excited. Ah. That told Eli all he needed to know. He lowered himself to the bed again, then on second thought inchwormed his way up higher until his head rested on the pillows. "Whatever you want," he said and meant it, though making the offer turned him light-headed. "You've got the wheel, remember?"

"As if I could forget." Zane surged over Eli and pressed his mouth to Eli's neck, kissing him hard. The first press of bare chest to bare chest made them both hiss, and the slick heat of tongue and teeth sent bolts of *want* to Eli's hardened dick. "Something I've been thinking about."

"You never stop thinking," Eli said, almost out of breath already, and wasn't that odd? Or not. "Tell me."

"I'd rather show you." Zane's hand drifted down to undo Eli's slacks and clumsily tried to nudge them off. Eli lent the man a hand, though the room temperature felt shockingly cold and brought goose bumps to his skin. He thought he knew where Zane was heading here.

And God, did he want it. "Really?" he asked, just to be sure.

Zane's eyes were fever bright. "One hundred

percent," he said. He kissed Eli, one rough press to his lips that almost stung, almost too hard and rough and lingering. "Say yes?"

"Fuck, yes," Eli said, voice gone baritone with need, already strung out. He watched Zane crawl backward on the bed, not between his legs but to the side, tugging his slacks farther down.

Zane stopped then, staring. Eli wanted to squirm. Women didn't do this, stare as if they couldn't believe their eyes. He had nothing to be ashamed of in the size department. That didn't worry him.

"Fuck," Zane breathed. He braced himself on the bed, and on Eli, and lowered his head. The fringes of his hair tickled Eli's stomach and hid what he was doing from view, but there was no mistaking the first tickling touch of a tongue to his cockhead, or the sudden, engulfing, wet warmth of an eager mouth.

Eli jackknifed up. "Oh, *fuck*!"

Zane pulled off. "What? Should I stop?"

"Hell, no." Eli pressed his hands to his eyes. "Do that again."

And Zane did.

"Ah -- *God*. Zane." Eli wanted to see. He fought between letting his eyes slam shut to feel it better in darkness and straining to keep them open, only Zane's damn hair was in the way.

Zane chuckled, sounding lower and more confident. All the stress in him had dissolved. The bad stress, at least. Eli could see a sheen of sweat on his back as the muscles flexed. He drew off with a wet sound, his lips tickling and his breath warm on Eli's dick. "Guess that means I'm doing it right."

"Get back in there." Eli reached down, trying to brush Zane's hair aside. He succeeded in haphazardly tucking it behind Zane's ear. Maybe that was better, maybe not, because when he was able to get a look at his cock sliding between Zane's lips -- Christ, he was going to come, come hard, and they'd barely started. He ground his teeth and clenched his hands into fists in an effort to calm down.

As if that were remotely possible. Eli had known Zane was a smart man and that he learned quick, but *fuck*, who'd have thought he'd pick up on this quite so rapidly? It wasn't perfect, too much saliva and the occasional scrape of teeth, but Zane licked away the sting.

"Thought about this, huh?" Eli gasped. He'd never been quite so grateful that his bed's headboard had slats on it that let him reach up to grasp them and hang on.

"In detail." Zane's hand left Eli's hip and disappeared between Eli's legs. His hair fell forward again, but Eli couldn't be bothered noticing or being annoyed because that was Zane's hand cupping his balls, balancing them gently and playing with the lightest of touches.

Might have figured Zane would pick up on his hot spots right away too. Eli swore and pushed at Zane. "Stop, fuck, stop. I'll come."

"Want you to," Zane murmured. He dipped his head. *Christ*, that was his tongue on Eli's balls, tracing figure eights. "Yeah. Thought about this a lot," he said between shallow breaths and harsh swallowing sounds. "Sometimes even before."

That hit Eli like a hammer between the eyes. They hadn't even -- he hadn't thought -- and Zane had -- He groaned and gripped the headboard's slats tighter, their edges cutting into his fingers as Zane got back to business, wrapping a fist around Eli's cock and drawing what his fist didn't cover between his lips.

The sounds were messy and too loud. Eli jerked as his stomach muscles contracted. He held himself still with a mighty effort, wanting nothing more than to lift his hips and fuck Zane's mouth. Ride his face. An image filled his mind of coming on Zane's face, striping his pretty lips and cheeks with cum that'd roll down in heavy drops. That he'd lick off. Eli groaned with the effort not to move, but he felt his cock surge and fill impossibly tighter.

"Hair," he said, grinding it out. "Tuck your fucking hair back and let me watch."

Zane drew his tongue up the length of Eli's dick, teasing, then slowly, ever so slowly, tucked his hair firmly behind his ear. "I'll get a rubber band next time," he said, keeping his hand moving.

"Shave your head."

Zane laughed. "Not happening. I've got to rebel somehow."

This isn't rebellious enough? Eli didn't ask it out loud. He had other things crowding his mind and drowning his senses. *Now* he could watch properly, and the sight of his dick slipping in and out between Zane's lips was -- God, he didn't have the words, only a growing tightness in his belly and in his balls.

He almost snorted when the random snatch of thought came to him: *If it's over fast, so what? We get to do it again whenever we want.* His toes curled, and he grunted, pushing up.

Zane took the thrust almost smoothly, only coughing once. He did pin Eli's hip down with the hand he wasn't using to brace himself. Maybe as punishment -- though Eli wasn't about to complain -- he slid down till his lips touched his hand and sucked, drawing his cheeks hollow enough that Eli could see the bulge of his cock inside.

Eli wanted to ask if Zane had practiced on bananas or something. No one could be this good without some prep work. God knew Eli was sure he wouldn't be. Fuck. He didn't care. What he wanted more was to get his hands on some of Zane. Or any part of him. He shifted his leg and found, with his knee, the hard fullness of Zane's cock. Not much contact as contact went but he could remind Zane, intimately, that it wasn't just Eli up for grabs here.

Zane spat out Eli's dick and arched his back. "Oh, God."

"Turnabout's fair play," Eli said, or meant to. It came out as a long groan, shuddering with amazement. So maybe he didn't know what he was doing. Playing it by ear seemed to be working just fine. He tugged awkwardly at Zane's slacks, working them down inch by inch. Had to stop every time Zane's head bobbed and wet heat engulfed him, and kept fumbling every time he looked down at his cock, so huge and fat. Had he ever been this hard? Looked fucking huge, rigid and rock solid and straining to come.

Zane drew off and began to work Eli with his hand and his hand alone, though he kept his face close enough to rub his cheek along the slick shaft. "Close," he said, breathing shallow. He gave Eli's balls a quick, clumsy grope, licked them, licked Eli's cockhead. "No clue what I'm doing."

"Could have fucking fooled me," Eli managed.

Zane laughed. It was that, and the light that glinted in his eyes, and the slick twist of his wrist -- who knew, but it was all too much, the roughness of his grasp and the rasp of his stubble against Eli's inner thigh and the surge his cock gave in Zane's hand. Eli couldn't hold it back -- fought, but couldn't -- and he was coming, just like he'd imagined, his cum striping

Zane's face in creamy lines. Zane opened his mouth to catch some on his tongue.

He came back to himself with Zane's cock throbbing against his palm and Zane kissing him, the taste of his own cum thick and salty on Zane's tongue, Zane's lips bent in a broad grin even as he kissed Eli sloppy and eager.

"Not bad for a beginner, huh?"

Eli tried to remember how to breathe.

He knew he didn't have to reciprocate. He wanted to. Made all the difference in the world. Though his arms felt like rubber, and his legs no better, he pushed at Zane. "Get on your back," he said, roughed out through the aftershocks of orgasm. "Now."

Zane let himself be tipped over. Once arranged to Eli's liking, he indulged himself with a good long stare into those gray eyes, trying to say everything he couldn't out loud, and shoved harder, pressing Zane into the mattress.

Clumsily he managed to wriggle over Zane and to pull his legs wide apart. The slacks, still half on, got in his way. He hesitated, thought about pulling them all the way off, but was distracted by his first clear sight of Zane's cock. Good God. Had his looked like that to Zane? Dark, heavy, shadowed beneath where his balls hung tight and so full.

He had to touch. Slowly, curiously, Eli weighed them in his palm. He stopped abruptly when Zane groaned and jerked up, throwing his arm over his eyes, his breathing more panting than not. "Please," Zane begged, and that was more than Eli could take, ever.

"Shh," he soothed, stroking Zane's thighs. "I've got you. Just -- don't expect this to be good."

Zane's snort of amusement broke down the

middle. "Eli," he said, remarkably clear. "Have you ever had a *bad* blowjob?"

Good point, and be damned if Eli could be bothered. He took a deep breath, closed his eyes, and found his place. Let it happen.

Zane's cock didn't feel like what Eli had expected. He'd thought he'd be stunned by the texture or by the taste, that he'd flinch away automatically, but no, God no. He didn't taste like a woman, but it wasn't bad, just different. And the flesh felt like flesh, even if it jerked and strained upward when he bumped it with his lips, curious, testing.

The head slid over his tongue. Reflex made Eli swallow, made him draw in his cheeks. He'd have liked to say it was easy then, but there were teeth and a hiss of pain, a shambling "sorry," and Zane's fingers scrabbling against his head to guide him. Zane shook like a tree in the wind beneath him, hanging on by a thread.

I did that. He's almost there because of me. Be damned if that didn't make a man a little crazy. Eli drew his lips over his teeth and to hell with how silly he thought it looked, and sank as far down as he could go. Back up, messier than Zane, letting his tongue skate the length on upstroke and down, saliva dripping from his lips, then saliva mixed with precum. Zane moaned and tossed from side to side, his fists knotted in the comforter and his neck arched, his back arched, his skin shining with sweat. Eli slid a hand over Zane's stomach to hold him down and ground him.

Zane tossed his head, his hair making *swish-swish-swish* noises on the pillow. "Eli," he said, a note of unmistakable warning in the word. "*Eli --*"

Now or never. He couldn't swallow, he'd choke, but he wanted to see. Eli lifted up and off and breathed over Zane's cockhead. "Come on," he urged, figuring out fast how jerking off worked in reverse, giddy with the power of it. "Come on, come on, let me see --"

"God, Eli -- oh, fuck -- ah, *ah* --" Zane ground his hands over his eyes, his mouth opened wide, and he buckled from the middle. Cum spurted, landing thick and creamy on his flexing stomach muscles, dripping down to the V-cut of his oblique muscles, lost in the crease between groin and thigh.

Eli followed it, wanting to taste as much as he'd wanted to see. He touched his tongue to a drop in fascination and startled when a fresh splash landed on his cheek. That he licked automatically, fascinated by the taste.

He had nothing else to give. Dropped his head on Zane's hip and let go, every muscle and seemingly every bone giving way at once until there was nothing left of Eli but a puddle of a man with lungs that wouldn't stop, breathing as if he'd just finished running a race.

Eli supposed, in a way, he had. And he'd won.

Zane tugged sloppily at him. Eli, dazed and thrilled by the success of what he'd managed without any coaching, shambled and wriggled his way up. He thumped his head on Zane's chest and groaned. "Was that us?"

"Think so." The rise and fall of Zane's chest with his ragged breathing reminded Eli of being at sea. "Why haven't we been doing this all along?"

"Wasted time," Eli said, his eyelids falling shut despite wanting to keep them open, to turn and look at Zane and maybe kiss him again, long and slow. He thumbed Zane's navel instead, feeling himself falling toward sleep. TKO. "So you really thought, sometimes…"

"Yeah. But not that it'd be like this," Zane said, faraway and stoned.

Eli knew exactly what he meant. "Never too old to try something new, huh?" he cracked around a tremendous yawn.

"Hey." Zane tweaked Eli's ear. "This was better than Paris."

That was almost -- almost -- better than watching Zane come. Eli hummed, satisfied, proud of himself and figuring he deserved to be. Strange days, these. The sky was green and the grass was blue and down was up, but be damned if he didn't think he liked it better this way.

"Worked it out together," he said, nuzzling Zane's stomach with the last of his strength.

"That we did." Zane shifted, curling toward Eli. "Best stress relief I've ever had."

Eli laughed. "Good. My work is done here."

Zane switched to finger combing Eli's hair, a move so soothing that Eli could no longer cling to wakefulness. "Better not be."

Chapter Seven

It became a habit of sorts, this thing between them. On and off, as "on" as possible. One full week from the first night, Eli woke alone in bed five minutes before his alarm clock was set to go off.

He blinked his eyes open in semidarkness, the first of the dawn's light beginning to shade away the dark of the night, and turned from side to stomach, one arm coming out to stretch across the sheets beside him.

Wait. Eli grunted and patted the empty space. Why had he slept on the far side and not the middle, and what was missing from this picture?

Ah. Zane. Still, it took him a moment to adjust to this new reality. Eli flipped from stomach to back and gazed at the ceiling, vision slowly coming into focus.

"That was us," he said in an echo of Zane's words the night before, and every night since the first. "Not bad, my friend. Not bad at all."

But where the hell had he gone? Eli glanced at the pillow scrunched up beside his and, as well as the dent where Zane had tossed and turned -- the man was a restless sleeper -- he saw a semi-crumpled scrap of paper torn from the back of a journal.

Classic Zane. Eli chuckled as he retrieved the note and strained to read it in the slowly growing light. Not hard. Zane wrote in large, blocky print, and he'd chosen a fat marker.

ELI,

RAINCHECK ON POSTPRANDIAL DELIGHTS. FINALLY TOUCHED BASE WITH SOMEONE WHO COULD BE SWEET-TALKED INTO PLAYING GENEROUS DONOR.

The free clinic. Eli's hopes rose. Zane knew some strange people, but they did tend to have money and egos, and if there was anyone on the planet Zane couldn't coax around to his way of thinking, Eli hadn't met them yet.

He patted the pillow. Case in point.

SORRY I HAD TO TAKE MY CAR.

Damn. Eli had left his at Immaculate Grace the night before, both of them too impatient to get somewhere private to be bothered taking separate vehicles and getting separated by traffic. He guessed it was public transit for him. For that, Zane owed him one.

Eli had a fair idea of how he'd like to collect.

MEET YOU AT THE HOSPITAL. BRING BREAKFAST?

LOVE,

ZANE

"Postprandial delights?" Eli shook his head, amused. "Zane, Zane, Zane, you are one strange bird. Your loss. I was going to make pancakes."

His loss too. Call him old-fashioned, but in his admittedly not-recent history of sleepovers, Eli preferred the classic send-off with a good, hot breakfast and some half-awake kisses by the coffeepot. He looked forward to that with Zane. Maybe next time, and wasn't that something else? Knowing there would be another chance.

Eli climbed out of bed, barely feeling the chill of the floor beneath his bare feet. He did take note of it on outlying areas, more accustomed to sleeping in sweats during the Chicago winter. Sweats and possibly a parka, depending on how low the mercury dropped.

The random thought occurred to him: that'd be one bonus to taking a job down south. Huh. He'd all but forgotten the Duke Medical School question by now. Still, Chicago at heart or not, there were definite advantages to warm weather, such as not waking up with a nasty case of dicksicle.

Eli stretched, yawned, and hit his alarm clock as it began to shrill. "Shut up." He stumbled forward in search of clothing. Stumble became hop became scramble. Jesus Christ, it was cold.

His undignified shuffle led him to the small desk where he kept a laptop, mostly used for reading online journals in bed when he couldn't sleep. Zane had apparently helped himself and left it turned on, Google window in the browser. Tsk. Wasn't like him to be so careless. Eli bent over the desk chair, taking note of his shirt draped there.

Perhaps Zane had had other things on his mind. Eli wouldn't mind thinking so. He reached to shut the laptop down -- and stopped. The toolbar's search pane showed the last key words Zane had searched for.

Paris culinary arts.

Now why... *oh.* Eli spun the chair around and sat, dropping his chin on the back. Christ.

He knew the flare of sparks in his gut was jealousy. Possibly a little hurt too. Didn't mean anything, though, did it?

Or maybe Zane had had more on his mind than a sloppy, hot blowjob. Maybe he'd spent the night thinking about how Eli compared to lush curves and bohemian black braids.

"Fuck." Eli kick-slid out of the chair. Enough. He'd be late for work.

* * *

"I heard you were looking for me the other day?"

Eli looked up with a startled jerk. "Taye. Didn't I tell you once about sneaking up on a guy?"

Taye hung on to the pole as the elevated train started forward. He swayed a little with the choppy motion but still grinned. And quite a grin it was, white amidst a face decorated with some alarmingly colorful bruises.

"I don't think I'm being out of place here when I ask what the hell happened to you."

"It's pretty obvious, don't you think?" Taye nodded at the empty seat next to Eli, a minor miracle at this hour on the train. "May I?"

"You'd better. Let me get a look at that eye." Eli was already reaching for the penlight he kept in his pocket. "Can you even see?"

"It's not that bad." Taye pushed him gently but firmly away as he sat.

"Not that bad, my ass." Eli frowned. No wonder Taye had taken the day off. He'd have scared the patients. "Okay, I won't push it."

"Thank you." Taye sighed. Looked like his mind worked along the same tracks as Eli's -- was Holly right with her whole "you're so alike" spiel? -- because once the pressure was off, that was when he caved. "Some bistro employees took exception to Richie's lifestyle. I happened to be there at the time."

"Be damned." Signed, sealed, and certified. Eli liked this kid. He had spunk. "Do they look worse than you?"

Taye's pride was almost visible. "Damn right."

"And Richie?"

"Got away almost without a scratch." Taye's pride in his lover was equally strong. "He's little, but he's fierce, and the way he puts it, being closer to the ground than those other dicks is an advantage in a tussle where you fight dirty and hit low."

Eli winced, but in approval.

"Then again, he's out of a job now."

"A fine excuse not to go back to that bistro."

Taye laughed. "True. But he's a damn good

waiter, and he's a good cook too. He's out looking for jobs. Speaking of looking, what did you need me for?" He tapped the cell phone-shaped bulge in his coat pocket. "I had a raft of messages."

"Forget about me," Eli deflected quickly. He and Zane, heck, they seemed to be working things out fine enough on their own. No need to burden Taye with fast-fading insecurity on how to please a guy in the sack. "Holly was the one fretting and wringing her hands. I just backed her up."

"Uh-huh." Taye's eyebrow tried to quirk. Didn't quite make it, what with the shiner distorting his face, but he got his point across. "Not buying it, and I've already talked to Holly. You, I wasn't able to touch base with last night."

Ah. Eli coughed. He'd set his phone to vibrate so it wouldn't jostle him and Zane out of their cocoon of silence, and after that he'd forgotten. Sloppy, very sloppy. Also a dead giveaway.

"Uh-huh," Taye said, his one good eye dancing. "What did you need?"

Damn it. Persistence. "It's not a big deal," Eli hedged. A sharp nudge to his shoulder from another passenger's giant, blocky purse reminded him of where they were: very much in public. Christ, he'd almost forgotten. "We can talk later."

Taye shrugged and glanced around at the crowded car. "That's the thing about the train," he remarked, seemingly at random, though Eli knew better than to believe a drop of innocence out of this one. "Look around. Not only do people not pay attention and not care, they're *actively* blocking out everyone else. There's a guy a few rows up who's talking to the itsy bitsy spider crawling up and down his 'waterspout,' and no one's batted an eye."

"Certainly not you, Mike Tyson," Eli shot back. He rubbed his nose. Taye did have a point, and he *could* let rip. If he wanted.

"No one cares," Taye returned.

"Your patchwork face says differently."

"I'd black the other eye if I needed to. Some things are worth it. Eli, you're a man who fights his own battles too. Forgive me for pushing, but you were a cop. Then a med student in your thirties, an intern, and a new doctor in your forties. You're not the kind of guy who backs down from a challenge."

Eli growled low in his throat. He might want to pop Taye another one right now for being an aggressive little bastard, but the kicker was that he wanted more to spill the weight on his mind. Surprised the hell out of himself with that desire, but there you had it. If there was one person he could trust to spill this to besides Zane, it'd be Taye.

Wanted, but couldn't manage to force a word past the blockage that rose in his throat when he tried.

"Maybe later," he muttered at last.

Taye nodded as if he'd expected just this. As if he was prepared to wait. "Suit yourself."

"I will," Eli said, and promptly felt five years old. He rolled his eyes.

"I know I'm being pushy," Taye said quietly. He nudged Eli's foot. "I figure that's what a guy like you needs."

"Come again? I thought I was Mr. Rough, Tough, and Ready to Rumble the way you see me."

"You are. You talk with your machismo, not from here." Taye tapped to the left of his breastbone. "It's a guy thing; I get it. We don't do the heavy emotional stuff. Which is why most of us get in the kind of trouble we do."

Eli glared dourly at Taye. "You sure you're on track for internal medicine? I'd think again. It's like talking to Holly Junior here."

"I've been considering that."

Enough. Eli's natural rough good humor got the better of him. "There's no squashing you, is there?"

Taye grinned cheekily, with one cheek. Christ, as black and blue as he was, odds were good he'd *still* scare the patients. "Witness the proof. I get knocked down, I get up again."

"You're young. Resiliency comes with the territory."

"That's an excuse. But hey, this is me dropping it." Taye held up his hands, palms out, just in time for their stop to be called over the train announcement system and the car to jerk to a halt. "If you ever want to pick it up again, you know how to reach me."

"Unless you're being pasted to the floor of a bar or used as a homophobe's punching bag."

"Like I said. Some things are worth it. I love Richie." Taye raised one shoulder. "That's all there is to it. For me."

"I thought this was you dropping it." Eli made exaggerated jazz hands and nearly clipped an impatient passenger in the elbow.

"I think you know me better enough already not to believe that."

Eli snorted. "Touché. Hey." He stood and gave Taye a hand up. "I'm working on it. I'll work harder. Like you said. Worth it."

Funny how Taye's pride extending his direction went a long way toward shoring up that good feeling and determination. "I have a pool table," Eli blurted.

"Say again?"

Christ, he really was sorely out of practice at

extending the offer of friendship, Zane excepted. Eli cleared his throat and tried again. "I have a pool table. First thing I bought for my place when I had a decent paycheck again."

"I like a man who has his priorities straight."

"Straight, hah. Anyway. You and Richie should come over some night, if you play."

Eli knew Taye picked up right away on how rare that invitation was. "I'd be honored," Taye said, offering Eli his hand to shake on it.

Eli did, quickly, then dealt out a firm nudge to get Taye moving off the train. "Shake a leg; we're going to be late."

He trudged behind Taye, wincing out loud at the blast of cold air once off the train. It could have gone worse, that talk. Could have gone a hell of a lot better too. Wanting to say things, that was huge for Eli.

Not being able to get a word of any substance out, that was hugely worrying. Eli hadn't known it'd gotten this bad. Not that he planned to shout his business from the rooftops anytime soon, especially not after seeing Taye's colorful patchwork face, but...

What was this going to mean for Zane and him in the long run? Call him pessimistic if you would, but Eli doubted it'd mean anything good.

* * *

For all that, Eli *did* have a little extra spring in his step during the first couple of hours on the job. Fate smiled down upon them, one of those rare, golden moments in a hospitalist's life where patients were mostly cooperative, incoming cases weren't too rough, and he actually had time to toss back a cup of coffee and, once, make a bolt down to the cafeteria to grab some bagels and bananas for Zane's breakfast.

"I hear the two of you finally found your way

together," Holly remarked in passing when she found Eli in the doctor's lounge, making quick work of his own share of the food. She stole a bite of Eli's banana, pinched neatly off the end rather than bitten into. Dainty touch, grip like steel. Eli found himself fairly glad he was keeping other lengthy objects out of her reach.

"Who, me and Taye? He's a good kid."

Holly smiled like the Madonna and bent to kiss Eli's cheek.

"What was that for?"

"Oh, nothing," she said, rubbing a smudge of professionally understated gloss off his skin. "I'm proud of you."

"Bah," Eli grumbled, nudging her on her way. She laughed at him.

His encounter with Diana went better. She might be as loud and uninhibited as a motorcycle cavalcade, but you did know where you stood with Diana. "Gimme," she said, grabbing his banana. The fruit, not anything else, but from the way her sharp teeth snapped deep and fast in the innocent flesh, Eli decided he was suddenly very glad he'd found and fallen for Zane and not her.

"Christ, it's like watching a piranha fall upon a cow carcass."

Diana flipped him off and finished his banana. "Those bagels up for grabs too?"

"Hands off." Eli guarded them. "They're for Zane. He's been awake since God knows when, and you know him. He's forgotten food exists, let alone that he needs it to survive."

"True enough." Diana still stole a bite and popped it in her mouth. "Don't glare at me. I'm a lady."

"If you're a lady, I'm a Bengal tiger," Eli informed her. He watched Diana lick her lips, idly noting that it did nothing for his libido -- and mouthiness aside, Diana was indeed a fine-looking woman.

Huh. A thought came to him. If anyone in this place had her finger on all the pulses, it would be this firecracker eyeing his bagel with hungry intent.

He pushed the remnants of the food over to her. "For a price."

"As long as it's not my firstborn, name it. No smart comments. I'm still fertile."

Eli cringed.

"No better way to make any man cringe." Diana snickered at him and bit into the bagel. "What did you want to know?"

What would be the harm in asking? "I've heard a buzz about a teaching position going at Duke University," Eli said as casually as he could. "A couple of the doctors seem to be getting pretty worked up. What's it all about?"

Diana gave Eli a flat, level look and named a salary that would have made Eli choke on his bagel if he'd still been eating. "Jesus Christ. No kidding?"

"Nope. This is serious business. Not to mention a chance to get in on some cutting-edge research, serious grants, and relative peace and quiet in which to concentrate on medicine rather than dealing with HMO bullshit." Diana sat back and shrugged. "You graduated from Duke, didn't you?"

"Guilty."

"God, you must have hated it down there. If I cut you open you'd bleed pure Chicago." Diana wrinkled her nose at him. "It'd be something, though, wouldn't it? To show them you could not only do it, but come back and kick their asses at it."

She'd taken the words right out of Eli's head. Externally, he nodded and made a noncommittal noise. "Who's head of the search committee? Might be someone I know."

Nice. Smooth. Eli patted himself on the back even while wondering what the hell he was doing.

"Umm…" Diana drummed the tabletop, lips together in a thoughtful moue. "Got it. Dr. Kazaran. I keep wanting to call him Dr. Kazoo."

"You would." Eli stood to rumple her hair.

Diana slapped him away. "I am not your kid sister. Do that again and you'll be pulling back nubs." She blocked his path when he tried to dodge around her. "Hang on. Why did you want to know about Duke?"

"Idle curiosity."

"Uh-huh." Diana snorted. "Can I have the rest of your coffee?"

"Woman, anyone would think you hadn't eaten in days."

"I'm a doctor. When do you think the last time I had to sit down to a proper meal was?"

"What about your date last night? Didn't you get to chow down then?"

Eli knew as soon as he'd asked that that hadn't been a wise question. Diana cackled wickedly at him. "No." He walked away at speed. "No details about your sex life allowed within my hearing."

"Your loss!" she called after him, already tonsil-deep in decent coffee. Eli struggled to keep a straight face until he'd made good his escape.

Dr. Kazaran. Eli knew the guy. Stuffed shirt on the surface, but if you surprised him with some ingenuity or a new take on an old problem, you were on your way to the top of his respect list. Eli had done that once or twice back in the day. Maybe more than a couple of times.

If he applied for the job and Kazaran remembered him... hell, he'd have a shot. More than. Eli hesitated in a juncture of hallways, one that could lead him back to the floor, one that could take him to an elevator down to the hospital library where he could do some more research, maybe fire off an e-mail to Kazaran.

Just to see if he would be considered good enough. That was all Eli wanted.

What could it hurt? Eli made the decision and headed library-ward, remembering a moment too late that he'd left Zane's breakfast behind to be seized upon by the ravening hordes. Damn.

* * *

Eli should have known better. After the brief lull of the early morning, the hospital piled it on in spades as payback. The five minutes he'd had to shoot a hasty e-mail Dr. Kazaran's way were the last he had to himself for most of the day. Four p.m. found him with a lunch of a power bar mostly a faded memory, a dangerous imbalance of blood in his caffeine stream, and a hell of a headache from losing a couple of hit-and-run victims.

In other words, not in the best frame of mind to tackle anything personal.

Still, the sight of Zane propped up against the wall beside an elevator, mostly asleep on his feet, made him brighten and turned his day a little better.

"There you are."

As romantic greetings went Eli could have done better, but it was the thought that counted. Zane got that. His sleepy gray eyes popped open, and though bloodshot, they showed an immediate pleasure at seeing Eli.

He reached for Eli, though, and God help him, Eli didn't get a chance to think before his body stepped back for him out of reach.

Pleasure gave immediate way to irritation. "I have leprosy now? Thanks."

Fuck. "I'm sorry." Eli knew that wouldn't count for much. He tried to ease back in, finding his comfortable space, the one he'd been accustomed to back when everyone only thought they were schtupping each other instead of knocking boots in truth.

Zane didn't seem appeased. Rather he was on edge, and it looked like Eli had jarred loose a day's worth of building irritation.

"I'm trying," Eli said, keeping it low. "You've got to give me time here."

Zane snorted, then sighed. "Right. As you wish."

Eli detected a note of sarcasm there but let it pass. Clearly treading lightly was the way to go. Problem there happened to be that Eli hadn't had such a marvelous day himself, and his own nerves were frayed. "Fuck it, Zane, I said I'm trying. What do you want from me?"

"What do I --" Zane snapped his mouth shut. "This isn't the place."

"My original point." The doctor and the friend in Eli assessed Zane's state of weariness that aggravated the man's temper and didn't like what they saw. "You've been running yourself ragged all day, haven't you?" He took a chance and laid his hand on Zane's arm, very close to the hand -- though not too close -- and whispered, "I missed you this morning."

See? Trying.

Zane seemed to sense that. He relaxed a fraction. Unhappiness of a different sort replaced aggravation. "Yeah, for all the good it did me."

Damn it. "No luck with the possible donor?"

"Nope. Apparently they've thrown in with PETA. Did you know that meat is murder and baby fish are actually better known as sea kittens?"

"They believe what they believe. Since when do you scoff at personal credos?"

"Since they'd rather drop half a mil on protest vigilantes than health care for people who have no fucking insurance, that's since when. Get off of me." The elevator dinged.

"Christ, Zane." Eli caught him again, truly worried now. "You keep losing your cool like this and you're going to rupture something."

Zane ground his teeth audibly, counted to ten under his breath, but at least he was trying. "Look. I've had a day of amazing shittiness. Then I see you, and frankly, I want to hug you. Hell, I'd like to kiss you. Just a peck, even, to remind me that there is more to life than fighting a losing battle against administration."

"Zane, keep your voice down." Eli's temper was faring no better at this point. "Look at me. You think my day's been any more of a treat?"

"I know it has." While Eli gaped, Zane carried on relentlessly, and despite all tiredness, that laser stare hadn't lost a single watt of pinpoint intensity. "Because you love this. All of it. One battle after another. On the streets, in Immaculate Grace's hallowed halls, it's all the same to you. You're helping people, and you fucking love it."

"Zane," Eli said, holding on to his temper with the last of his patience. "Either calm down or we go our own separate ways until you're ready to act like a grown-up again."

Zane scoffed but fell silent. Not that Eli was about to let his guard down. He waited, counting the seconds. The elevator came, proved empty, and went on its way.

By then, Eli thought he felt comfortable enough to shoulder bump Zane. "How about we take the stairs? Keep moving, keep limber."

"Yeah, okay." Zane turned with Eli and made for the stairwell. "So I'm an ass."

"Nothing I didn't already know." Eli wrapped one arm around Zane's shoulders. This, he'd done before. Still felt risky but he knew it was safe. "It's okay. Work it out together, right?"

Zane covered Eli's hand with his own and squeezed, which he hadn't done before, but no one was looking, so what the hell. "Remind me of that when I need it, would you?"

"That promise, I can make." Eli elbowed open the crash bar on the stairwell. "Come over to my place again tonight. I'm in the mood for something home cooked, and if you've eaten all day, I'll be very surprised."

"Hmm." Zane's general good humor seemed to be on its way back. "Is that all that's on the menu?"

Speaking in a sort of code worked well enough for Eli. "I was thinking dessert too," he said, feeling extremely brave and surprisingly smug about it.

Yet another thing he should have known better regarding. Confidence too easily transmitted to hubris, and Eli was well aware that karma lived for moments like these.

Zane chuckled. "God, I feel so domestic," he remarked. "Let's take it again from the top. How was your day, honey?"

"Actually, it had its good moments." Eli let go of Zane to grasp his stethoscope in both hands and tug thoughtfully. "You've heard about the Duke job, right?"

"Some gossip here and there." Zane paused, a sharp sort of turn spiking his mood. "Why?"

"No big deal. I know the guy spearheading the search. One of my professors. We got along well back in the day. I sent him an e-mail to say hi and to get some more info about the position. Zane, what?"

Zane had not just dropped Eli's arm but shoved him, hard enough to knock a breath of wind out of him. "Fuck you, Eli." He backed up, turning on his heel at the last possible second before falling down the stairs, and started down them at a fast, seriously pissed clip. "Fuck. You."

What the *hell*. "Zane, wait up!" Eli started after him, but not even his longer legs could catch up with Zane on the move. "Zane!"

* * *

Thank God for the late-afternoon shipments at the loading docks, way back in the part of the hospital where anyone not authorized to be there really, really shouldn't be. Without his coat or gloves, the cold hit Eli with the force of a shock wave.

It'd done the same for Zane, who'd stopped long enough for Eli to regain some ground and then had to dodge his way through burly men carrying massive boxes and finally appeared to have given up at the far edge. In safety, at least. Relatively speaking. He'd dug a pack of cigarettes out of his pocket and was trying to light up, no easy job in the cutting wind.

Eli made it to Zane in time to reach for the cigarette with the intention of snapping it out of his mouth, thinking better of it just in time, and blocking his path instead. "Explanation. I want one. Now."

Zane glared. "You know, that's rich coming from you."

"Enough. Talk to me. I mean it."

Zane scoffed. He turned inward, looking somewhere far away, gone someplace Eli couldn't follow on foot. Damn it. Eli hated more than anything to see Zane looking so lost.

"Where did this unravel?" Eli asked. "I'm honestly confused here. What did I do?"

"Duke University," Zane said, though who knew what he was thinking. "Great job. Great opportunity. Halfway across the country from this. Me. Without so much as a by-your-leave. Are you getting the picture now?"

Ah. Eli's stomach plummeted. He hadn't thought. Really should have. *Idiot.* "It's not like that. I haven't even properly applied."

Zane shrugged, bleak as a Detroit November, and managed to get his cigarette lit. "Yet." He blew out twin streams of smoke, too worked up to hear a word Eli might try to get in there. "You know, Eli, I love you, but sometimes I really fucking don't like you. You just throw that out there, like what we've got here is fucking nothing."

Eli stood utterly still. Wanted to ask Zane to repeat himself. Couldn't make the words come out.

Zane covered his face with his hand and growled. "So. Fucking. *Thick.* Eli, I swear to God --" This time, when Zane moved, Eli let him pass. "If you get a clue, you know where I'll be."

"Zane," Eli called after him. "Come *on*, would you? Give me a hand here."

Zane's dark stare was the only answer Eli got,

leaving him there nonplussed in the middle of increasingly surly deliverymen who weren't impressed by the lover's spat in their midst.

Irony. Eli savored it. Tasted bitter. "What are you looking at?" he asked, heading back into the hospital to finish his shift.

Chapter Eight

Seven hours and three major traumas later, Eli drove himself home. Or that had been the intention. He ended up outside Zane's condo instead, where instinct had guided him. So be it. His heart had pointed him home, as did the rest of him, and whatever it took to make this right...

He pulled his cell phone from his hip pocket, blew on his fingers to warm them, and hit speed dial.

"Zane? I'm parked outside."

"Eli, for fuck's sake..." He could see a shadow passing in front of Zane's window and an obscured gesture that he'd bet good money was Zane shoving his hand through his hair. All too easy to picture Zane right now pacing a hole through the floor, his strings wound too tight and in need of someone to steady him.

"I'm not leaving. We got ourselves into this. Maybe me more than you this time, but it's still the both of us that have to figure it out."

Silence on the other end of the line. Eli knew he'd grabbed Zane's ear.

"Let me in already."

Another long pause, but Eli knew how to interpret Zane's various hushes. This one was reluctant and stubborn, but finally giving in. The hardest to achieve once Zane had his mind on something. Absolutely crucial here.

Eli prepared himself for it but didn't expect the body-melting rush of relief when Zane said, finally, "Okay. It's late, though. Past eleven." He stopped. Surprised silence. "When did it get to be past eleven?"

Eli chuckled, too relieved to be aware of any dignity. "Usually happens right after ten. That's when the big hand is on the --"

"Oh, shut up." A laugh. Good! "Wait. You're not

just now getting back from the hospital, are you?"

Eli grimaced. "Guilty."

A thoughtful and worried pause this time. "You've got to slow down."

"I think I'm done with going slow," Eli said as honestly as he could with all the different ways that could be taken. He heard a small, indrawn breath from Zane and let his out in relief.

In the window, he thought he saw Zane settling down on the end of the couch next to it. We're like a pair of teenage girls, he thought, amused. Or not. He could imagine Zane's silky hair, sure, but the sprinkling of gray and paler shading at his temples did a hell of a lot more for Eli's libido than the thought of giggles and curls and fruit-flavored lip gloss. As it should.

"What happened to keep you so late?"

"Same old, same old." Eli switched his phone from hand to hand to rub them on his legs to keep the circulation up. Christ, he hoped Zane let him in soon. He was freezing his nuts off out here. He made a disgusted face when he came across a patch of something stiffly dried on the knee of his scrubs. "Oh, that's lovely."

"What?"

"Still in my scrubs. I was so fucking spaced I didn't even think to shower, much less change to my streets. You had me all tied up in knots, you know that?"

"Yet you're here," Zane said.

Eli was better with the silences, not the words -- *quelle surprise*, that -- and it took him a second to interpret this. "Where else would I want to be?" he asked, stating the plain facts. "After a rough day, all I want is to go home."

Zane sighed. Didn't sound entirely happy about that. "We need to talk."

"I know. Just -- not yet. Okay? Give me this. Hell, give yourself a break too. We work hard, we need some comfort zone time before we jump into the heavy shit. And speaking of which, I'm going to storm your shower before these scrubs develop sentience and crawl away on their own."

"Oh, that's pleasant." Zane was truly laughing now. Mission: accomplished. Eli could see the man in his mind's eye, the crinkles at the corners of his gray eyes and the laugh lines around his mouth. "As fresh as a spring daisy in a meatpacking plant, are you?"

"Such charming imagery." Eli propped his elbow on the steering wheel. "What are *you* wearing, Casanova?"

He hadn't intended that particular sally to come out in so many words, but once spoken, a thing couldn't be unspoken... and from the charged crackle of this silence, Eli thought he might not mind.

"Hey. I asked you a question," Eli said softly. "Tell me."

"You're not kidding?" The shadow in the window moved. "You want to --"

"What better way to keep warm? And you know as well as I do, makeup sex is fantastic."

Eli pictured Zane rubbing his hand over his nose and chin. Tempted, not yet too sure about this, but temptation was winning out. "You know this doesn't fix anything."

"True. It'll still be fun, and I need this. No," Eli said, correcting himself to strict honesty, "I need you."

"God, Eli."

"We'll talk later," Eli promised. "Do this for me now."

"Talk about anything we want to?"

Eli knew that meant "anything *I* want to" and was, he felt, rightfully worried, but he pushed the concern aside for now. "I promise, and you can hold me to it."

A small pause, a long sigh, a small chuckle, and Eli knew he'd won. "All right. Only because fighting makes me horny too."

"We are a pair, aren't we?"

"In many ways." Eli thought he could definitely see Zane relaxing in the window now, his head probably tipped back to rest on the couch arm and his legs splayed, the phone trapped between ear and shoulder with both hands free. His nerves and his pulse both jumped, not in a bad way.

This was actually something he'd never done, not with Marybeth, not with any of the women he'd had a fling or a thing with ever so rarely. He'd never even thought of it.

Now he wanted it badly enough to taste.

"You never did answer me," Eli said as he tucked his own phone between his ear and shoulder and thanked all holy powers for tinted windows and the absolute don't-give-a-shit-ness of the few pedestrians out at this time of night. Not that he wanted to give a thought to them. "What are you wearing?"

Eli heard rustling. Zane getting comfortable? He let himself imagine the scene in more detail. Zane's body relaxing, legs spread. He'd have one foot planted on the floor for balance. Maybe a hand resting on his stomach. Not at the good stuff yet, but working up an appetite by teasing himself with the potential.

"I remembered to change when I got home," Zane said, sounding almost sleepy. Not bored. Entering a zone. "Sleep pants. Soft flannel, the ones you said you liked once."

Eli remembered those. Kitten soft, washed and worn and well beloved. They hung low on Zane's hips, his new favorite look for the man, and caressed his ass. The words "plaid flannel" wouldn't have been a turn-on before, but now? Now the lumberjack look appealed.

"Tell me more." He widened his own seat, giving himself room to move if he needed it, and damn well planned on that coming to pass.

"A plain T-shirt," Zane went on. "Gray. V-neck. No logo, just plain."

The words themselves, not so much with the sexy. It was the low purr entering Zane's voice, the slight edge of nervousness mixed with the slowly rising enjoyment, that tripped Eli's trigger and encouraged the swelling in his groin.

A silence, not a planned one. "This is new for me," Zane admitted. Almost embarrassed. "Well. I have done this before."

"Jerked off?" Eli asked, deliberately provocative. He was scared out of his mind too, but someone had to take the wheel, and the way he saw it, it was his turn. "Trust me, at forty years old, you qualify as a professional."

"Oh, baby. Talk clinical to me." Zane laughed. "I meant phone sex."

Eli rested his hand over his groin, not pressing down yet, just giving himself some heat and light contact. "If you know what you're doing, then school me. Tell me more."

"Mmm." Zane's eyes would be closing right now, or going half-lidded. Eli exhaled with enjoyment over the visual and let himself do the same. "It's not what you think. The person on the other end of the line always had a script and got paid by the minute."

Eli's heart ached briefly for the loneliness in that admission, and then surprise, and then filled with a new resolve. "You've got me now."

"You've mastered the art of phone sex?"

"No, but if you hum a few bars, I can fake it." Eli shushed Zane's amusement. "Trust me. I've got you." He took a deep breath to center himself, relaxed fully into his seat, and rubbed his palm against the rise in his scrubs. "Tell the truth. You like this?"

A small hitch in Zane's breathing. "Yes. God, yes."

Good. Eli fingered the drawstring of his scrubs. "Tell me about it," he said, roughly, not a suggestion but an order. "Put your hand on yourself and tell me how you feel."

"Christ, Eli."

"Do it."

Eli waited, listening for every nuance in Zane's breathing. He knew, as if he were there watching, when Zane made contact. The smallest, most intoxicating whimper and the shudder made him grind up. "Zane. I'm waiting."

"I know, I --" Zane sounded frustrated. "I don't know where to start."

"You don't have to. Listen to me. Do as I say."

"*Eli.*"

"That's it. Do you have your hand on yourself? Not inside your pants just yet. Just outside. Just feeling it. Tell me."

"Hard," Zane said. "The things you do to me without even trying, Eli."

"Ah-ah-ah. Tell me the physical. I'll show you how." Eli rubbed himself, feeling the shaft and balls react to the friction, his toes tightening with the pulse of pleasure. "I'm humping my hand. Up, hard. Hard as stone."

"Goddamn, Eli." Zane's breath was ragged. "Okay. I'm looking down. Trying to. Want to watch."

"Good. Good start. Keep going. Run your finger in a line up, and down, the way you did with me. Fuck. Do you know what that did to me?"

"I remember." *There.* There was the note Eli had been waiting for. Arousal and excitement and the low hum of sensual enjoyment. "I'd wanted to do that for I don't know how long. To look at you, feel you. Taste you."

"Christ. Okay. Look. Touch. Tell me what you feel. What you're thinking about."

"Thinking about you," Zane said immediately. "Rubbing against my hand, imagining it's yours."

Eli's turn to be struck breathless. He tugged his scrubs waist open and slid inside. Into his boxers too, closing his fist around his cock. He held it there, just a solid fist, and imagined it was Zane. He could smell Zane's skin and feel the warmth of his body pressed close.

"If I were there," Eli said, "what would you do with me?"

Zane groaned. "God, I don't know. Strip you. Get those clothes off and look. Take my time. You don't believe it, but you are so fucking gorgeous, Eli. Strong. Built tough. Old scars. I want to put my mouth to those and see how the texture's different under my tongue. Taste the salt of your skin."

Eli had to grit his teeth and ride out a rush of too-much need. His body had gotten used to Zane's, and he wanted the real thing, not this pale imitation, but for all that, this got him more worked up than he'd anticipated. "Then what?"

"Uh-uh. Your turn. You. What would you, to me --"

Eli loved this part. Listening to Zane fall apart the only way Zane should. And out here, in the fantasy, he could be bold in a way he hadn't yet managed, and it worked. "I think I'd unwrap you, piece by piece. Pull the shirt off over your head and smooth your hair down. I'd spend minutes, maybe hours, kissing you. Wouldn't stop until our lips were sore."

"Then?" Zane begged.

"Then I'd lay you down. On your bed, your couch. No. Bed. Somewhere I could see you, every inch. Could spread you out." He wondered... "Maybe tie your hands to the bedpost so you couldn't get impatient and make a grab for me."

Zane's laugh was startled and breathless, but his moan told the whole truth. "Kinky."

"I could be." Not this time, though. "I'd take off those pants. Slide them down your legs. Off. Throw them aside. Smooth my hands down your legs. Push them open so I could see."

Zane made a noise that didn't have a name, but Eli could hear the desperation. "I can't do this."

No, no, no, that wasn't the plan. "Yes. You can." With an effort, Eli stilled his hand. "Keep going. For me."

"You *idiot*," Zane said with fondness. "I meant I can't see the point in doing this fifty feet from each other when I want you *here*, now. I want to do this in real time. Come in, Eli. Come in and stay. Hurry."

He didn't have to ask Eli twice. Thank God.

* * *

Eli opened the door to Zane's apartment, gladder than ever that he had his own key. Inside, the lights were off. He frowned, momentarily thrown and even a little disappointed. He'd hoped to see Zane spread out on the couch in abandon, the phone maybe still by his ear, his eyes shut tight and his breathing tight.

"Zane?"

"Shower first. Then meet me in the bedroom," he heard. A soft *click*, and low light rolled out into the hallway. "Get a move on. I want you in here."

It was possible Eli had never showered faster in his life.

Naked and still mostly wet, he padded to Zane's bedroom on bare feet, his footfalls silenced by the thick carpet, and pushed open the door that Zane had left open a few inches.

Opened the door and stopped in his tracks, riveted. Christ. Zane lay in bed with one arm thrown over his eyes and the other beneath the thin sheet he'd draped over himself, the motion of his hand on his cock so gorgeously obscene that Eli's gut tightened and he grunted in surprise as much as arousal.

The corner of Zane's mouth lifted, more grimace than grin, but hell. Worked for Eli. Zane slowed the pace of his strokes. "Figured I'd save us some time."

"Figured you'd drive me crazy, you mean. Sadist."

Zane didn't deny it. His lips parted fully, a breath rattling out between them.

Eli suddenly couldn't wait a second longer and crossed the distance as fast as possible. Found himself with his knees on the bed, braced at the end and drawing the sheet down, off Zane's body in a smooth ripple of dove-gray Egyptian cotton. Silky and thin in his hands, it still smelled of sex and man. He pressed the sheets to his nose and breathed in.

"Oh, *fuck*," Zane groaned. He held his cock still,

drawing Eli's eye to it. "See what you did?"

"God, yes." Eli had gotten used to the sight by now. More than that. He anticipated. From this angle, it looked different. Length and girth, flushed dark, with a thick vein standing out ropelike, the fat head peeking through the circle of Zane's thumb and forefinger.

He had to get closer. Action followed thought, and he crawled up Zane's bed, relieved as hell that he'd saved time by getting naked. Zane's skin was too hot against his, even fresh from a steaming shower.

The press of skin to skin made them both hiss and flinch, then melt into each other. Eli warmed fast, faster still when he found Zane's mouth with his and took the kiss he'd wanted. Zane's arms slid beneath his, finding purchase on his back and digging in, kneading, when Eli slid his tongue between Zane's lips to tease him, to drive him crazy.

Zane hooked his ankle around Eli's and bent his knee, jostling them closer. Eli could feel the hard press of Zane's cock aligned by his. Christ. So good. He deepened the kiss as if he were trying to climb inside, and maybe he was. He could drink Zane down and never stop.

Never, that was, until Zane let go of his back with one hand and slipped it between them, fumbling to get a grasp on both their engorged dicks. He couldn't manage to coordinate a grip around the girth of both, but the attempt made Eli's muscles contract and drove him down, the instinct to fuck too powerful to ignore even if he'd wanted to, and by hell, he didn't.

So easy to find a rhythm here. His cock skated through the crease of Zane's hip, along the V-cut of muscle. Yet -- somehow, not enough -- what could he --

Zane licked Eli's lip, then bit it and sucked the bit

of flesh into his mouth. He let go with a pop. "What do you want?" he whispered. "Anything. All you have to do is ask."

A thousand possibilities filled Eli's head. He wanted them all. How was he supposed to choose?

Zane's dazed smile broadened. "Or I could give you a hint."

Eli kissed that mischief into submission, and down Zane's neck, across his chest. Kissed Zane quiet, and moaning, and rising up to meet his thrusts down. The skin of their bellies was slick now with sweat and precum. Eli's balls drew tight. He let go to breathe, and to try and gain some control, not that he thought that was going to happen.

Only then did he ask, "What's the hint?"

"Huh?" Zane looked stoned or turned on beyond reason. The jerk of his hips was a pretty good clue which was the case. "Oh." No repressing Zane for long. "Raise up. On your hands and knees. Trust me."

"That's always risky." Eli bent to suck one of Zane's nipples, curious. Not like a woman, not at all, but goddamn if Zane didn't react more strongly than any of the women he'd ever been in this position with.

He threw his head back and shouted, pushed at Eli's head, and wrestled him free. "*Don't.* I'll come."

"That'd be a bad thing?" Eli tried to get back down there. Too addictive, and too fascinating to find Zane's hot spots.

"*Yes.* Because it's my turn, and I'm showing you what I want." Zane pushed at Eli. "Do it. Up."

Eli groaned but did as he'd been ordered. Up and braced on his knees. He got one long look at Zane beneath him, the dark red sex flush spread down his chest, the slick mess of precum on his stomach, and the stiffness of his cock lying flush and full against his hip.

Not a long enough look -- he could spend forever staring -- but then, Zane grinned wickedly and wriggled over. On his hip, on his stomach, his ass turned up and his face hidden in the cross of his arms. "Want this," he said, barely louder than a rasp like stone on stone. "Do you?"

"*Oh,*" Eli breathed. Okay, this far ahead, he hadn't thought. Damn, but he wished he had. He spread his hands over the cheeks of Zane's ass and squeezed. "I don't -- I didn't bring anything --"

"I've got lotion. Lube. Everything we need." Zane sounded desperate, as if speaking through gritted teeth, and Eli felt his pain.

"I won't hurt you." He let himself trace the cleft, just a tease, a promise of more to come. "Too worked up to make it good."

"I need --"

"So do I. Next time." Eli's head whirled, searching for answers to the question. "Lube. Give it here. Can't fuck you, not yet, but I can do this."

Zane reached, an awkward stretch, to the bedside table and fumbled it open. He almost dropped the lube, a new pump bottle. Eli rescued it, then stretched over Zane to snag a condom out of the drawer as well. He held his breath as he made fast work of sliding the latex on.

"What are you doing?" Zane shivered, the ripple riding down his back.

"Like this," Eli said, rough and dry.

"Like how?"

"Shh. You'll see. Or you'll feel." Eli squirted a good dollop of lube in his hand -- knew enough to rub his palms together to warm it up -- and before he could stop and think, or hesitate, he slid his slippery fingers between the cleft of Zane's ass cheeks to slick him up.

Had to stop and grind his teeth and count to ten backward when Zane made a noise like a desperate animal and canted back in search of more.

"I've got you," Eli soothed. He rubbed lube over the condom, getting himself good and slick. Pushed one arm under Zane to lift him up and to wrap his hand around Zane's cock. Zane moaned and pushed into his grip. Eli held himself steady with the greatest of effort and slid his cock into the cleft. No farther, but inside where it was warm and slick and tight, down through the valley and not stopping until his cockhead nudged Zane's balls.

"*Fuck,*" Zane groaned. He struggled to get higher, swore when Eli pushed him into the right position, and began to pant when Eli thrust again.

Fuck was right. No more thinking. He saw Zane in sensations, not visuals. The flex and clench of his muscles, the salty sweat on his back, the tightness of his ass. Eli forgot to pay proper attention to the reach around, remembering only when Zane sobbed and covered Eli's hand with his, bearing down. Too much to remember at once, too much of everything, yet not enough. Instinct, powerful and guiding, drove him through that wet heat again, again, never stopping. He could feel the end building, white heat burning bright as molten iron.

"Close?" he asked, jacking Zane fast and hard, the *snick snick snick* of his hand far louder than their ragged breathing. He drew back and held it, though the effort made his legs ache and shake. He stroked Zane's cock and pressed his thumb on the head. Listened to him shout, and though they'd been here before, it was still a shock and a thrill to feel Zane freeze and the stream of cum flow down his fist to drip heavy onto the sheets.

No holding back, not any longer. Eli set his hands, one slippery with cum, on Zane's hips and held him still. He lost his head and everything else, stroking faster, as fast as he could. God, he wanted to see. Next time. Sweat dripped into his eyes, making them sting and screw tightly shut. Almost there -- almost --

His cockhead caught on the puckered rim of muscle, bumped and held, and the orgasm charged out of Eli. He shouted, making the walls echo, and bowed forward to slam his forehead to Zane's back as he came.

He held it there as long as he could, wanting it to last forever. If it was always this good, then it was worth anything else. And not just this. The whole Zane package. Given freely, they were all his.

It was what he'd always wanted, even if he'd never known that. Now all he had to do was keep it.

Chapter Nine

"Not exactly how I'd seen this night working out." Zane accepted the warm, wet washcloth Eli laid on his stomach and swabbed both haphazardly and lazily, his grin as loopy as if he'd just gotten off a roller coaster. Eli supposed in a way he had. Adrenaline, endorphins, amazement that he'd lived to tell about it, and the urge to shout, "Again!"

Eli chuckled at himself, took the washcloth back and did a proper -- better, anyway -- job of clean-up. That done, he collapsed on his back. In the wet spot. Bah; he couldn't be bothered to move. He held one arm out at his side, silently beckoning Zane in.

Zane laid his head to rest over Eli's heart. "Going like a rabbit's," he said around a yawn. "Some kind of vigor you've got there, old man."

Eli slapped Zane's ass. "I'll 'old man' you."

"Yes, please," Zane murmured, Cheshire-cat smug.

"Not yet." Eli made sure they were both comfortable and that he had Zane pinned firmly next to him. "Ready to tell me what all that earlier was about?"

Zane groaned. "Afterglow, Eli. Learn to enjoy it."

"I will once I've got this straightened out." Eli didn't let go. "I can start, if it'd help." Some things became clearer after a man had worked off all the frustration that clouded his head. "Point one. You were pissed because I threw out Duke like it was a real option."

"Point one," Zane acknowledged. He'd slumped against Eli but hadn't gone anywhere, so Eli still counted that as a win.

Eli kissed the top of Zane's head. "I'm an idiot. This came as a surprise to you?"

Zane's shoulders shook with amusement. "Not really. But hell, I'm an idiot too sometimes, so I can't throw stones. My wants aside, I shouldn't hold you back. It's a good opportunity, Eli. Damned good. Anyone who's kicking ass and taking names like you are as a hospitalist would be a much bigger fool not to be tempted."

"I'm not," Eli insisted.

Zane shrugged.

That wouldn't do. Eli gave Zane a small shake. "I'll swear in blood if I have to, but I hoped I'd already done that with other bodily fluids."

He could feel Zane's nose wrinkle against his chest. "Afterglow. Do I have to get a dictionary for you?"

Eli thumped him between the shoulder blades. Not hard. He didn't have the energy. Afterglow, hell. After a good round of sex like that, *not* falling into a coma was the big challenge.

Zane was quiet, then sighed. "Okay. I believe you."

"*Thank* you." Eli had the feeling this wasn't over quite yet. Not a great sensation, but what good would it do to pick a fight over picking a fight? He let it go. For now. "Your turn. What's got you so worked up that you're barking at shadows?"

Zane shook his head, the tips of his hair oddly rough on Eli's bare chest. Too much agitated pulling on them, Eli guessed. "What do you think? The clinic. It means that much to me, and you know it does. Out there, medicine is as real as it gets in this city. Working men who can't afford a specialist looking for a last hope."

Eli pulled Zane an inch or so closer to him. "Don't think I don't remember."

Zane wasn't done. "And not just men like you. There are mothers who come in carrying kids for whom a shot means the difference between life and the alternative. Punks who need to be tested and don't have anywhere else to go. Scared people. Desperate people. It's ugly and it's harsh and it's beautiful, being able to do something that matters more than a tidy little nip and tuck."

"It's pretty real in the hospital too, Zane. We deal in life and death same as the clinic."

"For people who can pay. I just... I spend my time in the clinic because there, that's the last place where I enjoy my career."

Eli swept his thumb from side to side on Zane's back. "What are you saying?"

"I don't know. No. I do." Zane tangibly gathered his strength, then looked up at Eli. Though he had to crane his neck, he made eye contact. "If it weren't for you, odds are good I'd have left medicine years ago."

The confession took Eli's breath away.

"It's true," Zane said, steady now that he'd made himself start. "Working with you is the only thing that keeps me getting up in the morning and walking in those doors." He propped his chin on Eli's ribs and rubbed the point beneath one nipple. "Duke, the clinic, that's not all I was pissed about."

"I got the feeling," Eli said. All he could do was hold on. This, he hadn't even been able to think about, because it was just too much. "What you said. In the loading dock. You said you loved me."

Zane did not break eye contact. "I did, and I meant it."

"Zane --"

"No. Hear me out." Zane used the point of his chin to make sure Eli didn't move. "I have loved you for maybe a year now."

"Jesus Christ, Zane." Eli didn't -- What did he do with that? "You never said."

"You wouldn't have listened. Or you'd have misunderstood me." Zane laid his cheek on Eli's chest but otherwise held steady. "I wasn't planning on -- this," he said, caressing lower, firm and possessive. "I don't think I knew it would be this kind of love too. Except when I thought about Diana and Holly teasing us and I couldn't get it out of my head. And then I started to dream. Once I did, I couldn't stop. And that's that."

Christ. Loved him? Not that he didn't feel it too, inside, but to bring it out in the open... Eli couldn't. Not yet. All he could do was tighten his hold on Zane and try to say with that what he couldn't otherwise.

Zane finally let his eyes fall shut. "I know you," he said quietly. "It's okay. I can wait, if you think you'll get there in the end. Waited a year already, right?"

This mattered. Eli swallowed, the sound loud and painful but necessary because the lump in his throat was choking him, and nodded. Because that wasn't enough, he pulled Zane tight and said, rusty raw, "Yes."

"That's all I can ask." Zane relaxed. Mostly relaxed. "Do you know why I told you the story about that woman in Paris?"

Eli tensed. He'd hoped not to hear any more about her. "No."

Zane bit him, just lightly. "Because I wanted you to know what kinds of people I fall in love with. The ones who step in and take me out of myself. Who aren't the ones I'm supposed to love. Plain folks with no bullshit. Who care. Who can feel passion." He turned his face from Eli. "The ones who make me feel something good. There was her. Almost twenty years later, there was you."

Eli let his hand fall atop Zane's head. He smoothed Zane's hair down. "Lonely life."

"It was," Zane said. He rose to balance himself on one arm and leaned over Eli, face above his, his breath warm on Eli's cheeks. "Not anymore. It matters, Eli. So much. You want to keep it private? Fine. I shouldn't have pushed."

"Hiding isn't your way."

"But it is yours." Zane pushed Eli down. "Whatever it takes. I just need you. Don't leave me."

"Shh." Eli knew what Zane needed. He guided Zane down to him. "Like I said before, I've got you."

And I am never letting go.

* * *

"Now this is more my style. These? They are my people." Eli swabbed the last of his toast -- plain, white bread toast, bad for you, even worse when it'd been fried -- through the last drops of egg yolk from his two sunny-side ups and reached for the ketchup to better attack his hash browns. "I think I want bacon too. The absolute hell with good health, and I know what I'm talking about. I'm a doctor."

Zane had to put down his mug lest he either choke or spill. He dabbed at his mouth with a napkin. Eli took a moment to enjoy the sight of Zane bright and energetic and, dare he say it, happy. "You're in a rare mood today."

"And why shouldn't I be?" Among other things, they'd gone nearly two weeks since the blowup over Duke and enjoyed smooth sailing since then. "With this food? I'm in heaven. That's where I am."

Richie reappeared from behind the grill, red

kerchief doing its best to constrain his wiry curls. He flipped Eli the finger. Taye, returning to his seat at the end of the diner table, laughed and offered Zane a high five. "That's what you get for trying to be cute."

"Ah, don't hate the player because he's good at the game." Eli popped in a bite of greasy, salty, delicious hash browns and washed them down with coffee he knew Richie had made. A little touch of the good life down here with the salt of the earth. Perfection.

"How's he finding the adjustment?" Zane asked Taye, taking his own pancakes much more slowly but with thoughtful appreciation.

Eli watched with interest. Taye seemed to be a force unto himself. Wherever Eli went, there Taye eventually turned up. Fate, kismet, karma, luck, whatever you wanted to call it. This was only the second time since that first god-awful brunch that Zane and Taye had spent more than a hot moment together, and so help Eli, he wanted it to go well.

Taye, eating toast with grape jelly, grinned a purple grin. "Like a duck to water and a congressman to the cash pot. Would you believe he gets better tips here?"

Eli stopped with a forkful of potatoes hanging in the balance. "Since when do cooks get tips?"

"Exactly his point. We rich folk can be stingy bastards." Without looking across the table at Eli, Zane stole the forkful. "Good God. Are these just a vehicle for ketchup?"

"Essentially? Yes." Eli closed his eyes and let himself soak in the noisy clatter of the diner, the cheerful shouts of the regulars, and the smells of the food he'd woken up to year after year. Not that it was a dump; as diners went, Richie had found employment in one of the nicer of the breed. Clean as the proverbial whistle, bright, airy. But they knew how to feed people the way doctors said you never, ever should. Perfection.

He tuned in halfway through a conversation between Zane and Taye, who perched on an extra chair at the end of the two-man table as casually as if he'd always been there, though he was bumped or jostled every half minute by someone passing through.

"So, my specialty track for my medical residency. Clinical psych. Holly II, he called me." Taye feinted a mock jab at Eli, who jabbed back. "I'd thought about it before, but Eli was the one who made me consider the option seriously," Taye said, folding his hands under his chin. "What do you think?"

Zane took the question in equal solemnity, treating Taye to the full force of his gaze. Unlike the first time they'd met, Taye returned it inch for inch. Eli hung out comfortably on the perimeter, full and content.

"I think it's not quite you," Zane said at last. "I've seen you in action. You have a cool head in a crisis, and true, you might get some of those in clinical psych, but I think you'd be happier in the long run out where there's more adrenaline pumping."

"Hmm. Not sure I agree, but I'll take it into consideration." Taye took that well. He dug into the inner pocket of his jacket and withdrew a flyer, a folded packet, and a brown envelope. "This is the other option I'd been thinking about." He pushed the papers over to Zane.

Eli read the logo upside down. His eyebrows rose. "Doctors Without Borders?"

Taye nodded. "When I've got more experience under my belt. I think I could fit there."

Zane was already eyeball-deep in the literature. "You could do a hell of a lot of good," he murmured, mostly absorbed. "What about Operation Smile?"

"Also a possibility."

Huh. Eli tapped the side of his thick coffee mug. "What this, what about that, but -- what about Richie?" he asked, watching the young man behind the grill. He understood better now what Taye saw in Richie. The starry-eyed way the two acted when they were together, even when they were being discreet.

He guessed that was what you'd call love. No. He knew it.

"We've talked about it." Taye made to take the papers back, then shook his head. "You keep those for now. I'll get them back later." To Eli, he said, "It'll be a while before we decide where to go and when. I need to finish my residency and so on. Richie's at Kendall College, School of Culinary Arts. We're both making our way."

Zane raised his mug to his lips. He'd been about to say something but drifted off briefly and then swore his way out of it when his pager thrummed.

"Some things never change, huh?" Eli nudged Zane's foot with his under the table.

Zane gave him a curious but interested look. "Sometimes they do." He checked the pager and grimaced. "Unfortunately, not this. I'll be right back."

Taye waited for Zane to clear the area before turning to Eli. "Okay. Why did you really want me in on this breakfast?"

"What, you're assigning hidden agendas to me now?"

Taye shrugged and waited.

"It's almost like you know me." Eli sighed. He dabbed up the last bite of hash browns and licked his thumb. "Where do I go from here? *Don't* say anything about me asking for help. It took a steel worker's breakfast and a hell of a lot of pep talking before I could do it, so let's just skip that part."

Taye eyed Eli thoughtfully before nodding. "Okay. I need more to go on, though. Where are you now, where do you want to be, that kind of thing."

"Now? Now, we're good." Eli had to hide his ridiculously fond smile behind his hand. "Sort of. He wants… Hell, he's not saying it that often anymore, but he wants to be able to show affection in public, and I…" He sighed. "You know me well enough to know I'm something of a cripple that way."

"Mmm." Taye pressed his knuckles together. He'd almost healed up from the walloping he'd taken, though it looked like he'd carry a scar with him over his cheekbone. "You want me to teach you how to overcome that?"

"Yes."

"I can't."

"Excuse me?"

"Not because I don't want to. Understand that. It's just that people are people. Join the heavily populated club. If you're not comfortable being affectionate outside the home, then don't."

Eli could feel his skin suffuse with heat. "That's not the point," he said, low. "I want to. I just can't seem to make myself. I get the urge -- I freeze. Deer in the headlights. Zane's putting up with it, he's great that way, but for the first time in my life, I want to lay it out there, and now… I find I can't." Good mood dimmed and appetite finally gone, he pushed his plate away from him. "That's what I need help with."

"Okay. Give me a minute." Taye rested his chin on his hand and watched Eli. Eli fidgeted under the observation and thought to himself that Zane was wrong. Taye had been born for clinical psych and shaped from some primal clay to be Holly's protégé.

"Enough, already."

"There are no easy answers," Taye said, sitting back. "There is one piece of advice I can give you. Maybe it'd help."

"Lay it on me."

"Hey, Taye! Come over to the counter for a minute?" Richie called from behind the grill.

"Go on, go on." Eli shooed him. "We can finish this some other time."

"We can." Taye drummed a quick tattoo on the tabletop. "But once begun, better get it done. My advice is to tell Zane himself how you feel. Tell him that you love him."

The breath whooshed out of Eli. "You don't start small, do you?"

"We're way past the starting block," Taye told him, getting to his feet. "Once you've said it, things change. It might be easier then. Might not. Even if it doesn't, you still should. It's something people need to hear." He dodged aside to let Zane back into the booth. "See you two later."

* * *

Zane slid into the booth, already reaching for his mug before his ass properly hit the seat. "That was oddly like meeting the parents."

Eli smirked. "Can't get anything past you, can I?"

"You want the pair of us to get along, don't you?" Zane swirled his mug instead of drinking, watching Eli with an intensity that suggested the answer mattered more than Eli might have thought, though he wasn't sure why.

"He's a good kid. He'll make a great doctor. And

he reminds me of you."

"Funny." Zane cracked a grin. "He reminds me of *you*."

"So I've heard. I still don't see it, not really."

Zane shrugged that off. He slid the Doctors Without Borders literature Taye had left closer, falling back into his reading. "This is... I don't know." Eli could see him zone out over one of the pictures, stroking it lightly with his fingertip.

Eli couldn't help but notice Zane's pager had been turned off. "Something up?"

"Administrative bullshit, more axes showing up to hang over the free clinic. I really, really don't want to talk about it. I'm having a good breakfast and apparently making new friends." Zane flicked his fingertips to the side. "Leave it for now."

"Uh-huh," Eli said. "You can't get anything past me either, you know."

That got Zane to look up, nose wrinkled. "You'd be surprised. Come to think of it, you were plenty surprised, and not that long ago."

Fair point. Eli didn't mind the nudge, not like he might have. Funny how things changed, wasn't it? Besides, he had other things on his mind. Zane studied those brochures with something in his eye that Eli had become accustomed to seeing only when they were alone together. Took him a second to put a name to it: *yearning*.

"That really hits your buzzer, doesn't it?" he asked, poking the paperwork.

Zane sighed and pushed the sheets away. "I'd be lying if I said it didn't, and I'm not going to do that with you."

"But?"

"No but. Well. Sort of." Zane tracked his visual

way back to the top brochure. "Hear anything back from Dr. Kazaran?"

Ah. "Nope," Eli was happy to report, sorry he'd ever sent the e-mail in the first place. "The man probably doesn't even remember me. I'm not going down to Duke."

"You could do some good there."

Eli raised an eyebrow. "Playing devil's advocate now?"

"Not really." Zane stroked the DWB brochure. "Did you ever think…"

Eli had no idea where Zane was heading with this. "Think what?"

"Mmm." Zane was too focused elsewhere. "These guys… seems like they're out there doing what I wish I could. We're days away from the final chop at the free clinic. Maybe not even that long. DWB is making a difference. I'm just marking time."

Something odd began to gather in Eli's chest. "Zane…"

"I'm not going to do it." Zane finally tore himself away with a firmness that Eli knew well. Decision made. "I have things to keep me here."

"Christ, Zane." Eli searched for something comforting to say and only managed to come out with, "Shame they don't have something like this for the inner cities."

"They used to. Give us a few days, and we won't." Weariness replaced Zane's enthusiasm. The man was a regular chimera, and it was a hell of a job keeping up.

But there *was* one thing he could do that'd lift Zane's spirits. Eli hoped.

Here goes nothin'. No prompts, no demands. With one arm under the table, Eli reached toward Zane and nudged Zane's hand at rest on his knee. "We'll figure out something," he said, holding Zane's eyes as he took Zane's hand.

Zane looked as if he'd been singed by lightning. "Eli?"

"It's not much, I know." Eli laced their fingers together. "But it's a start."

Zane squeezed him, tighter than expected. A good clench. "It's more than you think it is." He took a pen from his pocket and scribbled three X's on a napkin. "Two can play at this game," he said, pushing the napkin toward Eli. "What do you think?"

"I think I --" Eli's throat closed. Damn it. "I think you're worth it," he said instead. *Sorry, Taye. I'll get there. Soon. I hope. Because you're right, it is true. And because I want to.*

"You don't have to, you know," Zane said, gentling his hold. "I already know."

"Nothing past you." Eli raised his mug to clink it with Zane's. "Thank God for that."

* * *

Yeah. Funny how things changed.

Eli leaned on his elbows, reading the e-mail for the -- fourth, fifth time? An innocent stop in the doctor's lounge and the borrowing of Diana's laptop to check an article -- well, no one could resist checking their e-mail, could they?

He wished he had.

Dr. Jameson,

Of course I remember you, and I must say that it is a pleasure indeed to hear from you again. You were one of my most promising students, though if you are as I remember, you are even now scoffing at the notion.

True. Eli ran his hand through his hair. He wasn't anything special. He was old. Not ancient, but c'mon. No hotshot on his way up.

Scoff if you must, then, but I am not the only faculty member who spoke highly of you. It takes great courage to return to school later in life, and even greater determination to succeed. Graduating near the top of your class and putting in their place those still so young they have a shine to them -- that takes talent.

Eli wished to God he could stop reading this. Wished even more that he didn't want to believe it. Dr. Kazaran, the tough old bastard, had never outed with something like this back in the day. If he had, Eli wouldn't have considered touching base, crazy salary and grand opportunity in the offing or not. Wasn't as if he planned to apply, after all.

Except Dr. Kazaran had taken that out of his hands.

I am most pleased to hear of your interest in returning to our medical college. In my estimation, you would be an excellent fit, and I intend to refer this matter to the search committee, among whom are many who remember you with equal admiration.

Christ.

I will contact you shortly with their response. Indeed, Dr. Jameson, I do hope that you will strongly consider joining us.

My best to Marybeth.

Sincerely,

Alexander Kazaran

Eli closed the e-mail, deleted it for good measure, and snapped the laptop shut.

Perhaps with more vigor than was wise. Diana, glazed out over a chart, blinked up at him. "Watch the casing, would you?" She got a good look at Eli and tilted her head. "That's not a good face. What's up? The amino acids you were looking up stage some kind of palace revolt?"

"That makes absolutely no sense, Diana."

"I've been on my feet -- so to speak -- for twenty fucking hours, Eli. I'm entitled to be as random as I like." Diana propped her cheek in her hand. "I ask because I care, and because you look -- I don't know. If you were a patient, I'd be calling for a nurse right about now. What's wrong?"

Eli pressed his fingers to his temples and tried to think. For all the good it did him. "Let me get back to you on that one."

"You do that." Diana took her laptop back and tucked it into its carrying case. She patted Eli's hand. Clumsily and with obvious lack of practice -- God, her beside manner left a lot to be desired -- but he could tell she meant well. "If Zane doesn't take proper care of you tonight, page me and I'll come kick his ass clear up to his tonsils for you."

Eli laughed. Diana winked. "Now that's more like it."

"I think it is," Eli said. "And I think I know where I want to be instead of here."

"Now that's what I'm talking about." Diana shooed Eli toward the door. "Go, go. Do something good. Balance out whatever fucked you up in there," she added with a wave at her computer. "And don't worry. I won't check the cache."

"Deleted it."

"I'd have to say that's probably a good move." Diana smiled at him. A real smile. It made her look younger and a little wistful. "All joking aside, Eli, what the two of you have... It gives me hope."

"Yeah," Eli said, pushing Dr. Kazaran to the back of his mind and letting Zane come to the forefront. There. Felt better already. Though he'd have to tell

Zane about this, and that wasn't what he'd call good anticipation. Still. Honesty above all, and better to get it out now than have it come around with sharp teeth later. "Me too."

Chapter Ten

Eli let himself into Zane's apartment. They traded about, fair being fair. Minus the pool table Eli guarded with his life, he did have to admit he liked Zane's digs better. A slightly better class of rats, leather furniture only a man with none of his five senses wouldn't enjoy, and now some damn good memories layered on top.

"Honey, I'm home," he wisecracked as he toed the door shut behind him.

Zane waved from his position stretched out on the couch, arms crossed under his head. He'd loosened his tie and rolled up his shirt sleeves, taken off his shoes, but was otherwise ready for anything. Right now, that seemed to be lying still with his eyes closed, listening to something jazzy and bluesy wafting from his speaker system. Eli glanced at the iPod dock and wished, for a moment, they still did records. A phonograph and a scratch every now and then would make the picture perfect.

He let himself lean on the door frame and look his fill. Zane's hair fell smoothly away from his face, spread out on the couch arm. Little grayer than it'd been a few weeks ago, but no less soft and touchable. A dark shadow of stubble, just enough to work up a beard burn, shadowed his cheeks. Eli could make out the firm cording of muscle in his arms, and then, of course, there was his chest, leading down to his stomach and to the neat fly of his slacks.

He lingered there a moment longer. Because he could, and because he knew perfectly well that though Zane wasn't watching him, he knew exactly what Eli was up to.

Then, to Eli's own surprise, he found himself skimming back up to Zane's face. Narrow upper lip, full lower, well-shaped nose, sharp cheekbones, smooth forehead. He fingered his own face, finding it rough-hewn and too strong in comparison.

Didn't matter as much as it used to, and Eli barely gave it more than one thought, too busy studying Zane. The vague sense of curiosity coalesced in a sudden understanding. He'd always known in a general sort of way that Zane was a good-looking man. Lately he'd come to the intimate knowledge that, for a guy, Zane was hot.

He'd never before realized that Zane was beautiful.

Zane stretched and yawned. He turned to look at Eli in a way that floored him. "Welcome home. Come here," he said, beckoning. "Listen to this part. The trumpet solo."

Eli didn't. He was still back there on the word he'd spoken earlier, and Zane had spoken now. *Home.* It was where the heart was, after all.

The temptation to go and sit by Zane, to let what came naturally now and which Zane casually but clearly invited -- that was a strong pull. Tonight, Eli thought he wanted more. Something... he didn't know. Something, dare he use the word, romantic. Mushy. Whatever, just something to show Zane how much this meant to him, to have a real home.

An idea came. "Hungry?"

Zane took the question in stride. "God, yes. Breakfast is a long-ago memory. I was thinking we could order in. I've got a taste for... hmm. Comfort food."

Perfect. Best opportunity ever. "Stay here. You're too pretty a picture to disrupt." Eli blushed hot while he said it, but the words did make their way out, so he'd call that a victory, as he would the slow roll of happiness that warmed Zane once he'd said them. "And you have a CD's worth of jazz to appreciate. I'll go get us dinner."

Zane blinked. "No kidding? You wouldn't rather…" He patted his hip. "In case I wasn't clear, I was making the offer."

"I want to give you something else that matters," Eli said. "I want to make you happy, not just fucked."

Zane smirked. "Such a way with words. Hey." He stretched out his arm. Eli could not help but cross to take it, and to bend down and kiss Zane once, just once. Zane was smiling when Eli drew back. "You're one of the good ones, Eli."

"Bah."

"Someday you'll believe it too. We might be too senile to know what the hell we're talking about by then, but I can wait." Zane stretched out, lazy and contented as a cat.

I want it to be sooner. One step at a time, though. "Give me carte blanche on what to bring back, yeah?"

"Of course. I trust you."

And didn't that kick like a mule to the chest? There had been something Eli had intended to share with Zane. Damned if he could remember it now, not with his stomach rumbling and Zane spread out in the manner of a feast.

"I'll hurry," he said, backtracking toward the door. If he didn't, he'd forget food, and that wasn't the goal.

"Do," Zane murmured, losing himself in the music. "Maybe I'll whip up something for dessert by the time you get back."

Eli swallowed roughly. He doubted Zane had chocolate cake or tortes in mind, damn fine cook though he might be on his own turf. "Is that a fact?"

"It is." Zane's lips curved like the Mona Lisa's.

"Then I'll hurry." Eli wanted to kiss Zane again, but somehow the anticipation seemed sweeter than diving in for immediate gratification. There was one advantage to being older when first trying this. No, two. For one, appreciation of the journey. For the second, appreciating properly what he had. "Back before you know it."

Zane gazed at Eli through soft gray. "I'll be here." His look was a kiss, one Eli tucked close to his heart as he headed back out into the Chicago night and the cold, cold rain that he noticed almost not at all with that kiss held close to keep him warm.

Only when he hit the corner that'd take him to the restaurant he had in mind did Eli remember he'd planned to tell Zane, right away, about Dr. Kazaran's e-mail. It'd have to wait, but he wouldn't forget again. Food, fun, truth. More than likely, the kind of sex he couldn't get enough of. Love.

What could possibly go wrong?

* * *

"Couldn't stay away, could you?"

Richie. Manning the counter by himself, no less. Eli draped his soaking jacket on a wall hook above a rubber mat. "You're a fine one to talk. Haven't been here since this morning, have you?"

Eli doubted it. Richie looked fresh and as rested as one could in a busy diner. Twenty-four hours and it never seemed to slow down. And they said New York didn't sleep. Try Chicago sometime.

Richie waved off the mild concern. "I crashed out for a few. Besides, Taye's on tonight too. What am I going to do at home by myself?"

"Sleep some more?"

"Nah. We need the money." This close to Richie,

Eli could see shadows beneath his eyes. He wondered, worried, wanted to make them an offer of help if they were in real financial trouble, but Taye was a proud man and he didn't doubt Richie was the same. Richie tried to make light of it. "You know what interns make. If I bust my hump, the tips I get here bring us just about even."

"Can't earn much money if you're worn out."

"We're young; we'll cope." Richie did seem cheerier now that he didn't have to maintain a cool, remote, and discreet 'tude. "Don't worry so much. I've got it covered. Though maybe not if I keep chatting." He flipped a clean hand towel over his shoulder. Eli could have seen now, if not before, how well Richie and Taye matched. "So what can I get you?"

Diner food was diner food was diner food, but there was always a chef's special, and if Richie was the chef, it had to be good. "Throw me some suggestions, would you? Dinner for two, me and Zane. I'm looking for something made for enjoying on a cold night. Something that'll stick to your ribs, but not like a slathering of concrete."

"Comfort food," Richie said with a decided nod. "Sit tight. I think I know what to get you -- if you trust my judgment?"

Eli considered that. Why not? The man made a masterpiece out of Folgers. "Consider yourself given carte blanche."

"Fantastic. Have a seat. Won't take long." Richie ducked behind the grill and got busy.

Eli tried to crane his neck to see what Richie was up to. Rustling wrappers and the sizzle of the grill could mean anything. He leaned on the freezer display in search of a better view. In that he failed, but the cold beneath his arm gave him an idea. "Do you do milkshakes here?" In season or out, Zane was a fiend for ice cream and only rarely indulged. Couldn't get much more into indulgent comfort than that, could it?

"Sure, we've got supplies. Really basic flavors, though." Richie popped briefly out. "Just got some fresh fruit in. I can dress it up some, if you're interested."

Eli chuckled. You could take the boy out of the bistro, but you couldn't take the cuisine out of the food-hearted. "Culinary school, huh?"

"As fast as I can. Milkshake?"

"Two." Eli made the peace sign. "Fruit's good. Just be careful you don't use strawberries," he called, having to raise his voice to be heard as Richie ducked away again.

"Right, strawberries, got it," Richie called back, almost drowned out by a rush and sizzle from the grill.

Christ, that smelled good. Eli closed his eyes and breathed deep, savoring the aromas. He could feel his need for a triple bypass growing, but in a place like this, who was able to care?

The bell over the door jingled to admit a crew of guys that looked somewhat familiar to Eli. The green and blue and magenta of scrubs peeked through their jackets. Though unsure if they'd recognize him, Eli gave them a wave.

"Jameson, right?" The tallest and leanest of the group, bespectacled and going bald, ambled directly up and shook his hand.

"Pearson?" Eli guessed. Not someone he regularly interacted with, and not someone he particularly cared to. Pearson had a look to him that suggested shiftiness.

"That's me." Pearson took a few seconds too long letting go of Eli's hand, trying to squeeze too hard.

Jeez. Talk about your masculine insecurities. "What are you doing down here with the rest of us peasants?"

"Hey, don't look at me. My friends have rarified tastes. I'm teaching them that plain and simple is just plain good."

"Right on. Hey, uh -- cook guy?"

Eli snorted. *Cook guy.* If this kind of diner was Pearson's familiar stomping grounds, he'd eat an empty soup can without salt.

"Be with you in a sec!" Richie shouted back. He waved at them over the back of the grill.

Pearson rolled his eyes. "Attitude, huh?"

"You're one to talk."

Pearson was the kind of man who'd take that as a compliment, and did. He pounded Eli on the shoulder, again too hard. Christ, this guy had issues. "Yeah, well. Some stereotypes are true, huh?"

"Beg pardon?"

Pearson leaned in and stage-whispered. "Bitchy queen. C'mon. You can't tell he's a little light in the loafers?"

Eli put a couple inches of distance between himself and Pearson. "You don't say. Know that for sure?"

"Please. It's obvious." Pearson thumped his hands together and chafed them to warm them. "So, where's your wife?"

Not this again. Eli took another inch's distance away. "Marybeth? Austria."

"Wait, you're married for real?" They'd drawn the attention of Pearson's cohort now. "No shit, man."

"Let me guess. You're talking about Dr. Novia?"

"You two are always together. Ah, c'mon, don't give me that look. Learn how to take a joke." Pearson elbowed Eli, all hail-fellow-well-met. "He's about ready to have a meltdown, isn't he?"

Enough. "Not my business and not yours."

"Jesus. Touchy, touchy." Pearson backed off. "Look, I'm sorry. You know how it gets when you've been awake for this long. The brain gives way, and the tongue cuts loose."

Eli couldn't argue with that. "Fair enough." He sighed in relief when a waitress, cute and blonde and obviously not in favor of Pearson and his gang, slid him a full cup of coffee and a surreptitious pat to the elbow. Apparently he had backup of his own. Good to know.

Richie shouted to him over the racket of the grill and the increased background hum of customers and the ringing of the till. Christ, it'd gotten busy all of a sudden. For the life of him, Eli couldn't make out a word. He gave an exaggerated shrug, made Richie laugh, and figured it couldn't be that important. Probably just passing the time.

"So you should come to a game with us sometime," Pearson said, picking right up where he'd left off. "I hear you like the Cubs."

"Who doesn't?"

"The guys and I, we try and get there at least once a season."

"Sure, me too." Eli hated this kind of inane chatter, more so from this particular source. He puzzled it over. Why were Pearson and his crew getting on Eli's nerves so? Diana dished out far worse on a daily business, with Holly a not-so-distant second. He wasn't sure.

No, strike that. He knew exactly what bugged him. These guys? They didn't know him, and they weren't sure they liked him. Eli knew he didn't care for them.

If you took the good food out of the equation and compared this place with the raucous customers to the *home* he had waiting for him -- Zane, jazz, quiet, leather couch, sleep -- wasn't any bit of a contest.

Richie called to Eli again. Damnable distractions. "What?" Eli cupped his hand around his ear.

The blonde waitress who'd slipped Eli his coffee interpreted. "Your order's almost up. Give him five to make the shakes and you're good to go."

Eli gave Richie the thumbs-up.

"Isn't he great?" She didn't bother being discreet. Eli figured Pearson and his crew probably annoyed her as much as him, and more often. "And his boyfriend is adorable. You should see the two of them together."

"I've had the privilege." Eli made sure Pearson was distracted. "So he's really out?"

The waitress nodded.

"And that's not a problem?"

She shrugged. "For some people, I guess. That's their problem."

Huh. Eli absorbed that, lost in thought until paper take-out bags were coming his way and he'd started to make a path to the till. Then Pearson followed him. Son of a bitch.

"Can I help you with something?" he asked, a curter approach than he'd normally take with a colleague but not in the mood for nonsense.

"Don't take this the wrong way, okay?" Pearson propped his elbows on the counter next to Eli.

In Eli's experience, those words invariably meant, *I'm going to insult you now.* "Uh-huh," he said as he handed the waitress his credit card. She made a sympathetic face. Richie stood at the back of the grill, quiet again, listening.

"*It's not just you anymore,*" Eli heard echoing in

his head.

"You spend a lot of time with Novia," Pearson said. "A lot of time. Maybe more than you should with one guy. If you don't want people to get the wrong idea, that is."

"Do they?" Eli did not look at Pearson.

"I guess some, yeah."

"Like who?"

"I don't know. People."

Aggravation, divided attention, and eagerness to get home to Zane made Eli's tongue sharper and coarser than usual. Honesty tasted as good as the diner's blue plate special smelled. "Like you, who I barely fucking know and don't really give a shit about?"

"Hey, don't get your back up. I'm just trying to give you some advice. So who's the food for?" Pearson eyed the soup containers and greaseproof bags. "Fuck, you've got enough for an army."

"I have a man-sized appetite," Eli said dryly.

Richie's lips twitched, the kid doing his damnedest not to grin. He winked at Eli.

Maybe it was that which gave Eli the courage, or maybe it was being sick and tired of this bullshit. Looking at Pearson and listening to him, a guy Eli probably would have liked in pre-Zane days -- plain and simple, a man who said what he thought -- it was like looking through a dirty mirror. Smudged and smeared. Who he'd been.

Not who he was becoming. Frankly, he liked the new him better.

"No, seriously." Pearson rattled a bag, then laughed at the two tall milkshakes in Styrofoam cups the waitress added to his pile of loot. "Got a hot date while your wife's out of the country?"

Bite me was what Eli wanted to say. What he chose to say was, "Nope. She and I are divorced. Dr. Novia and I are spending the night in together." *Fuck, I cannot believe I just said that.*

No. No excuses. No explanations, either. No losing his cool until he was out the door, please God. What was done was done. "Excuse me, gentlemen."

Well, he'd hoped he could make Taye proud of him. Looked like he'd made a start.

Chapter Eleven

By the time Eli got back home, he was chilled to the bone and couldn't feel his fingers. So good to get into the warmth, and even better to see Zane up and at 'em, busy poking around in his kitchen for plates and silverware.

"Finally. I was about to resort to eating my own arm." Zane's stomach rumbled audibly as he rounded the kitchen island with his arms loaded. He cracked up at the sight of what Eli held. "You've got icicles in your hair, and you bring me a milkshake?"

"Funny guy. Richie made them."

Zane hastily shed his load of flatware on the coffee table and made a grab. "That's a different story. Bring that over here."

"My pleasure." Emboldened by... whatever it was that had happened at the diner, Eli put his double armful on the coffee table and caught Zane by the bicep. Pulled him in for a quick kiss, one that went a hell of a lot further toward warming Eli clear down to his toes than the central heat. "I gave him a blank check with the food itself. No idea what we've got."

"Treasure hunt," Zane said. He returned the kiss with interest, finished with a light slap to Eli's hip that Eli recognized -- and enjoyed -- as a temporary rain check, and sat to dig through the goods.

"It's Richie. It's going to be good."

"Why else do you think I'm going after this like a pirate with gold in sight?"

Eli found a place on the couch and pulled Zane down next to him, the food in easy reach of both. He was in the process of reaching for a bag that smelled like heaven when he caught a look at what Zane was wearing and had to stop, cracking up. "Where in the holy hell did you find that shirt?"

Zane beamed at him and turned from the waist to display his tie-dye. A line of Grateful Dead skeletons boogied their way across at sternum level. "You like? I haven't worn this since college."

Eli smoothed down the wrinkles on the sleeve. "I can see that. I doubt you've washed it since then, either. Smells like patchouli with just a hint of weed, for Christ's sake."

"What can I say? I was rebellious in my youth." Zane's leaning over to kiss Eli seemed perfectly natural. "I'm feeling my oats tonight. Still fits, right?"

"Fits and looks good." Eli found a container of what looked like tomato soup, popped off the lid and took a taste. He moaned in appreciation and pushed the cup at Zane. "Try this, now. Campbell's never tasted this good."

Zane gave it a try. "Oh God. Amazing. What'd he add? Dash of lemon, dash of cracked black pepper -- "

"Don't know, don't care." Eli stole the container back and set about the busy work of draining it dry. "Think we could hire him as a personal chef?"

"And deprive the world of this? I'm not that selfish." Zane uncovered a wrapped sandwich that released heady, fragrant aromas of cheese, butter, and bacon. He gazed at it in wonder. "Kill me now."

"Only if I can have your sandwich."

"Uh-uh, get your own." Zane took a thoughtful bite, then made an orgasm face coupled with a sensual moan that Eli already knew were reserved for the best of all possible delights. "My God. My sweet God. Eli, I'm sorry. I'll also apologize to Taye. I'm running away with Richie tonight. We'll hit the Canadian border by morning."

Eli shoulder checked Zane. "Don't joke about

that."

Zane's hand landed briefly on Eli's thigh. "Don't worry about it." Grilled-cheese breath kissed his ear, followed by Zane's lips. "I know when I've got it good."

"Damn well better." This was better than a holiday morning. Eli checked the milkshakes and only there was he slightly disappointed. He'd thought the color was the lid, but no. They were very... white. "Vanilla. Huh. He'd said he was going to fancy them up."

Zane switched his sandwich to one hand and studied the shake close up. "Unlikely, unless it's white chocolate."

Eli took a tentative sip. "Nope. Plain old vanilla." A thought occurred. "Maybe he was trying to help. Nothing 'fruity.'" He made sarcastic quote fingers before realizing that might not have been such a good idea. The last thing he wanted was to bring that nastiness in the diner here, into his sanctum. "Don't ask. I don't want to tell."

Zane furrowed his forehead. "Don't ask what?"

"Already you disrespect my wishes." Eli sat a little closer to show he meant the words in jest, but he couldn't help the abrupt stiffness in his shoulders.

He should have known he couldn't fool Zane. Ever. "Ah," Zane said, poking the straw in his milkshake. He took a hearty bite of his sandwich. "So what happened while you were out?"

"Is there any getting you to drop this?"

Zane considered that. "Not really."

He should have known that too. "Some of the doctors stopped by while I was there, and they mouthed off. That's all. Eat your sandwich while it's still hot."

Zane dropped his sandwich on the coffee table. Might have seen that one coming. Eli rescued it and stuffed a bite in to keep his mouth busy. Dear God indeed. You couldn't call this "grilled cheese." It wasn't Gruyère and Dijon and pancetta on fancy bread, more like Swiss and cheddar and bacon on white, but be damned if it wasn't better.

He chewed industriously, hoping Zane would stop watching him with the narrow-eyed laser focus. "What aren't you telling me? Ah." His forehead smoothed. "They gave you a hard time, didn't they? About me."

"Fine. You want details?" Eli sat back heavily and let his hands fall to his lap. "It was bound to happen sooner or later." He tried to ignore the rising pounding of his pulse, and the nerves in his gut that reacted ill with the sandwich and soup. "I'm not sure what they deduced. I'd say they weren't brain surgeons, but with that group, they might have been. Not that that means they know jack shit about anything else."

"Eli. Stop deflecting." Zane squeezed his knee. "I need to know what happened. It's --"

"It's you too. I know." Appetite gone, Eli pinched the bridge of his nose. "They made insinuations. I didn't refute them."

Silence from Zane. A quiet that went on long enough that Eli frowned and turned to look to see exactly how Zane had taken that.

He'd not known what to anticipate, but it hadn't been a look of near wonder and a slowly growing smile, one of the rarest of all of Zane's smiles. Something soft and shy and almost boyish.

"Don't go thinking I'm a hero. I've never been that scared in my life, not even in the force."

"There's courage, and then there's courage," Zane said obliquely. He leaned in to kiss Eli, not on the lips but on the forehead, and while he was there settled into the curve of Eli's arm. Eli wrapped it around him without thought. "Are you okay?"

"I'm not sure."

Zane rubbed his head against Eli's shoulder. "Still."

Eli stroked Zane's hair. "Still. So we'll see what we'll see. Probably? Nothing will come of it. Nothing more than the usual, anyway. A hefty handful of gay jokes, maybe some panties snuck into my locker. Bah."

Zane could probably feel the faint tremors running under Eli's skin. "Do you know what courage means?"

"I think I have a pretty good idea."

"Maybe not." Zane's head rested over Eli's heart. "It means doing what needs to be done despite being scared shitless. You make me proud."

Eli blushed to what felt like a bone-deep degree. "Bah."

"Someday you'll learn to take a compliment. I'll keep trying." Zane stroked the back of Eli's hand. The "good" that Eli had felt before when coming in unannounced, and the immediate sense of hominess, both rolled easily back in under Zane's touch and the soothing sound of his voice. "You know there'll be more than talk this time."

Maybe so. Didn't mean Eli wanted to talk about it. "Leave it for now, Zane. Just for now."

Eli didn't miss Zane's small sigh or the resignation that passed through him. "I'm not good at living a lie, Eli," Zane said. "Is it so bad of me to want to be like this without worrying?"

"Bad, no. Realistic, yes."

Zane sat up straight and tugged his T-shirt down. "Realism is another word for cynicism, and they're both fucking overrated." He rummaged through the bag. "He threw in two pieces of chocolate cake, even."

"Zane --"

"No, forget it." Zane tried to grin. He didn't fool Eli for a second. "Like you said. Not now. This is good food, and I'm starving, so I'm not going to waste it." He softened. "We have time. I do. And I love you."

Hearing it again, spoken with deliberate intent, hit Eli no less hard than the first time he'd heard the words. "Zane," he said, the name not so much a word as a sound carried on breath. "Zane, I..."

Zane pushed his leg to Eli's, one solid line of warmth. "It's okay," he said, though Eli had the clear picture back now and knew it really mostly wasn't. "I can wait. You brought me a milkshake. I want to drink it before it melts."

"Here." Eli offered Zane a plastic spoon from the bag. "Just in case." It was a shitty substitute for what Eli wanted to give, and knew he did, but couldn't. He sucked firmly on his own straw and focused on the taste of sweet ice cream sliding cold and smooth over his tongue.

Zane said it before Eli could, just as surprised. "That's not plain vanilla. I still feel like a five-year-old chugging this instead of good scotch --"

"Liar. You adore shakes."

"I've got to admit it's tasty."

"Not half bad, no." Eli pried off the lid of his Styrofoam cup and used his straw to sift. Toward the bottom, he spotted the hidden treasure. "Huh! Fruit on the bottom. Leave it to Richie. I swear that guy could whip up a feast out of a dried cheese rind and a half box of crackers." He prodded the fruit. "Blueberries. Very nice." Over the sound of Zane taking a hearty slurp, he asked, "Did you get the same?"

There was a pause. The sort of pause that made Eli turn his head fast. What he saw -- Christ. Color drained from Zane's face, betraying a sheen of sweat that disappeared under fast-rising red.

The cup dropped from Zane's hands.

"Zane, what the hell?"

Zane didn't answer. He made the kind of noise no one ever, ever wanted to hear from someone they loved and shoved at his sides.

"What are you doing?" Zane couldn't answer him. He thumped at his hip pockets, his hands clumsy, and Jesus Christ, his breathing wasn't good. He was locked in some faraway place Eli couldn't hope to get near.

Fruit. Oh, shit. No, no, no -- Eli looked, just to be sure. Zane's shake had spilled over the floor, and there they were. Sliced red and perfect and juicy. Strawberries. Just the juice would have done it, and if Zane had swallowed a sliver --

Zane's breathing made Eli think of fists tightening around flesh. Fighting. Losing. He swayed. Eli caught him. Only just, and Zane clawed at him, making it impossible to hang on. With uncoordinated arms that were beginning to seize up, Zane thumped his hip, searching, finding nothing. His eyes rolled back in his head.

EpiPen. Christ, that stupid shirt -- Zane didn't have the EpiPen on him, and what the fuck was wrong with Eli that he hadn't thought --

He dashed for Zane's jacket, hung neatly on a chair. Dragged the chair over on its side but couldn't give less of a fuck. The slim black EpiPen case was tucked in the inside pocket, too little for Eli to get a grip on, and Zane was far, far too still by now.

Eli wasn't the praying type. He shot a quick one to the man upstairs as he sent the medicine into Zane. Phone. Fuck! That he had in his own pocket, and a good thing too because be damned if the EpiPen was working. Too late? No. Hell no. He wouldn't let it be too late. He dialed 911, wedged the phone under his ear, and tried to remember he was a doctor.

"Anaphylactic reaction," he said, interrupting the dispatcher's opening lines. He garbled the address and had to repeat himself. "For fuck's sake, get a move on."

The dispatcher did what she could, and so did Eli. All he could. It had to be enough. Had to be.

If it wasn't, the last thing he would have said to Zane was... nothing. Silence not filled with *I love you*.

God. Eli started CPR, and he kept praying.

* * *

Eli stomped his feet to keep them warm and cupped his hand around the lighter flame to guard it from the wind, lighting his fourth -- fifth? -- cigarette. Zane's stash. Who knew why he'd grabbed them on his way out of Zane's apartment. Who knew why he'd lit up? He didn't smoke, never had. The smoke burned like hell going down.

Almost like he couldn't breathe.

Eli took a lungful and held it. Every time he closed his eyes he could see Zane fighting to breathe. One sliced-up strawberry they'd found in the bottom of the cup. Just one was all it'd taken. Fuck.

A nurse elbowed open the crash door to the outside world. He knew her. Bernice, he thought her name was. "Dr. Jameson." She held her gloved hands up so she wouldn't contaminate them. "No smoking on hospital grounds. You know that."

Eli blew out his smoke and snapped in a vicious drag. "I want to see him."

He'd asked before. Repeating didn't help. "And I already told you no. You need to stay out here and let us do our jobs. You're a doctor. You know all of this."

"The hell you say. He's my -- Bernice, come on."

"Stay here. Put out your cigarette and wait." Narrow nosed and pointy chinned, with her hair slicked tightly back, Bernice looked all face and no smile on her small lips. All business. They'd worked together before, and he'd liked her then.

"You're boning me, Bernice. You talked to Pearson, didn't you?"

"Who? You mean that prick with the glasses?"

"See?" Eli pointed at her with the tip of his cigarette. A scratchiness in the back of his throat made him want to cough. "You're trying to have it both ways. Treating me like a doctor and like a family member."

"Far as I'm concerned, you're family. You're off duty, and the two of you are like brothers. I'm not having you in here getting in the way."

"So this is your call, not theirs?"

"Dr. Jameson, do not discuss semantics with me. I don't have time, and you're too worked up to come in. End of discussion."

"The hell you say. I kept Zane, Dr. Novia, going until the paramedics came." And Christ, he'd never be able to forget that. He'd see it in his nightmares for the rest of his life. Zane, always full of life and tempestuous emotion, as colorless as wax and as limp as a rag doll. "Bernice, I'm begging you. I won't even come in. I just want to be there."

"You don't know when to quit, do you?" A shout from behind Bernice got her on the move again. "*Stay,*

Dr. Jameson. I mean it."

And then she was gone, just like that, Immaculate Grace swallowing her back up. Eli dropped the mostly burned-out remnants of his -- Zane's -- cigarette into a puddle of slush and lit up another with shaking hands.

Christ. It'd been years since he'd been on the other side of the swinging doors. The memories weren't pleasant, and now he understood what he hadn't before, even as recently as this afternoon. What Zane felt. He knew now, in his bones, the brokenness of a place where you learned to sever your heart at the door when you wiped your feet.

* * *

A taxi barreled to the curb. Diana scrambled out almost before it'd come to a complete stop, tossing cash at the driver. She flipped him off, slammed the door behind her, and made tracks toward Eli in heels so high she could have broken her neck.

The throat was an amazing thing. So fragile, really. Everything in the human body was. The things that could go wrong with one little...

Diana snapped the cigarette out of Eli's hand and took a deep drag. "Eli, what the fuck? What happened?"

Cold seeped in abruptly, making Eli shiver and tighten his arms around his chest. "Zane. Strawberries. It was an accident. I didn't --" He didn't even remember calling or paging her. "They won't let me in."

Diana stood back and studied Eli. Her eyes narrowed, and her lips pursed. "No kidding. I can't say I blame them."

The injustice of that struck hard and cut deep. "You too, huh?" Eli took the cigarette back and drew an angry jerk of smoke. Shredding his throat. "Then what the hell did you come down here for?"

"Asshole. Give me a chance to explain myself. You look like shit, you're not being reasonable, and *no*, I don't blame you. Zane is --" There she stopped. "You've seen it from the other side. People who care get in the way."

Eli laughed, as bitter as Zane sometimes sounded. "No shit." The cigarette was halfway burned down. "So, what? You came to spank me?"

"As if. We both know I'm not your type."

"Don't make me laugh. Christ." Eli's head pounded. "Why *are* you here?"

Diana had to stretch up on tiptoe to twist his ear, but she managed, and lightning fast too. "Idiot. Why do you think?"

For the first time, Eli saw that she'd thrown a lab coat on over her sharp dress clothes and clipped her hospital ID to the lapel. A stethoscope hung around her neck. "Let them try to keep *me* out. I'm on call tonight. As far as I'm concerned, someone just called me in."

Eli's lips were numb. Inside, he could hear raised voices, and they could have been for anyone, anything, but he wasn't thinking. Couldn't make his brain work. "You're a cardiologist."

Diana made an impatient noise. "Do you want me to go lend a hand or what?"

Anything he could say to that wasn't good enough. Eli took Diana by the shoulders, pulled her to him in a rough attempt at a squeeze and kissed her forehead. "Yes. Please. Go."

She pointed into his face. "As long as *you* stay. Got me? And for God's sake, get some coffee to wash that smoke down with. If you're going to brood and pace, do it right."

"Diana, please." Eli wanted to yank the door open and push her inside.

"I'm gone." She reached for the pack. "No, give me one. Stick it in my pocket. I'll be back out as soon as I can, and I'll update you. *Stay.*"

Eli was gladder than anything that she'd be in there, that she'd help, but fuck if that didn't leave him alone in the cold dark. Again.

* * *

Eli checked his voice mail as a matter of habit. Call him old-fashioned, but he still wasn't totally on board with trusting a phone company whose CEO was young enough to be his son. Who knew how many calls he'd missed, spaced out in the darkness, floating in a sea of smoke as gray as Zane's flattest stare?

No messages.

Frustrated and in need of something -- anything -- to do with his hands, Eli checked for texts. Nothing. E-mails.

There he found something. A communication from Dr. Kazaran. Marked "high importance." He thumbed the touch screen, motivated by a sort of sick curiosity.

The search committee would like to schedule an interview…

Eli hit Delete. *I cannot deal with this right now. And I don't want it.*

Don't want anything but Zane, safe and sound.

* * *

At least until a second taxi disgorged its passengers at the curb. One of them was tall and blonde and slim, moving with quiet grace but still covering ground at a decent clip, followed behind by a dark, silent panther of a man.

"Eli." Holly was suddenly there, hugging him, smaller but infinitely stronger right now, smelling of balsam and lilies. "I came as soon as I could."

His arms went automatically around her. "Holly. What are you doing here?"

"Diana paged me. And called me from the taxi. You know Diana." She let go enough to look Eli in the face. "How are you?"

Keith, Holly's husband, came up as a sturdy presence behind him. They barely knew each other, but he offered Eli a firm shake, the good kind, the one where a guy had nothing to prove and offered no more than simple solidarity.

"How is he?"

No words came. All Eli could do was take Holly's small, cool hand and hold on.

Holly took that in her stride. "Diana's in with him? Good. She'll find out what's going on now. Tell me what happened then."

"Milkshake. Fucking stupid in this weather. Fruit cut up on the bottom."

"That much I did know." Holly's gaze was calm but intense, not letting him dodge. "Diana called Taye too, and Taye called me. He's with Richie right now. Richie's beside himself."

"Yeah? He can join the fucking club." Eli pulled away from Holly. "I'm going to kill that kid. I *told* him no strawberries, and he fucking --"

"Eli. Stop. We will find out what happened, but you're not thinking clearly right now, and that's why neither Taye nor Richie are here." Holly didn't let Eli withdraw. Just like Zane. Unlike Zane, she closed back in as relentlessly calm as ripples smoothing over a rock thrown into a lake. "You know they're doing the right thing not letting you in."

Eli was thoroughly tired of hearing that, but with Holly, who couldn't be argued with and couldn't be lied to, he couldn't deny the truth. "I know."

"Are you calmer now?" Holly rested her hand over his heart again. Checking his pulse, Eli thought. "Good. That's very good, Eli." Christ, she had a soothing voice. "Put your cigarette out. We'll go inside to the doctor's lounge where it's warm, and we'll get you something to drink."

"And then?"

"And then we wait. If you like, you can pray."

"I'm not the praying type," Eli said, nevertheless flashing back to how many times he'd done so on the way from Zane's apartment to Immaculate Grace, following in his own car because they wouldn't let him in the fucking ambulance.

"Ah, ah, ah," Holly cautioned, grounding Eli until he came back. "Breathe with me. There, that's better." She waited for him to steady himself. "Don't make yourself sick too, Eli. Zane will be fine."

Eli scoffed. "Don't patronize me. Anaphylaxis is serious fucking business, Holly. He could die." Christ. Saying it out loud…

"He could," Holly agreed, the living embodiment of that serenity prayer that infected the world. "I don't think he will. Do you know how people fight harder when they have something to come back for?"

She wouldn't take no answer for an answer. Eli nodded.

Holly cupped his cheek. "You see? Zane won't leave you."

He covered her hand. No more denials. What did they matter? "Everyone does know, huh?"

"Not everyone. Some already made up their

minds a long time ago. Some will still simply believe you're just close friends. Whatever truth is told is up to you, Eli."

"Goddamnit, Holly."

"Shh," she soothed. "Keith, help me get him inside. It'll be all right. I promise."

God help him. Eli wanted to believe her so much that he almost did. And if a woman like Holly said a thing would be so...

* * *

Then maybe it would be so.

Eli stood in the doorway to Zane's room and watched him from a distance. "Still," he said to Keith, who'd shadowed him even when Holly left to check up on Taye and Richie. "So still. Look at him. You wouldn't know he's alive if it weren't for the machines."

Keith nodded without a word. Still on a respirator -- just to make sure, Diana had said, words he'd delivered himself to too many people to count -- Zane was almost as pale as the sheets drawn up to his chest, his arms lying slack on the outside. An IV trailed from the back of his hand to a dripping bag of Eli didn't know what. Couldn't remember the name, too wiped out to think.

"I want to go in," he said to Keith. It was like talking to Holly in a way. They fit together. So many people did, and he'd never seen it. "But my feet are stuck to the floor. Isn't that the damnedest thing? Now that he's okay, I should... Christ, Keith, what does that say about me?"

"I think just that you're human." Keith kept one hand on Eli's shoulder to steady him. "He'll be okay. You too."

"Almost wasn't." Zane had flatlined. They'd

have called it if Diana hadn't been a pushy bitch and ignored their scolding to get the job done. If it weren't for her...

He couldn't even finish a thought. Christ.

"Almost isn't, is," Keith said, and Eli was tired enough to laugh at that. "Take your time. He'll be here."

Eli snorted. His mouth tasted like stale cigarettes and sour coffee and an ineffective Tic-Tac. He stank, and he had a streak of tomato soup on his sleeve. No. Strawberry juice.

"Or maybe you should sit down." Keith caught Eli before his knees gave out. As he guided Eli to the visitor's chair inside the room, he kept up a low, steady monologue. Eli only caught bits and pieces, but he did hear this clearly: "It's natural, Holly tells me. All that adrenaline. It's going to leave you shaky. Sit down and breathe."

"Fuck." Eli sank his head into his hands. "I feel like an idiot."

Keith shrugged. "Doesn't seem that way from here."

Eli craned his neck to look up at Keith and turned somehow in the middle of the move to look at Zane, and once he'd looked there, he couldn't look away. So quiet. So still. Respirator taped to the lips Eli had kissed -- Christ, was it only a few hours ago? He thought it might be close to dawn outside.

"Never know what you've got until it's almost gone, do you?" he asked. Rhetorical question. Keith still nodded.

A thought, somehow sharp and clear, pierced its way through Eli's mind. "Keith," he said, looking for the right words. "You do something with computers, right?"

Keith chuckled like a cave bear, a low rumble just as easily mistaken for a growl if he hadn't gently thumped Eli's shoulder. "Like you do something with medicine, yes."

"Sorry."

"Don't sweat it. You've had a rough night."

"Not as rough as some." Eli rubbed his cheek against the grain of his stubble. *Google search: Paris culinary arts.* There was someone else who needed to know. Not just this, but all that Zane had become. What kind of man he was. "Could you do a favor for me? There's someone I need to track down."

* * *

The sun had risen fully, shining unforgiving even through the blinds by the time Diana came by. Eli would have thought he'd be asleep in his chair by then. He wasn't.

One look at her and Eli knew she didn't bring good news. His heart jumped into his throat.

"Stop. It's not about Zane." Diana crouched beside him. She barely came up to his ribs that way. "He's doing great. They'll have him off the respirator in a couple of hours, probably."

Eli had to clear his throat, a raw and nasty sound, before he could respond. "Whatever you've come to tell me isn't anything good either, is it?"

"Not so much." Diana took his hand. "I figured you should hear this from someone you wouldn't want to punch in the nose. After all, you owe me."

More than he could ever pay. Eli steeled himself. "Let me have it." He expected to hear he'd been fired for causing a scene. Maybe reports that a mob was out for the queer doc's head. People laughing at their expense. Whatever.

He didn't even think about the possibility of

what he got.

"The free clinic's closing at the end of the month. No money," Diana said. "I'm sorry."

The last bit of wind Eli had left in his sails whooshed out. "Fuck. It never rains but it fucking pours, doesn't it?"

"Such a fucking filthy mouth." Diana pressed his hand between both of hers, more of a slap than a caress, but gentler than Eli had gotten from her at any moment he could remember. "Are you with me?"

Eli rarely saw this side of her, the competent doctor, and the tea and comfort were more Holly's forte, but Diana was trying as hard as she could and they both knew it. Everyone in their own fashion. Made the world go 'round.

Diana waited to be sure before she drew a deep breath and nodded decisively. "I'm telling you because you have to be the one to tell him when he wakes up. Don't let him hear this from anyone else."

Eli's chest ached. "Diana..." He wanted to tell her. Everything. It wasn't enough of a thank you; still, it'd be something.

"Shut up." She pinched the inside of his wrist. "Like I don't already know. We all saw it, Eli. Long before you two did. Why do you think we pushed so hard? Not for shits and giggles. Though there were plenty of those."

Eli started to laugh. Once he'd begun, he couldn't stop, and Diana joined him. They slumped in place and hooted like a pair of hyenas until the charge nurse came to snap at them, because sometimes you got a choice in how you cracked, and this was a hell of a lot better than screaming.

In its way.

* * *

It'd been twenty-five, almost twenty-six hours since Eli had last slept. He was used to it, but be that as it may, adrenaline peaking and fading did take its toll. He'd almost drowsed off still in the visitor's chair when a stir of movement from the bed brought him as wide awake as an alarm shrilling in his ear.

Zane's gray eyes were open just a crack. He tried to turn his head to look at Eli. Be damned if that twitch of his lips wasn't him attempting a grin. "Is this where I say you should have seen the other guy?"

"Jesus Christ." Eli didn't think. Wouldn't have wanted to. He was on his feet and leaning over the bed without remembering how he got from one to the other, the only thing he gave a damn about being touching his lips to Zane's. His were dry and cracked, but Eli tasted salt.

It took a second before the clumsy thump at his side registered as Zane trying to soothe him. "'S okay," Zane rasped, his voice all but a frayed thread. "I'm okay."

"Fuck you," Eli said before he had to push his face into Zane's shoulder and stay there until his eyes stopped watering. It made it worse, or better, when Zane fumbled to touch him and hold on, murmuring scraps of sound that Eli knew were comfort.

Finally he could withdraw. Roughly wiping his face on his sleeve, he kissed Zane once more. The chair was within hooking reach of his leg; Eli caught it with his ankle and drew it to the bedside. "If you ever scare me like that again, I'll kill you myself."

Zane laughed without sound.

"Keep snickering at me and I'll do it now." Careful of the IV, Eli threaded his fingers through Zane's and held on. "I'm too old for scares like this. Don't do that to me again."

Zane's voice had deserted him completely. Christ, what kind of doctor was Eli if he couldn't remember to caution Zane not to try to talk after he'd had a respirator all night, only taken out an hour ago? "Shh," Eli warned. "Don't pay me any attention. Just being maudlin."

You're entitled, Zane mouthed. *It's okay. Promise.* Then, almost sending Eli's temper through the roof, *How's Richie?*

"How's Richie? Fuck that; where's Richie? Better be across a state line by now or I'll --"

Zane shook his head as sharply as he could and shaped a firm *no* with his lips. He winced when the thin skin cracked.

Something Eli could help with, at last. Some nurse, not Bernice, had placed a cup of ice chips by the side of the bed. Eli fingered one out and ran it across Zane's mouth. "Lie still and rest up, would you? You're giving me more gray hairs, and those I don't need."

The corners of Zane's eyes crinkled. He tongued the ice into his mouth and tucked it into his cheek. *The gray is sexy.*

"How you can laugh about this? Swear to God."

Zane squeezed his hand. *How are you?*

"Too old for this." No. Wrong. Eli sighed. "I don't know. Better than you?" Still not thinking -- deliberately, because he didn't care anymore -- Eli lifted that hand to his lips and kissed the back, below the IV needle. "All I know is I'm here and I'm not leaving."

Good, Zane said silently. He rested on his pillow and gazed at Eli, visibly growing sleepy again. Or so Eli thought. He blinked, once and again, and for the first time the reality of where they were seemed to sink into his medicated daze. His eyes widened until Eli could see the whites, and he tried to pull away from Eli's hold on him, a firm grasp that no one could mistake for platonic. *Hospital.*

"I know." Eli didn't let go. "I've been here like this for most of the night, and guess what? I don't fucking care."

He wasn't sure how Zane would react, but by God, for once tonight something went Eli's way. Zane blinked again, slower, and this time when the smile curved his lips, it was a pretty sight. He squeezed Eli's hand and clumsily drew his thumb over the joint of Eli's thumb.

It was what he said that almost undid Eli. Again. *Thank you.*

"Don't," Eli said. He bent to kiss Zane's cheek, then his forehead, and then again his lips. "Get better and get home."

He didn't -- couldn't -- tell Zane about the free clinic. Not yet. Zane would hear that from him, but not now. He had one more thing that he needed to get out, and he would not lose this chance, not again.

He bent, put his lips to Zane's ear, and whispered. "Hey. So I'm an idiot, and it took me a while to figure it out. But I love you."

Zane's hand tightened on Eli's to the point of pain. A tear, the kind a tired man gave way to when he had no other choice, slipped from the corner of his eye and down through the salt-and-pepper over his temple, down to his ear, where the salt trickled over Eli's lips. He couldn't see Zane's lips to read them, but he knew what Zane was saying.

Thank you.

Chapter Twelve

"You're coddling me."

"I am not." Eli tossed the blanket he carried at Zane instead of laying it across his lap as he'd intended. Zane didn't need to know that. So he forgot himself on occasion.

Zane lifted the blanket in one hand and the mug of tea with honey Eli had fixed for him in the other and grinned at Eli in his old irrepressible way. "Absolutely. It's obvious to the untrained eye how very much you're not coddling."

Eli turned the cup of tea he'd made himself around in counterclockwise circles. He bit his tongue twice before he gave up the effort to keep it in. "Give me this one, would you?"

"Eli." Zane scooted forward on the couch, knocking knees with Eli, who sat on the matching leather ottoman. "I'm not going to break. So I have to take it easy for a couple of days. Don't start treating me like I'm fragile."

"Yeah, well. You didn't see yourself loaded into that ambulance," Eli muttered. "It's good tea. Don't let it get cold."

Zane sighed. He bumped his head against Eli's. "Don't think I don't appreciate it. It's just... you know how I am. How I feel about being waited on hand and foot."

Eli did know. He'd heard stories about nannies and, on one memorable occasion, a valet. How much money Zane's family had, he didn't know, but it was a hell of a comedown to be living in a midway-rent Chicago apartment and burning the candle at both ends as a hospitalist.

There was a reason why he hadn't called any of Zane's family while Zane was in the hospital. Zane might have forgiven him the strawberries, but never the family. He wondered what Zane might think of what he'd asked Keith to do… and stopped right there. No sense borrowing trouble. The online search of a random Parisienne with almost nothing to go on would turn up empty, anyway, no matter how good Keith might be.

Eli sat back, better able to discuss this if he were looking at Zane's face instead of getting a close-up view of his ear. "I'm not being paid to do this. I want to. Makes a big difference."

"Hmm." Zane eyed Eli, then sighed, rolled his eyes, and swigged tea. He licked a drop off his lips. "This actually is good."

"See? I've got you." Eli propped his elbows on his knees and balanced his mostly empty mug by the handle.

Zane drank slowly. He still spoke with a raw sort of edge, his throat sore and likely to be for a few days to come, and the honey and lemon in the tea would do him a world of good as long as he didn't bitch away the benefits. Eli kept his mouth shut so as not to encourage chattering but pressed his knee companionably to Zane's and let him get on with it.

When Zane began to toy with the mug, Eli knew the brief, comfortable silence had passed. He didn't expect what Zane asked to fill the quiet, though. "Did you ever do this for Marybeth?"

"If you're asking if I think you're a girl, then no." Eli chuckled at the disgusted look Zane threw him. He let himself slide his caress higher up Zane's leg. "The last thing I think you are is girly. Marybeth? She joined a Polar Bear Club somewhere around my second year of residency. I don't think the woman's been sick a day in her life. No, wait."

Zane propped himself on the couch arm and looked intrigued.

Eli needed something to do with his hands. He pushed his mug onto the coffee table with a *clunk* and slid into his newly accustomed, much more comfortable place at Zane's side on the couch. Pulling Zane's head onto his shoulder, he sighed, finally feeling at ease. "She sprained her ankle once. Wasn't long after we'd first gotten married. Laid herself up for a couple of weeks -- bad sprain -- and I didn't have anywhere near as much time as I would have liked to take care of her."

"Why?"

"Rookie police officer." Eli shrugged with one shoulder and chose to focus on finger smoothing Zane's hair away from his face. "Why do you think? I was barely home, period. She got better. I always wished I'd been more there for her."

"You did what you could."

"Isn't the road to hell paved with good intentions?" Eli took Zane's empty mug away from him. The twist brought him into a position where he could watch Zane face-to-face. "Not that this is what caused it, but if you smoke again, I'll finish the job and choke you myself. Understand?"

"Trust me, I hadn't planned on it." Zane rested his elbow on the couch arm and his cheek in his hand. It distorted his smile but made it no less fond or well-intentioned. "See something you like?"

"You know I do." Eli wanted to reach for Zane, to at least kiss the man, but Christ, he wasn't any too sure he could keep it to a PG-rated peck. Four days since they'd had some time purely to themselves, and while four days wasn't a remarkable dry spot and Eli wasn't a teenager anymore, there was something about

Zane that drove Eli as crazy as if he were eighteen again.

"If you're thinking what I think you're thinking, then yes, please," Zane murmured, his own gaze wandering and -- Eli still wasn't used to this, though he liked it -- hungry.

Eli wanted. Did he ever. But... "Not yet."

"I'm *fine*. What do I have to do to prove it to you?"

"Start talking like Han Solo instead of Darth Vader, for a start."

"Funny guy." Zane folded his arms. He looked amused, tolerant. "Get it out of your system. I'll still be here when you're done."

"Yeah, and I'm not going anywhere either." Eli pulled Zane back to him. He had yet to hear back from Kazaran regarding the voice mail he'd deleted. And the subsequent e-mail. Thanks but no thanks. There'd been a moment when he'd wondered if the temptation was going to be a problem. Now? Not a chance in hell.

Though there was no way of knowing what was going on in Zane's head, his mood, ever mercurial, shifted abruptly to the sort of intense thought that often made Eli uncomfortable on the other end of the laser stare. "I need to tell you something."

No good ever came of a conversation that started with those words. Eli braced himself. "I'm listening."

Zane delivered the news face-to-face, the way the best doctors did. No punches pulled. "I'm quitting Immaculate Grace."

No punches indeed. One-two to the gut, leaving Eli winded. "Come again?"

Zane kept going. Slow and firm. "I've had time to do some thinking. Not to get you wound up on the 'Zane is delicate right now' train of thought, but this, what happened... Life is too short to waste being miserable. I've been trying to figure out who I am, and what I want."

He started to cough. Too much talking. Eli wanted to jump up and make some more tea, but he doubted his ability to move even if Zane had let him go. He settled for thumping Zane on the back instead. The touch eased him enough to find words. "Who you are is a doctor. One who still cares. I can't let you walk away from that."

Possibly the wrong word to use. "Can't, my ass," Zane scoffed. "I'm not done. I'm not leaving medicine. Just the system. I don't fit there any longer. Maybe I never did, and I didn't know before now."

"But --" Christ, what could Eli say? *Don't leave me*? Pathetic, even if it was true. "I understand you. I just don't --"

"Eli." Zane reined him in. "I know the free clinic is closing."

Jesus Christ.

"You never told me. You were going to, I know, and I honestly don't blame you for not bringing it up yet. It's a hell of a thing."

"How did you know?" Eli asked, feeling adrift, like he'd missed half the conversation.

Zane offered him a tip-tilted grin. "Because I was there."

Ah. Now it made sense. Eli wished it didn't. Sometimes people were fully aware of their surroundings when, medically speaking, they were far, far away. He knew that. "So you heard it all, huh?"

"I did." Zane's hand found Eli's. "I can't stay at a place where things like that happen. You say I care. I do. Probably too much. I am who I am, and I have to go where I can make a difference. That's not this hospital. Do you understand me?"

The bitch of it was that Eli did. He tried to make light of it. "It's not going to be the same in that old dump without you."

"I know." Zane's light caress stilled. "You're thinking so loud, and your body language is screaming, Eli. Calm down. It'll be okay."

"You think?" Eli took a deep breath to steady himself. Helped, some. Not as much as he'd have liked. From day one, Zane had been... there. Hard to imagine him somewhere else, though truth be told, he should have seen this coming. "Where would you go? Private practice?"

"That I don't know. Maybe." Zane rubbed his chin. "I could volunteer. Fuck knows I don't need the money."

Eli didn't mention this, not usually, but now his edges were raw. "I would have thought you'd rather panhandle than dip into the family coffers."

Zane jerked away from him. "Fuck you. That's not what this is about. I don't plan to sponge off anyone. It occurs to me that it'd be a kick in the pants that'd sting for years if I used some of that cash to help those who need it. Hell, I should have been doing as much all along."

"What would you live on?"

"Look around. Do you think I've used all my salary over the years? Leather lasts forever if you take care of it. I wear plain clothes, eat plain food, live a simple life. If I'm careful, I can make my savings go for long enough to figure out what comes next."

"And any ideas there?"

"Honestly? No. Well. Some." Eli could tell that Zane was getting worked up, his color rising. "I could... teach, maybe. You gave me that idea. One good thing to come out of the whole Duke fiasco, right? No, don't interrupt me. I could -- I could find a position at a university. Try and pound some compassion into youthful bulletheads."

"Huh. I can see that." So why did Eli have a feeling that wasn't the first choice in Zane's mind? He knew Zane well enough to be almost certain when he had something he wasn't letting on. "Try again."

Zane scowled. "Cut the sick guy a break."

"Oh, so now you're pulling that card, are you?" Eli's temper had begun to rise. He reined it in with an effort. "Fuck. How about we don't fight. Deal?"

"Bah." Despite the scoff, Zane let Eli pull him back in. With his head at rest on Eli's shoulder, Zane let fly with his second sucker punch. "Heard anything lately about the job at Duke?"

Eli's teeth gritted together. He made himself relax. "Not a thing, and I'm not too interested in chasing after Kazaran for updates. I've got other priorities."

Zane stirred, almost restlessly. "It's a good position."

"That'd take me away from Chicago. And you." Eli put his hand on Zane's head to keep him there. "Neither is an option." Christ. He could feel the bubbling mix of thought and emotion churning through Zane. "What's going on with you?"

"It's the opportunity of a lifetime," Zane said, somewhat muffled by Eli's hold on him. "Don't put me in front of it."

"The hell I will." Saying it once hadn't made further repetition any easier; still, Eli needed to repeat himself and would as often as possible. "I don't give a damn anymore about the job of a lifetime. You, me, that's -- harder to come by. I love you. That's bigger than any job."

The fight surged out of Zane. "Goddamnit, Eli." He let all his weight rest on Eli. "You're a chump."

"You didn't already know that? Maybe I am. But I know what I want now." Eli made up his mind. "And I'll be here while you figure out what you want. I promise."

The knock on Zane's apartment door startled them apart. "What the hell?" Eli stood, automatically going to get it for him.

"Eli, I can answer my own door," Zane protested, already working his way to his feet.

Eli pointed sharply at him. "*Stay.*"

"I'm your dog now?" Zane settled, though not happily. More in the disgruntled vein. "Arf. Arf."

"No. You're my patient."

Zane's eyebrows shot up. "Really? Okay, then. That's so much better. I thought you were my friend. My lover."

Eli stopped in front of the door, his still-raw nerves fraying fast. "Are you trying to pick a fight?"

Zane grumbled under his breath and looked away.

Fine. Let him suit himself. Eli bent to take a gander through the peephole. He drew back with a hiss. "The fuck they say. Turn off the lights. We're not home."

That got Zane's attention. He sat upright again. "Now you've piqued my curiosity. Who's there? No, wait, let me guess." He tapped the cleft in his chin.

"Sherlock Holmes, you're not. Would you hush already? They'll hear us."

"The walls are so thin in this place they hear my neighbors wondering why we're being pussies about answering the door," Zane retorted. He assessed Eli's expression. "You look like you're ready to murder in cold blood. It's Richie, isn't it? Richie and-slash-or Taye."

Eli glowered. "They're not welcome here."

"It's my damn apartment, Eli." Zane sighed, some of the defensiveness draining away. "They came because I told them they could. Should."

"You *what*?"

"I'm the one who got it in the neck, no pun intended."

"Good. It wasn't funny." Eli still saw Zane, pale and still, every damn time he closed his eyes. He crossed the room, back to Zane, and caught him by the chin to lift his face and kiss him once, hard, trying to get his point across. "It isn't just you who's been through hell this past week. Do you see that?"

"I know," Zane said. "And that's why they're here. If I can forgive them, you damn well can too, and Taye thinks the sun shines out of your ass."

"Excuse me?"

"Don't let a mistake fuck up a good friendship. Neither of us have so many that we can let them go on a whim."

"I'd hardly call what happened a whim --"

"Eli." Eli could tell Zane had reached the end of his patience. "Let them in."

Eli threw his hands in the air, literally as well as metaphorically. "Fine. Fair warning: if they cross a single line, I'm putting my foot up their asses."

"Now who's the dog?" Zane made faux snarling noises.

Damn him for making Eli smile, anyway. Eli firmed his mouth into the best attempt he could work up at a neutral expression and, only because Zane asked, opened the door.

Richie wasn't a big man in the most generous of assessments. He looked smaller now, almost as pale as Zane had been, and as miserable as a puppy left outside to shiver on a doorstep in the rain. *Ah, jeez.* Taye stood behind Richie, but with one arm around him, guarding him. Bigger and stronger but no less unhappy.

"Eli," Zane said behind him. "Please."

Only because Zane asked. Eli stood aside and waved them through. He shut the door behind them but didn't lock it, and stood with his back to it with the knob in easy reach. So call him overprotective. He could live with that assessment.

"Thank you," Taye said quietly. He stood between Eli and Richie, a positioning Eli thought no less intentional than his own guarding of the door. "We won't be here long."

Eli could just see past the pair to Zane on the couch. He'd propped his head in his hand and studied Richie and Taye as he'd done with Eli countless times. He didn't say a word. Waiting.

Richie, with his hands stuffed in his pockets, was the one to give first. Hell, Eli had the feeling he'd barely been keeping it in, Taye the only thing that kept him steady. "I'm sorry. I need to say that first. You don't know how sorry."

"I think I might have an idea," Eli rumbled.

A sharp look from Zane quelled him. "Okay," Zane said. "Apology accepted." He brought up a hand to stop Eli from speaking. "My wrong. My decision. No arguments."

Eli kept quiet and seethed.

Richie didn't seem to buy it any more than Eli. Taye just looked blank, though he tightened his hold on Richie. Richie leaned into it a fraction. "You can't just -- I almost killed you."

"So tell me why."

Now who had been taking lessons from Holly? Eli rolled his eyes. Yet for all that, he'd admit to a certain curiosity that hadn't entered his head before. What *had* happened?

Richie looked uneasily between Zane and Eli, fighting some internal battle. Eli almost softened toward him. Hell, how could you keep the hate up against someone who looked that torn apart? Richie gave way. "The grill. They get loud. Sizzling fat, exhaust fans. And I had my mind on making something decent from what supplies I had on hand." He laughed, bitter. "You're both terrific guys, and I hear so much from Taye. I wanted to do the best I could."

Zane nodded. "I'm listening. No one's yelling. Go on."

Taye glanced back at Eli, so obviously assessing him that Eli automatically bristled. He made himself flatten his prickles. Zane had been right with one implication. This wasn't Taye's fault. Still, you could hardly separate the two once you'd seen them together.

He wondered if people thought the same of himself and Zane.

Richie squeezed his eyes briefly shut. "God. Okay. I heard Dr. Jameson say 'strawberries.' I was distracted, and the noise, and -- I thought he was asking for them, not warning me. I should have made sure."

"Huh." Zane mulled that over. Then, as if it were that easy, he nodded. "All right."

Taye moved to Richie's side. Not as a stronger defense, but in a position of solidarity. It came abruptly to Eli that if Taye had had to choose between Richie at home and Eli at work, the decision wouldn't take him a hot second.

And the kid had grown on him. Eli wouldn't say he'd passed pissed yet, but...

Zane glanced past him at Eli. "Eli, this is my choice to make."

"Not all of it," Taye corrected. He was the one to face Eli, not Richie, but Eli supposed that was as it should be. "Dr. Jameson?" Eli knew Taye knew what was going on inside his head.

Eli started to reach for the doorknob. Halfway there, he stopped. Fuck. Zane had gotten to him. What kind of guy would he be if he held a grudge against Zane's wishes?

A human one, Eli thought darkly. He let go of the door and lifted his hands, showing Zane that the next move was all on him. What now?

Zane fired the look right back. Ah. So the next move was Eli's. Eli hesitated, torn. Finally, he whoofed out a breath and stepped away from the door. "I still owe you both a smackdown," he informed the pair as he walked toward the kitchen. "I'm making more tea. Do you want some?"

Chapter Thirteen

"That was... the best way I can think to describe it is 'different.'" Eli rinsed the last of the mugs and turned it upside down on a cloth to dry. He wiped his hands on his hips and looked over his shoulder at Zane.

Zane rested obediently on the couch with his head propped on his arm, watching Eli work. "Different is the only way *to* describe that, I think." He fingered a small scuff on the leather. "I liked it."

"Beats linen tablecloths and a harpist, huh?"

"And then some," Zane said, deep feeling evident. "You done in there? Yes? Good. Get back in here and play human blanket."

"Are you cold?" Eli was already on his way to a hall closet for a throw or a quilt.

Zane's laughter stopped him. "No, idiot. Just missing you."

"Ah." Eli propped himself against the wall facing Zane, just to spin the teasing out a little longer. He had a warm glow going on, not unlike the light and cozy feeling a man occasionally got after two or three shots of good whiskey. Unfamiliar, somewhat, and exactly right. "I was here all night."

"And so were Taye, and Richie, who has to be half hummingbird the way he goes once someone's gotten him started." Zane changed position somehow -- it didn't look any different to the untrained eye, but to Eli's he softened and hardened, sinuous, beckoning with means other than words. "I liked them. They're gone. I'm still missing you."

"So it's that way, is it?" Eli let himself be pulled into Zane's orbit. Zane tugged him down before he was ready and finished with Eli sitting on the floor between Zane's knees, wincing between chuckles.

"Give a guy some warning, would you? I'm too old to go horsing around."

"I wouldn't say that," Zane murmured. He kissed the top of Eli's head and tweaked his ear. "Wouldn't even be tempted."

"Sounds like you're tempted to other things."

"Of course. I'm with you."

Eli's face heated.

"Take the compliment," Zane chided, giving Eli's ear another not-so-gentle twist. "Better hurry up and swallow that down, because I'm not done yet."

"Ah, Zane, c'mon --"

"Shush." Zane covered Eli's mouth with his hand. Eli could feel the warmth of Zane's breath on the top of his head. "I don't... ah, Eli. I'm not used to this, okay?"

"Used to what?"

Zane pressed his lips to Eli's temple. "Getting what I want. Need. Dreams coming true."

Eli closed his eyes. "I'm no one's dream, Zane."

"Wrong. Sometimes..." Zane slowed his movements, coming to a near cessation. "Sometimes I wonder how long it can last. You know? I wonder if maybe it's one last shout before I go completely gray and wander off into the silver years alone."

"Why the hell would you think that?"

"I don't know if I'm enough for you." Eli didn't have to see his face to know Zane stared off into space, lost in his head. "Or if I can keep being enough when there's still a whole world out there for you."

Eli shook Zane free and fought upright to take Zane's chin in his hands and give him a shake. "Don't you ever let me hear you say shit like that again. Understand? The only way anyone's prying me out of this is over my dead body and with a crowbar. Christ, that you can ever go there after what we've just --"

Zane covered Eli's mouth with his and silenced him with a kiss. "Okay," he said, breath to breath. "Okay. I'm sorry." He pressed his forehead to Eli's and chuckled. "You know, I'm proud of you."

Eli wrinkled his nose, the best he could do in regards to expressing a good, old-fashioned scoff and asking *why*.

Zane couldn't read minds, but he did know Eli and had his explanation ready. "For giving in," he said, letting go. "For not playing the ass and holding that grudge against Taye and Richie. For letting me make my choice."

Eli fidgeted. "They're good kids. They... *oh*." He rubbed the back of his neck, motions slowing and then stopping when Zane took over for him and did a proper job of the massage. He moaned then and let his head drop to give Zane room. "Christ, that feels great."

"I am a man of many talents." Zane kneaded away tension and knots Eli hadn't known he possessed, though he should have. "You were going to say something about those two. What?"

"Oh, boy." Even with all that had passed between them, Eli still wasn't great at saying these things. Not like Zane. "They're something else, you know? The way they love each other. Blows my mind. Holly and Keith too. I think Diana is shit out of luck, though."

Zane snorted. "I think you might be right, but what she loves is the chase. She's happiest on the prowl. Some people are like that."

"And all of us, all the different kinds, we all make the world go 'round." Eli sang the last off-key, some snippet of a long-ago campfire ditty. "Boom de yada, boom de yada."

"Someone's punch-drunk." Zane stopped massaging and tugged the collar of Eli's sweater. "Up you go."

Eli hated the loss of the massage, but when Zane was right, he was right. He still grumbled to keep up appearances. "Better make this worth my while."

"I plan to."

Well. If it was like that -- again -- still -- then moving was worth it. Eli slid into the space by the couch arm that Zane opened for him and lay back with his head propped up and Zane mostly draped over his torso. Their legs tangled companionably together.

Great moment until Zane spoke. "I *am* proud of you," he said. "Roll your eyes all you want. It doesn't change the fact." He cupped Eli's cheek and sighed, soft and needy, when Eli turned his head to press a kiss to Zane's palm. "You... ah, Eli. There's not much I wouldn't do for you, you know that?"

"Including kicking my ass when I need it?"

"Especially that." Zane's habitual study of Eli deepened. Eye to eye, their lashes almost tangling, as did their lower legs, Eli indulged in a flight of fantasy that made him imagine he could see himself reflected in Zane's pupils.

He shivered.

Zane's first kiss was light, almost not a kiss at all. It caught Eli's attention more effectively than an assault. Zane didn't do shy. "Kiss me," Zane said, and that was even stranger, the way he spoke. Hesitant. "Don't -- don't ask. Just kiss me."

Not being allowed to ask drove Eli crazy. He bit his tongue.

Zane chuckled and kissed him again, still barely there, a brush of lips and air. He'd sobered when he drew back, and there was almost something wistful about the way he moved. "Nothing I wouldn't do for you," he said. "Do this for me."

Eli didn't like the note in Zane's voice, though he had no idea what it might be. "Is something wrong?"

"Not right now, no. Everything's as it should be." Zane pressed his finger to Eli's lips. "I'm fine. I just want this."

Eli gave up -- for the moment -- and gave in to the need to touch. He slipped his hands beneath Zane's sweater and skated them up Zane's warm sides. "How much do you want?" he asked, gone husky.

"Whatever you can give," Zane said, bending for a third kiss. When he spoke, his lips tickled Eli's. "I want it all. I want you to fuck me."

"You're sure?" Of course he was. Eli knew that. He still had to ask. He needed to hear the answer.

Zane nodded, his chin bumping Eli's. It was enough.

Eli traced lines over Zane's face as he pulled himself together. "Three conditions. One? Don't talk." He kissed Zane as lightly as Zane had kissed him to make his point. "Save your voice."

Zane didn't seem inclined to argue. More fond and indulgent, and the wistful look had gone from his eyes. He raised one eyebrow and gestured for Eli to continue.

"Two, you let me do all the work. I mean it. You want this, then you let me take care of you."

That had an unexpected effect. Zane's breath skipped in through slightly parted lips, and his pupils dilated. He nodded, once, a clumsy jerk of his chin. *And*? he mouthed.

"Smart-ass. Always finding a way around the rules," Eli chided. He kissed Zane to take away the sting and because he wanted to and because he could.

"Three." Mirth, successfully cloaked, finally made its way out. "Three: promise you'll respect me in the morning."

It was hard to make roaring laughter silent, but Zane managed it. Of course he could. He slapped Eli on the hip.

Eli took him by the wrist. "Are you going to do as I say?"

Zane swallowed. He nodded, tense with an anticipation Eli could feel.

"Good." Eli pushed Zane up, helping him find his footing. "Fourth condition. We do this in a proper bed. I'm not falling off the couch halfway through."

Zane's smile emerged, broadened, and he inclined his head again. He took Eli's hand and let him lead the way.

* * *

Once in Zane's bedroom, Eli left the door slightly ajar. Why, he couldn't say. Maybe he was just done with closed doors and cloaks of secrecy. It felt right, and that was what mattered. He turned on one light, just the one, a small lamp that cast no more real illumination than a fat pillar candle.

Zane stood by the bed, waiting for him. As Eli watched, Zane's fists tightened briefly. He inhaled and let the air out slowly. Eli understood. Want it or not, this was still scary as hell.

Wanting it made a considerable difference. "I've got the wheel," Eli said, the deepness of his tone taking even him off guard. "We still figure it out together." He waited for Zane's nod before he went on. "Let me undress you."

Zane bowed his head. Eli could see the smile. As good as a green light.

Zane's clothes came off one piece at a time, Eli

guiding the sweater over his head and smirking at the static cloud it made of his hair. Smoothing that down and kissing his lips once the hair was cleared away from his face. Kissing farther down, beneath his hair, along his neck, one hand bracing him, with his thumb stroking the dent between Zane's collarbones.

"Ahhhh," Zane sighed, one long stream of air. He wavered and caught himself on Eli, who let Zane find his balance again before gently pushing him back. Pants. Those had to go. He went to his knees and reached for belt and zipper.

Zane didn't seem to know what to do with his hands before they settled on Eli's shoulders. Eli looked up at Zane, met and held his gaze rather than watching what he was doing. His hands had learned the skill by now, and he took his time. Dark slacks and formfitting boxer briefs skimmed down Zane's leg. No shoes or socks to get in the way, but Eli still rubbed his thumbs over the arches of Zane's feet.

Both were breathing a little faster and shaking a little harder when Eli rose to his feet. He smoothed the tremors away by kissing Zane and being kissed, until Zane clung to him, pliant.

They'd been headed here all along. It'd just taken some time.

He nudged Zane to the bed and guided him down. Zane improvised and slid backward on the rumpled sheets to prop himself on his elbows and watch Eli shed his own clothes. That he did with considerably less finesse, being otherwise distracted. As he watched, Zane stroked himself with the kind of motion Eli knew was meant to make it feel good but last.

There was an odd half second of embarrassment then, and then again when Eli stepped out of his jeans and stood naked before Zane. It passed when Zane beckoned, still silent, and Eli crawled onto the bed with him. Skin against skin made him hiss, and Zane too, a lusty breath that Eli swallowed up in a kiss.

Zane undulated beneath him. Eli got that, why he had to. Hot, hard, urgent -- a man needed friction, and his body sought it no matter what the brain said. Not that he figured Zane was doing a lot of thinking right now. Hell, for that matter, Eli was receding into instinct, only hanging on enough to make sure Zane was still good.

He found a place for his thigh between Zane's, the crease of Zane's hip already glossy with sweat, a snug channel he could thrust up, made slicker by precum. That, he could have done for hours, if Zane hadn't made an impatient noise.

"Hey. I'm in charge." Eli bit the tip of Zane's nose.

Zane grinned unrepentantly and nodded to his right, at the pillow they hadn't yet touched. Eli got the message: *look underneath*. He did and came up with a small, unopened bottle of lube and a condom. No, three condoms.

"Christ." Eli had to laugh. "Been planning this all night, haven't you?"

Zane inclined his head, utterly satisfied with himself.

"Pretty sure of me, weren't you?"

Zane tilted his head to the left as if to say, *And your point is?*

"Three condoms, though? Might be a little overambitious."

At that, Zane shook his head and grew serious again. He took the condoms from Eli and tossed two aside. Tugged open the packet and reached for Eli in silent request.

He shrugged, unrepentant, when Eli tapped his cheek to remind him of their deal. *Together, idiot*, he shaped with his lips.

Eli pushed Zane's arms down to his sides and indulged in the longest, deepest kiss so far, not stopping until Zane was breathless. The goodness of it drove out the shreds of nightmare from the last time Eli had seen Zane falling apart and made this the best it could be. Better than.

He took the condom from Zane. "You and me?"

Zane closed his eyes. *You and me.*

Eli knelt up to slide the condom on. Zane followed, slicking it down his length and following with a palm full of lube that he applied slowly, tantalizing Eli.

"Tease." Eli pushed him away. The need to come was there on the horizon but rolling in slow. Still, he wanted this on his terms, and he knew Zane did too. For whatever reason. "Give me the bottle and lie on your side."

Zane's forehead creased in silent question.

Eli stroked Zane's shoulder. "Trust me," he said. The idea had come to him in a series of erratic flashes, no real start or stop that he could pinpoint, but they hung tight and he knew: this was the way. He helped Zane into position, then lay behind him, also on his side. They fit together like this.

Zane rasped out a breathless laugh. "Seriously? I'm the little spoon?"

"Shh." Eli lifted Zane's knee. The angle was odd before they braced his foot on the mattress. The movement exposed him to Eli, whose heart stutter-stopped in three broken beats before he could move again. "If I hurt you," he muttered, slicking his fingers, "you let me know. If you don't --"

"I will." Zane arched back into the first press inside. "Promise. *Ahh*. No, don't stop. Good noise."

"Glad to know." Eli couldn't look. Urgency picked up speed, and it became more of a struggle to go slow, to take his time. He butted his forehead to Zane's back and closed his eyes, and let sensation be his guide. Stretching him open, taking his time, amazed at how the human body reacted.

Unable to resist, he wiped his hand on the sheets and reached around to stroke Zane's thigh, which shook with either nerves or impatience. Probably both. He ached to grasp Zane's cock and rub, to get him as hard again as he'd been before the intrusion of fingers. Natural, he knew, but he wanted that craving back.

Zane huffed, an impatient sound, and pulled clumsily away to rummage in his bedside drawer. He came back with a much smaller bottle that he shoved clumsily back at Eli. Eli snorted at the label when it came into focus. "Hand sanitizer," he said, muffling his laughter in Zane's skin. "Christ, what a Boy Scout."

"You love it," Zane said, moving in a slow, steady sideways wave that brought him brushing deliciously against Eli. "Use it or don't, I don't care. Fuck me."

Christ, it still wasn't familiar to hear, but the plaint went to Eli's head, his heart, and to points farther south. He caught and held Zane to keep him still. "Knee up. Like that." He slicked his cock with lube, his hand with cleanser, and positioned himself where he wanted to be.

He had to ask. Just once more. "You're sure?"

Zane growled. "*Do it.*"

Eli dug his fingers into Zane's arm for balance, for control, and did what Zane wanted. What he wanted. He held Zane still, whispering, "Breathe, breathe," when the push made Zane cry out sharply and stiffen. Soothed him with kisses over his nape and shoulders until Zane let out a long breath and nodded.

Seemed never-ending, going so slow, Zane adjusting an inch at a time. Sweat dripped into Eli's eyes when he was fully seated. He teased his way down to find Zane half-hard. "Still okay?"

Zane's muscles shivered, but the noise he made wasn't one of pain. "God, yes. Good. Move."

Eli slipped his arm beneath Zane's and wrapped his cock in his fist again. He stroked once, up, and down again, slow and steady. Zane hardened for him, breathing quickening, and when he was fully rigid, Eli finally -- finally -- let himself move.

Holy Christ. He hadn't thought it would be like this. Nothing like a woman, even coming in this way. Zane's legs were strong, and his hips flat, his stomach hard, no curves to grasp but all the better for it, or maybe just because he was *Zane*. Eli gritted his teeth and fucked in a little deeper, a little faster, testing Zane's limits and his own. He soothed Zane with whispers and gentled down when he went too rough, but God help him and them both, it wasn't easy.

Zane growled again. "I won't break."

"I know." Eli bit his nape. "I want it like this."

Zane groaned. He rolled his head on the pillow, and then on Eli's arm when Eli slipped it beneath his head. Eli rested his hand over Zane's heart and felt the hammering.

"I've got you," Eli said, fucking with gradually less care and more abandon, a little bit at a time as he could handle it. Goddamn, Zane felt amazing around him, a smooth tunnel that grasped and clung. He withdrew only long enough to slick on more lube and to stare in amazement at where he'd been. "God."

This time the slide in was effortless, but Zane's abrupt jerk and shout almost threw Eli. "What?"

Zane punched back at him, breathless in his laughter. "Prostate. Idiot. Do it again. That -- there -- *oh God* --"

Eli set his teeth into Zane's shoulder and grasped his hip. He'd leave a mark there. He wanted to see every mark when he woke. Gentleness was overrated sometimes. Faster and deeper, forgetting to stroke Zane's cock, stopping the one to remember the other until Zane knocked Eli's hand away and took over.

"Don't worry. Just keeping it warm for you." Zane moaned. He arched, so close that Eli could see it rising as did the color in his skin. He bit his own lip, tasting blood, and when the shift of his hips hit that sweet spot again and Zane shouted, Eli couldn't take it anymore.

"Going to," he huffed, hanging on to the edge. "Zane --"

"Do it, yeah. Do it." Zane tried to crane his neck. "Want to see."

"*Christ.*" Eli thought fast, clouded, and let his body do the work. He slid out, though the shock of cooler air and loss of friction made him groan. "On your back, move, hurry." He shoved Zane into place and knelt above him, stripped the condom off, and pumped hard into the tunnel of his fist, fast, wrist burning and knees aching but not ready to end it -- not yet --

His toes curled. Almost there.

Zane reached for Eli and brushed the flat of his hand over Eli's cockhead when it surged through his fist. "God, I love you," he breathed.

Enough. Too much. Eli shouted and fell forward,

catching his weight on one arm, and shot. He felt Zane sucking marks on his skin, and the push of Zane's cock against his stomach. Zane's body contracted, drawing up tight, and Eli knew what that meant. He knocked Zane's hand away from his cock and replaced it with his own, breathing heavily into Zane's ear and muttering sounds that weren't words, urging him on.

He'd never heard anything finer than Zane's keening cry when he came. Never seen or felt anything that could compare, and in the little bit of his head that could still think, knew he'd never find anything close to this good again.

Worn out, he draped himself atop Zane, heedless of the mess that would stick them together, and let the breath and shakes drain out of him. Zane moved clumsily to cup the back of his head and pull him into a haphazard kiss, mouths moving together without rhyme or reason, just the touching being enough.

"So," Zane said, the first to recover. His lips quirked. "That was us, huh?"

"Damn right it was," Eli said, resting his head on Zane's shoulder. "And worth the wait."

Chapter Fourteen

"Here." Zane wrapped Eli's hand around a warm mug that smelled not of coffee, but of some fruity blend of tea. "Made this for you."

"I can see you did." Eli tried a sip. Not bad. "And why aren't you still in bed? Doctor's orders." He patted the space beside him on the couch, where with the curtains drawn back and the shades open, he had a hell of a view of Chicago at dawn. "Since you're awake, you might as well."

"Generous of you." Zane being Zane, he ignored Eli's placement suggestion and parked himself on Eli's lap instead. Straddled him, the mug carefully balanced between them, at perfect level for sharing.

It was so sweet Eli's teeth hurt. He wouldn't have traded the moment for the world.

He drew Zane to him by the nape and kissed him good morning, flavored with hot tea, honey, and a hint of spice. The momentum jostled Zane, who winced out loud.

Eli stopped immediately. "Sore?"

"Little bit," Zane admitted before waving that aside. "It'll pass, and besides. Worth it."

"Glad to hear you think so."

One of Zane's eyebrows crooked wickedly. "I could go into detail if you liked about how worth it and list reasons why."

"Thanks, no need. I was there, after all." Eli didn't know whether to blush or to brazenly enjoy. He chose the latter. Why not? The sun was shining, he had a lap full of best friend and lover combined in one attractive package, and as far as Eli was concerned, it would be a terrific day.

He did admit to some curiosity. "If you save that list for later on, say, tonight, I'd be inclined to listen then. Pointers, you know."

"Pointers indeed." Zane flicked the drawstring on the sleep pants he'd lent Eli. "I'll give you pointers."

"That goes without saying." Eli wrestled Zane -- gently -- and eased him off. He felt the strain of a good hard fuck himself, even if he hadn't been on the receiving end, and he wanted to take this morning slowly. "Sit still. Enjoy."

Zane had to have been feeling better. He tapped his foot with excess energy. "Why?"

Eli reeled Zane in. "Because I like lazy mornings with the one I care enough to send my very best."

Zane laughed. Mission accomplished. More, when he slowed to an easy grin, Eli could see a smoothing of his forehead and a sort of calmness pass through his gray eyes in place of the quicksilver, rapid-fire thoughts Eli had seen over the past few days.

He stroked Zane's hair over his forehead. "What's been on your mind lately?"

"That, I would think, was obvious." Zane used Eli as leverage to pull himself up. He kissed the top of Eli's head with a loud, ringing *smack*. Amazing, really, how familiar and comfortable that had become. How welcome.

"You're fooling no one. Hey." Eli caught Zane's arm. "Are you with me?"

Zane made an annoyed face. "Don't push it, or I'll have to punish you."

"I think that's more your style than mine."

"Don't knock it until you've tried it, pal." On his feet, Zane stretched, popping his neck from side to side. Eli grimaced at the sight and sound, but on the other hand, he could see Zane's old energy flowing back in, and that was nothing to sneer at.

"So they say about sushi, yet I have still to

experience the desire to try raw fish." Eli shuddered. The mug they shared between them was empty save for the dregs, which he drained. He hitched up to playfully slap Zane's ass. "Since you're up, how about a refill?"

"Since you have two functional legs, go get it yourself." Zane gave an exaggerated bow, ending with a doublehanded point to the kitchen.

"Tastes better when you pour it."

"Oh, hell no. I'm not June Cleaver in pearls." Zane laughed as he scoffed. "Just for that, I'm leaving you to fend for yourself while I go down and get yesterday's mail. *Alone*, thank you very much. Ah-ah-ah. If I'm well enough to get fucked, I'm well enough to handle a few flights of stairs."

"As long as you're not running scared. That was my job, and I'm done with it."

Zane shrugged. "I just need to stretch my legs some. I'm restless."

"Okay, fine." Eli considered himself man enough to admit when he was being overcautious. Sometimes. "If you're not back upstairs in fifteen minutes, I'm coming after you."

"And the status quo continues. With minor alterations." Zane pulled Eli to his feet, all the better to kiss him, then pushed him gently back down. "Watch the sun rise. Commune with the wonders of the Chicago skyline. I'll be back soon with a sheaf of what will no doubt be junk mail, and we'll pick up where we left off. I promise."

* * *

Not quite as promised. The slam of the apartment door jolted Eli out of a reverie he'd fallen into watching the sun and the city. Chicago. No place like it on earth.

He checked his watch. Eleven minutes. "Faster than I expected," he called to Zane.

Zane did not respond. He carried a thicker stack of mail than Eli would have expected, three or four days' worth, and slapped it down one piece at a time on the end table by the couch. His lips were pressed together in a thin white line.

Eli struggled to sit up straighter. "Christ. Zane, what happened down there?" The worst flashed through his mind. Harassed for dual male sex shouts keeping the neighbors awake. Maybe he'd been threatened. "Zane, talk to me."

Zane ignored him. "Bill," he said, waving one envelope in the air. Down it went. "Bill. Flyer for the new Cantonese delivery place. Please donate to our political campaign." *Slap. Slap. Slap.*

Eli couldn't help noticing more than a few pieces went down without comment. He'd have asked if Zane hadn't stopped at the very last one, a thin envelope addressed by hand, its ragged edges already proving it'd been opened. He wondered, for half a panicked second, if it was a note from Kazaran. The old guy could be devious when he wanted, and Eli wouldn't have put it past someone to offer Zane's place as a backup address when the earlier sign-for-delivery had gone ignored.

Turned out that wasn't the case. It was worse.

Zane threw the envelope at Eli. It flew with surprising velocity. Something heavier inside. A photo? "Want to explain this?"

Eli kept one eye on Zane, concerned, while he checked the postmark. Not North Carolina, thank Christ. New York. What the hell in New York could have --

Oh. The photograph fell out of the envelope and

ended faceup on Eli's lap. He'd never seen this face before with his own eyes, and she was older than Zane had described her, but all the elements were there: startling green eyes fringed in dark lashes, loose black braids falling over the shoulders of a pristine white chef's uniform. A smile that was bright enough to light up the world, and more than a hint of delighted mischief in the dimples of her cheeks.

Be damned if Holly's husband wasn't as good with computers as he claimed.

Damned indeed.

No letter lurked inside. Eli checked the back of the photo.

I have missed you and your crazy American bullshit, Zane. I never thought to hear from you again. How did you find me? I am in New York. Call me, or visit. I will cook you better food than I served in Paris, and there will be no strawberries, that I promise.

In fond memories of good times,

Yvonne

"It's a pretty name," Eli heard himself say. "She's beautiful."

"No shit she's beautiful. I told you so." Zane jerked the photo out of Eli's hands and tossed it behind him. "What the hell were you thinking, contacting her?"

"For one, that you'd be glad to hear from her." Eli could feel cold iron settling into his backbone. "I wanted her to know what a good man you'd become."

"Fuck." Zane sat heavily on the couch arm, far out of Eli's reach. He suddenly looked older than his years, not younger. "When?"

"When do you think? When I thought you might not be here that much longer. I got Keith to look her up. Guess he's better at what he does than I'd thought."

Zane made a disgusted noise and rolled his eyes to the ceiling. "Eli, I swear to God. You had no right."

"Excuse the fuck out of me. I thought you were dying. Maybe already dead. So she wants to hear from you. I'd figured this would make you *happy*. The way you spoke of her, I could hear and feel how much you missed Yvonne." Eli could see Yvonne's picture lying on the carpet behind Zane, faceup, still smiling in that moment frozen in time. "Your turn. Why's this got you so mad?"

"Not mad. Just --" Zane rubbed his forehead. "I told you about her to get some closure. Not because I was yearning for her. What, do you think that now I've had my jollies getting ass fucked that I'm going to go running straight for some Parisienne --"

Eli had a hard time believing his ears. "Are you trying to pick a fight?"

Zane's chin came up, making what he said an appallingly obvious lie. "No."

"Sure. I'm fooled." Eli stood and moved toward Zane. Zane held his ground. Definitely in a fighting mood. "Why? What changed? Twelve minutes ago all was right with the world. I'm not planning on sending you to Yvonne, and I'm sure as hell not giving you up."

"Even for Duke University?" Zane crossed his arms and gritted his teeth with a *clack*. He nodded stiffly at the haphazardly fallen stack of mail.

Eli glanced and sighed. Figured. *Never tell yourself you're out of the woods until you're picking your teeth with the splinters.* A letter from Kazaran to Eli at Immaculate Grace, redirected here, just as he'd feared. "I'm not pursuing the job."

Wrong thing to say. Zane pounced with the

precise surgical coolness of a scalpel. "Then Kazaran did offer you a good chance. Don't lie to me. Did he?"

"Yes."

"And you're not going after it because..."

"Why do you think, and what the fuck did I just say? I'm not leaving you." Eli tried to catch Zane and calm him with touches. No go. Zane evaded his grasp. He stayed mostly physically put, but Eli could feel him slipping away fast behind a glass wall.

"Maybe that's what you say," Zane replied eventually, still and cold. "What if I'm not letting you stay?"

Eli stared at Zane. He wiggled his finger in his ear. "Come again? I know I couldn't have heard that right."

Zane shrugged, shoulders stiff. The thing about glass walls -- they were strong, and if you tried to punch through, they'd slice you to confetti, but you could see right through them. The struggle so recently vanquished had returned to his face. Eli could see the fight going on within.

"Zane, talk to me."

"If I told you to go, would you go?"

Didn't require any thought to answer that one. "No. Because I'm not a dammed idiot, and I'd have to be one to know you don't want me leaving. Zane, for fuck's sake." Eli tried to reach him physically again. "What do you want me to do? Apologize for looking up Yvonne? I'm sorry. Let you kick my ass for keeping the Duke mess to myself? Go right ahead. Whatever it takes."

Zane shook his head, but Eli was secretly, angrily glad to see the move was a struggle for him. "I want you to go."

"And I said no." Eli broke through the keep-away force field Zane had whipped up around himself and took him by the shoulders to shake some sense back into his lover's -- his friend's -- head.

Zane was like stone under Eli's hands. Unmoving, but with tiny fault lines. Weeds grew through cracks in rocks, and if Eli was anything, it wasn't a hothouse flower but a tough, sturdy weed.

"Fuck you," Zane said.

"If you like." Eli pulled Zane to him, but it was like trying to shift a statue. "Tell me why I should go, and none of this bullshit about Yvonne or Kazaran. Either you tell me why you're spoiling for a fight or I find out the hard way. Get me?"

"You really want to know?" White dents appeared on either side of Zane's nose. Stress lines. "Whether I want you to go or not is not the point. You need to go. For your own good."

"And here we are again with me knowing I couldn't have heard you right. Where did you get that kind of idea? Also, I'm forty-fucking-three, and I don't need you making my decisions for me like I'm a child."

"I know you're a man."

"Damn right I am." Eli took Zane by the chin and kissed him, hard. Zane's lips remained cold and pressed together hard, unyielding, but Eli felt Zane shiver and it gave him just enough hope to be going on with. He pushed his luck and dragged Zane fully to him, body to body, kneading Zane's back and the top of his ass. Working him the way he'd learned, waiting for that moment when Zane would groan and melt into him --

Didn't work out that way. Almost. Almost didn't count in a battle zone. Zane struggled free, and he fought dirty, biting Eli's lip sharply enough to draw blood. "Don't do that again."

Eli shoved the sting away and wiped his mouth with the back of his hand. "Then tell me why." Internal hurt made him ask, "Who's the one running scared now?"

Zane shoved his hands through his hair and yanked. "The job, Eli. Okay? It's a damned good job. For you to turn this down because of me is --"

"Is what I want to do. Or suddenly that doesn't count?"

"It's a fool's move," Zane said flatly. "You're nobody's fool."

"Right. That's why I'm not buying what you're selling." Eli made to sweep up the letter from Kazaran and tear it in half. As he did, the pile of mail scattered and more than one return address jumped out to catch his eye. "The fuck." He sank to a crouch, picking up envelopes and reading the labels. "Doctors Without Borders. University of Chicago. Of New York. Of Colorado. Colorado, Zane? Really?"

"I told you I was thinking about teaching."

Things were coming together for Eli, and he didn't want to believe them -- didn't -- but the anger seething through him made it hard to think. "Not running scared. Sure. And pigs are going to fly past the window any second now."

"Goddamn it, Eli." Zane sat. "Don't make this harder than it has to be. I'm done arguing. I'm not letting you turn down a job like Duke, and I can't stay at Immaculate Grace. I'm done there."

Where Zane led, Eli followed. He sat on the ottoman, mirroring Zane, who wouldn't look at him. "So, what? You want me to take the job even if I don't. Say I do. I take it. You're done in Chicago. We both move to North Carolina. You love warm weather. We could make a home there, you and me. Fresh start."

Zane wanted that. Christ, did he ever. It came off of him in waves. Still, he shook his head. "No."

Eli wanted to throw his hands in the air. "And why not?"

"How long did it take you to admit to anyone here that we were together? What did it take? It's life or death with you, Eli, and I can't do that again." Zane's weariness made him look so old. "Who I am. That's what I'm looking for. And it's not a 'roommate' or a 'buddy.' If we moved down there together, I know that's what I'd be. Think about it. That wasn't what you immediately figured?"

Eli had. Force of habit, cowardice, common sense, all of the above. "You want the truth? Yes. But I wouldn't."

"Easier said than done and you damn well know it, and I can't force you, but I won't live a lie myself. This *is* for your own good. See that, Eli. Please."

"No. None of this is for my own good if I lose you in all ways. It's not just this thing we have between us. You're my friend, and I don't make those easily. The hell I'm giving you up without a fight."

"Do what you like." Zane pinched the bridge of his nose. He'd gone from speaking in a roar to a rasp. "I've made up my mind. Hate me now if you want, but you'll thank me later."

"The hell I will." Eli tried one last time to grab Zane, but Zane jumped away. Scared. Eli could tell from the whites of his eyes and the growing fault lines in his stony mood.

"It's not just your choice," Zane said with the flat ring of finality.

"Nice way to throw that little ditty in my face. Want me to repeat the chorus? 'We work it out together.' This is you making my choices for me, and that's not happening."

"No? Stop me. Leave my apartment. Now. And don't you fucking dare look back."

Eli could hear Zane's heart cracking. Amazing considering the sound of his own nearly deafened him. He could see the reasoning. He couldn't see the sense.

And he didn't know what to say.

"Go," Zane ordered -- no, begged.

What the hell could Eli do? Either shout and do something he'd regret, or get away and regroup.

He wouldn't hurt Zane. Never take that chance. He went, but he promised himself as he closed the door behind him that he wouldn't stay gone.

There had to be a way to fix this.

* * *

Eli wasn't as fast a thinker as Zane, but give him just enough light to make his way by and lead from his heart and he'd get there in the end, one step at a time.

Occasionally, faster.

Eli hadn't even cleared the parking lot of Zane's complex before he had his phone out, dialing. When Zane picked up on his end, Eli knew it was him but heard nothing except a weighted sort of silence that asked, *Please don't do this.*

Tough. And he wanted to keep mum? No problem. Eli had plenty to say. "I know why you're doing this," he began, angry and not bothering to hide it. "Not because of a smoke screen. Not because you don't want this 'us.' Because you *do.*"

Zane's small, caught breath told the truth. Spot on. As Eli knew it would be.

He eased out into traffic and scrolled the window down, knowing Zane would hear the sounds of a busy road carrying Eli away. Cruel, but he had to be, to be kind.

"Eli --"

"Uh-uh. I'm talking now. Here's how I see it, Zane. You've always been that poor little rich boy. Family and cash like a weight you don't want dangling off your shoulders, because it doesn't buy happiness. And you don't get what you want. Like the clinic. Maybe like me, not for keeps, is what you're thinking now."

"Eli, stop."

"No. This is where it gets rough. On top of that, you don't usually let yourself have what you want because you feel guilty about having more than others. Only this time, you did. And it scares the shit out of you. You were trying to pick a fight. Lost your nerve."

"Goddamnit, Eli!"

"I am not giving you up. I will not lose you. Took me too damn long to get here to walk away with my tail between my legs."

Zane rallied. "It wasn't -- I meant it about not living a lie. I can't."

"You might not have noticed, but I never said I *would* ask you to hide, you dick. Tempted? Sure. I'm human. Follow-through? No. For you, I would come out. Again. As loudly as I needed to."

"I can't believe that."

"Figured you'd say as much." Eli took a right onto a much busier road, the roar of traffic almost deafening him to Zane's replies. "Watch and learn."

He could still detect wary alarm just fine. "Eli, what are you going to do?"

Ha. Look who's ahead of the game. "Wait and find out." Eli disconnected and threw the phone on the seat beside him.

Sometimes anger was a destructive force, only good for doing wrong.

Sometimes, though, if you could harness that head of steam? You could pull out a last-minute home run.

* * *

He could have asked Diana. Holly. Taye. They'd have backed him up, sure. Eli needed to do this himself. Any other way, it'd lose momentum and, above all, meaning. A man worked hard for what he wanted.

For Zane, it couldn't be any other way.

But Eli knew Zane as well as Zane knew him. He didn't act at first. Zane would have expected that. The first cold night alone in his bed, Eli almost gave. When the sun came up on him, still alone, he almost gave in. Didn't, though, and glad of it.

Now, with a day and a night behind him and Zane looking over his shoulder? Now was the time to strike, surgical and clean, to cut out the poison.

* * *

"Whoa! Easy there, Cap'n." Diana tried to block the entrance to the staff lounge. She assessed Eli in one quick swoop, raising her eyebrows at Eli's casual street clothes and overgrown stubble. "Glad you're not supposed to be here today looking like that."

"Like how?"

Diana bit her lip thoughtfully. "Like a badass."

"Yeah?" Eli scraped his stubble against the back of his hand. "Good. I'm not in the mood to play nice."

"No shit." Diana planted herself foursquare in the door. She glanced over her shoulder, though, a dead giveaway. Behind her, Eli could see quite the tableau laid out for him: Holly on the couch in briefly paused yet utterly earnest mode. Taye leaned on the far wall, arms crossed and chin stubborn. He wore his heart on his sleeve, so Richie might as well have been there too.

They didn't matter so much as the man in the middle, the one crouched to pick up a filing box crammed with crumpled lab coats, scrubs, and other detritus of a career he'd decided to chuck down the drain.

Like hell was Eli letting that happen to what he and Zane had together.

Problem: he had a stubborn female barrier to get through.

Eli rested his hands on Diana's shoulders, not to hurt, but to make sure she knew he meant business. "Diana. You're half a foot shorter than me and at least less than half my body mass. If I need to, I can and will pick you up and put you down somewhere that's not in my way."

"I'd like to see you try."

Eli thought she might mean that, and not in the sense of a hostile dare. Diana looked as torn as he'd ever seen her, as if her position as barricade was something she'd drawn the short straw to get. She wavered between looking at Zane, frozen stock-still, and Eli, building up another good head of steam. "Fuck it," she said, letting go of the sides of the door. "I'm too old for the equivalent of chaining myself to a tree."

Though he'd meant to charge straight through, what she said gave Eli pause. Might as well ask. No. He needed to ask. Where Zane could hear him. "So how much do you know?"

Diana rolled her eyes. "You're seriously asking me this. What do I know? Jack shit. Doesn't mean I can't guess, and I can read the writing on the wall just dandy. It's not exactly in small print."

Good. Exactly what he'd wanted her to say, out

loud, where Zane could hear. "How long have you known?"

"Honestly? Pretty much always. Long before either of you did, dumb-ass. We weren't *teasing* you, we were whacking you with giant clue-by-fours. Christ!"

"You were right to." Felt good to say it out loud. Better than he'd expected it might. "I love Zane," he said, out loud, loud and proud. Pitching his voice to carry.

Zane finally looked at Eli. Wide and panicked, a perfect picture of a deer in the headlights. Eli grinned, and he didn't know how it looked, but it must have been fairly savage because Diana took a quick step back.

"I'm also way too old to get bulldozed. Unless I ask for it." She held up her hands in surrender.

"Diana." Eli bent to kiss her cheek. "You are only as old as you feel, and you? You'll be young forever."

"Flattery will get you everywhere." Diana tugged Eli's shirt sleeve. "He's been ranting about Duke. What's up with that?"

To her, Eli had only to say what he'd told Zane. "Wait and see." He pulled his cell phone out of his pocket and waved it at her. "Kazaran's on speed dial five," he said, knowing he had Zane's full attention. A different sort of alarm, one tinged with confusion, entered the mix swirling in the near-visible dark clouds around Zane.

"What are you doing?" Zane asked, the first words he'd spoken to Eli in over a day. Felt like longer.

"Taking the wheel," Eli replied. He tapped the speed dial and waited for his call to complete. Half expecting voice mail, the answering gruff voice on the other end took him directly back to his university days with the single drawl of a simple hello.

Even better. Eli hit Speakerphone and held it out so everyone could hear. He could sense an audience gathering behind him -- hospitals were hell pits of gossip. Best of all. No going back.

"Dr. Kazaran, hello. It's Eli Jameson."

"Damn my hide. I wondered if you'd dropped off the face of the earth."

"It's been a hectic few days," Eli said, his gaze fixed on Zane. "I'm calling about the interview."

"I would hope so. We're looking forward to seeing you here again."

"Thank you, sir. I'm honored." Eli did not look away. "There are a few things you'd need to know first."

Dr. Kazaran rumbled. "I can't say I'm surprised. You always did take a unique approach. Very well. Let's hear them."

"I wouldn't be coming down there alone," Eli said. He could hear stifled gasps and murmurs and the slipperiness of what was probably money changing hands behind him. Screw 'em. He had eyes for Zane alone. Zane, who'd gone blanched-strawberry white and was shaking his head, slow then fast.

"Oh? Of course, your wife."

"Not my wife, Dr. Kazaran. She and I divorced some years back."

"Ah. I'm sorry to hear that." Dr. Kazaran hesitated. "Fiancée, then? Lady friend?"

"Gentleman friend," Eli said, loud and clear. "Dr. Zane Novia. He and I are involved, and I would have no plans to leave him behind."

A longer pause. "Be more specific, if you would."

Karma had its bitchy side, but every so often, it paid you back for the rough stuff, and in spades. "He's my lover," Eli said. "And my friend. He and I are a two-for-one deal."

Silence. "I see." More silence. Eli counted his heartbeats and watched Zane climb clumsily to his feet.

He waited for Kazaran to go on. The older man finally cleared his throat with a rough *harrumph*. Good at thinking on his feet, that one, and no bullshit either. "Your personal life is personal. I see no reason to concern myself further with the finer details. However, I feel I must warn you that many other faculty members wouldn't be quite as accepting. I assume you're aware of general prejudices."

"I am. When I can, I like to prove those prejudices wrong. Dr. Kazaran, half those people you mention thought I'd last less than a year in med school. Now some of them, they're the ones asking me to come back and research with them, side by side. Pretty impressive, huh?"

"I should say so." Eli thought he could hear Kazaran drumming his fingers. "Is there anything else you'd wanted to make clear before we arrange an interview?"

"There is." No going back now. Eli didn't want to. "I'm honored by the offer, Dr. Kazaran, but I must respectfully decline. I have too much to stay here for."

* * *

"You son of a bitch," Zane said over the *snap*! of Eli closing his phone. He wasn't blinking. The cat was backed into a corner and hissing with his claws out, but there was no getting out of this and they both knew it. Eli knew Zane wanted it. Knew him as friend and lover, could see the alarm fighting with relief, and so he let Zane vent his ire without offense. "You fucking idiot. What did you just do?"

"What I should have done a long time ago.

Ending what I shouldn't have started." Eli saw the path clear to Zane and started on that trek. Zane didn't move. "I'm taking what I really want instead."

"You just --" Zane finally moved, shoving his hand through his hair to leave it sticking up in manic directions. "You torpedoed your career, Eli."

"Maybe. Probably not. Either way, I'm not sorry."

Zane took a step back, and another, as Eli got too close. "Call him back."

"No. I'm done with that. You heard what I said. Where you go, I go. Not the other way around. But here's the difference."

Eli moved forward without breaking stride, breaching the gap between them. Backing Zane into a corner, literally, and not sorry about that either. He didn't stop until Zane was pressed into the kitty-corner of two walls, his back to them and his face to Eli.

This close, he could see the fine shakes in Zane's hands. The hope that warred with doubt and fear. Enough of both, and to hell with hiding. Eli laid his hands as gently as he could on Zane, bracketing his face and lifting his head. He knew his way to Zane's lips and kissed them. He didn't know for how long, only that it was enough time for everyone, inside and out, to fall utterly silent.

He could hear nothing but their breathing when he let Zane go. "I'm going to talk. You're going to listen. Understand?"

There. There was the hitch in Zane's throat and the expansion of his pupils. The strong man's fantasy of being controlled, fulfilled, and Eli had control. Zane nodded once, jerkily.

"We belong together. Always have. Always will. It took us a while to see that. You talk about me wasting my life? It'd be a hell of a waste if I lost you. You talk about you wasting your life? What would you be if you cut yourself up for me?"

That, Zane didn't want to hear. He looked sharply away.

Eli didn't let him stay there, guiding Zane back to meet him eye to eye, as they always should. "I'm not done yet."

"You never are," Zane murmured. Wasn't much, on the surface, but it was almost the final crack in the stone and the one Eli had been waiting for. He dove in. "I love you."

"Eli…" He didn't know if Zane was aware he'd taken Eli by the wrists and squeezed. "Don't go here if you don't mean it."

"But I do, and you damn well know it. I love you. I'll say it until my lips go numb if I have to."

"People can hear you."

"No, really?" Eli kissed him again, quick and hard. "They can see me too. Let 'em watch." He eased his grip and lowered his voice, only because this was the most important part and he wanted all Zane's focus on *him*, not the hospital.

Zane swallowed hard. He wanted to believe. So much. Eli could see that in him.

Finally something he could give. "What we have between us," he started, "I don't guess it'll ever be *easy*, but it's worth it because I. Love. You. And it's never too late to start fresh."

Zane looked at his hands as if in truth realizing for the first time where they were. His eyes darted back and forth. Eli could see his mind working, pieces clicking back into place and jumping ahead. "You son of a bitch," he said once more, but not as he had. Eli heard awe. Admiration.

"Beat you at your own game for once."

Love.

The tension in Zane eased, fraction by fraction. "Do you have any idea where we're heading?"

"Not a clue. And I don't care. We're off-road, and I'm fine with that. So there are bumps along the way, but not dead ends. Not with us. We've been headed here all along, and we can dig our way out of the ditches *if we stick together*."

Zane began to grin. Goddamn, Eli loved that impish side of him. "Are you sure you're not from Detroit? Or did you eat a car magazine for breakfast?"

"Shut up." Eli kissed him again, third time being the charm and so on. He hoped. So he saw was true. "You're never too old to try something new. I'm *young* enough to enjoy the drive for the sake of the journey. We'll figure it out together. You and me. What d'you say?"

Zane didn't respond in words but in the uncoiling of the tension that kept him taut and in a kiss that melted the rest of him in Eli's arms. Eli could work with that. He held Zane upright and kissed him deep, and long, and forever, and let the rest of the world disappear.

Epilogue

"About time you two showed up." Eli pulled back the house door to let Diana and Holly in. On second thought, he lingered, enjoying the sight of them on his doorstep. His and Zane's. A tiny house, so far in the 'burbs as to only be called Chicago by second cousinship, but theirs.

"You going to let us in or what?" Diana hitched a cooler higher on her hip. "C'mon. I want to get a look around. Plus you promised us an honest-to-Christ backyard barbecue, and I'm starving."

"So impatient," Holly chided. "We're late because we stopped to pick up a passenger." She nudged Diana aside to reveal Richie standing behind them, his arms overloaded with a heavy grocery box from which peeked homemade potato chips, sharply piquant relish, and pungent cheese.

Eli eyed Richie, who by now knew Eli well enough to grin cheekily at him. "Too small. Throw this one back."

"Eli, be nice."

"I'm an angel of light. Oh, look at that, Diana's flipping me off. So cute. Why'd you bring him?" Eli knew, of course, but he wanted to hear the answer.

"Because he's been at school all day," Holly said, a tolerant twinkle in her eye. "He deserves a treat."

Eli savored it. The more things changed, the more they stayed the same, and if you asked him, that wasn't so much a bad thing. "Lucky him, I've already got the big fish out in the backyard trying to light the charcoal."

"Holy shit, he'll burn the house down." Richie shoved the box at Eli and elbowed past. "Taye!"

Eli laughed until his ribs hurt. He waved Diana and Holly past. "Go, go. Hey, Zane!" he called. "Get out of the john already. You're pretty enough, and we've got company."

"You're not telling me anything I didn't already know." Zane strode out of the hallway and straight to Holly, then Diana, wrapping them up in firm hugs. "Don't get jealous."

"Me? Please. I know your type." Eli couldn't seem to stop grinning these days, especially not when Zane radiated happiness like summer sunshine. "I'm not threatened."

"Alas, he's right. You have no chance with me." Zane put a staged arm's length between himself and Diana. "Consider yourself shunned."

"Damn," Diana said, poker-faced. "There go my plans for a threesome."

Not even she could resist chortling at the face Zane pulled. "How anyone ever could have thought you were straight," she said, poking him in the side. "Or, well, straight since Eli came on the scene."

"Fucking amen to that. Get over here." Eli reeled Zane in to stand behind him so he could rest his chin on Zane's shoulder and wrap his arms around Zane's waist.

"My God. That is so cute I think I'm going into diabetic shock."

"Liar. You're melting on the inside."

"Melting on the fucking outside too." Diana fanned herself one-handed. "Are you two just cheap bastards, or doesn't this shack have central air?"

"All the amenities present and accounted for. We just wanted to torment you. Backyard." Eli waved her on. "That's where the action is. Go, go." Shouts from outside made him wince. "Then again, you might want to wait until either the fire's out or Taye and Richie have finished saying hello, whichever all the ruckus is about."

Holly covered her face with one hand and giggled. *Giggled.*

"What're you laughing at?" Zane asked, comfortable against Eli.

"Life in general." She tipped her head to one side, her smile calm again but not cooled. "Zane. You have a little..." she said, pointing at her cheek. And her neck. And her collarbones.

"This bastard likes to mark me. What can I say?"

"That it's about time?" Diana jostled her cooler. "Screw it. I'm interrupting young love out there before my arms break hauling around an ungodly amount of beer."

Zane perked up. Eli pushed him around to the side, all the better to enjoy the sight of his mussed hair, the pink beard burn on his cheeks, and the swollen redness of his lips. He was indeed as marked as Diana had claimed, and then some.

Diana squeezed her eyes shut. "Christ, tell me those aren't BJ lips. That's why the AC's off. Airing out the house."

"You don't ask, I won't answer," Zane sassed. He pulled Eli down for a quick kiss, slapped his ass, and whispered for him alone, "To tide you over until tonight."

Eli went back for seconds. "Back at you," he breathed in Zane's ear because he could. He sent Zane on his way with a spring in his step the likes of which Eli hadn't seen before, not even the first time they'd met, but which he wasn't without these days.

And they were good days, these. A house, a place to call their own. Eli still worked at Immaculate Grace. Zane was right -- he loved it, every minute of it. Zane? A couple months volunteering, and his job search had borne fruit. Part-time lecturing at U of Chicago, premed. Some would call that a hell of a come-down in the world. Not Zane. Not Eli. Not when it made Zane that happy.

"Get 'em while they're young," he'd told Eli once, over a cup of coffee drunk companionably together at the counter in their new kitchen. "Imprint the hell out of those impressionable young minds and teach 'em how to care. Maybe then they won't wait until they're closer to fifty than forty to --"

"Fifty, my ass," Eli had growled.

* * *

After that, the conversation devolved somewhat. Not that either of them had minded.

"Go make sure Taye doesn't torch the place. Clinical psychologist-in-training he might be, but chef he sure as hell isn't. Tell him to leave that to Richie and sit the fuck down."

Zane tipped his head back and laughed. "Your wish, my command."

"Damn right it is," Eli rumbled, just for the pleasure of watching the shudder of reaction wash through Zane. "I've got plans."

"I'll hold you to those," Zane said. He blew Eli a saucy kiss not precisely aimed at his face and turned to jog out to meet their group.

Plans? Yeah, Eli had a few. *They* did. One year here was what they'd agreed on. Summer after that, Taye and Richie would house-sit -- rent argued over and wrangled down to enough of a token to satisfy pride -- and he and Zane would be in Africa probably. Kenya. A summer of Doctors Without Borders.

Their life could -- would -- fall into a pattern. That didn't mean it'd get predictable. Or that it would ever get old. Zane? Zane kept Eli young. He got that now.

"Hey, slowpoke." Zane popped his head around the corner, his grin blazing bright and his T-shirt already sticking to his skin with the heat of a Chicago summer. Looking good enough to eat and eager as a kid. "Hurry it up or you're going to miss the party."

"No way is that happening." Eli pushed himself off the wall and toward Zane, pointed home. "Lead me to it." He kissed Zane behind the ear. "Lead me anywhere, and that's where I'll go." Forty-three years young, and he had the rest of his life to grow old with his best friend, his lover.

So maybe there was something to be said for pushy friends after all. And nothing at all to be said for setting the story straight.

And Call Me in the Evening
A Friends to Lovers Medical Romance
Will Okati

Eli's still not great at wearing his heart on his sleeve and Zane's still got trust issues, but they manage just fine. It's all good. Right?

Yes and no. When the doctors find themselves grounded between trips for Medicins Sans Frontieres, things begin to change. Zane's making plans for where they'll go next, but homesick Eli discovers the opportunity to open a clinic of his own in his old neighborhood. He'd have thought Zane would be all over that, but Zane's not listening. Meanwhile, there's trouble in paradise between protégés Taye and Richie, and Eli's ex-wife Marybeth has come back to town, bringing a heaping helping of hassle with her. Eli figures it's no wonder he's been having a heck of a time with chest pain -- which he hasn't told anyone about.

There's something to be said for setting the story straight, it's true. Eli knows he and Zane have a good thing going even if keeping it that way is the hardest -- and best -- part.

Chapter One

So there was nothing to be said for setting the record straight, as it were. Eli couldn't say he minded being proved wrong, not when Zane was both reward and incentive to turn his life around. Change might never be easy, but it was well worth a man's while.

But what then? After a guy fell in love -- with his best friend, no less -- what came next?

That, Eli had surmised, was the million-dollar question.

So far he figured he had about sixty-four cents' worth of answers. He'd get the full dollar eventually. Just took time.

Thank God Zane was the patient type.

* * *

Long time no see, Doc!

Eli frowned at the text that'd popped up on his phone. Unknown number, no name attached. He couldn't think of who might have sent it. None of the usual suspects had gotten new contact info recently.

Must be a wrong number, he decided. He stuffed the phone back in his pocket. *Out of sight, out of mind --* and he already had enough going on to keep him busy that night.

"Eli! Eli, over here." Across the street, Diana stood on her tiptoes, waving at him with the hand not holding a half-smoked cigarette.

Eli waved once to show he'd heard her, and put a few ounces of speed in his step to hurry over the crosswalk before the light turned. Didn't stop impatient city drivers from honking at him, but such was life in any city.

This city, though. He could have stopped directly under the lights as red changed to green and tossed his hat in the air like a refugee from the 1960s. Don't think he hadn't been tempted a time or two. Made him remember the days when he'd just finished with med school in North Carolina and come back home to Chicago a newly minted doctor. He'd damn near gotten to his knees to kiss the asphalt.

Diana took a hearty, satisfied puff on her cigarette and grinned broadly at Eli, speaking as soon as he came within earshot. "Look who decided to show up. I almost thought you weren't going to make it."

"I almost didn't," Eli admitted. "Got distracted walking around the neighborhood. It's not far from where I used to live." He nipped the cigarette out of Diana's fingers and tossed it neatly into a grubby ashtray atop a nearby trash can. "I'd heard you quit."

"That was my last one, you mannerless bastard." Diana pretended to glower at him. "You of all people should know bad habits are never that easy to break."

Didn't he just. Not that he'd *say* so. "And? So you've quit again, now," Eli retorted. Then relented enough to add, "Nice to see you again, Diana."

"Well played. Come here, you."

"Do I have a choice?"

"Nope." Forty-six and unashamed, still a hell of a looker in her gamine way, Diana drew more than a few appreciative looks when she got worked up. Either she didn't notice, or she took them as her due and ignored them in favor of first punching Eli in the biceps, then wrapping her arms around his neck for a brief hug that smelled of icy peppermint and a whiff of smoke. "It's good to see you again, Eli."

"You too." Eli wasn't much of a one for public displays of affection. Never had been, and try though he might, suspected he never would be. His cheeks and ears still warmed when he asked, "Where's Zane?"

"Downstairs, last I checked. He's looking good,

you lucky bastard." Diana dusted her hands off and took Eli by the elbow. "Shall we?"

* * *

"Downstairs" was a literal description, Eli discovered. Diana led him to a set of steps descending from sidewalk level to what might now be described as a basement but had likely once been the ground floor when they laid the cornerstone. Chicago settled, sinking deeper into its roots year after year.

The staircase hadn't been built for tall men. Eli had to duck his head to avoid bashing it against the sidewalk's edge as they made their way underneath the street. Plate-glass windows set alongside the stairs beckoned with their warmth, light, and the unmistakable smells of garlic, oregano, and sizzling beef. His stomach roared its appreciation. He hadn't had a decent chow fest in weeks. He hadn't meant to be back in town for a few weeks more, but drinking bad water while working abroad tended to upset the best-laid plans. He'd had to baby himself for a while, but now? *Bring on the beef!*

"I think I've been here before," he said, pausing to check the view -- and to scan for Zane. No sight of him, but the window didn't provide a full three-sixty angle. "Used to be a bar, didn't it?"

"A bar with a backroom poker night," Diana agreed. She elbowed the door at the foot of the steps open and gestured him past. "Damn good game too."

Eli covered his face with one palm. "You didn't."

"You thought I wouldn't?"

"Not exactly." Eli wouldn't put anything past Diana. "You obviously lived to tell the tale. I'm not worried about that. Did you leave the other guys any money?"

"Enough for cab fare." Diana winked at Eli

before pointing herself down a short hall with cell phone in hand. "Go on, already. I'm not the only one who's missed you. Glad to see you back, Eli."

And there she left him.

Eli took his time near the entrance. He could wish for winter weather -- stripping off gloves and scarf and thumping snow off of boots made for good occupation while sizing up a new place -- but no one seemed to notice or be bothered by his loitering. Low-key, they'd promised him. Zane knew the place of old and swore it was very laissez-faire. *"Run by locals. You'll love it, Eli. Trust me."*

Which Eli did. He trusted Zane with more than he ever had another, even his ex-wife, Marybeth. The more he looked back on his short-lived marriage... *whoo.* He hadn't seen Marybeth in years and wasn't sure what she got up to these days. Mostly whenever Eli thought about her, he hoped she was happy and left it at that. Even as happy as him.

Sometimes he wondered what she'd make of it, his being involved with a man. Being the lover of a man. He never had been quite sure how she'd react. Marybeth could be tricky.

"I'm here with a group," he said to the hostess approaching him. "Just point me to the party of rowdy doctors, and I'll find my way there."

"Which one?" she shot back without batting an eye. "This close to Immaculate Grace, we get a few."

"This one," a warm voice said next to Eli's ear, almost brushing his skin. Knuckles bumped his lazily, and a shoulder jostled Eli's. "He's with me."

Zane.

Eli's heart rate kicked up a notch. He would have liked nothing better than to do a one-eighty turn and press his lips to Zane's. He'd had his mouth on every inch of the man's body in the privacy of their home, and in tents, and once -- just once -- behind a tree broader than both of them put together, in a forest where almost no one had ever been, while the rest of their small party slept like they'd been drugged.

And yet he still couldn't handle one little kiss in public -- about which, frankly, he did give a damn. Zane swore he understood. Zane wasn't given to lying, not even to make someone feel better. Sometimes, Eli had his doubts.

And sometimes, he could give himself a little kick in the ass. He hooked his pinkie around Zane's forefinger and squeezed. "Yeah," he said, looking the hostess in the eye as he slowly and with his face on fire let the rest of his fingers tangle with Zane's. "I'm with him."

Zane's shoulder nestled more firmly against Eli's. Eli could *feel* the approval. The hostess glanced back and forth between them, then grinned. "Mazel tov. Follow me, gentlemen, unless you know the way?"

"I should. I've been here for what, almost an hour already?" Zane cocked his head and made a curious gesture at Eli's flank. "Your pocket's buzzing."

"Is it?" Eli clicked his tongue in annoyance and checked the readout.

It's been a long time. How are you doing?

Still no name attached.

Zane peeked over Eli's shoulder to read. "Think they've got the wrong number?"

"Odds are." Eli shrugged. "Curious, though."

"Hmm. Should I give you something else to think about?" Zane winked as he stepped in front of Eli, hips fluid as a salsa dancer's. "Let me know if anything comes to mind."

Irrepressible son of a... Not that Eli minded. He

enjoyed the view. Zane had an open, friendly face with his striking gray eyes and disheveled dark hair shot through with more silver than in older days. Not as long as it had been, but long enough to gather in a short ponytail that curled over his collar. He'd shaved that morning, elbow to elbow with Eli at the bathroom sink, but where Eli's stubble was already long enough to make a scraping sound when scratched, Zane's was only a faint shadow. They were as unlike each other as two men could be, one raised in an ivory tower and one down on the streets, one a doctor who'd hated it and one a former cop turned doctor who couldn't have loved anything more.

And yet they'd found each other. It still blew Eli's mind sometimes. When he tallied up all the years Zane had waited for him to get his act together, it did the rest of his head in.

"You two are so cute together," the hostess said, her grin not fading a bit. "Just for reference, your party's at the round table by the center fireplace. Enjoy."

Zane waited for her to turn her back before he bumped a quick kiss to Eli's temple and dropped a casual arm around Eli's shoulders. "What kept you? I was getting ready to send out a search party. Don't tell me I steered you wrong with the directions."

Eli relaxed, tension ebbing away. He missed this when he didn't have it. "Your directions were fine. The day I have to ask someone else how to get around in this town... Anyway. Table?"

"In a minute." Zane checked Eli's eyes and color and reflexes with a few quick passes, finishing by pressing the back of his hand to Eli's cheeks and forehead. "Still a little warm," he said. "You should be in bed, you know."

"So should you," Eli retorted. He rolled his eyes at Zane's broad, naughty wink. "Yeah, yeah. Not like that. In bed, recovering."

Zane hooted at that. "Oh really, now?"

"Wiseass," Eli grumbled, hiding his smile.

Zane knocked elbows with him companionably, pointing him left at what Eli guessed to be the most easily navigable path through the tables, though those were mostly empty at this hour. They'd meant to gather for supper, but a one-hour nap turned into two. Such was the way of good intentions. Eli had woken an hour ago to a note with directions to the gang's new favorite watering hole.

"You're feeling better, I take it," Eli remarked.

Zane stretched, arms over his head, tugging at his elbows. "Almost a hundred percent. I'll be back out there before you know it. We'll be," he corrected. "Both of us. Though whether or not we'll survive the teasing is up for debate. 'Physician, heal thyself' is likely to be the least of it."

Eli winced. He'd lived down a few humiliations in his day, but having to be helicopter-lifted out of Brazil and flown a few hundred miles clinging to his stomach lining and the straps on a stretcher would go down as one of the most unpleasant experiences he'd known to date. At least he hadn't suffered alone, not that he'd wish illness on Zane.

Still, Zane had very nearly snapped back. Just like a rubber band, and good as new. Eli? Better, but not yet at his best. One of the nurses had suggested brightly that relearning his limits was all part of getting older. Eli grumbled under his breath at the memory. Older, his ass. Forty-eight wasn't *old*. He preferred to see it as just hitting his stride. God knew he still had too much to learn to let himself give way early to age and consider himself *old*.

Zane chuckled. "God, your face," he said, affection in his tone if not overtly in his touch to Eli's elbow. "You'll be fine when you stop pushing yourself every step of the way."

"Thank you, Zen Master."

"I live to please," Zane said with a much slyer sort of wink, the kind he usually saved for the bedroom. Seeing it out here in the public arena made Eli catch his breath.

Another thing nurses said to him, or rather asked: did he know how lucky he was?

Damn right, he did. And the thought of ever losing that made his blood run cold. So even if the thought of getting better only to turn right around and go back left Eli prickling with doubt, like hell would he ever breathe a word about it. Especially not to Zane.

"Couple weeks, three at the most, and we'll be on top of the world," Eli said. "Stand back and watch us go."

"That's what I like to hear." Zane took a hard left that landed them at a round table. "And here we are. Look who I found, Holly."

Holly was on her feet before he'd finished speaking, or before Eli had finished pulling out his chair. A calm, elegant blonde with the soul of Sigmund Freud and an uncanny way with prescience, their clinical-psychologist-slash-den-mother ruled the roost, and everyone knew it. She took a different approach to hugging than Diana, pausing first for a good X-ray look at his face, particularly his eyes, and resting her palm over his heart -- a sneaky way, he'd learned, of checking his pulse rate.

Whatever she saw didn't exactly seem to please her, but she let it go for the moment to smile at him.

"It's so good to have you back in town. You've been missed."

"He's one of the good ones," Zane agreed. He nudged Eli toward a different seat. "That one's Taye's," he explained at Eli's curious look. "Not that he's sat in it more than once all night, but I live in hope. And in thirst. Mind if I…"

"Do what you've got to do," Eli said. Truth be told, no matter how little he liked it, the short walk had nearly winded him, and he wouldn't mind sitting for a few minutes to get his breath. He very emphatically did not look at Holly or let her catch his eye before Zane walked away, tousling Eli's hair in lieu of a kiss.

He could *feel* her analyzing him. He held up one finger. "Don't."

"I have no idea what you mean," she replied, sunny and calm as a perfect day of golf. "It's good to see you again, Eli, truly. Do you two have plans for your unexpected vacation?"

"Zane's picked up some lecturing at the university. Filling in for someone who had to take compassionate leave, all hail the irony."

"I see. And yourself, Eli?" Give credit where credit was due -- Holly stuck to her guns like a champ. "Will you go back to Immaculate Grace in the interim?"

And there was the rub. "Not sure," Eli said, clipped and brief. "Still waiting on word." Though that word might well be no, and Eli knew it. They might very well not take him back at all. On the one hand, he couldn't blame them. Every time he hopped a flight with Zane, he came back needing to brush up and reintegrate.

On the other hand, what he'd do without his job as a hospitalist, he didn't know and didn't want to know. Even thinking about it gave him the cold chills, which he was more than certain Holly was aware of right down to the molecular level.

"I'll find something," he said, gruff in his embarrassment. "Don't worry about me."

"Affection can't be turned on and off like a faucet, Eli. If it can, then it isn't affection at all, and you are a very dear friend." Holly patted his hand with her smaller, cooler one. Though she frowned when she discovered the dry roughness of Eli's skin, at least she forbore to comment. "Ah, Zane. Hello again. I thought you were placing an order."

"I did. And then I came back here to effect a rescue." Zane sat lightly on the chair next to Eli. "He's just got some color back. Don't try and probe his brain before he's ready."

"I can take care of myself, you know," Eli objected. "I thought you were going to find Taye."

"And find him I did. He'll be here in a few. Kid looks exhausted. If he wants to finish his pint in peace, more power to him."

That was Zane all over, Eli thought. Kinder to others than he was to himself. Kind enough to put up with a grouchy old bear like Eli, at least.

But within limits. Zane's stomach rumbled. "Then again, I might head over and see if I can get him to shake a leg. I'll put in an order for appetizers while I'm at the bar."

"Could have done that before," Eli said mildly as he could. "Up, down, up again. You're like a yo-yo tonight. What's up?"

"Sorry." Zane grimaced in abashed apology. "Just feeling restless, and my mind keeps resetting to a different time zone. Better that I burn off the energy now."

True enough. Zane had never liked sitting still when he could keep busy. Probably didn't help that he wasn't as tied to a pager as he once had been. It'd been months since Eli wore a pager. He still reached for it without thinking. He flexed his fingers, itching for a suture kit or a stethoscope or at the very least a butterfly bandage. Come to think of it, he could understand Zane's itchy feet tonight a little better.

"Go on," he said, punctuating himself with a fond knuckle to Zane's ribs. "Bring me back a beer, would you?" His stomach would feel better with something in there to get to work on, and if he regretted the choice later, he'd take his lumps like a man.

Zane raised an eyebrow but didn't otherwise question him. "Your usual?"

"You know me well." Eli watched him wander away and held up his finger a second time. "Still don't, Holly."

"All right, Eli. You win. I'll give you a pass for the rest of the night." Holly glanced around. "Where's Diana gotten to?"

"Eating someone younger than her alive for an appetizer, probably," Eli suggested. "Last seen on her cell, headed for the ladies'." He paused, tapping the tabletop in thought. Meddling wasn't his thing usually, but… "Everything okay with her? She was smoking again."

Holly's eyes crinkled when she smiled. "Diana is, as ever and always, utterly Diana. Sometimes more than is good for her. I do hope you took her cigarettes away."

"Just the one. She said it was her last."

"And you believed her, didn't you?" The seat Eli had very nearly occupied scooted out with a scrape of wood on wood. Taye dropped into the chair with a decided lack of grace and a heaping helping of tired bonhomie. "Welcome back, Eli."

"Taye." Eli held up his fist for a bump, though he felt like an idiot. Taye's laugh said he'd noticed and didn't mind. "How's tricks?"

He'd finished his residency not long after Eli and Zane went on their latest tour of duty, and Eli would have expected no less than good-natured exhaustion from a man transitioning from student to authority figure. Even in clinical psychology. Or possibly especially in clinical psychology. He'd lost ten pounds, easy, possibly as much as fifteen, and he'd been a lanky so-and-so as long as Eli had known him. He'd cut his reddish hair far shorter than usual. Nearly a buzz, which made the weariness that rounded his shoulders stand out like the skyline by night.

Taye and his longtime partner, Richie, housesat Eli and Zane's suburban home while they were away. While they'd offered to clear out upon the unexpected return, he and Zane had decided to use their city apartment and leave the kids to it for now. It'd be a hell of a thing to try finding another place on a moment's notice, and they'd kept the city apartment for just such emergencies.

The suburban home had a damned good bed with a very fine mattress. Eli had made sure of that. Taye, however, looked as if he'd been sleeping on a pallet of half bricks and straw.

"What the hell happened to you?"

A pointy-toed shoe rapped Eli's shin below the table. Above the table, Holly looked as calm and poised as if she were made of chinaware. Taye thumped back in his seat, his mood taking on a deeper shade of pale blue.

"What?" Eli gestured at Taye. "I should ignore it? You look worse than I do, and I'm the one with an ICU bill. Buy a new mattress or something, kid, would you?"

Holly put her head briefly in her hands. Taye made a face that might have been halfway to the beginnings of a rueful smile. "Just as good with tact as ever, I see," he said. "Is that Zane's influence?"

"Oh, hell no. Don't try to psychoanalyze me."

Taye shook his head. The faint grin lingered. "I didn't say he was a bad influence. More just the opposite. You're a lucky man, Eli."

"Luckier than I deserve, and that's enough of that." Eli pointed at Holly. "This one's already let me have it with both barrels. I call immunity for the duration."

Both Holly and Taye got a chuckle out of that one. Eli imagined it was much like the sound tigers made before they leaped upon their prey. Wiseasses.

"Seriously, though --" he started.

Zane tugged Eli's earlobe. "Incoming, and the food's not far behind."

Saved by the bell. Eli made room for his partner to sit. "Think you can park it in neutral long enough to eat?"

"I could eat a bear with all its claws," Zane said. "Heads up, guys." He cleared space for a waitress to deposit a tray of something that smelled of starch, tomato sauce, and heaven inside a crispy deep-fried crumb shell.

"Damnation. Good thing we're here with a cardiologist." Eli snagged the first bite before the returning Diana could have her wicked way with a morsel of what turned out to be breaded, stuffed mushrooms.

His groan of pleasure made Diana's grin turn positively feral.

"Set him loose on homemade fortune cookies sometime," Zane said, unbothered. "Now that's fun for everyone."

"In bed," Diana murmured in a not at all stage whisper.

Zane ignored her with great aplomb. He turned sideways in his chair to cast his sole regard on Eli, who lifted his chin and returned the favor, and was rewarded with one of Zane's quieter, no less radiant smiles. "I guess you are feeling better, if you can eat like that."

"Told you I was." Eli swallowed and cleaned a trace of spicy sauce from the corner of his mouth with the tip of his tongue. The way Zane looked at him, good Christ, what it did to his blood pressure -- and everything below the belt. He settled for clapping Zane on the shoulder and taking up the velvet-headed dark beer Zane had brought him for a deep, thirsty draught. "I'm good, I promise."

"Glad to hear it," Zane said, settling back with a nod of satisfaction. "I ordered three appetizers for everyone to share, so save room. The best is yet to come."

"Richie joining us?" Eli asked, popping another bite-sized morsel in his mouth.

The brief silence that descended, broken only by the sound of chewing, was as thick and unpleasant as a blanket of dull black dryer lint. *Okay... interesting*. Eli cocked an eyebrow at Zane, asking without words what the hell had just happened.

"Richie's too busy in the kitchen to come out," Taye said a beat or two into the awkwardness. "He sends his regards. And extra sauce for the appetizers.

He --"

The kid went quiet and rubbed at his mouth, looking away. Holly and Diana exchanged knowing glances. Diana frowned and shook her head at Eli in warning to keep his yapper shut about it.

Trouble in paradise, then. Good to be aware of, but not at all good to know. If any couple should have been solid... *Damn.*

"I'm not giving up," Taye said. Though he wasn't looking at any of them in particular, he got every man and woman's attention surer than a cattle prod to the gut. He lifted his chin and settled his shoulders. "And he can't convince me that I should give up. He's worth fighting for."

Holly laid her hand over Taye's. Diana knocked shoulders with him. Support and approval, and a double dose of it too. Eli couldn't tell what Zane might be thinking. He wasn't entirely sure about his own reaction. Admiration for the kid's stubbornness, maybe, and a dash of wondering if he might be setting himself up for one hell of a trip to heartbreak hotel.

His phone buzzed again. Good Lord. Whoever that was, they wanted to make contact in the worst way.

They could wait.

"Eat before it gets cold, would you?" Eli chose the fattest of the mushrooms and dunked it in spicy sauce before offering it up between thumb and forefinger, and though it made his mouth dry, pressed the bite to Zane's lips. "It's good stuff. Try for yourself."

The reward was worth the risk. Eli could live with the cooing from Holly and Diana, and the surprised gratification and delight that glowed in Zane's eyes made for a far finer result. He put up with

Eli's emotional stoicism, but he loved this kind of stuff. Made him light up like Christmas. A pretty sight, and not one he saw all that often.

Eli *did* know how lucky he was, thank you, and he could do with more of that. Pinning his heart on his sleeve never came easy, but he could try. Come hell or high water, he'd try harder.

Watch him and see.

Chapter Two

Eli stopped at the top of the stairs to wait for Zane and checked the text that'd come in during dinner.

Too busy for an old friend?

Hmph. Eli tapped out a reply.

Think you might have the wrong number. Who is this?

There. He'd see what whoever-this-was made of that.

Eli breathed deep, savoring the unique bouquet of the city on a warm spring night. Diesel, humanity, and a faint hint of the Great Lakes. Granted, something of an acquired taste and not for those with overly weak stomachs, but to him it was manna all the way.

God, but he loved this city. Better still, his energy levels had risen into the red after exceeding the recommended daily dosage of starch and carbs. Not his usual sort of thing but not bad, not bad at all. He'd have to come back. Maybe make a regular thing of it --

Except they'd be off again as soon as they both proved hale enough to hit the jet stream on an airport tarmac. Didn't seem to matter whether it was summer or fall -- boarding tunnels were always cold.

But the travel made Zane happy, and Eli didn't mind so much. Not enough to put on the brakes.

"Walk you home, Doctor?" Zane took the last three steps at a light, quick jog and grinned at Eli. Made him look ten years younger when he did that. Almost boyish, despite the growing number of silver threads in his hair. A passing pedestrian, one sporting a suit far more tailored than anything Eli could afford, took a second look at Zane and nearly walked into a flagpole.

Eli glared at him and at his polished shoes. *Hands*

off.

Zane didn't seem to notice. He never did, no matter how many admiring glances came his way, and the one time Eli had drawn his attention to it, Zane had asked how Eli knew the admirers weren't watching *him* instead. Eli had spent a week picking up the pieces of his blown mind after that one, and he didn't care to repeat the experience.

Right now, at least, Zane's eyes were all for Eli, and as far as Eli could tell, Zane liked what he saw. "Look at you, waiting like a gentleman. What's the occasion?"

Gentleman, was it? Eli could do genteel if he put in the effort. He crooked his arm to offer Zane his elbow. "No occasion. Just escorting a friend home."

Zane raised an eyebrow at the elbow. He shook his head, gave a quiet chuckle, and bumped shoulders with Eli instead. "You're in a fine mood, Romeo. Care to stop for coffee on the way home in that little Greek place that does the good espresso?"

"I could do coffee. And, what? I shouldn't be romantic?" Eli asked, though he'd have to admit to a small amount of relief Zane hadn't taken him up on the offer. "Or would you rather the other way around?"

"Hmm. You could lean on me if you wanted. I wouldn't say no." Zane nudged Eli to start him walking away from the restaurant, pointed toward the elevated train station. "On the other hand, your color's better. You're certainly feeling well enough to eat like a racehorse in training."

Eli ran one hand down his admittedly long, narrow face. "I feel as if I should take offense."

Zane rolled his eyes. He knew how to tell the admittedly subtle difference between Eli's teasing and his sober moments. One of the reasons they'd become friends in the first place, back in the day. "You don't look like a horse to me. But if you were, I suppose that'd make me the jockey. It's not inappropriate. I seem to remember you giving me one hell of a ride a few weeks back."

"A few weeks?" Eli frowned. "It hasn't been that long, has it?"

"And? Not complaining, Eli." Zane turned to walk a few steps backward. He raised one shoulder in a casual shrug before turning again to match Eli's pace side by side with him. *Damned nimble...* Eli grumbled internally. His steps were starting to lag a hair more than he liked. "You were ill. I was more concerned with getting you back to fighting fit before I dragged the saddle and bridle out of storage."

"I think you're mixing your metaphors, there." To pleasant mental effect, yes, but still.

"Am I? Blame it on the burgundy." Zane gave a contented sigh. "Nice cellar they had on them. We should go back if we get the chance." As quickly as he'd showed his pleasure, he shifted gears into a more serious mien. "So, Taye and Richie. I have to confess I didn't see that coming. You?"

"Not as such," Eli admitted. "Taye sounded like he had a game plan, though."

"Maybe so, but I still wonder." Zane had the look of a man lost in concerned thought. He reached for his pocket in the last remnant of his old smoking habit. Three years, and never a light. Eli couldn't have been more pleased, although sometimes he wondered if he'd been fair to ask. Everyone *should* have a vice to call their own. Kept them human. "You can't tell me you're not concerned."

"I never said I wasn't concerned," Eli protested mildly. "Taye's not the kind of guy who appreciates someone poking their nose in, that's all. He'll work it out, or he'll come around looking for help in his own time. Best to let him do things the way he's comfortable."

"Is it?"

"You think otherwise?"

"Maybe." Zane tapped his pocket absently. He grinned at Eli. "If no one ever pushed anyone, where would you and I be? Hmm?"

Eli laughed. At best, his laughs were short and sharp, but Zane appreciated them well enough. "Fair point."

"There you have it," Zane said, content. He leaned briefly against Eli's shoulder, as good as a kiss. "Eli?"

"Hmm?"

"You make a difference," Zane said. "Just so you know."

Warmth suffused Eli. Good old Zane, he thought. Then --

"Weeks, really?" Eli asked.

Zane laughed.

"Yeah, yeah, yeah." Eli tucked his hands in his pockets and held still a moment to study Zane while he ran backward through a calendar in his head. Be damned if Zane wasn't right on the money. It'd been weeks. No wonder every move he made in the restaurant hit Eli where he lived.

Time to remedy that too.

When consolidating their assets four-odd years ago, Eli and Zane had wrangled it over and chosen to keep Eli's old place when they'd bought the house, instead of liquidating as they had Zane's condominium. Closer to the hospital and not too far from the university, it made for a decent crash pad on the nights when they'd rather sleep than ride the rails. Or do other things besides sleep, which Eli hoped Zane would remember.

Eli caught Zane by the wrist and held him there. "I'm not in the mood for coffee."

"That's a first." Zane frowned at him. "Are you sure you're all right?"

Eli's cheeks warmed. It was a hell of a thing, to be on the downhill slope to fifty and still fully capable of a blush. Zane brought out all manner of different sides to him and always had. Hopefully always would. "I feel fine. Cross my heart, so stop worrying."

Which was, ever so slightly, an utter lie, but not for long.

Eli reached up to brush the backs of his knuckles against Zane's cheekbone, feeling his heartbeat speed up. "More that I'd like to have you, and I'm not in the mood to wait."

Zane's eyes rounded, but his grin popped up and widened. "Eli?"

"Hmm?"

"You could have just said so in the first place."

Relief tasted sweet. Eli wrapped one arm around Zane's shoulders and gave him a contented jostle. "I'm saying so now, aren't I? Onward, friend."

* * *

Eli's key stuck in the lock, the tumblers stiff with disuse. He scowled at the thing and gave it a good jiggle. "Remind me to get some oil for this, would you?"

"You say that every time."

"Because I keep forgetting, every time."

"Eli, Eli. What am I supposed to do with you?" Zane draped himself companionably against Eli's side. For all his energy, he looked a shade more worn than before they'd left the restaurant. Good idea to come here, then, and not just for the one reason.

Though that "one reason" was admittedly well to the forefront of Eli's mind. He gave the recalcitrant lock a firm rattle and grunted with satisfaction when the tumblers finally turned. *Aha! Gotcha.*

The familiar smell of *home* hit Eli in the solar plexus when he locked the door to his West Side bolt-hole behind them. He'd lived there for the better part of twenty years, cop and then resident and then doctor, before Zane gave him the nudge he'd needed to get a move on with his life and his heart. When he'd thought about his future back then, he'd imagined himself firmly rooted within the comfort of those walls until they carted his grumbly ass off to the nursing home.

Course, he'd figured on sharing space at the home with Zane, both of them old men demanding some kick to their applesauce. Eli ran his palm down the familiar old door frame and chuckled. Funny how life turned out, wasn't it?

Zane ambled ahead of Eli, stirring up the thin layer of dust as he went. He tugged at his tie to loosen the knot. "Speaking of forgetting, I never can remember if I've left the right clothes here, or if what I want is still packed up, or lost in shipping, or out in the suburbs. Are we getting old?"

"The hell you say. Age is all in the mind." Eli reached for Zane as he passed. He managed to snag the trailing end of the tie. "I hope you meant to save dressing for later."

Zane tilted his head and undid the knot completely. "What do you think?"

"I think guessing games are the surest way to get in trouble."

"Smart man," Zane said approvingly. He slid the

tie free of his collar and wound the end around Eli's wrist. "I hope you also think that an unmade bed and wrinkled sheets are not the surest way to a man's heart. Otherwise I'll have to educate you."

"Pfft." Eli was familiar with this particular quirk of Zane's, and he certainly didn't mind fresh, fluffed bedding. He gestured expansively at the bedroom. "Be my guest."

"Give me five minutes, then." Zane used the tie to tug Eli close enough to kiss. His lips were warm and soft, his dark shadow of stubble scratchy.

Eli brought one arm up to wrap around his waist and hold him there, sturdy and solid and still so real it startled him sometimes. "Five minutes. I'll time it on the clock."

Zane crinkled his nose and gave Eli a light push. "The clock's batteries must have run down. Unless it did take us three hours to walk from the El and it's two-thirty in the morning."

As tired as Eli felt after such a short walk, he honestly wouldn't have been surprised, but no. Traffic outside rattled and hummed at its usual near-midnight pace. He could have told time with his eyes closed, gauging it by the streets outside these familiar windows. He made an absent noise and waved Zane toward the linen closet. For his part, he made a detour into their kitchen to snag a handful of antacid tablets. *Damned bacteria.*

Hopefully just the bacteria, anyway. He'd hate like hell to get an ulcer. His dad had been plagued with those, and Eli took after his father's side of the family.

The crunching mint tabs between his teeth helped. Feeling idle then, content to let the slow burn of arousal take its time growing from ember to flame, Eli meandered toward the sitting room's single window over the couch. Looked like the suspension on the rolling blinds had broken to send them shooting up to halfway-open. *Tch. Shoddy goods.* He reached for the pull cord with one hand while undoing the buttons on his shirt with the other --

And stopped. He rubbed a circle of dust away from the pane, then knelt on the couch cushions for a closer look. *Huh.* He hadn't noticed the locked and barred storefront just across the street. It blended in, sure, but he fidgeted uncomfortably at thinking he'd been so far out of it as to miss this.

"Bed's made. I think we might be out of chocolates to put on the pillow," Zane said behind him.

"Somehow, I think we'll live." Eli flicked the latches holding the window shut and gave the sash a tug upward. "Do you remember the drugstore that used to be across the street?"

"'Used' to be? Damn. They still did malted milk. Those were the best in summertime." Zane sounded wistful. "I got them to make me an egg cream once by promising I'd never tell."

Doctors did indeed take the most health risks of any subcategory of men, in Eli's experience. "You and your creamy sweet drinks," Eli chided. He listened with one ear to the sound of Zane's steps coming closer. His skin tightened with a pleasurable ripple of sensation. Just like Pavlov's dog, him. It'd taken long enough.

"Any idea how long they've been shut down?"

"From the looks of things, maybe a month or two." Damn this economy. Eli had fond memories of stopping at the soda counter on his way home from a long shift, back when he and Marybeth made these walls reverberate with the vehemence of their cat-fighting.

God bless her, wherever she was and whoever she happened to be with this month. The woman had earned her stripes and her payout. If Eli looked back at the time they'd spent together, he could see -- now -- how he'd always held something of himself in reserve. She'd blamed the job and hadn't been wrong to do so, but by Eli's reckoning, that was only the first layer.

He'd been waiting, even though he hadn't known it, and he damn sure hadn't recognized it in the gray-eyed doctor at a free clinic, the one who'd treated him like a person after a bullet stopped his career in law enforcement cold.

Come to think of it... *Hmm.* A storefront like that would make an excellent spot for a neighborhood clinic. If they were planning to stay long enough, Eli would have liked to help get one started.

Almost a shame, really.

"You have," Zane said, "the craziest body language. Eli." Warm hands landed on Eli's shoulders. Zane dug in with his thumbs to massage away the stiffness to either side of Eli's neck. "Did I ever tell you? Can't remember if I did or didn't. Not always, but sometimes I can damned near read your mind by the way you shift forward or back." He ran his fingertips into the short hairs curling over Eli's nape and ruffled them up. "It goes without saying that I approve."

Eli hummed and tilted his neck back to give Zane a better angle. "Don't stop."

"I won't if you won't."

"Deal," Eli said around a groan of satisfaction when Zane hit *just* the right spot. "Damn. Fine hands on that man. You could be a doctor with hands like those."

Zane had a better laugh than Eli, in Eli's opinion, warm and hearty as spicy chili on a cold day. "Sweet talker."

"It's a gift." Eli leaned forward, bracing his crossed arms on the back of the couch.

Now, he could have turned around to give Zane the eye. He knew -- or felt reasonably sure -- Zane waited for him to do so. But Zane wasn't the only one who could extemporize.

"Come and see for yourself," he invited, widening his kneel. "What am I thinking now?"

The radiant warmth of Zane's body heat covered Eli's back in a blanket. Zane settled against him almost lightly, holding back by the barest of margins. "I hope to God it's the same thing I'm thinking."

"Take three guesses, and the first two don't count." Odd angle be damned. Eli twisted about to glance over his shoulder and whistled. "Looking good, old man."

"Old, my ass," Zane said. He settled more firmly against Eli's back, and from what Eli could tell -- not an inconsiderable amount -- was happy to be there. The fact that he didn't have a single stitch of clothing on made it all kinds of handy in gauging his state of mind. "Were you deliberately teasing me with the stuffed mushroom?"

"Might have been." Eli grinned. He nudged the question of the drugstore out of his mind. He had better things to think about just then. "Depends on whether or not you liked it."

"Take three guesses," Zane mocked, his mouth warm and tasting sweetly of the peppermint candy they'd gotten with their share of the bill. "Or you could just kiss me. I think I could settle for that."

"You could, could you? What if I'm not in the mood for settling?" Eli pushed back, nudging Zane out of his way, and when Zane least expected it, caught

Zane around the waist and pulled him forward. Neither of their backs would thank them for the fancy dancing, but Eli considered it a worthwhile tradeoff for the satisfaction of Zane's delighted yelp when Eli tossed him bare-naked onto the couch and came to a stop that suited him between Zane's knees.

Zane thumped backward, just this side of out of breath. "Hot damn, Eli."

"You like? There's more where that came from."

"Better be." Zane settled his bare feet flat on the carpet, worn down to the weave here and there but still soft, still comfortable enough. He nudged Eli's shoulder with one knee. "I don't know what's gotten into you tonight, Eli, but feel free not to stop. Unless you want to aim me at the bed next."

"I could do that," Eli said. He stroked against the grain of the short, wiry hair on Zane's calves, and up, past the knee, and against the soft inside of his thigh. "Or I could do this."

Zane hummed and relaxed deeper into the couch. "You could, at that. But to what end?"

"Is that a challenge?"

"It's not a guess." Zane laid his hands on his thighs, palms up. His cock rested full and dark, to the left. Not completely hard, but getting there damned fast. Faster when Eli bent his head to blow warm air against him. He put one arm against Zane's waist to hold him steady and rolled his shoulders, pleased, when one of Zane's hands found its way to his hair. "Eli..."

"That's my name." Eli touched the tip of his nose to a small mole, the kind they used to call a beauty mark, on Zane's hip. Want it as he might -- and Christ, but he did, his own cock straining behind a barrier of boxers and formerly pressed trousers -- he still had to take the smallest breath before diving in. Sometimes out of disbelief, and sometimes in amazement that after all these years, this was them. He wondered if Zane ever felt that way still, or if he had before.

Better not to dwell on it. Better still to show the man that Eli could learn, given time.

"Hold as still as you can," he said, stroking Zane's lean hips with both hands. "Doctor's orders."

He closed his eyes and took Zane's length deep into his mouth.

Zane's stomach muscles flexed and jumped, and his fist knotted too tightly in Eli's hair. Eli could not find it within himself to care even the slightest bit about the minor sting. "Oh," he groaned. "Eli, fuck. Eli. *Eli.*"

Eli breathed deeply through his nose, taking in the scent of warm skin and that undeniably *male* smell both like and unlike his own. The closest he'd ever come, before Zane, was tasting his own cum. Everyone did that at least once, or so he'd heard. He'd thought for sure he'd hate the taste and compare it to a woman's flavor, but not so. He'd learned to like Zane's salty-clean skin on its own merits.

And by damn, there wasn't much that could go to a man's head like knowing, from experience, what it felt like to go so hard as that. What the need for another felt like, burning in his gut, to see and feel and taste that in Zane and know it was because of him. He made Zane crazy. Woke the need to fuck within him, and that wasn't too shabby at all.

Eli might have started to learn the ins and outs of how to give a blowjob late in the game, but Zane made a good teacher, and he led by example too. Pulling out the stops was natural as turning on a tap now. Eli held his fist around what of Zane's cock he couldn't get into his mouth, and put his mouth to good, wet, messy use on the rest. Spit dribbled down his fist and into the tightly crinkled nest of hair that tickled his knuckles. He chased the wetness, licking up what he could and letting the rest drip where it would.

"Holy *fuck*, Eli!" Zane sounded both breathless and dazed. His thighs trembled, muscles gathered in tight bunches beneath the skin from reaction. He pushed at Eli's shoulders, first clumsily and then with intent. "Eli, my God."

"Not a god. Just an old doctor." Eli kept his hand in place as he winked up at Zane. "Not bad, eh?"

"I'll be the judge of what's next to godliness." Zane's cheeks puffed as he exhaled. He tugged clumsily at Eli. "Bad? No. Better if you'd come up here. One is the loneliest number. I want my hands on you too."

"Do you?" Eli murmured. His knees wouldn't mind, to tell the truth. The left one popped in protest as he stood, and whether it or Zane and gravity were to blame for his falling forward he'd leave up to the judges to decide. Didn't matter, really; Zane made a fine cushion, if a laughing one, and he was more than strong enough to guide them both down on the couch itself.

For the moment, they lay side to side. Could have gone either way, putting Zane or his back, or… or Eli.

Eli caught his breath. Anticipation hitched in the back of his throat, and frankly it took him off his guard. They'd done just about everything together, him and Zane, but not that. Zane cracked jokes about making up for forty-odd years of missing out on cock and being too greedy to share.

Which suited Eli well enough. He hadn't missed

out for lack of bottoming, or so he'd thought. Now, though. Now he wondered…

Though not for long. Zane's eyes crinkled at the corners. He thumbed Eli's mouth with rough affection. "BJ lips look good on you."

"Glad to hear it." Eli stretched his legs, not so incidentally tangling his feet with Zane's, and let Zane guide them over to rest with Zane beneath him. He tucked the notion of changing places aside for the moment. Time enough to come back to that later. "Want to put your money where your mouth is?"

"Maybe later, when you're not spoiling me for choice. God help, Eli…" Zane slipped both hands beneath Eli's belt and his boxers too, settling firm and warm on his ass. What there was of it, anyway. Between the two of them, Zane was the one with junk in the trunk. Nice round cheeks, still firm, still good to the touch.

Though Eli was, admittedly, rather more interested in the other side of the man.

"You make me feel like a kid sometimes," Eli said. "Only sometimes. Not when we're naked."

Zane's grin dazzled him. "Which was the point I'm trying to make." He kneaded Eli's ass like a cat on a mission. "As in, too many clothes. Take 'em off, Doc."

"Hmm. I could," Eli said, bending his head to press his mouth to the side of Zane's neck. He nibbled at the light stubble and enjoyed the way Zane groaned when he hit the sweet spot. Enjoyed even more the noise Zane made when he found his way down between them and took Zane, still slippery-slick and harder than ever, in hand.

Zane lifted them both with the arch of his back. When Eli came down, he settled with one thigh pressed between Zane's, and his cock tucked snug against Zane's hip. Zane opened dazed eyes. "Or you could do that," he said, throaty. "Or you could do a hell of a lot more of exactly that."

Suited Eli down to the ground. He rolled his hips, meaning only to test for any zipper friction that might get in the way, but -- *good goddamn*. He stifled his groan against Zane's chest and went for a second round. Fuck. Yes. That was the right stuff.

Zane undulated beneath Eli, rising and falling off rhythm at first, but Eli liked it better that way. Rough. Messy. Nothing but *need* and *want* and *now*. "Right there," Zane said, voice rough as raw wood when Eli shifted to the left. He locked his knees around Eli's hips. "Right there, harder --"

Eli squeezed his eyes shut. He couldn't have stopped if he'd wanted to, and he didn't want anything in the world except to keep on going. He could taste it -- almost there --

Zane made a small, almost animal sound deep in his throat, shuddered tremendously, and let go. Cum covered Eli's hand in thick gouts, soaking into Eli's trousers. Eli buried his face in Zane's shoulder and rolled his hips -- just... once... more...

There. Yes. "Fuck," he said between gritted teeth as the climax hit, belting him in the head and chest and everywhere else he could think to name. "Fuck, Zane. Zane."

Zane wound his arms around Eli's neck and butted their heads clumsily together. "God yes, Eli," he said, out of breath. "Damn. I love you."

There.

Eli had barely collapsed against Zane's chest before he started to laugh under his breath. *There, and so there!* Old? Who could call themselves old after a round like that? Not Eli. Old age could take that, stuff it in its pipe, and have a smoke. He pillowed his head on Zane's collarbone and let out a long breath of satisfied contentment.

It might have been minutes or longer after when Zane's chuckle made him open his eyes. "Guess I don't need to ask if it was good for you too."

"Nope. I like the 'too,' though. You get extra points for that."

"I live to please," Zane said. His eyes were sleepy but warm with affection when Eli raised himself on his elbows for one more kiss. "Now that you've had your way with me, Doctor, how about you take me to bed?"

That, Eli could do.

* * *

They didn't make it to the bedroom straightaway. First a detour into the bathroom -- while Eli didn't so much mind coming in his pants like a randy teenager, he had a dedicated objection to waking up stuck to his underwear. Zane teased him. He could, the naked so-and-so. That was all right. Let him have his fun. They got where they'd meant to go, in the end.

Zane hit the bed first and lay near-bonelessly, barely making the effort to wriggle under the sheets he'd considerately turned back earlier. He lay on his stomach, his back bare and exposed above the careless toss of the top sheet. Sliding in beside him, Eli reached to tug the selfsame sheet up and drape the blue cotton over Zane's shoulders, smoothing it down with long, thoughtful strokes. "Not bad, eh?" he asked again as he splayed his hand wide over that smooth skin. "Not bad, you and me."

"You'll do," Zane said drowsily. "Plenty good enough to be getting on with."

Eli frowned. *Hmm.* Not old, check. There might

be snow on the roof, but there was a fire in the furnace. But enough to satisfy? Seemed as if he could have done more. Zane knew Eli wasn't any great shakes at the great romantic gestures, yes, but...

"Eli?" Zane gazed at Eli through heavy lids. He brushed his thumb across Eli's wrist. "Watching you think is like biting into tinfoil. Don't try so hard, would you? Because you're not fooling me, you know."

"I'm not?" Eli tried -- and, he thought, failed -- to keep up. "Fooling you with what?"

"Don't try so hard, you dope. If I didn't already like your cranky, stubborn ass..." He broke to yawn wide and mint scented, and patted Eli's arm on the way down. "Go to sleep, Eli. I'll see you in the morning."

Eli thumped Zane's shoulder in return. "Same to you." He waited for Zane to drowse off before reaching down and picking up the trousers he'd fetched into the bedroom with him. Old habit dictated he check his messages one last time before he slept. It was tempting to let it go for one night, but he'd never be able to sleep. The thing about old habits was how they all died hard.

He had one new text. *Hmm.* His mystery caller from before, no doubt.. Eli opened the message.

Sorry, I'm using a pay-as-you-go phone. I lost the other one in Austria. That sounds like a song, doesn't it? Anyway, you should be able to call me back at this number.

No name attached. Eli scowled at the phone and had his finger ready to tap and consign the message to the trash when a second notification chirped at him.

I'll forget my head next. Sorry, Eli. It's Marybeth. Give me a ring.

Eli dropped the phone with a clattering *thunk.* "Hell!"

Chapter Three

Eli woke to the steady, sturdy growling of Chicago morning traffic. Even with his eyes closed, he could pick out the patient rattle of garbage trucks, gruff shouts for a cab on the corner, and the *thud-thud-thud* of footsteps on the sidewalk. Old women sweeping their stoops, kids jostling and catcalling on the steps when they should have been in school.

He rolled to his back and sighed, content. His town. His people. Make no mistake, he loved their house out in the suburbs, packed to the gills with Zane's high-class leather furniture and all the detritus of everyday life, but... *No place like home, Dorothy.*

Sheets as soft and familiar as the back of his hand clung to his bare chest and thighs as he shifted position and cracked his eyelids open. Strong sunlight sifted through the blinds and caught the screen of his open laptop, turning it into a blazing mirror. Eli squinted and shaded his face. Light at that angle meant... *hmm, what? Ten o' clock, or close enough.*

Holy shit, but he'd overslept. Eli sat up with an abrupt tangling of the sheets and made a grab for his alarm clock. He swore again when he rapped his knuckles good and hard on the nightstand. Ten fifteen.

"Zane?" Eli swung his legs over the side of the bed and stopped to groan when the rapid-fire movement made his head thump out a warning. He hadn't had that much to drink the night before. Just one beer. Admittedly one beer in a hell of a large glass, but... "Zane, you still here?"

He'd better not be. Eli knew Zane's schedule at the university down to the fine tick of a keystroke, and if Zane was still in his apartment and not in class, his ass would be --

"Toast?" Zane poked his head through the open

bedroom door to ask.

Eli shot him a semibaleful stare through one screwed-up eye. "How did we sleep so late?"

"Forgetting to set the alarm clock tends to have that effect." Zane crunched down on a triangle of toast and clamped it between his teeth as he shrugged into the sport coat Eli remembered his leaving in the sitting room the night before. Toast still tucked in his mouth, he made a series of muffled, random noises culminating in a question mark that Eli presumed to be an offer of sharing his breakfast.

Eli's acid-burned innards answered the query with a decided *no*. "Any coffee?"

"If you don't mind sharing my cup, sure," Zane said, swallowing the last bite of toasted bread. He pivoted at the waist, damn near graceful as a dancer, and ducked back into the bathroom to retrieve a mug that he passed off to Eli.

Eli sniffed at the contents. Still hot enough to steam, but half-empty. "Swear to God, your mouth must be made of asbestos."

Zane laughed. "You're one to talk." He dusted his hands off and ran them quickly through his hair. The five-finger styling system. Eli knew it well from days gone by, before he'd started keeping his short enough to make do with a lick and a promise whenever he was in a real hurry. "Am I presentable?"

Presentable? Yes, and then some. Would that Eli, too, had a job to hurry out the door for.

Spilled milk. Don't whine about it. Eli shook his head but let the smile that wanted to come out change the shape of his mouth. He pushed himself back onto the bed with his back against the headboard, careful not to spill the coffee during the move. Aced it too. He sipped more carefully than Zane might have and still burned his tongue. "Gorgeous," he said, "and you know it."

Zane liked a compliment as much as the next guy. Sometimes he still looked surprised when Eli came out with a prettily turned phrase like that. "What *has* gotten into you?"

"Don't look a gift horse in the mouth."

"Or it'll spit hay at you." Zane looked down, realized his buttons were done up in the wrong holes, and started to undo them with a mildly irritated noise.

Eli shot a guilty look at his phone, still on the floor where he'd dropped it the night before. He didn't dare touch the thing yet -- especially not with Zane in the house.

Marybeth? What the ever-loving -- seriously, now. What does she want?

He had no idea, and he didn't much savor the idea of explaining it to Zane. Zane never had gotten along as well with her as he did Eli. Better not to trouble him, Eli decided. Surely he could deal with the problem just fine by himself.

Eli put his coffee on the nightstand and beckoned. "C'mere, you. Hurrying never gets you in anything but trouble."

"Amen to that." Zane stole the mug for a swig as he came to stand by the side of the bed, then stood still to let Eli do the tricky work. He kept a wary eye on Eli that warred with a boyish grin. "You're thinking about getting me back in there with you, aren't you?"

"Would I do such a thing?"

"Yes, you would." Zane ruffled up the tips of Eli's hair, the motion slowing from playful to thoughtful, and finishing with a light squeeze of Eli's shoulder. "You actually would. You're something else, Eli, you know that?"

Eli's ears warmed. "Don't go making me out to be something special. I'm just an ordinary guy."

"Ordinary is the least of what you are," Zane informed him. He drained the mug and set it down with a gentle thump, then chucked Eli's chin to get him to look up. His kiss was light as a breath and quick as a thought, and tasted of coffee. "Walk me to the door, former copper. Might as well do the job right from start to finish."

* * *

Not that it was what one might call a *long* walk. Eli weighed up the ebbing thud of his headache in his temples versus the opportunity to snag a fresh cup while the pot was still hot plus the advantages of saying good-bye to Zane minus the frustration of finding clothes, and decided the odds were in his favor. Especially if he forwent the clothes.

Zane arched an eyebrow but didn't look displeased. Eli resisted the urge to preen. One damn good thing about globetrotting -- it kept a man in shape. He might not have abs, no, but neither did he have any hint of a spare tire. Although he did have some gray in his happy trail. He scowled at the offending line of hair so hard he nearly missed Zane's chuckle.

"You're just noticing that now?"

"I usually have other things on my mind when I strip down these days."

"True enough." Zane led the way, but slowly, walking backward. He plucked a lightweight stadium blanket off the sofa and tossed it at Eli. "So you don't frighten the neighbors, even if they've seen it before."

"You planning to keep me on display in the open door for any length of time?"

"Would that I could, Eli." Use must have eased

the stiffness in the tumblers of the door's old lock. Zane flipped the deadbolt without trouble and propped the door open with one foot. He waited for Eli to wrap the blanket around his waist like a towel before taking hold of the loose tucked knot to tug Eli close enough to kiss.

Eli rubbed his knuckles along the stubble on Zane's jaw. He cleared his throat, abruptly embarrassed enough to be gruff. "Go on. I'm not writing you a doctor's note explaining why you're late."

"Such a hardhearted bastard," Zane said with a faux-disappointed cluck of the tongue. "What're you up to today while I'm at the salt mines? Anything planned?"

"Nothing carved in stone." And more was the pity. "You know I don't like sitting still."

"Even so..." Zane's forehead crinkled slightly when he frowned. "I'm not entirely thrilled with your color, and you seem sluggish."

"Charming. Thank you."

"I scold because I love." Zane bumped his knuckles as lightly as the brush of a butterfly's wing against the point of Eli's chin. "You should get some more rest."

"You thought I'd do what, instead? Start training for a marathon?" Eli huffed. "Don't worry about me. I'll rest for a while if it'll make you happy, but then I'll hit the gym or go pester the higher-ups in Human Resources at the hospital and see whether or not they need someone for locum work."

"I'd advise skipping the gym. Walk if you must." Zane looked dubious still -- and mischievous. "Or you could call Taye. See what kind of trouble the pair of you could get up to left to your own devices."

"Ah-ah-ah." Eli held up a warning finger. "No meddling in this corner. You're starting to sound like Holly and Diana."

"Would that be so bad?"

Now he was just trying to yank Eli's chain, and barely holding back on the shit-eating grin. "All things considered? Yes." He gave Zane a firm push outward. "I'll be fine. You know me. I land on my feet. You, on the other hand, are moving toward almost too late to bother with leaving, so unless you're serious about me holding you back, get a move on."

"Slave driver." Zane stole one more kiss and tweaked Eli's ear as a grace note. "Rain check on the rest. See you tonight."

* * *

It hadn't been exaggeration or hyperbole to warn and remind Zane that idleness had never set well with Eli. Leave him to his own devices for too long, and look out, here came trouble.

Pouring a cup of coffee kept his hands too busy for the devil's work for a couple of minutes. Stepping into clean if slightly dusty jeans and pale coffee button-down from the closet occupied him for another three hundred or so seconds.

After that, so help him if Eli had a clue what to do with himself.

Mug in hand -- good dark roast with a drop of cream and a spoonful of brown sugar -- he meandered toward the couch, meaning to park it and put off a final decision of the day's agenda until he'd drunk it down to the last drop.

He should do something about Marybeth right away. He knew that.

Instead, he found himself at the window instead, mug in one hand and flicking the blinds open with the other. His eyes had not deceived him the night before. The old drugstore across the street was as gone with the wind as Rhett and Scarlett.

Eli sipped his coffee meditatively as he looked down at the empty storefront. A couple of hand-lettered signs still hung in the windows, but they'd faded from bright blue to a dull near gray above empty display shelves no doubt choked with dust. A chain and padlock rusted around the front doors.

Shame, that. A real shame. Eli would never tell Zane as much, but Zane wasn't the only one who'd cajoled an illicit egg cream from the soda fountain. He'd been curious. Sue him. Frankly, Zane could keep the creamy drinks and their attendant risk of salmonella, but there'd been something damned comforting about knowing he had only to cross the street if he needed something in the dead of night.

Ha! Eli had almost forgotten that. Not long before Marybeth left, she'd sent him on a midnight run for rubbers. He'd *run* too. Hormones and libido and the things they did to young -- well, younger -- men, eh? He took a deeper swig of his coffee as it cooled, and rubbed his thumb and forefinger together. A small scar, too little to notice unless he deliberately looked for it, marred the first knuckle. He'd hurried so that he'd pinched his hand in those doors and not realized he was bleeding until the sleepy-eyed cashier cleared his throat and tossed a box of Band-Aids on the counter next to his packet of Durex.

Such an idiot he'd been. Eli shook his head and chuckled at the memory. Damn lucky he hadn't gotten blood poisoning or a bigger scar. Less lucky now, when he'd run out of antacids and could have used one. Whether it was the thought of Marybeth that set his gastric juices to souring or damage done with too much Italian the night before, he couldn't say for sure.

He'd have a few choice words for the whims of fate if he *did* have an ulcer.

Eli thumped his chest in discontented dissatisfaction. A man should feel better after a good meal and a night's sleep, but honestly, he could have gone back to bed and napped half the day away.

Probably ought to go get himself checked out, he thought. Such a pain in the ass, though. It'd be handy enough to have the necessities of life close to home.

A location like that really would make for a decent neighborhood clinic. Better than decent.

Eli forgot the coffee growing cold in his cup as he studied the empty storefront. It wouldn't hurt to take a closer look, would it? Where was the harm?

* * *

STEFFON REALTY. Vandals had done their best to deface the sign, but enough remained to let Eli take down the information. Of course, nothing would come of it as such, but who knew? He might run into someone at Immaculate Grace who'd take an interest. Better to keep the information ready at hand.

In the meantime --

Given the track record of his life, Eli wasn't even slightly surprised to glance up and see Taye rounding the street corner as he saved and closed the note file. Hell, he'd gone so far as to buy a second bottle of water from a kiosk on his way from point A to point B. He held it out by the neck and waited for Taye to reach shouting distance. "I wondered when you'd turn up."

Taye shook his head, amusement mingling with weariness. "I'm not that predictable."

"Maybe you're not. Everyone else in your life is."

"Sometimes I wonder," Taye said with a snort. He uncapped the water but played with the top instead of drinking. Beads of condensation ran down his fingers. Christ, and it wasn't even noon yet. Another scorcher in the city. Global warming central started down on the streets. "If you're headed to the hospital, mind if I tag along?"

Eli didn't mind as such. He had his doubts as to whether or not Taye could keep up. Eli eyed the kid up and then down, letting him know he was doing it without going so far as to lay hands on the man. Contrary to what others might think, he'd developed a sort of friendship over the years with Taye. He still didn't see the resemblance between himself and the younger doctor that others claimed was there, but they got along well enough.

He hammered down on his half-empty water, still cold enough to make his palate ache with the brumal bite of it, and asked between sips, "So who called you? Zane or Holly?"

"Neither of them, if you'd believe it."

"I might have trouble swallowing that, yes."

"Good thing you've got some water, then," Taye said. He nudged Eli forward, setting them both on the path that'd lead to a nearby El station. "If you were waiting for the store to open, you might have been there a while."

"Funny man." Eli drained the bottle and crumpled the plastic. He tossed the empty in a trash can as they passed it. "If you're not drinking that, I'll take it."

Taye shrugged. He wiped condensation off on his sleeve and made the trade-off. "It's true, you know. No one asked me to check up on you. I did call your house to find out if you'd left yet, and then Zane when no one answered. Got him on his cell, but he made no suggestions. This one's all on me."

"Interesting." Eli eyed Taye with a dash more intent. As tired and heartsore as the kid looked, he kept up the walking pace just fine. Even made Eli work to match stride with him. "Which compels me to ask why. As I'm sure you know."

"I couldn't help noticing you still seemed to feel pretty rough last night. I know from personal experience by now what awful patients doctors make. No way you'd go get checked out on your own, so I figured I'd make a house call." Taye cracked a grin that made him look as young as his years. "I always did want to do that."

"Everybody's got to have a dream," Eli said. He shrugged uncomfortably. "I'm fine, kid. I know myself well enough to make the call. That's without taking Zane into consideration. He wouldn't have let me out to play if he thought there was any real reason for concern."

Taye made a noncommittal noise. "It's never a good idea for doctors to treat their loved ones. Not enough emotional distance. You should get a workup by someone who's not invested in wanting to spend a night on the town with you. Did he check your blood sugar?"

"And that's enough of that," Eli said, irritated. He'd hoped when he was younger that one day age would soften the quick strike of his temper. Alas for all things not meant to be. "Zane's a better doctor than that. Give him the credit he's due. Who are you to ask, anyway, Quincy?"

"Quincy?" Taye frowned. "Come again?"

For Pete's sake. Talk about feeling his age. "Never mind." Eli found he had almost gotten halfway down the second bottle of water. "Drop it, if you would. All of it. Please and thank you."

"At least some things never change," Taye said, his grin lingering. "The sun will rise in the east, deep-dish pizza is always a good option, and Eli is grumpy."

"Glad to be a touchstone of normalcy."

"You were the one who said everyone has to have a dream," Taye replied placidly. Point and match. Truth be told, Eli didn't so much mind. Taye had perked up to no end while trading friendly jabs, the banter putting a dash of color in his cheeks and a hint of the old familiar spark in his eye. Suited him better than dispirited monotones, for sure.

Eli stopped at a streetlight, glad of the chance to catch his breath. Not far now to the El. It'd feel better than it should to sit down. "Speaking of feeling rough..."

"Don't ask me about Richie." Taye had gone as stiff as if Eli had rammed a poker up where the sun didn't shine. Eli half expected him to cough and spit out fireplace soot. "I mean it."

"Okay, okay." Eli raised both hands. "Far be it from me to push. It's not as if I get pushed around by the well-meaning all day long."

Taye snorted. He might have cracked a glimmer of a smile. "The day anyone pushes you, Eli, will be the day the sun rises in the west."

"Try walking in my shoes for a day, and then smile when you say that."

"No deal," Taye replied. He tried to smile as he traded quips, but the tension in his shoulders made an almost painfully palpable knot, even from where Eli stood. "Come on. We're almost at the station."

So be it. Eli wouldn't push for more. Much more, anyway. He caught up to Taye in three steps and offered a conciliatory shrug. "Just letting you know the option's open."

"I know." Taye sighed. "For what it's worth, if I were going to talk to anyone about it, it'd be you. Can I have the rest of that?"

Eli had barely three sips' worth of water left in the second bottle, and serious doubts as to the amount of backwash compared to original product content, but hey, it would be Taye's funeral. "Knock yourself out. You look like you could use some hydration yourself."

"Not as much as you." Taye pinched up a bit of skin on Eli's wrist. The fold stayed half a second longer than it should have. "Seriously, Eli. Aftercare matters even when you're back home."

"You were saying, about not being pushed? Richie should --" Eli clamped his mouth shut. "Hell. Believe it or not, I had no intention of going back there."

"I do believe you." Taye glanced sideways. "Even so. You might never admit it, but you're dying of curiosity, aren't you?"

Eli turned his hands palms up as his sole reply. "You ever visit the soda counter at that old store when they were still open?"

"Not that I know of. Why?"

"No real reason. I'd been thinking it'd make a good location for a neighborhood clinic. Maybe headed up by someone young. Not you, being as you're a busy man, but still."

Taye rolled his eyes, but Eli would take what he could get. "Stop it before you hurt yourself."

Eli smirked internally. *Bingo*. He didn't need to know, no. On the other hand, if he got the scoop first, he wouldn't mind being ahead for once.

"It isn't much of a story," Taye said. He gestured for Eli to go ahead of him on the metal stairs up to the El station and waited to reach the top before he spoke.

"Or rather, it's just about the same story everyone tells. Things get rough a few years in. You either make it through, or you don't."

Eli frowned. "Any luck pinpointing the source?"

"No," Taye said, his smile falling away. "I've tried, believe me. He's tried. I don't think it's anything either of us have done. That'd be easy enough to handle. I'm always busy, and he's not busy enough. He's had trouble holding on to a job these past few months. I ask him why, but as far as I can tell, he doesn't know the answer himself."

"No ideas at all?" Eli asked, skeptical.

"I'm not sure. No, that's a lie." Taye crumpled the water bottle and sent it sailing into a trash bin. "There's this anger in him that I can't touch. He's always been a live wire, but it's different now. He's too quick to flare up. It isn't aimed at me, but that doesn't make it easier to live with."

"And you the clinical psychologist."

"He says that too." Taye dry washed his face. "So there you have it. My life in summary."

Eli didn't go in for too much of the touchy-feely -- he'd rather let Zane handle that -- but he put one hand on Taye's shoulder to give him a friendly jostle. "Sucks to be you, kid, but if anyone can find a way out of the hole, it'd be you."

He got a genuine grin out of Taye for that one. Good enough to be going on with.

"And not that you've been sharing --" he started.

"Heaven forbid," Taye murmured. "But?"

"*But*, any time you want to..." Eli made an expansive gesture that included the better part of his old neighborhood. "You usually know where to find me."

Taye nodded. He looked a little better, Eli

thought. Not chipper, but not glum. "I may take you up on that. Your pocket's ringing, by the way."

"Is it?" Vibrating, at least. Eli hadn't noticed. He checked the display just before the call went to voice mail. "Zane. Ten'll get you twenty he forgot something he needs today."

"Better call him back," Taye said. "You're right about that storefront, I think. It would be a great spot for a neighborhood clinic. I'm not the one to spearhead something like that, but I'll pass the word around and see if anyone's up for taking the bait. Oh, and Eli?"

"Hmm?"

Taye had the grace to look sheepish where Diana might have smirked or Holly petted him. "Run a basic hematology panel? I promise I'll leave you alone if you do."

"Somehow, I have a hard time believing that too, but fine, fine, fine. If it'll make you happy." Eli laid a hand on the kid's shoulder. Despite it all, he did know what he owed, how much, and to whom. Without Taye to talk some sense into him back in the days before he and Zane became an item... well. They wouldn't be an item now, would they? "I'll take care of it this afternoon. You have my word."

He'd talk to Holly and Diana later that day too. Point them in Richie's direction and see what good they could manage when they put their minds to it. He and Zane could take Taye's half of the affair and set about some good old-fashioned wrangling.

And then -- once he knew "what" and "why" and had identified the cure for future reference, just in case -- Eli figured he might just be ahead of the game.

Chapter Four

The door to Human Resources was shut. Eli tried the handle, giving it a good jiggle just in case the whole OUT TO LUNCH sign taped to the door was a prank. Because that was likely to happen. He shook his head in resigned frustration and reached for his phone. Better call Zane back now.

Zane picked up on the first ring. Were they still called that, when there wasn't any "ring" to them? Eli wondered. "Eli?"

"Nope. They call me Cool Hand Luke."

Zane's snort of laughter made Eli grin. "Sure they do. Everything okay? The day you don't answer the phone right away even in a dead sleep is the day I worry. I trained you better than that."

"You and every other drill sergeant who missed his calling and decided to train newbie doctors instead," Eli said, wanting to hear more of that amusement. Call him an addict if you liked. "I'm fine, Zane. Stop worrying so much. Do I look like I'm that close to death's door half the time?"

He peered at his reflection in the shuttered window of the door to Human Resources. He could stand to shave, maybe, but otherwise he looked just about the same as ever to himself.

"On occasion," Zane said. Trust him to be honest, if nothing else. *Huh.* "Sue me for worrying."

"Yeah, yeah, yeah." Eli leaned against the door. Strange to think it, but this was one of the things he liked best about intimacy with another man -- trading insults and teasing that really meant *I love you.* "What do you want, chief? I'm busy doing nothing."

"Far be it from me to interrupt." Zane sounded slightly harried now, though Eli didn't think the frustration was aimed in his direction. "Forgot a few things back at the apartment. Like lunch, or money to buy any with. The university canteen doesn't extend credit based on a man's good looks, sad to say. Also, one of the buttons on my shirt just gave way. Some ex-cop got grabby with me last night."

"You don't say. Hope you gave him hell."

"In a handbasket, and then some. Tie? Lunch? I've got an in-box jammed with egos that need deflating. If I turn my back for a second, they'll rise up in mutiny and drown me. I'll owe you."

"I'll think of some way for you to pay me back," Eli said, straight-faced.

"A man can hope," Zane replied, equally Sunday somber. Eli could just imagine him touching his lips to keep them steady. "See you in a few, Eli."

Eli chuckled quietly as he ended the call. He could pick up lunch for both of them at the Greek place they'd missed out on the night before. Zane would do anything for well-made souvlaki and warm flatbread with tangy hummus, with a diamond-shaped morsel of sticky honey-sweet pastry for dessert.

Or if they were closed, hell, food carts were thick as snow on the ground these days. As were kiosks where a man could buy anything from rubbers to roses to the daily news. Clinics weren't exactly sprinkled about like salt and pepper, but if one knew where to look, they wouldn't have too much trouble finding one.

Better to accept the whole tempting, frustrating notion as a pipe dream and move on. Get himself good and fit for heading back into the world.

Ah well.

Eli switched his phone off before he made for the stairwell that'd take him down and out. He'd promised to deal with the Marybeth situation later, true. Which didn't mean obsessing with her *now*. The last thing he needed was another text popping up when he handed over Zane's lunch.

What Zane didn't know wouldn't hurt him, after all.

* * *

Then again, as sayings went that one had a few obvious drawbacks.

Warm crinkled paper bags in hand, Eli studied a university floor directory mounted between a set of blue-enamel-painted elevators. He did remember which building Zane's temporary office was located in. Not a part associated with the medical college, but that was understandable enough. They'd save the cushy digs for those with tenure or influence.

Influence. Zane could have all he cared to, if he were willing to make more use of his family name. Eli understood why he preferred not to. Especially his mother's family. Ice water for blood and steel razor blades for tongues. Sometimes it baffled him how Zane had turned out a decent, affectionate human being. Eli wasn't too sure he'd have managed the feat.

Tenure... ah now, that would be another story. Eli figured a guy like Zane could go plenty far on his own merits. Give him a lever, and he could move the world; he had a peculiar genius that way. Not if he kept moving around, no, but that was his choice. Eli wouldn't stand in his way. The man had had enough barriers and barricades in his life already.

Eli scowled at the map. It couldn't have been *less* helpful if it'd been printed in reverse Esperanto.

Set at an angle to the elevator -- presumably where a receptionist could keep an eye out on the comings and goings of students and faculty -- Eli sniffed out a pair of what looked like student interns huddled over a messy stack of manila folders. Young enough for the remnants of acne, old enough for tongue piercings and attitude. He knocked on the frame of the open door to get their attention. "Dr. Novia's office?"

The female half of the duo blinked bleary eyes at him. Eli thought he recognized the look as the hasn't-slept-in-days special. The male -- Eli would hesitate to call him a "man" just yet -- had enough pep in his step to frown. "Who?"

Eli juggled the paper sacks jammed with gyros, black olives, crisp spanakopita, and soft warm flatbread to keep from dropping them. He'd bought too much, and he wondered now if he ought to have a visitor's pass. He wasn't sure if they did that here. "I'm looking for Dr. Novia. Zane? Midforties, interim lecturer?"

"The lecturers are in the basement," the boy said, visibly dismissing Eli from his consideration.

The girl gave Eli a dose of wary consideration. He'd looped Zane's tie loosely around his neck. Possibly it looked a little less professional and a little more eccentric than he'd intended. "Are you supposed to be here? I mean, does he know you're coming?"

He did last night. Eli kept the riposte locked behind his teeth. "No, I thought I'd surprise him," he said with his best deadpan. "Yes, he knows. He left some odds and ends behind this morning. Just want to drop the stuff by his office, and I'll be on my way."

The girl's lips formed a silent O. Eli could feel his face heat up as he watched her put two and two together. So she hadn't known. No reason why she should, he supposed, and no reason why he should care, but the tiny nose wrinkle inclined him to dislike her more than reason allowed.

At least she elbowed the boy quiet when he sat up, clearly ready to let loose with some kind of question that would require a dressing down in response.

Eli made a beckoning gesture. "No? If you're done, then, you said the basement. Want to look at the directory and be sure?"

An older fellow -- maybe in his early forties -- appeared in an office door behind them. Tall, lean, horse faced. A full head of hair mostly unmarred with gray and a neatly trimmed beard. Eli ran a hand over his own chin, wondering briefly if he should try and grow one again. Never did work out well. "Can I help you?"

"I'm just looking for Dr. Novia," Eli said, thoroughly weary of the shenanigans -- and wary when the professor's face lit up. He had far too many teeth, all of them a cosmetically unnatural shade of gleaming white.

"Zane, of course." The professor ambled casually toward the students. They winced but paid him far more attention and respect than they had Eli. "I know Zane. He's a good man. Are you a friend of his?"

"Something like that," Eli said, narrowing his eyes. "And you are?"

"Dr. Pedersen. Art history." He grinned at Eli as if they were old buddies. "I've had lunch with Zane a couple of times. It's amazing how much he knows about early Spanish --"

"Is it really," Eli said. "Lunch, was it?"

"Um," the girl said. She squeaked quietly. She flipped a folder open and ran her finger down the page. "It's the second floor, actually," she said. "Room 214."

Kids these days. Jeez. "Glad we got that sorted

out," Eli said. God help the future of the country if this was the next generation they had to depend on. He turned his back on the mini-gaggle of academics and made for the elevators, pretending he couldn't hear a hushed rush of whispers spring up the second he looked away.

So he'd behaved like a jackass. Hell with it. Tenure was overrated.

* * *

The numbering system on office doors made as little sense as the maps that supposedly pointed one there, but Eli found Zane sooner rather than later. So help him, if he'd ended up wasting half an hour trudging around the basement…

Zane had a small office stuck squarely between one belonging to, if the signage was to be believed, an adjunct professor in English Lit who favored patchouli mothballs and a lecturer from Mathematics who barely looked old enough to shave. The adjunct had accidentally or purposefully spilled a stack of paperwork into a messy cascade that edged into the corridor.

Eli preferred Zane's domain, once he got an unobstructed look in the door. Cool and neat, floors uncluttered and lights turned off, blinds rolled up to let the natural sunlight in. Zane half sat on a desk that'd been pushed under the window. He had a pen in one hand, a test paper in the other, and a belly full of frustration. Eli knew the look.

"Kids these days," Zane said without glancing up. His lips quirked. "I wondered if you'd gotten lost."

"How'd you know it was me?"

Zane beckoned Eli in with a wave of his pen-bearing hand. Dots and blots of red ink marred his palm. "I didn't, exactly." His stomach rumbled. "But I do know the smell of Greek spices, and hope springs eternal." Finally, he laid pen and paper aside and made eye contact, easy and pleased. "I'm guessing you didn't get my voice mail, though."

"The one you left before I called you?" On the wall next to the door, Eli found what he supposed to be a guest chair doing double duty as a journal storage unit. He shifted the lot aside to a new temporary home on the floor to give himself room to perch. While he was down there, he blotted his face against his sleeve. *Whew*. Hot today. He'd worked up a sweat en route.

"No. Here, let me." Zane crouched to scoop up the journals before they made like dominos. He moved with the fluid easiness of a man half his age, popping up and down with nary a creak or crack from aging joints. He tapped the journals together to neaten the edges and stacked them on an empty shelf. "I'd thought maybe we could go out and get something together, or walk around the block and pick up a to-go. You haven't eaten yet, have you?"

Not to speak of. He'd thought the Greek place would tempt him, but he had no real appetite. Still, to say so would be to invite concern. Best avoid that.

"Too much Italian last night. I think I'm still full," Eli said in excuse for himself. "Who's Dr. Pedersen?"

Zane blinked. "Who?"

Eli relaxed minutely. Zane wasn't much of a dissembler. Lunch, forsooth. "Dr. Teeth."

"Ohh, that one." Zane wrinkled his nose. "He's nosy as a bloodhound, but he's mostly harmless. You ran into him? Are you sure you won't eat?"

Eli raised one shoulder in a slight shrug. "More like he ran into me." He broke open the bag and offered Zane one-half of a gyro, keeping the other portion for himself. He could nibble. "If it'll make you feel better."

"It will, actually. Cheers." Zane lifted the sandwich as one might a glass and saluted Eli. He took a giant bite that left a dot of mysterious sauce on the corner of his mouth and mumbled something unintelligible through the crumbs. "Hnruf garf?"

"I take it that means the selection appeals to Sir." Eli shook his head, amused. He fished out a napkin and dropped the paper bag to hand it to Zane. "You're supposed to eat the food, not wear it."

Zane shot him the finger but took the napkin Eli offered and patted his chin. "Mmm. God, that's good. Manna from heaven."

"Glad to hear it. After all, I bought it with my own two hands. And that's without the trouble of transport. Uphill. Both ways. In the snow."

"Idiot." Zane swung his calf out to nudge Eli affectionately with the tip of his shoe. "Do you remember those 'love is' posters from a couple decades back? Love is still-warm junk food, regardless of transport through snow."

Snow would be fantastic, Eli thought. He sneaked a second napkin for himself and patted his forehead. Building maintenance must have not gotten around to shutting boilers down for the advent of warmer weather. How Zane could stay cool as a cucumber beat the hell out of him. "Mind opening the window?"

"Sure, no problem." Zane twisted easily at the waist to flick open the latches and crack the lower pane open a few inches. "Must be hotter outside than it looks. I was thinking about snitching a lab coat, actually, but there's no harm in fresh air all the same. You didn't get my call before, then?"

Eli shook his head with absolute honesty. Must have come in after he'd turned his phone off. *Damn*. He made a show of checking the blank display. "My fault. Don't worry about it. I ran into Taye and got distracted. He worries as much as you do sometimes. Said I ought to go get a basic blood panel drawn."

Zane made a thoughtful noise. "Getting a new baseline might not be a bad idea," he said, then one-two following up with, "Batteries dead?"

"Who knows? I consider myself lucky that I know how to turn it on and off."

"Luddite," Zane said with a cheeky grin that -- thank God -- seemed to signal his letting the phone question drop at last.

"You're a fine one to talk." Eli found a more comfortable position on the chair, one that cradled his hips just right. *Ahh. Much better.* "Too bad I did miss the message. I could have gone for a stroll around my old stomping grounds."

"They'll still be there later. We'll make time for it. You get homesick when we're away for too long. I've noticed, you know," Zane said, turning momentarily serious. He capped the water and tilted his head to watch Eli, fondness softening the firm line of his jaw. "I'd have a hard time not noticing as much. I do know what you give up to come abroad with me. You should know it's appreciated."

Eli shrugged uncomfortably. "No one's twisting my arm."

"Nevertheless." Zane crumpled his empty sandwich wrapper and looked pointedly at the half in Eli's hand until Eli made himself take a bite. "Someday you'll learn to take a compliment."

"I wouldn't hold my breath." Eli resealed the wrapping on his portion of the gyro -- his tongue liked it, but his stomach didn't -- and bent to dig in the bag for a packet of baked Sriracha potato chips. He wasn't sure, but he seemed to remember Zane had loved those when they first came out. Fiery as they were, possibly he only loved to hate them, but when they'd caught Eli's eye he hadn't been able to resist buying them.

As Eli bent, he caught a flicker of movement in his peripheral vision. Red plaid and cheap gold. Smelled like nosy students to him. The kids from reception? Eli growled under his breath, annoyed.

"Ignore it, Eli," Zane said. He'd noticed them too. He looked rueful and tired but more tolerant than Eli. He always had been. "They're mostly harmless too. Let them do their thing. They'll be out of the way all the quicker, and better that they go with the whole story than a concoction of suspicions."

True enough, Eli supposed. That didn't mean he had to like it. He tossed Zane the chips with an overhand throw and, after brief consideration, winged the baklava in its greaseproof paper his way too. "You think knowing the truth stops people from embroidering as they please?"

"Of course not. I'm just not sure why it should bother me enough to care what they think." Zane exhaled quietly, leaving Eli uncomfortably feeling as if he'd disappointed Zane more than usual.

And why should that be? Zane knew his faults and foibles better than any other man alive. Eli kneaded at the back of his neck in mild but growing frustration. "I don't care what they think. I..." He didn't like anyone knowing his business. Period, full stop. He shifted position, making to cross his legs but not able to get the right leverage in the low office chair. Giving up, he ran an impatient hand through his hair. "Forget it, would you? It doesn't matter."

"I'd very much like to, but to forgive and forget requires a certain degree of 'live and learn.'" Zane crumbled off a bite of baklava but didn't eat it. "You know, this is one thing I don't miss about Chicago. You're touchier in the city."

Eli scanned back over his memories and wasn't sure he could see the difference. "Am I?"

"This time around, you are." Zane snaffled the phone out of his hand before Eli could blink.

"Hey!"

"Thought so," Zane said, apparently missing Eli's grab for the phone. Sure, now he could pick and choose. "Aha. You must have turned it off. Most people butt dial. Leave it to your bony hips."

"No harm, no foul," Eli said, making another unsuccessful swipe. His ears were hot. "Give it back. I'll listen to your message now."

"Hold your horses. Let me check and make sure everything works."

Eli had never put a password on his private phone. He'd never seen the need before. Possibly something he should have invested the five minutes in making happen. When Zane thumbed the readout to life, the pip that announced a waiting voice mail gave way to the tinkling factory-standard chime of a text.

Given the pale grimness that descended in a cloud to mask Zane's face, Eli didn't have to work hard at guessing who that text might be from.

He held up one hand, finger pointed at Zane. "Whatever you're thinking, it's not like that."

"Isn't it?" Zane's tone was unreadable. Not that that fooled Eli, especially not when Zane tossed the phone into his lap. Whipped it, rather. Eli barely caught the unit in time to keep it from bouncing off and hitting the floor. "I'd like to hear how it is, then.

Because to be frank, Eli, as it stands it's a little hard to misinterpret."

Good God, what had Marybeth said? Eli flicked the display back to life.

She'd figured out how to make the texts display her name as the sender. *Super.*

Not sure if you're getting these? I'm at the Sun Hotel, room 2113. Give me a call, Eli.

Eli groaned. "Okay, let me explain."

"Sure," Zane said, still far too calm. "You might want to read the second one first, though."

"There's a second one?" Eli tapped his thumb against the screen. More from luck than design, he hit upon an icon that slotted the second text in front of the first.

Just like old times, isn't it? Looking forward to seeing you again, Eli. XXOO Marybeth.

Seriously? Eli covered his face with one hand. Somewhere out there, Diana was laughing at him, and unless Eli missed his guess, the two students lurking outside had been joined by a third of indeterminate gender. Whoever they were, they boasted both a fauxhawk and death wish enough to cock their head for better listening.

"Signed with a kiss." Zane made a clipped gesture at Eli. "Feel free to jump in and elaborate at any time."

It looked pretty damning. Eli wouldn't deny that. But neither would he sit still to be accused at Zane's leisure. "It's not what you think," he said, jabbing at the air between them, "And it's not what it looks like. *Not.* I have no idea what Marybeth wants, but I have no intention of seeing her. Okay? But even if I did plan to pay her a visit, then so what? My ex-wife's being in town doesn't mean I'm going to switch seats on the bisexual train."

Zane laid the crumpled bag down. "Excuse me?"

Now what? "For fuck's sake, Zane. I said, that doesn't mean I'm going to --"

"Right." Zane brushed crumbs off his lap and stood with neat, precise movements. "That's what I thought." He turned his back on Eli and made for the desk proper, buried as it was beneath stacks of paper and periodicals. He took up a stack of stapled quizzes and another pen as he went. "If you're done with lunch, you can find your own way out."

Eli gaped at him, indignant question marks firing so fast and thick he wouldn't have been surprised if they'd appeared over his skull like in the cartoons. "Do you want to tell me what I did? Because I'm not seeing it."

"Exactly." Zane wouldn't look up from his papers. "Eli," he said, very measured and far too calm, "I do love you -- and I don't give a damn who might be listening to me say that --"

The students clustered outside scattered like guilty mice.

"But right now, I think you and I need to part ways for the afternoon before I say something I regret speaking, or you say something I regret hearing."

"Zane," Eli said in protest. "*Zane.* Come on."

Zane ignored him. His pen scratched over the paper.

For God's sake. Eli kicked the chair back harder than necessary when he stood, and though he glowered at Zane, he didn't make a dent in the man's nitroglycerin shell. He had no plans to entangle himself in Marybeth's life again, but he couldn't help remembering -- with fondness -- that at least he'd never had to play this kind of guessing game with her.

Almost enough to make a man want to --

Eli shunted the thought aside. *Hell with this.* He left Zane's office without saying good-bye.

The students, at least, had sense enough to avoid eye contact when Eli stalked back through the lower halls and slammed his way out the front doors with a little too much force. Who said people couldn't learn from their mistakes?

Chapter Five

The sign taped to the door of Human Resources hadn't budged in the -- what was it, two hours? Eli scowled at the paper, then deliberately retaped it cockeyed. He wondered if he ought to put a strip of tape across from door to wall. A sign could be left in place, but --

He clapped a hand to his face and sighed. Righteous indignation was one thing, and conspiracy theories quite another. Maybe the good folks inside were avoiding him. Hell, if Eli put himself in their shoes, he wouldn't be able to blame them. Their jobs couldn't be anything but thankless, trying to stretch zero money across a couple thousand paychecks. It had to sap the heart and soul out of a person.

But it still didn't feel any too good to stand in front of the firmly closed door, with nary a hint of hope in sight.

Really, it wasn't hard to understand how Zane felt sometimes.

* * *

Diana did not appear to be on the schedule for that day.

Eli scowled at the messy notations on the whiteboard with its multiple strike-throughs and smudges of dry-erase ink. Looked like she'd been, and then she'd gone. Figured, didn't it? Actually go in search of the woman, and she was nowhere to be found. Hope devoutly not to encounter her, and trip over her with every other step.

The flow of traffic through the nurse's station dodged around Eli. Most seemed to recognize him, and several gave him curious sideways looks, but no one stopped to say hello. Busy as bees in an overcrowded hive, sure, but he had no stethoscope around his neck or employee badge to validate his being there. He would have thought someone would ask what he was doing there. He would almost have welcomed a growl from a security guard.

Eli checked his phone. No new messages. Either Marybeth had given up, or she'd decided to bide her time. Part of Eli wanted nothing more than to cut to the chase, hit redial, and ask. The other part wanted to take off running for the border and not look back.

Which made no sense, not as such. They hadn't parted on the warmest of terms, but Eli wouldn't have called Marybeth an enemy. More like a frustrated friend who couldn't figure out any more than he could how things had gone so awry between them. He still didn't know for sure when they'd started to sour. Maybe it'd been coming from day one. Cops made bad husbands, or at least Eli the Cop had. Eli the Student made no better a showing for himself.

She'd put up with a hell of a lot from him, come to think of it. And taken it with better grace.

The way she'd smiled when she met Zane, now. Eli would never forget that. Not a warm smile. More like a sideways slant of her mouth, lips pressed together. The slant pointed up, so it couldn't have been called a frown or a scowl, but…

Women. If Eli ever managed to understand them, someone had better be there at the finish line to award him a chestful of medals.

Diana had never met Marybeth as far as Eli knew. Saint Peter have mercy. The idea made him shiver. Either they'd love each other, or they'd be able to see the explosion from space. Either way, not much of the hospital would be left standing afterward. TNT and a lit match, that's what they'd be.

Holly and Marybeth had gotten along like rum

and cola. That figured too, really.

Might as well see if Holly had gone home yet, Eli decided. Not that he intended to seek her out for the sake of counsel. But if he happened to find her, he could… pass the word about Taye. Right. That'd do.

* * *

Holly did not seem surprised to see him, which surprised Eli not at all when he made his way to the nursing station on the psych unit. Not all doctors were welcome to set up camp behind the station -- very few, come to think of it -- but Holly tended to insert herself in places and spaces in such a way as to make it seem as if she'd always been there.

"Eli, hello," she said, looking up from a slim stack of test results. She closed the lid of her notebook computer and stacked the papers atop it, readouts turned down. Eli appreciated the professionalism. He had no need to see. "What brings you by?"

Eli chose a nice comfortable storage file to lean against. "Looking for Diana, and I came up short."

"I see." Holly folded her hands demurely beneath her chin. "You don't have to loom, Eli. Let me find a seat for you."

Eyeing the busy to-and-fro of the nurses made Eli less than inclined to take her up on the invitation. They'd tolerate Holly, but not a long-legged interloper. Best not to push his luck. He waved a hand in silence to decline as politely as he could. The last thing he needed was Holly picking up on his pique with Zane --

And she didn't. Well. Not as such. Holly gave him a once-over that somehow managed to be both intrusive and polite. The lady had skills. "How are you feeling, Eli?"

Eli eyed her. "Reasonable, for my age. Why do you ask?"

"Your age is really quite comparably young," Holly said. "Or so you've always seemed to me. If you're old, I have to admit I'm getting old, and I'm not in a hurry for that."

Eli chuckled despite himself. "The day you're old is the day we can all hang up our hats and go home."

"And that won't happen anytime soon." Holly picked up a pen and held it loosely between two fingers. Eli kept an eye on her. He wouldn't put a little bit of voodoo or mesmerism past the woman. "What's on your mind, Eli?"

Hell. "You can't tell just by looking?"

She twinkled at him. "If I were that good, I wouldn't need to keep regular office hours. I do know the look, Eli. I'm glad to listen if you want to talk, you know. You can sit here, or we could go back to my office. Whatever you like."

Eli couldn't help backpedaling. "Nah. No need."

Holly sighed quietly but didn't look frustrated. Practice had made that particular aspect perfect, Eli supposed. "All right, Eli. Just as long as you know the option is open to you. Though I really would suggest you rest for a few minutes. I'm not sure I like your color."

"Just some heartburn. It comes and goes. I'll be fine." Darn Diana anyway for not being in. "I promised Taye I'd get a basic panel drawn down in the lab. He worries too much, but what the hell, if it'll make him happy."

"Mmm," Holly said. "You saw him today, then. How is he?" One blue eye closed in a quick wink. "I can't tell just by looking."

"Rough, I guess?" Eli gave in to the urge and snagged a rolling stool from under the station desk. He'd give it back if anyone asked. "Tired. Frustrated.

And yes, I'm talking about Taye, not myself."

Holly's nose crinkled when she laughed. "I think I've told you before how the two of you are peas in a pod."

"And I still don't see it."

"I suppose you don't." She patted his hand. "I think Taye and Richie do have what it takes, you know. I always have. Rough patches are a natural part of any relationship's progress. It'd be more worrying to come across a couple who never fought."

Eli blinked at her. "Seriously?"

"Of course. Conflict is never pleasant, but we're all only human, and such is the nature of the beast." Holly watched him as she spoke, never raising her voice above a pleasant murmur. "Learning the ins and outs of conflict *resolution* is the key to successful navigation of a love affair. Those who understand the knack of that are the ones who celebrate silver anniversaries. As Keith and I will do next year, did you know?"

"I see what you're doing here," Eli grumbled. He exhaled and ran a hand backward through his hair. "And if I have no idea what I'm doing wrong or right, or if I'm anywhere near figuring myself out. Where do I even start?"

"Where anyone starts with anything, Eli." She smiled at him. "At the beginning."

"Which is all very well and good," Eli said, keeping his voice level, "but that's my point. How do I know where the beginning even is? I'm clueless here, Holly. Throw me a bone."

"I'm trying. If you don't know something, then your first task is to find out."

"How, though?"

"*Eli.*" Holly laid her hand atop his, bringing him

to an abrupt halt. "By asking, you goose. That's it. All you have to do is *ask*."

Eli bit his tongue. And then…

Holly's smile widened just a touch as he slumped back. "Okay. Good, Eli. That's a place to start."

Eli shook his head in silence. Not denying what she said so much as resignation to its truth. Lucy van Pelt charged a nickel in her practice. Holly had probably done a decent side business in firstborn children to get this good. "Why do you have to be right so often?"

"A great deal of practice. And experience." She patted his wrist. "It'll be all right. I think you have it in you to be pleasantly surprised."

From her lips to God's ears. The least Eli could do was try.

She seemed to sense that and sat up straighter with one last pat to his hand. "You're not a patient, so I can't write the order for the blood work you wanted. However, I can put a word in with the hospitalist on call, and he'll get you set up for the next available. Will that do?"

Eli had to fight the urge to either rumple her hair or put an arm around her shoulders and hug her. "It'll do for a start. Like you say. Holly? I, eh…"

She winked at him and turned her attention back to her files. "You're welcome, Eli. Stop eating so much spicy food in the meantime. That'll help more than anything."

* * *

Eli opened his apartment door to the sound of running water. He shut the door behind him and stood with one hand on the knob, his head tipped to catch the direction of the noise. *Bathroom.* The shower.

So. He wasn't home alone. Though he'd stopped thinking of this place as "home" a while back in his everyday subconscious, at some point over the past few days he'd forgotten.

Could be he wasn't the only one.

Zane had left his tie draped over the back of the couch. As best Eli could tell, his shoes lay where they'd fallen when he kicked them off, probably while sitting down. He could imagine it easily enough. Zane, stewing as dusk fell, tapping a nail against the screen of his phone in a hummingbird tattoo of frustration and stubbornness and never calling. Finally seeking the comfort of warm water and white noise.

Eli might not know much, but he knew medicine, and he knew Zane.

Picking up after Zane took barely a minute. Even when piqued, Zane wasn't one to make a mess. Eli tidied away the discarded line of clothes leading to the bathroom -- and there he hesitated, listening to the noise from within. Not much of it. Water pattering against tile and skin, minimal splashing. Not washing himself, then, but only standing beneath the spray and getting dug too deeply into his own head.

All right, then. Eli rapped his knuckles once, twice, three times on the door, turned the knob, and stepped inside.

He waited by the door for his eyes to adjust. Zane had plugged in the night lamp instead of flicking a switch for the harsher overhead light. Eli preferred the softer deep-amber glow, himself, and it didn't take much getting used to. He blinked and saw Zane standing stock-still behind the frosted glass, water flowing down and around him, arrested in midmotion.

Eli inclined his head. He imagined frown lines popping up in Zane's forehead at that but didn't let that stop him and didn't explain himself. Better to show than to tell. Neatly, carefully, slowly, he undid the buttons on his shirt and shrugged the cloth off his shoulders and then the trousers down his hips, followed by boxers, watch, and socks. Nothing he hadn't done in a locker room; hell, nothing he hadn't done with Zane more than a few times.

Why it felt so very like a first time, he couldn't have said. He could sense every move Zane made, abbreviated as they were, watching him undress. When he finished, he put his palm on the handle of the shower door and pulled it open to release a puff of fragrant steam.

Zane looked at Eli, confusion and carefully repressed emotion clear as day, written in bold lines on his face to someone who knew him well enough to speak the language. Which, handily enough, Eli did.

He made a small gesture to the left. "Move over, Zane."

Zane looked from Eli to a washcloth that'd lost all its soap as he held it motionless against his chest. He folded the cloth in neat thirds and hung it over the cold-water spigot. Without a word, he stepped back under the spray, giving Eli room enough to join him.

Good enough for a start.

Eli shut the door to trap the heat and steam inside with them. Zane stood under the water and blocked most of it from reaching Eli, but that suited his purposes well enough. "Here." He picked up the shampoo from the nook where it lived and pointed the bottle at Zane. "Bend your head."

"Eli --" Zane started with a frown of bafflement.

"Bend your head," Eli said again. He poured a quarter-sized puddle of shampoo into the cup of his palm. "Please."

Zane exhaled, a gusty sigh, and did as he'd been asked. Though there wasn't much room in a shower not built for two to go backward or forward, he came a step closer to Eli. Better still, Eli thought. He guided Zane under the spray to get his hair good and wet before he laid hands on the man.

Zane sighed again, smaller and quieter, and shivered once before going quiet.

Okay, then.

"I'm not denying your right to be pissed off with me," Eli said as he rubbed soap and crisp cedar-scented foam deep into Zane's hair. "God knows I'm a master at stuffing my foot in my mouth. Hell, I wouldn't last a day in a relationship with myself."

Zane snorted quietly. Not quite a laugh, but not far from one. Good, even if Eli couldn't see his face behind the fall of wet hair that hung down to block his view. He lifted Zane's chin, careful to smooth wet hair away without letting soap drip and sting the man's eyes. They looked red enough already. Damn.

Eli took care to keep his touch gentle, but not so light as to let Zane turn his head if he had a mind to. "What I do have a problem with is you shutting me out without letting me know what I've done."

He knew why Zane did it. Repress and deny. It was how he'd been raised and just about all he knew before Holly, Diana, and then Eli wandered into his life.

But if Eli could change his ways, then so could Zane. It was only fair.

Still... baby steps. One move at a time.

Zane reached up to cover Eli's hand with his. "I didn't..." he started, then cleared his throat to try again. "I didn't know you considered yourself bisexual."

Eli bit back the growl of annoyed frustration that wanted to come out. It wouldn't have helped. He stiffened his fingertips instead and massaged Zane's scalp under the still-hot water, easing the soap out wave by wave. "I don't."

"And yet it's the word that jumped to the tip of your tongue."

"Maybe so," Eli allowed. He didn't know how to say this. Gruffness made him sound rougher than he usually did. "It'd be an accurate word. I was married to a woman for a good damn while, Zane, and that's not news to you. Hell, you were married too. You're the one who told me that story."

"I know. It's just..." Zane shook his head as he trailed off.

"It's just you keep waiting for the other shoe to drop," Eli finished for him. Which made sense, but -- what? Zane couldn't trust him? The frustration cut deep, and it must have showed, though Zane hid his flinch well. Would have fooled anyone besides Eli.

Zane's hair was clean enough to squeak under Eli's searching fingertips. He tucked wet strands behind Zane's ears, first the left and then the right, and watched Zane search his face for something only he knew how to identify.

Let him. Eli wasn't keeping a secret now. "I don't consider myself bisexual," he said. "I'm just Eli. And I'm with you. Does anything else matter?"

Zane closed his eyes. He covered Eli's hand with his own, resting against his cheek, and bowed his head once more. "No," he said, whisper loud in the quiet space of tile and water. "No, it doesn't." He pushed into Eli's hand. "Thank you."

"Okay, then." Eli lowered his head to rest against Zane's. "Try not to do that again, would you? I'm getting too old for this shit."

Zane's laugh rang out and echoed back, brighter on the reverb.

"What? You think this is funny?" Eli poked him between the ribs, a light tickle. He put one arm around Zane's waist to keep them from falling. "You're no spring chicken yourself, you know."

"Speak for yourself, Grandpa," Zane said. He mirrored Eli's stance, his arm around Eli's back. Shifting brought them closer, chest to chest and groin to groin. Zane's free hand wandered lower. "Or if you let this do the talking, well. It doesn't feel old to me."

Eli found the places where his hands fit just so on Zane's hips and jostled their bodies one against the other. "I could say the same thing about you."

"That you could." Zane took Eli's face in one hand and stretched up to kiss him.

Eli met him halfway.

He could feel the relief and release in Zane's shoulders and chest as he touched his tongue to Zane's. Slow and easy did it. Neither of them needed to be in any hurry. Zane hummed quietly and opened his mouth wider to give Eli room to play as long and lazily as he liked --

Though long and lazy did lead to consequences, Eli would have to admit. His breathing quickened into rough puffs and dragged inhalations, and his pulse climbed at a rapid, steady pace. When he stopped, his lips were pleasantly numb, almost tingling, and his cheeks felt raw with the rub of stubble against his face.

Eli remembered, then, what he'd meant to do the next time they had a few minutes and a notion to use them in play. He ran his fingertips against Zane's shoulders in a slow loop. Seemed so easy in concept. He wouldn't even have to ask out loud. Just turn round about and lean on the shower wall, head braced on his folded arms. Zane was a smart man. He'd figure out what Eli wanted.

But… not this time. This wasn't so much about that sort of give and take. Better to come to it from a steadier place.

They'd have other chances. Eli closed his eyes and let the impulse slip away on a breath of steam.

Zane didn't seem to notice. He skimmed one palm down Eli's back, wet hand slippery as silk as it came to rest over Eli's ass. "Hi."

"Hello yourself," Eli replied, slitting his eyes open for a look at Zane. God, but he was gorgeous. Sometimes Eli wondered why it'd taken him so long to see it and why it still surprised him. He feigned a nip at the tip of Zane's nose. "I know that look. You're plotting. Care to share?"

Zane's face had warmed with the kissing and with impish mischief. He took a double handful instead of a single and kneaded with a surgeon's light touch, not enough but more than plenty sufficient to get Eli's motor revving in first gear. "How are your knees, old man? Strong enough to hold you up?"

Eli blinked. Zane wasn't suggesting --

But he was. Gentle but firm, Zane crowded Eli to the back wall of the shower. Eli spared a moment to be grateful this wasn't a combination tub with a rim to slip and trip on. "Should I be asking about your knees?"

"They're in tip-top condition."

"I thought you might say that. Zane…" Eli caught him before he started his descent, checking for truth in the man's eyes. "You don't have to."

Zane took Eli's hand from its place beneath his chin and pressed his lips to the knuckles. "I know I don't have to," he said. "I want to. And I think you want me to as well."

He wasn't wrong.

Eli silently thanked the cool, wet tile of the shower wall for being there to hold him up. *He* had his doubt about his knees, but Zane took him by the hips to keep him steady, and with Zane's knees planted in front of Eli's hips, there was no chance he'd slip and fall -- not even when Zane ducked his head to take Eli deep in his mouth and envelop him in tight, wet heat.

"*Oh*... fuck," Eli sighed, dropping his head back. "Zane, God."

Zane kneaded Eli's hips roughly, making quiet noises that reminded Eli of the sound a cat made when it'd gotten the canary and the cream. Not inappropriate, he supposed. He groaned as he tried to hold back, keeping his hands to himself until Zane took them without breaking contact and nudged them to his head. Zane's hair did squeak, it was so clean. Good job well done, if he did say so himself.

Though forming words was beyond him at the moment. Eli closed his eyes and let himself drown in the steam and the slow, tugging pulls at his cock. He could feel the deep, rolling burn start low in his stomach, arrows making their way down and down and down, and hissed between his teeth as Zane coaxed him harder still. His toes curled into knots of knuckles and sinew. It took all the effort he could spare not to pull too hard at Zane's hair. Good. So good. God, so --

He groaned when he came, a basso growl that filled his ears and made Zane's shoulders shake with approval and amusement. When he pulled off -- and Eli could trust himself to look down and focus -- Zane's lips were cherry pink. Wet, neither of them seemed to have gray in their hair.

"Forgiven?" Zane asked. "Though that wasn't why I was upset with you. Not completely why."

Eli knew. It was still good to hear. He curled his fingers, beckoning Zane to stand and be kissed. Eli tasted himself in Zane's mouth. Funny how a man got used to some things. Learned to crave them, even. "Forgiven and forgotten -- if it goes both ways."

Zane landed a light slap on Eli's ass. "Close enough for horseshoes and hand grenades," he said. "We're never going to get it perfect, you know."

"And?" Eli frowned. "No one does. That's not what I was ever looking for. What?" Zane had burst into silent laughter. "No, what? I didn't say anything funny."

"So you think." Zane drew Eli in for one more kiss and one more slap to the ass before he leaned back to turn the slowly cooling water off. "Come on, you. We're nowhere near done yet. You can give me what I've got coming to me in bed."

Sounded like a plan Eli could roll with, even if he still didn't get the joke.

* * *

Later -- before he could slip into sleep, tempting as that was with Zane's head pillowed on his chest -- Eli jostled Zane lightly to catch his attention. "Still awake?"

"Just barely." Zane fluffed up a patch of Eli's chest hair. He stretched his legs and insinuated one foot beneath Eli's ankle. "Do I need to be?"

"Only a minute longer." Eli cleared his throat. "Just so you don't think I'm dodging, I want you to know I'm going to do something about the Marybeth question tomorrow."

He could feel the abrupt tension in Zane's focus

on him. "All right," he said slowly. "Any ideas what?"

"No," Eli had to admit. He ruffled up the soft hair at Zane's nape. "But I'll think of something. Promise. Okay?"

Zane's breath warmed the hollow of Eli's throat. Though he took his time about answering, Eli believed him when he nodded.

And that'd do just fine.

Chapter Six

"You're not leaving already, are you?"

"Would that I didn't have to." Zane tipped back the last drops of smoky espresso and slid out of his seat in the café booth across from Eli. It took some doing. Eli reserved serious doubts about whether these booths had been constructed by someone who understood the relative dimensions of a normal human adult, much less one with long arms and legs. "Oof. There."

Eli sat sideways, himself. Only way to keep from kicking his companions every time he took a breath. "Here." He tossed Zane the light jacket he preferred to a lab coat while teaching and watched Zane shimmy his arms into the sleeves. He wore a belt buckle of tarnished bronze that reflected the noonday light in a cloudy halo. A punch of pleased warmth hit Eli in the gut to realize it was one of his.

Zane did have a winning way of marking out territory lines.

Eli enjoyed the view as he leaned back. "Sure you have to go?"

Zane chuckled. "Dr. Jameson, I never. Are you trying to tease me into playing hooky?"

Eli gave that one due consideration. He popped a ripe cherry in his mouth, chewed, and swallowed, then folded his hands very seriously across his lap. "Yes."

Diana snorted.

Eli ignored her. No one else looking? Good. He flashed a quick wink at Zane.

Zane shook his head, apparently well amused by Eli's antics. "I'm not sure what's gotten into you today, but feel free to offer it regular employment and a steady wage."

"Funny man." Eli licked his lips, a sign of

nervousness that Zane picked up on. He caught Zane's hand for a quick squeeze and ran his thumb over Zane's knuckles. "Go do what you've gotta do. When do you get off, five?"

"Close enough." He'd piqued Zane's curiosity now. Eli could see it in the tilt of his head and curious angle of his eyebrows. "Why do you ask?"

"Ask me no questions, and I'll tell you no lies," Eli said. He bumped knuckles with Zane and let go. "The way I figure, that should put you back at the apartment by six. I recommend not being late."

"Oh, *do* you now?" The hook looked to be well and truly set. Zane adjusted the hang of his jacket on his shoulders as he studied Eli.

Eli gave him the best blank face he could muster. He'd have reckoned it to be about an eight out of ten. Maybe a six from the Russian judge.

Good enough to tickle Zane's funny bone, which had after all been more or less the point. Zane's smile widened as he thumped Eli on the shoulder. "Have it your way. But it'd better be good after a buildup like this."

Eli certainly hoped so. "Have I ever let you down? In the long run," he amended hastily. "On second thought, don't answer that."

"Too late. And no… you haven't, have you? How about that?" Zane thumbed the side of Eli's neck, as good as a kiss.

Diana made a cooing sound.

Zane gave Eli his wink back, with interest. "Until the evening, Doctor."

Hopefully so. "Go on, get out of here." Eli leaned back against the wall, watching Zane go. He held up a finger before Diana could speak. "*Still* no. Not a word."

"As if," Diana told him cheerfully. "Come on, Eli. Who do you think you're talking to?"

"Fair point." With Zane gone, Eli had enough leg room opposite to swing around and face more or less forward. "Although you know I'm not going to tell you."

"Not a problem. I'll get it out of Holly later."

Again, fair point. And just to prove that if you spoke of the devil, he *would* appear, when Eli glanced to where Holly stood in a quiet eave next to the restrooms, cell phone pressed to her ear, she sensed his regard and lifted one small hand in a wave.

Hmm. Eli tapped the tabletop and narrowed his gaze, trying to assess the implications of her demeanor. Hopefully she'd touched base with the contacts she'd sworn owed her a favor. Tickets to the theater and a reservation for two at a steakhouse hung in the balance. He'd owe *her* for more or less the rest of his natural life in turn, but what the hell. He'd give Zane a night out like he'd never managed before. Call it thanks, or call it courtship, or call it whatever you liked. Eli wasn't too old a dog to learn new tricks.

And maybe -- just maybe -- he'd have the stones to turn the tables in bed. Let himself be turned. The more Eli thought about it, the more he wanted to know what it was like to be taken. The thought lingered no matter where he went, pleasantly sharp like a new bruise he couldn't help poking. Zane seemed to like it well enough, and he liked Zane. Ergo...

As if she'd heard the inner commentary or picked up on the question marks dancing over Eli's head, Holly crinkled her eyes with amusement and offered Eli a thumbs-up.

"Devil woman," Eli muttered.

"Eerie, isn't it?" Diana asked. She nipped open a

packet of sugar substitute and emptied it into her half-full mug.

"That's rich, coming from you. You're her best friend."

"Still eerie." Diana tried the coffee and made a satisfied sound. She studied him for a moment. "You're looking better, Eli."

So Eli had seen for himself in the mirror that morning. Good to hear it from someone else. "I feel better."

Which he did. No headache, no residual fatigue that made his knees wobble, not a hint of the gray fog that'd made thinking more of a struggle than necessary. The nagging suspicion of an ulcer lingered, but at the back of Eli's mind, not at the forefront. He wouldn't have said he was ready to run a race or anything, nor was he quite as pink-cheeked as Zane, but he had more than enough zip in his line to be going on with.

"Do you?" Taye, as was his wont, appeared very nearly out of nowhere. Zane liked to tease Eli about not paying sufficient attention to his surroundings when encircled by these strange friends of theirs, but Eli would swear at gunpoint that there was more to it than that. Good thing he wasn't the jumpy sort.

Eli patted his chest. "Fit as a fiddle. Two fiddles, even."

Taye made an impressed noise and a dubious face. Eli flicked an empty sugar packet at him. "Sit down before you give me neck strain looking all the way up there. Thought you weren't going to make it."

"I almost didn't," Taye admitted. He took the seat Zane had so recently vacated, but considerately enough sat at an angle sufficient to prevent his knees from knocking Eli's. He wasn't quite as worn down with exhaustion as he had been at the Italian place, but neither was he bright-eyed and bushy-tailed, and his legs were longer than anyone else's. "Oof."

Eli felt his pain. "Don't make any sudden moves. Holly picked the place." Her price for keeping mum about the secret plans Eli had spent a hushed half hour discussing with her before Zane woke up that morning. If the price of successful collusion was a few contusions here and there, Eli could live with that. "Anything this fragile and uncomfortable has to cost a fortune, and if we break it, odds are we'll have bought it."

"Don't look at me. I'm perfectly comfortable," Diana said. "God, that's good coffee."

"You can taste it underneath all the sweetener?" Taye asked, eyeing the pile of empty packets at Diana's elbow.

Diana waved negligently at Eli. "Sue me. So! What's the skinny, Dr. Jameson? You've been shooting me covert looks all morning, and inquiring minds want to know what's up with that."

"Eh…" Eli stalled. Problem: the things he'd hoped to corral Diana to discuss and those he'd hoped to have a chance to chew over with Taye didn't exactly mesh. The idea had been more for them to be on opposite sides of the city when discussions happened. "Anything I'm about to say doesn't leave this table. Understood?"

"Eli opens up?" Taye looked impressed.

"Don't get too excited," Diana cautioned with a smirk. "It hasn't happened yet. Might not if we aren't careful."

Eli rolled his eyes. "Keep pushing your luck, would you?"

"I live to serve." Diana sipped her coffee and

made a face. "Cold. Think we could get some more --"

Timing peeked its head in, and for once it was on Eli's side. A waitress with tired eyes and a kind mouth cruised to a stop at their table. Must have seen Taye ambling in. "Can I get you anything?"

Taye glanced at Eli, who hid his relief and waved him on. "Don't worry, I'm in no rush," he said. "You look like you could use a square meal."

"Nicely done," Diana murmured. She spared the waitress a tomboyish beam of thanks for the refill, and zeroed in on Eli -- for once, outside of the hospital, almost serious. "No more stalling, friend. What's eating you?"

Eli checked to be sure Taye's eyes and ears were well occupied before he laid both hands and all his cards on the table. "Depends. If I ask you for the truth, I think I can rest assured you'll give it to me. Even if it's a truth I won't like and frankly don't want to hear. Am I right?"

Diana's eyebrows rose. "Conversation starters like that usually bode well. Are you and Zane --"

"We're fine," Eli said, brushing the concern aside. He'd gotten a bellyful of that from Holly and didn't feel in the mood for a refill just yet. Besides, they were fine and would be better still now that Holly had come through with the goods. "That's not what I wanted to ask."

"Then is it the Marybeth thing?"

"Yes," Eli said, not surprised in the least that she'd already heard. Very little passed Diana by. "Marybeth's not the issue right this second. God knows what I'm going to do about her in the long run, but that's not it either."

"Huh. Then color me curious." Diana wrapped both hands around her china cup and blew at the steam. Her gaze held steadily on him. He had her full attention and then some. "Let's hear it."

"The hospital. They're not going to hire me again, are they?"

"Ah." Diana sipped her coffee, then lived up to her word with regret, but with no apologies in her clear brown eyes. "No. Probably not."

Damn.

She must have noticed his grimace but carried through to the end. "As far as I can tell, they're looking to cut corners everywhere a corner can be cut. Take two residents who can cover your workload for roughly half your salary combined --"

"And who won't take off once or twice a year," Eli finished for her. He blew out a long breath. "That's what I figured."

"Sucks to be you." Diana nudged him under the table, almost gently. She put her cheek in her hand. "I'm not trying to trespass on Holly's turf, but are you okay with that? I wouldn't be."

"Do I have a choice?" Eli rubbed his forehead, then shook his head and sat back. "I didn't want to hear it, but..." He cleared his throat. "Appreciate your telling it."

Diana made a *hmm* noise. She glanced sideways at Taye, who had apparently gotten lost in the intricacies of the café's admittedly odd menu, and pursed her lips. "If I'd known he was coming, I would have suggested we go somewhere else," she said. Quietly, almost as if to herself. "Espresso at five bucks a pop? Come on. I could grind the beans myself and make it stretch for a pot."

Eli didn't like the sound of that. He eyed Diana. She didn't look like a woman who had fallen on lean times. Expensive-looking silk blouse, perfume with a flowery high note and a low tone of money-money-money.

She rolled her eyes. "Not me, you dope. Him."

Him being Taye. *Ah.* Now that Eli knew where to look and how, he saw it. The lab coat Taye wore had been washed and ironed with starch, but a frayed hole showed on the side pocket. And then there was the weight loss. And he wasn't focused on choosing biscuits over brioche for the sake of taste, was he? Nor did he order "just coffee" and excuse himself to the bathroom before the waitress could try to upsell him out of an interest in an ascetic lifestyle.

Eli kept his voice low as he watched Taye make his temporary exit. "How bad?"

"Bad enough." She grimaced. "If you two hadn't decided to stay in the city and let them finish out their sublet -- and I know it's pennies on the dollar, you big softy -- they'd have trouble keeping a roof over their heads. Student loans are a bitch of the highest order."

And didn't Eli know it from bitter experience? He waved in the general direction of the café's kitchen. "Richie's job doesn't help?"

"If Richie could keep a job, it might. He's not had a lot of luck there. Add that to Taye's losing sleep over relationship strain, and voila. Recipe for a nervous breakdown."

All in all, not unexpected, but worse than Eli had imagined. Shame on him for not putting the pieces together sooner. "Anything we can do?"

"Are you kidding? He's as bad as you for stubborn pride," Diana said. "Would you let anyone help?"

"Odds are he wouldn't, no," Taye said as he returned to his seat with a half smile Eli would describe as sheepish. He'd know better than most how picky-choosing annoyed restaurant staff, but what could he do? The waitress didn't seem to take it personally. Or so Eli hoped. "Help with what?"

"And you say you don't see the resemblance," Diana mused aloud, gesturing from Eli to Taye and back again.

"Because I don't," Eli said. Okay, so sometimes he did. Denying Diana was a hobby, and he had to keep in practice. "I'll go so far as to say everyone else does, but I think you're all imagining things."

"You get that too?" Taye nodded his thanks to the waitress bringing him a plain, unadorned cup of coffee. "I thought it was just me."

"I should be so lucky."

Taye wasn't paying attention. "One time someone asked me if I minded working at the same hospital as my dad," he told Diana. "Did you ever hear about that one?"

Eli squawked and sat up straight. "Hey!"

Diana clapped her hands together with a hoot of laughter. "No, they didn't. Did they? See, Eli? We tell you and we tell you, but do you believe us?"

"What did you say to them?" Eli demanded.

Taye subsided, albeit with a wicked grin. "Don't worry. I told them you weren't that old."

"Damn right." Not that he'd have minded, not as such. He and Marybeth never wanted kids, but it wouldn't have been so bad to end up with a son like this one. Eli coughed to ward off the ever so pointed question he could *feel* forming in Diana's head. "Not that age is a concern. Youngest kid I ever knew to have been responsible for a pregnancy was, what... eleven, I think? Maybe twelve, but I doubt it."

"You've been hanging out with the wrong people," Taye said. "I've seen younger come through with their own mothers seeking counseling."

"Another reason to thank God I am not in clinical psych." Eli raised his mug in salute. "All hail those who can do it, but they aren't me."

"It's a fine thing to know your strengths and play to them," Taye agreed. He sipped at his coffee. "I can understand being asked. You're a good friend. Most people misinterpret that. Sometimes to an advantage, like with you and Zane."

"Yeah, well." Eli fidgeted. "You have a father of your own. Most people do."

Diana shot him a disgusted look. Taye was kinder. "Yes, and I haven't seen him or my mother in ten years."

"Thought you'd just turned twenty-seven," Eli said.

"Yes," Taye said. "I did."

The numbers came together in Eli's head, added themselves up, and pointed a big red arrow to a tally that suggested Taye and his parents didn't so much get along. Kicked out of the house at just-turned-seventeen would be Eli's guess. He scowled mentally at himself. Christ, but he was slow today. He didn't need the threat of Diana's under-table discipline to prompt his gruff, "Sorry, kid. I'm an idiot sometimes."

"Not that I didn't already know that, but thanks."

Eli waved that off. "Anytime."

"Well! What did I miss?" Holly couldn't have timed her return better, hallelujah and amen. She clicked her phone shut and slid it into her pocket as she approached the table. "Eli, you're blushing."

"Nope. Just your imagination. Everything taken care of?"

"It's all set up," she assured him, patting his

shoulder. "Diana, if you're heading back to Immaculate Grace, I'll share a taxi with you."

"You read my mind." Where Holly patted, Diana punched, but the friendliness in the contact was no less evident or genuine. "That other question you asked, Eli," she said, smoothing back her sleek bob, "I'll put some thought into it tonight. Deal?"

"Deal." Inspiration struck. Eli plucked the check out of its tray before she could make a grab for it to claim her and Holly's shares. "Don't sweat it. My treat today, remember?" They could afford their espresso, yes, but Eli could live with shelling out for theirs as well as Taye's.

Holly understood before Diana did, but Diana wasn't far behind. Her punch softened into a nudge of approval. Holly sent him an approving nod behind Taye's back.

Hard to tell if Taye noticed. Possibly. It was the only kind of help Eli would have taken, back in the day.

Maybe they were on to something with their whole doctrine of similarities after all.

Chin propped on his hand, Taye watched the rest of their party make their escape. Eli would swear he could see him counting down in his head as he waited for the door to shut behind the ladies. "So. What was it you didn't want to ask me in front of them?"

"Way too incisive for your own good," Eli grumbled for the sake of form. Then, truly curious, he asked, "How did you know?"

Taye waggled his fingers. "Magic."

The sass startled a laugh out of Eli. "Punk-ass kid."

"Old fart," Taye returned with a sideways grin. "No, seriously. What did you want? I'm all ears."

Eli hesitated. The question had formed clearly enough in his mind -- *how do I ask Zane if he'd like a turn on the top, as I'd like to check out the view from below, so to speak* -- but now that the time had come to put it into audible words, he couldn't quite make them stumble out. His face burned. He blurted instead, "The clinic."

"The what?"

Damn. Eli backtracked. He hadn't meant to say "the clinic" as if it were a done deal. It'd just popped out that way. "I meant, the idea to use that storefront to set up a clinic. Anyone taken the bait?"

Taye didn't look as if he'd been fooled, but he allowed Eli the dignity of pretending otherwise. "No one yet, sorry."

Eli couldn't have said he wasn't disappointed, but as falling blows went, he'd had worse. "Eh. Bad idea anyway."

Taye frowned. "It isn't, though. It's a good idea. The neighborhood you live in is close to the hospital for a given value of 'close,' but still too far for some. People who can't drive or who can't take all day to wait. People without insurance."

"Preaching to the choir here." The kid's enthusiasm tempted Eli to set a match to the banked hopes that wanted to rekindle, and that might not be for the best. He'd be gone soon, following Zane, and that was as it should be.

Shouldn't it?

"I'll keep asking," Taye said, chin stubborn now. "I haven't had as much of a chance as I'd wanted to ask around, and I'll fix that." He raised one shoulder. "I've had a few things on my mind. As I'm sure you've been told."

Eli saw no point in dissembling. "You saw who I was here with. You think any secrets last for long?"

"True," Taye admitted, then hesitated. Making up his mind, if Eli were to judge. "I take it you've heard everything."

"Enough to get the gist. Not enough to see the big picture." Eli shifted to sit forward, assessing Taye partly from long-term habit and partly in renewed concern. He was a doctor. He couldn't help it. Nor did he want to. "You're not getting enough sleep. I know the feeling."

"I suppose you do, at that." Taye seemed to steel himself. "It's funny, you know? I'd wanted to talk to you about it, but I didn't know how."

"Me?" Eli had his reservations about *that*. "You sure about that? Ann Landers I'm not."

Taye's mouth twitched in a brief smile. "No. I think I could convince Holly to loan you a twinset and pearls, but clothes don't make the man. You and Zane are good friends. How did you keep that trust? I thought I knew, but lately…" He took a breath. "It's like he's disappearing on me. Going somewhere I can't follow."

Huh. Eli didn't know Richie as well as the ladies -- he'd kept hold of the distance set between them after Richie's mistake in the kitchen nearly cost him and Zane everything -- but from what he could tell, that didn't sound like Taye's partner. "Literally or otherwise?"

"Both." Taye ran a hand through his hair, quick and frustrated. "I asked him last night if he'd come to lunch today. He said he'd think about it. When I texted him with the location this morning? Nothing. Radio silence. I'm not so much like you that I can't admit I'm scared." He took hold of his mug with both hands and directed his stare to its black depths. "I want to know he's all right. That's all. If I could just get a handle on that… But when I try to get hold, he's not there. I don't even know where he is right now."

Oh, hell, Eli had a bad feeling about this. If it were him, he'd want to know, and yet…

Taye had noticed his indecision and pounced on it like a hungry cat. "Eli?"

Eli winced. "Come on, kid."

"No. You know something," Taye insisted. He had the reach to push into Eli's space from across the tabletop if he chose. "Eli, what?"

"I might know where he is," Eli said. "But you're not going to like it."

"I didn't think I would," Taye said, jaw firm. "Tell me."

And so Eli did, by pointing past Taye into the kitchen. "Right there, kid. I thought you saw him too." Like the Italian joint, when he'd seen Richie in the back, he'd just assumed it was with Taye's full knowledge. That'd teach him, wouldn't it? "He's been there all along."

Taye stood bolt upright, rocking the table. "*What?*"

Everyone heard him. Including Richie, who froze between counter and employee entrance. He had a gray Rubbermaid tub full of dirty dishes in both arms.

Taye's head of steam melted away. "Richie, what…" he started.

Richie finished the question for him with a concise if not at all happy answer. Hell, Eli would bet people could have heard from miles away the ringing *crash* as he dropped his armload of dishes and bolted as if his ass was on fire.

Not good.

Chapter Seven

Richie might be small, but by God he could move. Eli stopped chasing him at the mouth of the third alley, the one that'd lead them back to the thoroughfare they'd started from. He dropped into a half crouch at the exit, hands on his knees, sucking for air.

"Dr. Jameson?" Taye forgot himself sometimes under stress. He halted clumsily beside Eli, windmilling one arm to keep from tipping over.

"No good. He's already on the street."

Taye swiveled from the hips to kick an innocent paper sack into the wall. "*Fuck.*"

Which just about summed it up. Eli straightened and put two fingers on his neck to check his pulse. Going like gangbusters, Christ. He hadn't been idle long enough for half a city block's worth of running to wind him, had he?

"Did you see which way he went?"

Eli cast a weather eye over Taye. Neither fight nor flight, he judged. The kid had lost the impetus to run and settled down to earth with a *thump*, a dark blue fugue wrapping around his shoulders.

"I didn't. Sorry," Eli said. He shook his head to rid it of the irritating light prickle of exertion. "Does his phone have GPS?"

"I'm not going to track him like a lost dog with an ID chip." Taye didn't so much lean against the wall as let it hold him up. Lost dogs, eh? He was the one who looked like a puppy left out in the rain. Woebegone as hell.

"Kid..." Eli started.

Taye wasn't listening. "It doesn't make sense. If I've done something, he would tell me about it. If there was anything wrong, I should have seen it. I *know* him,

Eli."

"Aha. There. You see?" Eli clapped his hands to startle Taye's attention his way. Worked too. He hadn't known this particular idea was busy growing in the back of his mind before it flowered, but what the hell. Couldn't hurt and might help. "You know him. Don't judge him before you've heard him out."

"Judge him?" Taye gawked at Eli. "I'm not!"

"The hell you say." Eli finally had his breath under control, and a good thing too. He'd worked up a head of steam. He laid a hand briefly on Taye's shoulder. "Ask him what's going on. Have you done that? No? Yeah, didn't think so."

"Excuse me? You just saw it for yourself. He won't stand still long enough to *be* asked."

"And? He has a phone. So do you. Send him a text. It's a place to start."

"And if he doesn't answer?"

"Then you'll know more than you do now, but I'll tell you this for free. You know him. He wouldn't do these things without a good reason. All correct so far?"

Taye nodded, silent and puppy-eyed.

Well, sometimes a man had to hurt before he could start to heal. "So trust in that," Eli said. "God knows it's the pot calling the kettle black and we both might want to move before we get struck by lightning, but I say talk to him. Tell him you're freaking out. Then see what he says."

Taye bit at his lip for a moment. "What if I don't like what he says?"

"Then at least you'll know." Eli had just about enough strength left in his rubbery knees to make it out to the street proper, and double the pride needed to make sure he got there without stumbling. "Come on. Let's get out of here before we breathe in more germs than oxygen."

He wasn't Holly, who could soothe with a pat on the shoulder and a promise that things would be okay, but he wondered if that would have been what Taye needed. A call to action might be more his speed.

It was what Eli would have wanted. "Just do it," he said, feeling more like a doctor than he had in weeks. "That's all anyone can do."

* * *

Good advice, as far as it went. Would it work?
No clue.

Eli locked the apartment door behind himself and leaned against the cool strength of the cheap old wood. Old habits dictated he switch on the lamp within arm's reach, but after second thought, Eli declined to reach for the light. He toed off his shoes one at a time, kicking them into the shadowy corner where they wouldn't be in the way when Zane came home.

Home. Funny, that. Eli had trained himself to think of this place as a temporary stop in the road. He wouldn't need it anymore once Immaculate Grace officially let him go. He'd have a hell of a commute anywhere else. Might as well start the journey from their house in the suburbs.

Still, he'd hate to let this place go. Too many memories.

What can you do? Eli brushed his knuckles against the knob before pushing off and padding forward silently on socked feet. Zane wouldn't be back for hours, so he could... what? That was the question. Eli hadn't had an afternoon to himself in years, and it didn't take much doing to remember why. He hadn't been made to sit idle.

He dry washed his face in frustration. He'd rather be active, sure, but doing what? Staring out the window like a teenage girl, mooning over an empty drugstore of all the damn things?

He could turn around and make his way to Immaculate Grace. Set up camp outside Human Resources and pounce on the first person who peeked their head out. Make them give him an answer.

No real point to it, though, and Eli didn't much care for the notion of pinning himself to a target while waiting for the gun to fire.

What else? Dealing with Marybeth still lingered on his personal agenda. Eli dug his phone out and thumbed the screen to life. He winced. Too bright in the dimness of the room, ouch. His eyes stung as they adjusted to the white backlight.

A couple of new texts had come in. He hadn't noticed the chime of their arrival. Maybe it *was* time to hang up his hat if he'd started missing so much. No way he could keep up with a pager.

Good news, Eli. I've confirmed your reservations for tonight at eight. That should give you plenty of time before the ten p.m. showing at the theater. You and Zane should have a wonderful night.

Going by the timestamp, Holly must have sent that while Eli navigated the El. Fair enough. No one could hear themselves think while packed into the noisy, crowded cars. Usually didn't bother Eli. Today he'd had to breathe shallowly through his mouth.

Something about that struck him as wrong, more wrong than it should be, but when Eli tried to chase the thought, it swam away.

He checked the second text.

Do I have to pull your pigtails or what, Champ? I'm only in town for a couple more days. Give me a call.

And Marybeth. Eli pinched the bridge of his nose. Would he like to see her?

Actually... yes.

"Champ," he muttered, amused despite himself. God, but she'd always been a tough old bird. In a different world, he'd bet his lunch that she and Zane would have gotten along like gangbusters.

Which was the heart of the problem. They didn't live in a different world, and in this one, Eli would saw his hand off at the wrist before he'd give Zane reason to doubt him.

Hell. Sorry, Marybeth. Maybe Diana will come up with some grand scheme.

That was a more heartening thought than Eli would have imagined. It cheered him up fully enough to snag a day-old newspaper Zane had left by the TV on his way into the bedroom. He'd need work sooner than later, right? Truth. And that given, there was nothing like a good old set of want ads as a place to get started.

Just do it, indeed.

* * *

Sleeping hadn't been the plan. Like so many other aspects of life, sleeping happened regardless of any intentions to the contrary on Eli's part.

He blamed the jazz he'd tuned the inner sanctum radio to before settling down on the bed with pen and newspaper turned open to the appropriate page. Something he thought Zane liked to listen to, soft and smoky and growling sweet, with cool trumpets and warm strings.

He knew he was *falling* asleep. Before he opened his eyes, he had no notion of waking.

Hell, he didn't know he wasn't alone before his fist sank into the yielding bare flesh of Zane's naked stomach.

What? Eli blinked and shook his head, trying in vain to clear the gray mist that obscured his vision. Like waking up with cataracts. His pulse thundered far faster and rougher than it had in the alley chasing Richie, and his mouth tasted as if he'd licked the inside of a meat locker.

"Zane?" he croaked. Voice sounded worse than raw. Eli scrubbed at his face and managed, finally, to wipe away the spider webs in his eyes. He sucked in a noisy breath. "Zane, what the hell?"

"I was about to ask you the same thing." Zane picked himself up off the floor beside the bed. His eyes were wide as an owl's, and his body language screamed of wariness. He didn't have a stitch of clothing on him, and he held his stomach as he winced. "Good Lord, Eli. Are you okay?"

"I didn't --" Eli reached for him, remembered the sensation of striking skin against skin, and jerked back. "Did I hit you?"

"I'll say you did. *Oof.*" Zane prodded at his belly. "You're a strong old cuss. I'll tell you that for free."

And he wasted time asking if *Eli* was all right? "Zane, what the hell?" Eli said again, only then realizing his throat burned. "Fuck. Are you hurt?"

"So much for erotic surprises, but I think I'll live." Zane sat on the edge of the bed. "I can read your mind. Stop that. You were fast asleep, and I thought I'd be cute and wake you up with a kiss. Should have known better, so don't blame yourself. You've warned me plenty of times not to sneak up on an ex-cop."

"That doesn't excuse it. *Fuck.*" Eli tried to push himself into a sitting position. He'd knocked his want ads off the bed while he slept, save for one page that crinkled under his hand. Newsprint all over the sheets, perfect. He'd worry about the stains later. "You're sure I didn't hurt you?"

"I've been hit harder at work. So have you. You might have winded me, but I'll be all right. It's you I'm worried about."

"I'm fine now. Must have been having a nightmare," he said, pressing two fingers to his temple. Seemed like the upswing he'd been on earlier had packed its bags and hitched a lift to the border while he slept. "I can't remember."

"If it was a nightmare, then I'll be glad." Zane leaned over Eli and shaded his eyes. Eli knew from experience he'd be checking first the left and then the right for pupil response. "You gave us both a scare. I thought it was a seizure before you took a swing."

Eli batted Zane's hand away. The changing light made his head growl. He remembered with a vague sense of annoyance that he'd forgotten to follow up on firming up an appointment with Holly's hospitalist friend. Damn. He could have gone to see about that this afternoon instead of moping around and apparently sleeping the day away.

Handy it would be, to have a clinic close by. *Ah well.*

"Don't worry so much about me." Eli shook the static-wool irritation away and took the hand that'd sneaked back to check his temperature between both of his instead. He carried that hand to his cheek and let it rest there to pacify Zane and to enjoy the cool competency of his touch. Win-win. "Hand to my heart, I'm good. Stop dodging and tell me if I hurt you."

"Eli." Zane cupped his cheek and lowered his head to gently knock their foreheads together. "Practice what you preach."

"You knew my faults when you signed up for

this."

"And they are many." Zane settled onto the bed beside Eli and ruffled his hair back away from his neck. "Almost as much as me."

"Good thing we've got each other, then, eh?" Eli watched him. He felt odd. Almost half-asleep, but not unhappily. Reminded him of waking up early on a snow day back when he'd been knee-high to a grasshopper and eager to skip school. "I'm taking care of the Marybeth thing. I don't want you to worry. Okay?"

Zane brushed a kiss across Eli's head. "Then I won't. But Eli..." He hesitated. "Thank you."

"Anytime." It wasn't a lie, Eli told himself. He would leave Marybeth in Diana's capable hands starting tomorrow, so he could check that off his worry list. *Forget the past; enjoy the present.* Eli stretched up with one arm to pull Zane down for a repeat of the kiss, with bonus extras. Zane's shoulders were strong and his skin wonderfully cool, his confidence soothing and the rest of him inflammatory in the way Eli had learned to like.

"Mmm." Zane's lips touched his when he spoke. "I wouldn't wish bad dreams on anyone, but I can't hate the aftermath."

"It's got nothing to do with dreams." Eli sifted through Zane's soft salt-and-pepper hair, aware of how the silky strands caught on the calluses of his fingers. Zane bent his head to lean into the touch, almost purring. "I --"

Ow. Eli winced. Must have slept on his back wrong. The muscles twanged in protest.

"Oof. I felt that." Zane withdrew. He rested his palms against Eli's shoulders and frowned. "You're stiff as a board."

"I know. If you'd care to finish the job you started, doctor?"

The man did have a good chuckle, quiet and warm. "I'd rather you weren't half-crippled when we got down to the in-depth studies. Roll over. I think there's some cinnamon oil from that gift basket Holly and Diana gave us last Christmas still gathering dust in the linen closet."

Eli couldn't deny the temptations inherent in the offer of a massage. Normally, that was. Just at the moment, he wasn't certain he wanted to take the time. He'd rather lie there with Zane. Lie there and drift…

He blinked. "I didn't doze off again, did I?"

"Nah." Zane kissed his forehead. "Lose the shirt and the shorts while I go rummage."

No danger of his drowsing then. Awkward though it might be to wiggle out of his clothes without getting out of bed, Eli managed and occupied himself gainfully by watching Zane through the open bedroom door. Looked younger than his years, Eli thought. Especially if one watched him in gathering twilight, when gray hid itself in black. He moved lightly, his bare feet scarcely making a sound on the well-worn carpet, and swayed his head unconsciously to the silvery saxophone on the radio.

Eli remembered the first time he'd realized Zane was beautiful. Funny how every time seemed like the first. It never stopped surprising him.

No more or no less surprising than the look on the man's face when he turned to grin at Eli. Made Eli's heart do a hop-skip and a jump, catching in his throat. Making him hungry.

"You're looking at me as if you want to eat me up," Zane murmured. Seemed like he had an extra ounce of sway in his walk as he moved back to the bed in measured paces, sleek and prowling.

"Could be I do." Eli reached to take Zane's hand and give a pull, but Zane clicked his tongue and gestured for Eli to roll over instead.

"You found the gift basket?" Holly and Diana's sense of humor, sheesh. Although he couldn't deny it might have been worse. Holly swore she'd talked Diana out of doing their shopping at the adult toy store. Made Eli's cheeks burn just to think of the possible consequences. He sniffed the air. "Cinnamon."

"There is balm in Gilead after all," Zane said. He pressed oil-slick hands to Eli's skin. "Lie still. Let me take care of you."

Eli didn't answer, except in a moan. He butted his head into the pillows. "You're far too good at that."

"Or just good enough, I would say." Zane's voice matched the saxophone just right. Almost like a harmony. "I can feel it working already. That's my boy."

Eli waved lazily, brushing off the teasing. The massage was far too pleasant to be bothered with banter. "Mmm," he sighed into the pillow, the warm humidity of his breath bathing his nose and chin. He stretched in an X shape, arms and legs splayed, to give Zane more room to work.

"You look like a happy cat who's just found a sunbeam," Zane said with an almost audible smile. He slipped one leg over Eli's back and straddled him.

Hmm. Looked like Eli wasn't the only one enjoying this massage business, was he?

They'd be late. Eli shifted his hips in a vain effort to take some of the pressure off.

Zane's low chuckle rippled in his ears. "So it's like that. I see."

"Zane..." Eli twisted as best he could to look

back over his shoulder. "I could say 'I see' too, but... plans tonight. Big plans." And grudge it though he might, even if he'd only had a nightmare, it'd left him far more rubber-kneed than he'd like. "Maybe not a good idea right now."

Should have known he couldn't fool Zane. "Maybe, maybe not." Zane smoothed his hands in a double stroke across Eli's shoulders and resettled himself on Eli's hips. "Or I could do all the work. And you could lie there and let me take care of you."

Eli caught his breath between his teeth. That... yes, he could roll with that.

He must have responded in some way he didn't consciously recognize. Flexed his hips or his fists. Or maybe it was just the sound of his quiet hiss and the shudder he couldn't help, or the quiet groan that escaped him. Not a noise he'd make during normal working hours, no, but one they saved for the dark hours of the night when it was only him and Zane and not a stitch of clothes to spare between them.

He could feel Zane's surprise -- and even more so his quiet, ragged exhalation. "You like the sound of that," Zane said. His hands skated over Eli's bare shoulders. He rolled his hips once, down and against Eli's ass.

Eli's fists knotted tighter in the sheets. His face had caught fire -- he thought the tips of his ears would ignite -- but he'd gone hard as rebar, and so help him, he wanted to put that hard-on to use. Or put it up for Zane's use. Oh God, yes. That one. The second choice.

He blew his air out through his nose and rolled his hips again, deliberately pushing up against Zane.

Zane's mouth pressed hot against the back of Eli's neck. He'd stopped massaging and started kneading. Eli could tell the difference in the dark, you betcha. "I've got cinnamon oil all over my hands," he said on a rough laugh. "Probably could have planned ahead a bit better."

"Don't care," Eli said. He hid his face in the pillows and squared his shoulders for more leverage to rock back. He hissed between his teeth. It wasn't like he hadn't had Zane behind him before, mind. But not like this. With… intent. "Don't care about anything, but that you don't stop."

"I won't." Zane's mouth moved against Eli's neck between words. "Promise, I won't. God, Eli." He reached between them to adjust himself. Eli felt it, the slippery-slick hardness sliding into the cleft of his ass. They'd done this the first time they'd been naked in a bed together.

"Knew you'd… think of something. *God. Oh.*" Eli's stomach muscles jerked. He could feel so much more than he'd thought. Wiry pubic hair rough against his ass. Slick precum smoothing the way. Zane's strong, capable hands pinning him down. "Zane, fuck. *Oh.* Don't stop."

"Not stopping. Not." Zane pressed his forehead hard to the back of Eli's skull. He'd found his rhythm, though he kept slipping out of it, his hips too eager to keep the pace. Fuck, how long must he have wanted to do this? Maybe longer than Eli. "Never going to stop."

"Good. Good." Eli rolled his shoulders and pushed up. "Wish you'd --"

"Not this time. Don't tempt me. The way you feel, Eli."

"Not so… bad… yourself. *Oh.*"

Zane made a breathless sound, half hunger and half delight and almost a whole sob, if Eli were to judge. He drove harder, and without a hand to steady either of Eli's hips, Eli scooted forward an inch or two with each thrust. Jolts of sensation sent shock waves through Eli that made him think of the one time he'd tried surfing. Rising, rising, a slap of surprise, the bottom falling out of his stomach as he swooped down -- the rising hot need that made him roll his hips hard against the mattress. He wouldn't spare a hand for this, not when he needed both to keep him pushing back into Zane.

But Zane knew him. All too well. He snatched up the sheet and ground his right hand into the tangle of fabric. Pushed it underneath Eli, took him in hand, and sent him down like a mad dog given mercy. Eli shuddered and shouted, garbling them both, and soaked the sheet with cum. Muscles kinked and protested in his back, but nowhere near loudly enough to bother him -- then -- as Zane followed, messy and hot and filthy and fucking amazing.

He settled into the sheets. Could have happily drowned in them and sung hallelujah. His pulse still raced, and he was startled beyond words at what he'd done. What *they'd* done. After all that anguish... all he had to do was let it happen.

How about that?

"God help," Eli said, mouth dry. "Sweet baby saints. How'd I get this lucky?"

"I don't know. How did I?" Zane brushed a sloppy kiss to Eli's temple. He dropped his head against Eli's shoulder, sobering.

Eli let him gather his thoughts. No rush, no hurry, not for either of them.

"We're talking about this, Eli," Zane said at last. "Just so you know. Maybe not now, but soon."

"Fair enough," Eli said gruffly. "If you want."

Zane knew him well enough to understand what Eli really meant by the grumbling: *thank you.* "I do."

* * *

While Zane didn't fall asleep on Eli, it ended up a very near thing. If Eli hadn't jostled him when sneaking out of bed in search of a glass of water, they might have dozed the night away. As it stood, they had a half hour to tumble back into their clothes in a pell-mell rush to make the reservations. Zane teased for crumbs of info, but Eli kept it to himself. He patted himself on the back for that one. Let no man say Zane couldn't be mighty persuasive when he put his mind to it.

He'd done up his tie and crouched to lace his shoes when he saw Zane walking into his field of vision, socked and buttoned and shaved, dressed to the nines in fact, and looking good. Eli craned his neck to give Zane a good and proper once-over and wolf-whistled to show his appreciation. The man did know how to wear a suit.

"You clean up pretty well yourself," Zane said. He bopped Eli lightly on the top of the head with the fold of newspaper. "But you left your want ads on the bedroom floor."

"Ah." Eli grimaced. *Damn.* "Yeah, about those."

Zane smoothed down the hair he'd disarranged, slow and thoughtful. Eli heard no judgment in his voice, but plenty of thoughtful concern, when he asked, "Are you really that bored?"

Eli caught his hand and smacked a rough kiss against the backs of the knuckles. "With you, hell no. But with this time off... maybe I am."

"I thought you might be." Zane drew his eyebrows together. "What would you do, if you could do anything? Anything at all."

Wasn't that the million-dollar question? Eli pressed his lips tight as he thought. He could mention the clinic idea. Again. Why, though? Even if Zane did take an interest, their calendars were booked. No use crying over spilled milk, and no point in wishing for wings when you had a damn good horse.

Besides, he didn't want to spoil this.

"That's easy enough to answer." Eli nudged Zane back and stood, still clasping his hand loosely. "I'd go out with you tonight."

Zane shook his head. Eli could tell he hadn't fooled the man, but Zane let it go all the same. For now. And he looked pleased. Flattered. Everyone loved a compliment, all the more when it was sincerely meant. "Must be some night you've got planned."

"Don't I just?" Eli felt obscurely pleased at having diverted Zane's attention. "Or at least it'd better be, for all the time and effort that's gone into it."

"Now you're tickling my curiosity."

"Good. That was the goal." Eli offered Zane his arm, an antiquated courtesy that made Zane snort with amusement. "Chop-chop, sir. The town's not going to wait forever for us to paint it red."

Chapter Eight

Eli should have known the gods didn't like men to be too happy. He'd learned that lesson the hard way, hadn't he? Somehow, he kept forgetting. Taye would have given a philosophical shrug, and Holly would have had something to say about persistent, stubborn optimism being part of the human condition.

Eli never had been overly good at taking his lumps. That was *his* human condition.

But that much, he didn't know just yet.

They'd made a good start to the night, as Eli considered it. Nap, sex, and now food. A man would be hard-pressed to ask for more trimmings on the tree.

"You're not telling me where we're going," Zane mused. He walked side by side with Eli, hands swinging carelessly near his pockets.

Eli watched him in his peripheral vision, well pleased. "Nope. Not a word."

"Which leaves me with no choice but to put my thinking cap on."

"Do people who aren't five years old use that expression?"

"This one does." Zane elbowed Eli gently, sending him a half step off pace. "Shh. I'm collating data. It's a thinking factory up in here."

"It's *something* up in there, all right." Eli poked Zane's ear as mild but satisfying payback for the nudge. Damn, but life was good tonight, wasn't it? He eyed Zane's hand as Zane tucked one thumb into his hip pocket on the side nearest him.

It'd be better if he had the stones to take that hand, he knew. He wanted to. He almost --

Zane flicked it out of reach to snap his fingers. "Got it! Wait... no."

Eli snorted. He pushed his hands safely into his

pockets. "Keep on trying. You'll get there eventually."

"But will I before we get where we're going?"

"Mmm... possibly not." They'd come to a four-way intersection. Crossing any road at night could be considered an urban form of Russian roulette, but Eli would take his chances. He thumbed the button that'd send a signal to the stoplights. "I always wondered if these actually do anything or if they're giant placebo effects."

"You'd be asking the wrong man about that." Waiting for traffic lights to change always drove Zane a particular shade of bonkers. He fidgeted, checked his watch, and then -- as Eli had hoped -- cast about in search of distraction.

He zeroed in on the corner restaurant. Good taste, that man. The crisp charcoal and searing sirloin fragrance made for a heady perfume. Likely the music coming from within attracted Zane more. "Is that a live performance?"

Eli shrugged. In truth, he was a shitty liar, and glad Zane had turned his focus toward the smoked glass windows in their mahogany frames. "Could be. Sounds like it might."

Zane tried to peer through, smoked glass be damned. "Ella Fitzgerald," he said after cocking his ear.

"Hate to break it to you, but I think she passed a few years back."

"Her music," Zane said, though he had to know Eli was only yanking his chain. His fine-featured face had lit up from within with enjoyment of the sweet, mournful melodies. "God, would you listen to that? Gorgeous."

"Not bad. You know I can't pick a performer out of a lineup, but not bad at all."

Eli could see Zane wouldn't have minded standing there all night, but he sighed and thumped the wall lightly with one fist. "Ah well. We'd better hurry. It's nearly eight." He tapped his watch. "Really nearly eight. Are we going to have time to get where we're going?"

"Might do," Eli said. He backtracked past Zane and set his hand on the latch. "Depends on how long it takes you to walk five feet."

And if he'd thought Zane looked happy before...

A good start to a good night, indeed.

Once inside the sturdy mahogany doors, the sizzling beef and silky jazz permeated everything from floorboard to ceiling tiles. Zane's smile couldn't have been wider. Eli basked in it like sunlight. It'd taken him too damn long to realize life could be this good.

He lifted his chin to the maître'd manning a discreet podium between entryway and steakhouse proper. "Table for two. Should be a reservation under the name Jameson."

"Yes, sir. One moment, please."

Eli watched the man vanish into the inexplicable space where all restaurant staff seemed to vanish whenever anything got called into question. Much like interns and residents when they thought they'd screwed up. *Huh.* Eli frowned. Something about the way the guy had glanced from him to Zane didn't sit well.

Was he --

"Eli." Zane laid his hand on Eli's forearm. His eyes shone brighter than the stars. "How did you -- no, never mind that."

Never mind, his ass. Eli knew what Zane meant to say. How did Eli know he'd want to come here? Holly had told him. He'd never heard of the place before tonight.

He still hoped he would have thought, if he'd spotted it on his own, *that's Zane's kind of joint. I should take him there.*

"I guessed," Eli said. He covered Zane's hand with his. Briefly, but by God he did it. "Good guess?"

"One of your better deductions," Zane said. "A for effort."

Eli would have liked nothing better to kiss him then, and he thought it must have showed. The maître'd shot another hard look at him and then at Zane when he reappeared. "There are no reservations under that name."

Zane frowned. "Are you sure?"

"Check again," Eli said. A bad feeling had started to wiggle in his gut. When he looked past the maître'd's station and across the tables, he saw plenty of men dressed in jacket and tie... and plenty of women leaning on their arms. "Hey" -- he snapped his fingers --"I said check again."

"There is no reservation under that name," the man repeated. He had a voice like a robot and a face like a mask now. Absolutely nothing either hostile or even the slightest bit apologetic. "You must have made a mistake."

Zane wasn't slow to pick up the vibe, and he'd been raised to handle this kind of situation. "Right. Any chance of unmaking it?"

"Reservations must be made in advance. If you'll excuse me?"

Eli had a few inches of height advantage over Zane and the maître'd. He stood as tall as he could and narrowed his eyes at the reservation book. While he might not understand the diagrams or shorthand, he'd learned to ignore that gut instinct at his peril. "Excuse *this*. The reservation was plenty advance, pal. You want to look again?"

Robowaiter could not have cared less. "You may want to try --"

"Down in Boystown?" Crackling red heat rose behind Eli's eyes, knocking at the forefront of his tone and tightening his hands into the suggestion of fists. "Or maybe you were going to suggest a nice chicken sandwich? Newsflash. They don't much like our kind either."

"*Eli*." Zane took him by the elbow. "That's enough."

The maître'd's lip curled a hair. Just a hair, but sufficient to confirm Eli's suspicion. "You're damn right it's enough," he said, pulling his arm free of Zane's restraining hand. "Let's go."

* * *

Give credit where credit was due, Zane waited for the door to shut and the sound of jazz to fade into the background before he stood in front of Eli and fixed him in place with a hard look. "That wasn't necessary."

"Hell if it wasn't." Eli's temper smarted, roused and then denied a chance to vent. *Better be careful. Don't vent it all over Zane. It's hardly his fault.* "He had no right."

"Or maybe they did lose the reservation. It happens, Eli." Zane stood his ground. "And it's also possible that he scratched out your name. It doesn't matter."

Eli's head came up, quick as a strike. "It does. You of all people say that?"

Zane didn't much like that, but he returned fire. "Yes, me. It's not the first time. It won't be the last. Either here or far from home, there will always be people who don't like what we are. You know that as well as I do."

True, but --"Are you grinning?" Eli demanded. "Why?"

Zane's smile widened. "Because, you big idiot." He took Eli's elbow again and used it as a fulcrum to lean closer with. "You didn't deny it."

The wind zipped out of Eli's sails.

"The old dog can learn new tricks after all," Zane said. He knocked shoulders with Eli. "You don't know how glad that makes me, do you? Sometimes I wonder, Eli. I wonder if you know how lucky I am."

Eli couldn't have spoken if ordered to at gunpoint. He made a helpless, abbreviated sort of motion even he couldn't have interpreted.

But Zane spoke his language. "Tell you what. I think I have an idea. Feel up to following my lead?"

That, Eli could answer. He nodded once, rough and jerky.

And he let Zane take his elbow as they walked. Zane shivered once. Didn't seem like a bad shiver, though, and he was smiling still. Even had a hint of pep in his step as he led Eli back in the direction they'd come.

"I do," Eli said. He sounded like a rusty frog. "Trust you."

Zane's glance his way was as good as a kiss... and as naughty as a frat boy's. "Since when do you even know what Boystown is?"

Eli didn't mean to laugh, but it happened all the same. Who'd have thought?

* * *

And where did Zane lead him?

"The rooftop of Immaculate Grace," Eli said, turning in an ambling circle. "Why do I feel like I should have known?"

"You like it," Zane replied, confident and as it happened correct. "It's a clear night. We can't see the stars from up here with the light pollution from below, but I don't mind pretending."

"You wouldn't," Eli said. He draped one arm over Zane's shoulders. Narrower than his, as were the long bones in Zane's arms and legs and fingers. The hands of a man born to be a doctor. Eli toyed with the left, measuring it against his own in a moment of whimsy. "I'll wager you know all the constellations."

Zane crinkled his nose. "Hopelessly geeky, I know."

"Nah." Eli cleared his throat. "It's cute."

In answer, Zane patted Eli's hand where it lay against his collarbone. "Geeky and cute. I could live with that."

Yeah. Eli wouldn't mind it himself. He gave Zane a friendly squeeze as they meandered closer to the roof's edge. Looked like they had the place all to themselves that night. Must have been slow on the business end for once, because he wouldn't doubt they'd have company on a rush night.

Neither of them were supposed to be there, granted, but neither was anyone else, and they didn't let that stop *them*. Zane had pointed to the scratch marks marring the enamel paint on the security doors, showing where management had tried and failed to block off access.

"You can't stop human nature, can you?" Eli asked.

"Not even with dynamite."

"Dynamite. Interesting choice."

"I'm a bloodthirsty little bastard sometimes," Zane agreed with great good cheer. "Sometimes that's a good thing."

Eli wondered if Zane was thinking back to the last time they'd been on Immaculate Grace's roof. When he tried to remember the first big fight they'd had as a couple, his mind blurred the details. Either that was a mercy, or it was masochism. More than likely a mix of both.

"Sometimes," he agreed aloud. He stifled what he'd thought might be a cough and tasted the surprising bitterness of stomach acid.

Lovely. If commanded to view the situation through rose-tinted glasses, Eli might have said it was just as well they hadn't tucked into a steak dinner after all. Heartburn burned with a sullen blaze behind his breastbone and made swallowing a challenge.

Too much coffee at lunch. He ought to cut down, he knew. Neither of them were getting any younger. Eli patted his chest and winced at a particularly sharp protest from within.

Though Zane -- as he crossed his arms to lean against the roof railing -- looked as if he'd found the fountain of youth somewhere in his travels. It was altogether difficult to imagine him as truly old. Eli joined him, their elbows comfortably knocking together, Zane's body warmth plentiful enough to share.

Eli dug through his pocket for the minty antacid he'd thought to stash there on his way out of the apartment. One problem solved. He pushed his awareness of the discomfort to the back of his mind and left it there. Better to enjoy his night out. Even if it wasn't what he'd anticipated, he couldn't complain. He couldn't complain at all.

"I remember the first time I climbed up somewhere I shouldn't," Eli said, surprising himself and Zane too. Why not, though? "A water tower."

"How old were you?" Zane had his cheek tucked against one arm as he turned his head sideways to watch Eli.

"Fourteen. Me and a couple of kids from the old neighborhood. I don't even remember their names now." Eli laughed at the memory. "God, we thought we were kings of the world. You should have seen us, buzzed on half a stolen six-pack and egging each other on."

Zane chuckled. "How high did you get? All the way?"

"Hell no. We were barely off the ground before the cops who'd been watching us clicked on their flashlights and knocked us blind. I can still hear them laughing. Pissed me off to no end at the time, but we deserved it, little shits that we were."

Zane's shoulders were shaking and his eyes shiny, but his smile easy and carefree. "You were a hellion, hmm?"

"A trial to everyone who knew me." Eli let out a long breath and blew the shreds of nostalgia away. "Some things never change."

"Some things do." Zane stretched out his forearm in invitation.

After a moment's surprise -- because some things did change, and some things didn't -- Eli took it and laced their fingers together. "I am what I am," he said. "Sometimes I wonder why you put up with it."

"I have my reasons." Zane rested his head against Eli's. "Trust me, I'm well aware that I'm not exactly low-maintenance either."

"Bite your tongue."

Zane arched an eyebrow. "Eli, really?"

"Well..." Eli shrugged uncomfortably. "You're

human. I just don't think of it like that."

"You think of me as more than human? Ouch, okay, okay." Zane rumpled Eli's hair in retaliation for being ear flicked. "You're far too easy to mess with. You know that, right?"

"Don't I just."

One thing Eli wouldn't grow tired of was having someone to be quiet with when life allowed. He rested his head against Zane's and let the sound of the streets and of Zane's breathing fill his ears. Nice. More than nice.

His gaze fell on a blank blackness below them without registering, at first, the oddness of a dark spot in the cityscape. When Zane sobered, Eli's mind clicked pieces into place. From here, they'd been able to look down at the free clinic while its doors were open. He'd watched Zane through the skylight, once upon a time.

Zane rested his chin on his forearms. "I really thought we'd find a way to keep it open," he said. "It still feels like…"

Eli waited, letting his body language ask, *feels like what?*

"Like I could have tried harder," Zane said. All his focus rested on the low building, as hollow and empty as the old drugstore. It'd have the same kind of chains across its doors. Maybe plywood in the windows. Cabinets with leftover Band-Aids and forgotten cotton swabs lurking in drawers. "Like I should have done more. Only I didn't know what. I still don't. And I've tried, Eli."

"I know that." Eli didn't care for the creeping misery that made Zane's shoulders tight and his mouth drawn into a line. He put his arm around Zane's waist to anchor and steady him. "You did everything you could. More than. Some you win --"

"And some you lose," Zane finished for him. "I wish that'd been a win."

Eli idly drew his thumb across the smooth warmth at the small of Zane's back. He knew he should hold his tongue, or thought he should. But what if he shouldn't? "Me too," he said.

"Yeah?" Zane glanced sideways at him, seeming surprised.

"Yeah." Eli didn't quite dare look his friend in the eye. "Ever think about trying again?" He ran his thumbnail down the line of Zane's back. "Starting a clinic of your own, maybe. That'd be something to consider."

"I have, from time to time." Zane shook his head. He looked tired, and for once close to his age. "And no. I don't want to. I spent most of my life breaking my heart against one stone or another. I don't want to waste the time I have left chasing the impossible. Not when I like all the other cards I've been dealt. Working with Medicins Sans Frontieres. Our house. You." He closed his eyes. "It's a good life, Eli. It makes me happy. I couldn't ask for more."

And that was that, wasn't it? "Me either," Eli said. A life's worth of practice kept him reserved enough to hope Zane wouldn't notice the fleeting flurry of disappointment. "As long as you're happy."

"I am." Zane turned to cast his gaze over Eli. He took Eli's hand and pressed it lightly between both of his. "Are you happy, Eli?"

Eli returned the gaze. *Zane.* Friend, lover, partner. Home on two legs. "I am."

Zane's eyes crinkled at the corners. "I am a lucky man," he murmured. "The luckiest one I know. You have a good heart. Thank you, Eli."

Sheepish embarrassment made Eli gruff. "Yeah, well. Don't thank me too much yet. The night's not over."

"There's more?"

Eli took one last look at the free clinic and tried to put it out of his mind. That, and the nagging suspicion that it might be the last time he walked the roof of Immaculate Grace if they didn't hire him back. It didn't matter, did it? Not if he had Zane. "There's more, he asks?" He took Zane by the hand. "You bet there's more, and I have these tickets in my wallet. Follow me."

And no looking back.

* * *

"When you decide to do a date night, you don't do it by halves, do you?"

"A what?" Eli tucked the ticket stubs back into his wallet. *RENT.* Zane's favorite. A one-night-showing only, and tickets had been sold out for weeks.

Sold out for people who weren't Holly, anyway. Or, luckily for Eli, people who knew Holly and somehow managed to stay on her good side.

Zane looked like a kid at the circus. A pretty sight, and one Eli intended to enjoy for all it was worth. He couldn't say he was as much a fan of the close, too-warm air in theater corridors, smelling strongly of humanity drenched in cologne and coconut-oil "butter," but you took the good with the bad in this life.

"Date night." Zane tipped his head to one side. He laughed. "That's what this is. In case you were wondering."

"Huh. You learn something new every day." Eli rapped a knuckle against the poster for an upcoming event. He couldn't quite make out the print. Something to do with modern major generals. Zane could take himself to that one, thanks. Eli would do a hell of a lot for love, but Gilbert and Sullivan didn't make the list.

Zane didn't seem to mind. He squeezed Eli's wrist in his preferred public display of affection -- or if one were to speak honestly, their agreed-upon compromise. "You don't have to learn what you already know."

"Is that a fact?"

"Fact," Zane confirmed. "The other girls are going to be so jealous, you wait and see. Laugh if you will, but none of their boyfriends measure up."

Eli wasn't laughing. Not as such. "I'm not that good," he said. "Maybe good enough to know I could do better."

"Not sure how you could top this."

He didn't ask for it. That was what made Eli want to give it to him. Slowly -- and carefully, so carefully -- making sure he telegraphed every move despite the jostling of the crowd that pushed past them, Eli lifted Zane's chin. He bent his head and brushed his lips across Zane's. A genteel kiss. Discreet.

Zane stared at Eli as if Eli had hung the moon and turned on the stars. "You..."

"Me," Eli agreed. He took Zane's hand in his. To hell with the crowds. Zane's lips looked good enough that he wanted to see what a second kiss did to them by the low glow of the mezzanine. He bent his head, and --

A hand, not Zane's, landed on his shoulder. "Eli?"

Zane went very, very still.

"Eli," the speaker insisted, tugging him by the collar of his coat. "Son of a -- I thought that was you. Of all the places. I thought you hated musical theater."

Hell. He knew that voice. Eli's heart sank to the pit of his stomach, then did a one-eighty and jumped up to lodge in his throat. "Marybeth."

Chapter Nine

Marybeth was tall for a woman. She had strong arms and legs that went on for days. Small breasts, a narrow nose, and thin lips. Soft brown hair. Chestnut, he remembered she used to correct him, then turn right around and despair of her eyes being a muddy mix of green and hazel. Her second youth, as she called her life post-divorce, looked good on her. The lines in her face spoke of smiles, not frowns, and she'd lost the tightly wound boniness she'd sported in the last years of their marriage.

She wrapped those arms around his neck in a hug that smelled of flowery soap and Chanel No. 5. "I thought it was you! Eli, my God. How are you?"

At the moment? Choking. Good Lord, he'd forgotten how strong Marybeth was, and how unbending once she'd set her mind on something.

Eli tried to nudge her down. Swear to God, he did. Somehow, though, his arms didn't work right when he looked over her shoulder and saw Zane standing alone, stock-still, as if he'd been shot and gravity hadn't made him fall yet.

"Marybeth," he croaked again. He patted her back, glad he could only move awkwardly. "Can't breathe."

"Oh, you big baby," she scolded, swatting him. She settled down flat on her feet -- or as flat as a woman could stand in those ankle-breaker heels she liked -- and grinned up at him like a girl half her age. She always had done that, Eli recalled now. That smile had been the first thing he liked about Marybeth.

He couldn't lie. She wasn't Zane, but she looked good.

"Just a second," Marybeth said, popping back up on her toes to smack a kiss on his cheek. "There. I warned you that was coming."

Eli didn't dare look at Zane. He loosened his tie and managed a good step back from Marybeth. He hadn't been kidding about not getting enough oxygen, and Holly and Diana's butterfly hugs aside, he'd long since grown accustomed to clean woodsy soap and aftershave in his nose when he put his arms around someone. "What are you doing here?"

She ignored him. Or didn't hear him. "Look at you, Eli," she said, giving him the kind of once-over that made him feel uncomfortably naked -- sure, she'd seen it all, but... Her smile faded by millimeters. "You look like hell."

Christ. Leave it to Marybeth. "I'm fine," he said, trying to dislodge her hands from his wrists. "Just a shock, seeing you again. I hadn't expected to."

Eli tried to overemphasize that last and aim it in Zane's direction. Given that he still couldn't make himself look, he had no idea if the words reached their target.

"You look... healthy," he said, and could feel Zane stiffen. Sure, he heard *that*, didn't he?

"And you, my dear Eli, are still a flatterer of the highest degree." Marybeth cupped his cheek. Her fingers were colder than Zane's, and softer. She looked past him with a widening smile. "Knew it! As soon as I saw Eli standing there, I knew there had to be a reason he'd come to the theater without a gun actively pressed to his head. I could never drag him to anything less violent than a hockey game."

Eli winced internally and externally as Marybeth dropped his wrists to duck past him. Not hard to see Zane wanted to run for cover, but he didn't -- or couldn't -- move fast enough to avoid being swallowed in the same sort of happy-families hug.

"You look ten years younger than the last time I saw you," Marybeth said. Swear to God, Eli couldn't see anything in her except earnest bonhomie. She was *glad* to have run into them both. What the hell he should make of that, Eli didn't know...

She didn't know Zane as well as he did, and couldn't read through the lines of his hard-set jaw to the frozen fury cooking underneath.

"Marybeth," Zane said, to all appearances a perfect gentleman. "Last I heard you were in Austria."

"Austria was a few years ago." Marybeth punched Zane on the arm as if they were best friends. Her smile appeared guileless. "Let me guess. This one doesn't keep you up to date on all his comings and goings, does he?"

"Depends, I suppose," Zane said, poker-faced. Not even Eli could scan him clearly once he passed a certain point and they were coming up on it pretty damn quick. "He has a tendency to forget certain details sometimes."

Eli's face burned. So did his gut. Hell. So much for following the letter of the law. He'd have more ulcer than stomach lining left after tonight. "Marybeth, come on."

"In a minute, hon," she said absently, all her interest in Zane. Zane, who gritted his teeth so tightly Eli worried he'd crack one. "Well, you do look good. Whatever you're doing, you should share it with Eli."

"I'll take that under consideration," Zane said. "If you'll --"

"It's so good to see that some things don't change." Marybeth still had hold of Zane's hand, and Eli knew her grip strength all too well. "Do you two still do this often? Go out together?"

"Go out together, yes," Zane said. Shock ebbed

away. A wary edginess took his place. "And go home together."

Marybeth didn't understand. Eli could see from her faint frown that she didn't. If he could open his mouth before Zane did --

"We live together," Zane said. "We are together."

"Marybeth," Eli started. He stopped with a grunt as his gut twisted into a spiky-edged knot. *Fuck, that hurt.* "Zane."

Neither heard him. "Together," Marybeth repeated. She pointed from Zane to Eli. "You mean..."

"He didn't tell you," Zane said. "Okay. If you'd excuse me."

Marybeth had grip strength. Zane had something else altogether. He politely but absolutely effectively peeled her hand off his wrist and left her in the dust, staring unblinking after him. She pressed the back of her hand to her forehead. "Eli, what the --"

Oh, hell. Eli didn't have the breath to speak to her, to deal with the angry pain that made his throat burn, or to go after Zane. He could only manage one out of the three.

As he broke into a run to follow Zane, he could only hope to God *this* choice would count in his favor when time came for the gravedigger to make his tally.

* * *

Eli caught Zane just outside the side entrance to the theater, a door he guessed would be mostly used by staff and performers who didn't want the spotlight on them as they stole away. "Hold on a damn minute," he said. "It's not what you think, Zane."

"The hell it isn't, Eli." Zane shoved him, hard and meaning to knock him away. "Put another hand on me, and I'll take it off."

"Fucking hell. Fine." Eli raised both hands,

palms out. "Give me a chance to explain."

"Explain what? That you never told you wife we were -- that you'd --" Zane twisted away from Eli, pointed at the alley's exit. He struck the wall with one tightly knotted fist, hard enough to scrape the skin off the knuckles and maybe to break bones. Eli started toward him, pure reflex, meaning to stop him punching the brick a second time.

Zane's finger came an inch from putting out Eli's eye. "I said, *don't.*"

The slow-moving theater door slammed shut.

"Okay." Eli made himself stand still, and it took more effort than he'd thought. "Okay. Calm down. Talk to me."

Zane scoffed.

Thinking wasn't a walk in the park either. Eli's stomach had tied itself into Gordian knots. He swallowed acid that made him rasp when he spoke. "You're pissed. I get that."

"You think?" Zane's look made lemons seem sweet by comparison. "And 'it's not what it seems,' Eli? How exactly am I supposed to interpret what I just saw?"

Hell with it. Eli would risk losing a hand. He caught Zane by the arm. His muscles were tight and tense as coiled iron. Just as brittle too. "I didn't tell Marybeth. I meant to. It just... didn't happen."

Zane's face was a picture. "See, Eli, the thing is I believe you. I know you well enough to be certain it's the sort of thing you'd put off, and put off, and put off. Always thinking there'd be time to get it done tomorrow. What I'm still having trouble believing is that after all this time, you still don't get it. Eli, I swear to God, sometimes I want to shake you until your teeth rattle."

"Then do it." Eli kept a careful hold on Zane's arm but opened the rest of his stance as wide as he could. "Take a shot if you want. If it'll make you feel better. Just don't hit the wall again. You're going to break something."

"I've been punching walls since I was thirteen. I know how to take care of myself."

"I'd believe that about you," Eli said. "And I don't get why it's a big deal I didn't tell Marybeth. Don't glare at me like you wish looks could kill. What the hell, Zane? You didn't want me having anything to do with Marybeth. *I* didn't want anything to do with her. I'm damned if I do and damned if I don't. Is that it?"

"Eli…" Zane looked up to the heavens. "You are so fucking *thick*."

"Yeah. I am. It's an established fact. You're the one who gets bent out of shape every damn time."

"So I should just let you tra-la-la along until you stumble over your own feet and onto the right path." Zane's face had begun to close off again into hard, bitter lines. "If I didn't love you…"

Eli swallowed another bitter-sour mouthful of burning ache. "I'm sorry. I'm not just saying it either. Okay? I mean it. I try to be better, Zane, I do. I'm not good at it, but I try."

Zane shook his head slowly, wearily. "And that's your saving grace," he murmured. "No one can say you don't do that."

He didn't sound particularly happy about the fact, but hell, Eli would take what he could get.

If his mouth didn't do him in. "You thought I would cheat on you?" Eli couldn't help it; that *hurt*. "You really think I would?"

Zane wouldn't look at him. "It's hard to think

otherwise," he muttered. "She had her hands on you. She kissed you."

"I'm sorry, but did you not see what happened? Only way I could have dodged was by letting her fall."

"I saw enough."

"Sure you did." The stink of fake butter piping through air vents made Eli shudder. He'd bent over backward for Zane. Hell. And this was what he got? "If you want go there, I'll go there. Why don't we talk about things I've seen?"

"What?"

He looked *confused*. That son of a... "When were you going to tell me about Pedersen?"

"Who?" Zane stared. He shoved a hand into his hair and gripped his skull as if he thought it'd pop loose and fly apart. "Have you *actually* lost your mind?"

Eli's blood was up now. Hot and thick in his head, pounding in his ears. "If you really want to throw stones, I can throw a few of my own. Pedersen. The guy with the... the -- hell, I don't know his first name. The one with the teeth, from your college."

"Jabez? He's *married*."

"So were you. And so was I."

Zane had lost most of the color in his face. "If you think I would cheat on you, Eli, you can walk away right now."

No, roared the smaller, saner part of Eli's head, before the trammeling clubfeet of other, uglier thoughts stomped it into the mud. "Maybe I should. You'd be happier."

As still as Zane had gone before, he seemed far stiller now.

Eli would have been happy to lie down right there in the dirty alley. Swear to God. He was just that tired. He didn't have any more to give. "Maybe you should be with someone who can be what I'm not, Zane. If you're never going to be satisfied with who I am."

Zane said nothing. Looked like nothing Eli had ever seen before. Gut-stabbed. Throat-kicked.

"Or you can take me as I am," Eli said. "Not perfect, and never will be. Not the best at anything, and hard as hell to love. That's me. Take me or leave me, Zane, because I can't do much more of this."

"You son of a..." Zane pulled free of Eli and pressed both palms to his face. His knuckles were bruised and torn. "I'll be so *fucking* glad to get out of this city again. Bad things happen here. I need to be back where I belong."

"Where you belong," Eli said. He didn't mean to. Just came out like that. And once it'd ripped free, others followed. So help him, the indignity of being the only one in the wrong -- even if it was true -- galled worse than the squeezing burn inside. "Right. Because nothing ever happens when we're off God knows where and doing it all your way."

Zane stared at him. "Say that again?"

"You heard me. I know you're not a stupid man. Maybe I'm not the only one who's so... fucking... thick, Zane."

"I did hear you." Zane looked equal parts dangerous and fragile at that. He took one step forward without lifting his feet, nearly sliding on the concrete littered with old playbills. "I thought you liked working abroad with me."

Eli tried to keep it back. He did. But he couldn't. "Maybe I did once. But I don't want to go back."

There. He'd said the words. Six of them that landed with a hard and ugly slap that sliced the air between them.

"Say that again," Zane said. No color to him now. He might as well have been carved out of limestone. "Eli."

"I don't want to go back," Eli repeated. He didn't have the strength to hold himself upright, but let the wall bear his weight. "That might be where you belong, but I don't. I tried for you. Every day I'm away from the city is a day closer to coming home. You wanted the truth? There it is. Don't blame me if you don't like the way it tastes."

"Why..." Zane stopped. Eli could see him make himself start again. "Why didn't you ever tell me any of this?"

"I didn't want to rock the boat." Eli snorted. "So much for that."

"And you... you mean it, don't you?" Zane pressed his bruised hand to his mouth and spoke through the shield of his fingers. "No, don't answer me. I can see how much you mean it. You hate what we do that much, and you never said."

Eli could have answered him. Could have said, *yes, and I was going to keep on doing it because I love you.*

But now that he needed to, he couldn't say a single damn word.

"Fuck this," Zane said. White as chalk, cold as death. "Fuck you, Eli. Go to hell."

He turned his back on Eli and walked away. Clear to the mouth of the alley and beyond, taking a right turn into foot traffic and melting away.

And Eli? Eli let him go.

* * *

He shut his eyes, knotted his fists, and punched the fucking hell out of the wall behind him.

It helped Eli about as much as it'd helped Zane.

Which was to say, not at all. The shout of pain he locked behind his teeth choked Eli, and he felt the startling warmth of drawn blood follow fast after the shock of impact to his knuckles.

He couldn't fucking breathe. Again. Still. He reached for his tie, meaning to loosen the knot, and realized only then that it'd come fully undone already. When he tried to find the loose end, he missed.

What?

Eli's knees were made of rubber and gravy. They wouldn't hold him up. His shoes, damned slick-soled dress shoes, slipped from beneath him. He caught his back against the wall with a jarring jolt and a flare of pain that didn't come close to matching the ripping, tearing --

He pressed his fist over his heart. Hell. Oh, hell. *You idiot.* A fucking fine doctor he made.

His phone. He had his phone in one pocket. Except he'd turned it off so he wouldn't get any texts. Or had he left it at home? He couldn't remember. His hand wouldn't work to reach into his pocket.

The ground was cooler than he'd imagined. Hard and cool. The lights belled in and out; he closed his eyes to stop them hurting his head.

God, but he could do with something to drink. His mouth tasted of copper and cucumbers. Were there snakes in the alley? One of them had bitten him right in the chest. He needed… something. A doctor, but Zane was gone.

"It's okay," someone said. Shouted. In his ear. "Hey. Hey! Stay awake. It's okay, Dr. Jameson. It'll be okay."

Nice try, kid, he thought. *You mean well. You get points for that.*

He closed his eyes.

Chapter Ten

"What've we got?"

"White male, approximately fifty years old --"

I'm not fifty yet. Eli wanted to protest, but it was the damnedest thing how he couldn't make his lips move. The best he could produce was a barely there growl that came out sounding more like a cry.

"Probable cardiac event approximately fifteen minutes ago. Stabilized him in the ambulance."

"Family with him?"

"No. One of the kids working concessions at the theater found him when he was taking out the trash."

"Did he stick around?"

"Nope. Said he needed to make a call. Some kind of Good Samaritan, huh?"

Richie. Vague memories swam into focus. Short kid. Curly dark hair. A button nose. *Damn good Samaritan. I didn't find him. He found me.*

"Okay, on three. One -- two --"

Eli had seen the emergency department in action plenty of times. He'd never been on the receiving end. From his vantage point, he thought he could say honestly and fairly that it was a fucking rotten experience. Emotionally. Logically, sure, he appreciated they were too busy trying to save his life to worry about banging his joints transferring him from gurney to table, but he was too big a man to be tossed about like a rag doll. He couldn't help the groan that spilled from his lips.

"I know him. He used to work here. Dr. Jameson?" A light too bright to focus on blazed over each eye. "Patient is semiconscious and partially responsive. Get him back in a patient bay, start an EKG --"

The snake from the alley must have hitched a

ride. It sank its fangs into Eli's sternum and *gnawed* at him. He heard himself grunt and thought that sound would give him nightmares for a good damn while to come.

If he lived to have nightmares. What the hell?

"Zane," he said, or tried to say. The word didn't sound right. "Zane?"

"Oh hell. Come on, clear the way --"

"*Zane*," Eli begged. Where was he? Maybe at the university. Someone should call him. Richie must have gone to call him, but the university was in Brazil. Wasn't it? They'd just gone to Brazil... when? Eli couldn't remember. No, no. they'd come back to Chicago. Eli remembered that. He and --

No... wait. Zane had left him behind the theater. Walked away.

Something chokingly thick and heavy covered his face. Eli tossed his head, rearing away from the mask. The snake was eating him from the chest up and the skull down. It'd go after Zane next. Had to find him and warn him --

"Hold his shoulders. Dr. Jameson, stop fighting us. Dr. Jameson! Can you hear me?"

"No response."

"Who's he calling for?"

"No idea. Stabilize him now and worry about the rest later." A cold hand that stank of latex was choking him. "Sedation?"

"Probably should. And find out who he's trying to call."

The world belled out and belled in. He couldn't stop shaking.

"What in the goddamn hell is going on here?" a strident female voice bellowed. "Move over and get the fucking *fuck* out of my way."

Eli laughed, or tried to. He smelled cigarettes and White Linen perfume. The Good Samaritan must have made the right call. *Diana.*

He was still laughing when red velvet darkness drew the covers over his head and turned out the lights. Everyone should go out on a song, and it only made sense that his turned out to be filthy music to his ears.

* * *

Softness. Quiet. Cool, still air. Sheets that crackled beneath Eli.

No one around. Not a soul.

Eli couldn't open his eyes, but he knew he was alone. And then, he knew when he wasn't alone.

"Zane?"

No answer.

Eli forced his hand open from the loose fist it'd formed and strained to stretch his fingers wide, searching. If he could only reach far enough he might get lucky. "Zane?"

"Shh," the someone said. Thick and choked and breaking down the middle. Even so, their hand didn't shake when it brushed Eli's forehead. Cool lips touched his cheek. He knew that touch, he *did.*

Zane.

Eli sighed and relaxed.

"You… Eli, if you ever do that again…" Zane took a deep, rattling breath. "It'll be okay. I'll make it be okay."

When had it started raining? Hot drops fell on Eli's skin. When he tried to brush them away, he reached too high into the sky, and he pulled the night down on top of his head. *Damn.*

* * *

When he woke, Zane had gone. Had he ever

been there in the first place? Eli couldn't tell.

"I shouldn't be here," a man said quietly. Eli couldn't identify the speaker. Not with his head so fucking *foggy*. "Your friend Diana sneaked me in. She said I could stay for five minutes and I should make them count."

Eli's chest ached, a deep throbbing burn that went down to the bones and thrummed in his ribs. Felt like an elephant had parked it on his stomach and started digging for peanuts.

Someone -- the owner of the voice, no doubt -- had a cool wet cloth and was wiping his hands. "They're not really dirty. Don't worry. I used to do this for my grandmother when I was little. I don't think it does any good, but she liked it."

Eli couldn't say he minded. The voice had deft, gentle hands and moved slowly.

But he wasn't Zane. Where was Zane?

"You didn't know that," the voice went on. "No one does, except for Taye. I didn't tell him about my grandmother. She had a heart attack just like you, only she was alone when it happened, and I didn't find her until it was too late. Taye figured that out all on his own just from bits and pieces back when we lived in the shelter. He's smart, you know? Smarter than anyone."

Zane was smarter, Eli thought. Zane was a genius. That way he had of looking at people as if he could see right through them, and know what they'd do and when... terrifying, and wonderful. Both at the same time.

"I know Taye's worried. But if I hadn't been working, I wouldn't have found you. Maybe that makes up for it." The hands stilled. "Don't tell him. Please? I've almost got enough saved up. I promise I'll tell him everything then. I just want it to be a surprise. Okay?"

The voice sounded worried enough that Eli wanted to make that promise. *Sorry, kid. I'm not sure I've got much of a choice.*

"Don't tell him," it said again. "Dr. Jameson?"

Eli blinked.

* * *

Eli opened his eyes. Tried to open his eyes. He couldn't say he got very far before he decided *nope, not today*, and let them slide shut again.

Different hands, cool and soft with unscented lotion, held his. Delicate, they sifted through his hair and patted his wrist. "Eli," Holly said. "If you do anything like that again, I promise I'll kill you myself."

Eli believed her.

Where's Zane? he wanted to ask. *What happened?*

Holly always had been good at reading minds. "Zane hasn't abandoned you, Eli. But he seems to think you'd be too angry with him to let him visit, if you had the choice," she said. "He hasn't chosen to share why he thinks that is. Of course, I can guess, but guessing is never as good as the truth, when the truth needs to be told. It doesn't always."

It didn't?

"I can imagine what you'd have to say to that." She chuckled quietly. "I can also imagine very well that you'd tell Zane not to be an idiot, but then I wonder why exactly he wasn't with you when you were found."

Richie found me, he wanted to tell her. In case she didn't know. Good kid, that kid.

"If you'd like, you can tell me if you'd want Zane to visit." Holly's voice took on the encouraging tones of a mother coaxing her child to walk. "Would you like to do that, Eli? All you have to do is squeeze my hand once. Just once, to tell me what you want."

Want? He wanted Zane.

Eli opened his mouth and got as far as shaping a Z on his lips before he ran out of breath.

* * *

He dreamed a memory. First one of waking up in the old apartment, filled with all the new things he and Zane had acquired over the past four-odd years, and littered with the detritus of everyday life too, and then of a day not long before they'd left for the last trip out.

"It can't be four years already," Zane said as he folded laundry. He liked doing that -- something about the way the blankets felt and smelled straight out of the dryer -- and Eli didn't mind letting him have at it. "If you tell me it's closer to five, I'm going to start feeling way too old."

"Depends," Eli said. He propped one hip against the washer and crossed his arms loosely, content to watch Zane work. If Zane asked for help, he'd be on it like white on rice, sure, but Zane had his pride, and Eli had a secret guilty pleasure in watching the man go to whatever job he'd chosen to spend his time on.

"Depends on what?" Zane asked. Static from the freshly laundered sheets made his hair stand up and crackle like a surprised dandelion.

Eli snorted and broke pose to beckon him closer, trying to flatten the mess down into something that bore a closer resemblance to actual hair. "You look like a puffer fish. Depends on whether you count from how long we've known each other."

"Oh, that. I don't count from then."

"No?"

"Maybe I should," Zane said, content to let himself be played with. He leaned comfortably against

Eli and flicked bits of dryer lint off Eli's sleeve. "It's accurate, but it isn't quite right. There's a difference. I count it from the day you kissed me in the parking lot of an overpriced bistro."

"Hmm." Eli poked at a stubborn cowlick that threatened to fall square over Zane's forehead. "Seems more like you kissed me."

"That's how you remember it," Zane said. "I've got my own story, and I'm sticking to it."

"Suit yourself."

Zane hummed in response. Eli knew he didn't mind. He had always preferred to count from the day he walked into a free clinic and the doctor on duty shook his hand instead of looking at his chart first thing. It'd been the start of something good, only he hadn't seen it for what it was for far too long.

But if he were to count anniversaries the way Zane did, then... well, Eli would have to go from the minute Zane opened his eyes in a hospital bed. He'd nearly died, and come back to life.

Come to think of it, the second he'd said *I love you*, so had Eli.

* * *

"There you go. Bet that feels better, huh?" A light slap landed on Eli's shoulder. Big bark, little bite.

Hi, Diana. What brings you? Eli's eyes were dry and itched as if someone had packed crumbs under the lids. His throat was as raw as hamburger and felt as swollen as a boxer's right knuckles.

"Don't talk. They've taken the tube out of your throat, and you fought them. I could have told 'em you would, but when does anyone ever listen to me?" Diana's slight weight perched on the edge of the bed. She cleared her throat and sounded more like a doctor -- and a damn fine cardiologist -- than usual when she spoke. "I've got your chart right here, Eli. Heart attack. It wasn't quite as bad as it could be, but worse than I'd like. You're going to have to make *so* many changes to your lifestyle, and I guarantee you'll hate each and every one."

Eli tried to frown. *What... oh. Right.* He remembered the alley almost clearly now. He groaned, wishing he could stick his head under the pillow.

"Heh. I heard that," Diana said. "You know, you'd actually had several minor episodes?" She thwapped him lightly with what felt like a patient file. "You thought cardiac pain was an ulcer? I don't know whether I'm impressed by your stones or if I want to staple the warning signs of a heart attack to your forehead."

Neither would go amiss, in Eli's opinion. He grumbled under his breath despite the soreness of his throat.

"Don't worry, I'm not that awful. I'll wait for you to get back on your feet before I really start giving you hell." She sounded almost cheerful. "Zane, on the other hand, is wide open. Olly-olly-oxen-free."

Egads. Eli devoutly hoped Zane would start running now.

"Don't, eh..." Diana cracked her knuckles. "Don't lose your cool if he's not around as much as everyone else for a while. You know how he is. If you're bad about internalizing, he's worse. He'll come around."

From her lips to God's ears, Eli would have said if he could. Yeah. He knew Zane. God help them, this wouldn't be an easy one to get past, but he'd try all the same.

"He loves you, you know," she added after a minute. "Loves you like you're both princes in a fairy tale. Lucky bastard, aren't you?"

Eli wanted to laugh or to shake her hand. He settled for trying to smile. Good enough, he thought. Good enough.

* * *

Someone held Eli's hand, and it wasn't Zane. Small hands, tougher than Diana's, not as soft as Holly's. They'd been humming to him, a lullaby version of Top 40.

"Oh," someone else said. Eli's ears pricked up. "I didn't know you were here."

"I'm still listed as his emergency contact. Probably because he never thought to change it."

The man laughed, but not as if he thought what the woman said was funny. "That'd be like him."

"Wouldn't it just?" the woman asked. Marybeth. Eli recognized her now.

And Zane. But Zane wouldn't come. He remembered Holly saying so.

Must have been another dream, then. *Damn, again.*

"I'm glad you're here," Marybeth said. "I was going to track you down, but I don't mind someone else doing the legwork for me. You and I need to have words."

Uh-oh. Eli would have advised Zane that was the tone Marybeth took when she meant business. Since neither she nor he was actually here, he resigned them all to their fates and settled in to enjoy the show.

"Well? Come on in. I don't know much about hospitals, but I do know it's probably not the best idea to block doorways."

"If you want to… You don't have to say it, Marybeth." Hesitant footsteps edged closer. Zane sounded flat as a board when he said, "You're holding his hand."

"Points to you for noticing, genius. I'm holding his hand because he's been sick, and you weren't here."

"I had my reasons."

"I'm sure you did. Some of them might even be valid. Just in case you didn't hear me before, we need to have words. I'm not going anywhere. Are you?"

"Do you want me to?"

"Is *that* it -- Oh no. You... man. You male individual." Marybeth chortled, the exact same way she'd laughed when Eli accidentally broke a window over the sink trying to hang a half curtain with lace. "For heaven's sake, Zane. I didn't come back to town to try and win him over. Been there, done that, and burned the T-shirt."

It would take a yardstick to measure the depths of Zane's confusion. "But... he didn't tell you about us."

"Of course he didn't. Since when does Eli tell anyone anything? He keeps it all inside, and probably agonized himself halfway to this very heart attack." Marybeth clicked her tongue. "But Eli didn't have to tell me. I knew. Always. I knew before either of you did."

Silence of the stunned variety. Eli wouldn't mind getting up and stretching his legs, but he'd started to appreciate the windowless theater.

"Close your mouth, sweetie," Marybeth said. "Give me just a little credit. How could I not know? I could see the way you two lit up around each other the very first time he brought you home for dinner, and since when does a doctor become friends with a patient?"

"Not often."

"There you go." Marybeth took Eli's ring finger between her thumb and forefinger. Felt like a good-bye, and he remembered the confused regret he'd felt.

Then warmth enclosed his right hand. A firm hand, cool and dry, reassuringly strong. Zane.

Eli couldn't do much, but he gave it all he had and just barely squeezed.

"See?" Marybeth said after a moment. "That's pretty much all the answer anyone needs. He loves you, you big dope. He never loved me like that."

"But..." Eli imagined Zane tugging, frustrated, at his hair. "You're not okay with it. You can't be."

"Can't I? Listen up, champ. I'm not saying I wasn't blazingly pissed off at the time. Or that I didn't fight it for too damn long. *Or* that I wouldn't take a free left hook even now if you were gentleman enough to offer me one. We're in a hospital. No better place. I might add that *you* didn't tell me either, and I'll bet my finely toned ass you had a few chances you didn't take."

Silence.

Marybeth laid Eli's hand on the cool sheet. "But here's the thing. It took me years to learn, and I paid out the ass for the lesson, so pay attention. You can't tell the heart who and what to love, or even when or how. Try it, and you end up withered and wrinkled and cold and sour. Worse than an old lemon shoved to the back of the fridge, and me? I'd like to think I'm too good for that. So is he. And so are you."

Silence. Then --

Zane wrapped Eli's hand in both of his. "I see why he fell in love with you back then."

"He has good taste. You just have to be patient with the man while he figures out what he wants." Marybeth patted Eli's arm. Less of a pat and more of a light slap, but the affection translated well enough. "Now. This seat belongs to you. I don't know what the hospital makes them out of, but they must stuff them with broken ceramics and raffia. Sit down and keep him company. I've got a hatful of texts from someone named Diana to answer."

Zane laughed. If Eli could have, he'd laugh *and* groan. Oh God.

A-plus dream, that one. Eli bookmarked it in his memory to come back to.

Too bad it wasn't real...

* * *

"Now you're just being stubborn," a woman said. Eli had no idea which one.

The corners of his mouth quirked up. He kept his eyes shut.

They chuckled and smoothed the blanket over his stomach. "Well, you've earned a night's rest. Sleep well, Eli. We'll see you tomorrow."

We. Eli liked the sound of that.

* * *

"For once, you're going to sit still and listen to me," Zane said. He held Eli's hand lightly but competently. The man had a good touch.

Eli sighed through his nose and turned his head into the pillow. He listened through the air not smothered in hospital-grade cushion. Probably just another dream, but what the hell.

"Marybeth says she knew before you or I did. She's a smart woman, but she got that wrong. I knew the day I met you. Maybe not consciously, but somewhere in here, I knew. I never thought anything would come of it, and I made myself forget."

Yep. Classic Zane.

"When you kissed me... God, Eli. I didn't think

I'd ever have that. And I knew. Or I thought I knew. Deep down. I was always, *always* waiting for the second shoe to drop. For the day to come when you'd have had enough."

Never happen. Not truly. Eli stirred. Even if it was only a dream, Zane shouldn't sound that unhappy.

He didn't think Zane noticed his movement. Zane sounded as if he were far away, lost in his own head. "You have no idea what a good man you are, Eli. You don't like it when I say that, so mostly I keep it to myself. Learn to take a compliment."

Like that would happen.

"Take this one," Zane said. The way he sounded, Christ. It made Eli's heart hurt -- and trust him, he knew the finer, deeper shades of meaning in that old saying now. "Take this compliment, Eli, even if you are fast asleep, and remember it. You don't have to be good enough for me. It's never been about that. It's me who needs to try to be good enough for *you*."

Zane. Zane, don't.

Zane exhaled a long, ragged breath. "But I can do something about that, and I promise you, Eli: I will. You watch and see."

Didn't he get it? He had it the wrong way around. Eli opened his mouth to tell him so --

And closed it, keeping the thoughts he had to himself until he fell asleep again. A natural sleep, with no dreams.

And then he woke up.

* * *

"Five minutes," a woman said. "You can sit beside him."

"That's fine. I'm on shift in five minutes anyway," a man replied. "You're sure he'll be okay?"

"Down the road, yes. He gave us all a scare, but

he's on the mend now."

Eli raised a mental cheer. He knew the man's voice, if not the woman's. "Taye," he said.

He laughed at the startled yelp from the woman, for the sake of savoring the sound of Taye tripping over his feet en route to the bed. When he cracked his eyelids open and squinted to bring the lanky young doctor into focus.

Taye collapsed his limbs into the tiny chair and stared as if making a conscious attempt to dislodge eyes from sockets. "Good God, Eli."

"Yeah, yeah." Eli's throat still hurt, and his lips were dry as sand, but he had a thought in his head, and he didn't intend to let it go before he'd given it shape and sound. "Richie found me. You heard?"

Taye nodded. He hadn't combed his hair, and he looked like ripe hell. "He called Diana, and Diana called the rest of us."

"Not you?" When Taye shook his head, Eli made a *heh* noise. He couldn't sort out what had been dream and what had been real, but he'd take his chances. It all made sense now. "He came to visit me. Told me not to tell you."

Taye frowned. "But you…"

"Are going to tell you everything he said." Eli jerked a hand at him. "Sit down, and listen up."

The exasperating boy grinned. "You *are* going to be okay, aren't you?"

Damn right, he was. Too damn right. Starting now. And as soon as Zane came around, Eli would be giving him an earful.

But one thing at a time, hmm? *And first things first.*

* * *

Eli meant to tell Zane all about it when he came

around next. He would have too.

But the thing of it was…

Zane never did come back. Nor did he give any reason why.

Chapter Eleven

"Where did you get this bucket of bolts?"

Taye laughed. "It's not that bad, is it?"

"Depends on your definition of 'bad.'" The roll of shame from hospital exit to waiting chauffeur, now that was "bad," and the less said about it, the better in Eli's opinion. Now those wheelchairs, those were rolling death traps. The neat steel-blue compact might not be a showpiece, but she purred like a contented kitten stuffed with all the cream and herring it could ask for. "It'll do," Eli allowed.

Taye touched the dash with his knuckles, as if for luck. "It'll do just fine, at that," he said. "And you're welcome. The car is mine, actually. Richie's handiwork."

"No kidding?" Well now. There was news Eli hadn't gotten wind of yet. "How so?"

Taye paid attention to the roads -- good man -- but as he eased into traffic, Eli thought he could see how the past few days had made an impression on the kid's face, and for the better. The bruised weariness under Taye's eyes had faded to hints of lilac, and he showed the effects of a few good meals.

And he looked happy again. Content. Slightly bepuzzled, but it never did do to start taking too much good fortune for granted. Complacency killed more men than curiosity did cats, and you could take that to the bank.

Eli bit at a cuticle on his thumbnail. Zane hadn't showed up. Not once, since Eli woke up properly and all the tubes were detached. He'd been tempted to wonder if he'd dreamed all the episodes where Zane gave a damn.

It didn't sit right. Zane never hesitated to rip a strip off Eli when angry. The only time he made with the vanishing act was when guilt had its claws in him.

It wasn't his fault. Nor mine.

But how to convince Zane of that? Therein lay the problem, and Eli didn't consider himself any better at this relationship gig now than he had been at the start. Ergo, eager willingness to focus on anything beside himself on the ride home.

"I talked to him," Taye said after Eli counted off the third mile on the odometer between question and answer.

Eli smirked. "So that's what they're calling it these days?"

"That too," Taye said with a laugh. "Mostly just talking, though. With our mouths."

"Like I was saying."

Taye flicked a hand out to poke him. "Checking to make sure I'm not riding with Diana."

"If you did that to Diana, she'd have your nuts for a necklace." Eli rubbed his face. His skin had gone weirdly dry and tight after a few days stuck in a hospital room. He gestured for Taye to carry on speaking.

"Kind of you to let me get a word in edgewise," Taye said. "I know that's your way of saying you're happy for me, by the way."

Eli pretended to grumble under his breath. Funny, really. He wouldn't have thought the first day he laid eyes on the kid that he'd end up being the kind of friend Eli would take a bullet for.

Then again, he'd thought much the same thing about Zane, so there you had it.

Zane…

"He blames himself," Taye said, deliberately not looking at Eli.

"Yeah, well. Maybe so." Eli cleared his throat. "I

remember Richie saying he'd nearly saved up enough. For the car, I take it?"

"Mm-hmm. I know it doesn't look like much in the grand scheme of things, but now we don't have to beg, borrow, or catch the bus. Which from the suburbs takes half of forever. That's why I never saw him. He's been working three jobs. Taking on catering." Taye shook his head in what seemed like amazement. "That's why he kept getting fired. Falling asleep on the job. He'd meant to try and pay my college loans."

"Good luck there."

"No kidding. I'll be paying for those when I'm eighty. But he wanted to try. That counts for something. It counts for a hell of a lot, actually."

Damned right it did. "So you're good, then. The pair of you."

"Good," Taye said, "and getting better."

And if they were, then maybe that was a good sign for himself and Zane. Eli would take what he could get.

He almost asked Taye then. *Why didn't he ever come?* In the end, Eli kept the question to himself. The farther from the hospital they got, and the closer to home away from home, the less he was certain he wanted an answer.

Taye clicked on the blinkers and eased left. Eli sat up straighter. Huh! He'd gotten so wrapped up he hadn't realized they were making excellent time. The old apartment waited for him across the street. It'd be graceless to bitch about getting the last step wrong, so Eli buttoned that and kept it to himself. "What are you, training for NASCAR?"

"I got you here in one piece, didn't I?" Taye undid the clasp on Eli's seatbelt. The easy grin he wore sat well on him. Not boyish, if not yet fully grown, but getting there day by day. "It'll be all right, you know. In the end."

A nice thought. Eli appreciated the good wishes. "We'll see," he said as he eased out of the car.

"Maybe sooner than you think. I didn't drive you to your apartment. That's just a bonus. Look where I did park, Dr. Jameson. Turn around. See?"

Be damned.

Eli slowly stood and propped himself against the roof of the car, arms crossed on the metal. Lights shone through the drugstore window. If Eli looked closely, he could just about see someone moving around inside, near the back, where he could tell himself the distance was too great to make out for sure who it was.

Taye leaned across the now empty passenger seat, watching Eli. "It's okay," he said. "You can go in."

Eli found himself in the rare position of actually *wanting* to speak yet being struck dumb. "What the…"

Taye reached for the handle of the passenger-side door and gently but inexorably pulled it shut. "Go in and find out for yourself," he called as he eased away from the curb. "If you don't really know what this is, then *ask* him."

* * *

The chains had left their marks on the double door handles. Eli touched the faint stains rust left behind. Those would need to be painted.

But Zane had oiled the hinges. When Eli pulled the right door handle, it opened with never a squeak or a creak. The sharp chemical smells of floor cleaner and scrubbing bubbles made his nose twitch in preparation for a sneeze. He pressed a finger against his upper lip until the urge passed. Sneezing with sore ribs was an experience he could live without.

You're stalling, he told himself.

I know, he replied inside his head.

He saw the figure at the back of the store look up at him sharply, but they said nothing. *Zane.*

All the dust and cobwebs had been swept away. All the old shelving units had been ripped out too. Marks on the linoleum showed where they'd been. Just like scars. Everything had a memory attached. Eli diverted sideways for a look at where the soda counter used to stand. He could taste the cloying rich sweetness of the egg cream if he tried.

The counter itself, Zane had left standing. Just the right size for a reasonably well-stocked pharmacy, Eli couldn't help but notice. He swallowed hard, the knot in his throat the approximate size and shape of a baseball.

Zane carried on with whatever task he'd set himself at the back of the store, but Eli knew him better than to think he wasn't watching, waiting, wondering about how Eli would respond to this.

Eli ran a finger along the top of the counter. Right where he used to sit after a long hard day's work. "Is this supposed to go too?"

Zane didn't look up as he carefully laid down what Eli could see now was a carpenter's pencil, atop a stack of papers both yellow-old and crisply new. "I haven't decided yet. I'd asked Taye to come by and help." He drew his tongue uncertainly across the bow of his upper lip. "I didn't know you'd be out of the hospital this early."

"Neither did anyone else."

Zane almost smiled, but not quite. "I should have guessed."

"You know me," Eli said. "So Taye's helped. And Richie?"

"Where one goes, the other follows," Zane

agreed. He rubbed one hand against the other. "I... I'm told you're the one to thank for that."

"Purely by chance." Eli still couldn't wrap his head around the work in progress. He waved at the walls and the drop cloths and the cleaning supplies. "How?"

Zane took a deep breath. "One step at a time. I found the Realtor's contact information in your phone."

"You looked at my phone?"

Eli didn't mean it as an accusation. They'd have thought nothing of checking each other's messages as convenience or courtesy -- before -- and he'd barely bothered to wonder where his cell had gotten to. Maybe he should have.

Zane paled regardless, but he rallied like a champ. "Marybeth wanted to see if you had your lawyer's name in your contacts. To change the emergency listing from her to me."

"Good God."

"Tell me about it. I always thought she hated me."

"She probably did, way back when." Eli cocked his head. So that hadn't been a dream. Marybeth and Zane had actually made peace while sitting by his bed. Go figure! "She got better."

"Mmm." Zane stood straighter, though he held his arms crossed over his chest as if to protect himself. "Do you hate me?"

Eli jerked as if he'd been struck. Sure as hell felt like taking a fist to the gut. For Zane to ask -- and he meant it too. He'd thought Zane might feel some guilt, sure, but not like this. "No! Zane how can you -- *hell*. That's the one thing that never crossed my mind." The sharp shock ebbed into stunned hurt and something dangerously close to disappointment. "I thought you knew me better than that."

"I did. I do." Zane bit at his cheek. "It's just that I'd hate me after what I did to you."

"You didn't do anything."

"Exactly. When it counted, I had my back turned." Zane held his ground, but Eli could see how much effort it took to stand still. "I keep reliving that every time I close my eyes. I can believe *you* not noticing or understanding the warning signs --"

"Thanks for that," Eli said, stung.

"You know what I mean. I hope." Zane wrapped his arms tighter around himself. "But I'm a doctor too, Eli. There's no excuse for my not noticing that or -- or other things. Like your idea for a neighborhood clinic. I didn't give it enough credit."

"You thought we'd be going back in a month or so. It was a pipe dream. Even I knew that."

Zane made a minute gesture at the ceiling and walls. "And yet."

"And yet," Eli agreed. He took a longer look than Zane had indicated he should. "You really did all of this yourself? Not the heavy lifting. The planning. The buying."

"Mostly. That and the heavy work too. I needed to… I couldn't sit still."

No. He never had been able to, no more than Eli himself. Eli turned in a circle and imagined how the place would look when all the nails were in and a shingle hung outside. Pretty damn good. A little spit and polish, and they could make something good out of this place.

He realized he was grinning, and didn't know when he'd started, but was certain he didn't want to stop. "So this is why you didn't come visit me."

Zane's flinch was audible. Almost tangible. "I wasn't sure you'd understand. *I* didn't understand before I was halfway through tossing out the old display racks. When we were on the roof at Immaculate Grace, I thought, *you know, it isn't fair. I wish he'd thought of that sooner.* And I realized you had. It was me who'd dragged my feet too long. Eli?"

Eli turned from the soda counter to face Zane.

Zane held his head high, though his skin was pale and his hands uncertain. "If you don't hate me, then would you come over here and talk to me?"

All he'd had to do was ask. Eli nodded once and pushed himself off the counter, taking it one step at a time. Making his way back home where he belonged. He thought he understood now, perhaps more than Zane would have liked, and he had a mission to keep him up and running now. "I'll talk if you'll listen."

Zane swallowed hard. Eli's throat panged in sympathy.

First the bitter pill, the one Zane wouldn't like swallowing even if he did need to take his medicine. "I don't hate you. Don't ever say that again, or you really are going to piss me off almost past the point of return. Okay?"

"I understand," Zane said. His hands were shaking.

"Ah-ah-ah. None of that." Eli couldn't stand watching that, and if he could do something to stop it, then by God, he would. He caught Zane by the wrist, then by the hand. His hand still had the bruise from an IV port on the back, but he couldn't have cared less about that. He focused on Zane, who stared at him with those wide gray eyes that should never, *never* look lost or helpless. He was too good a man for that.

And for that matter, so was Eli.

"Look at me, Zane," Eli said. He fed Zane the second pill, the one that -- he hoped -- would slip down easier. He'd swallow one himself. "I've got no idea what I'm doing, okay? I never do. But I know I can't do it myself. Nor do I want to. If you're with me, then you *stay* with me. That's all I'm asking."

Zane shivered. "I want to," he said, looking away. His jaw worked. "And I will, if that's what you want. As long as you want me."

"And you think I'll stop someday." Hell. He couldn't help it. Eli would have to teach him better, then, and he wasn't done yet. "Not going to happen. Not even if you make me mad enough to punch the walls. Zane, I knew you were high-maintenance. I knew you were raised to hide and deny, and honest to God, sometimes I think that's partly why we get along." He let go of Zane's hand and reached up to cradle his cheek. Stubble scraped against his palm as Zane leaned into the touch. "And I know you don't think you're allowed to be happy. Tough. I have been, and I am. With you."

"Eli." His name slipped free on Zane's startled breath.

Eli pressed on. God knew if he let himself be interrupted when he'd find the stones to do this again. "You might have had to shepherd me along at first, but once I got my footing, then I walked in with my eyes open. And it's not as if I think I'm perfect. I'm worse than you are." He tapped Zane's lip with his forefinger. "Shush. *You* try taking a compliment for a change."

"I'm sorry," Zane said. His lips tickled Eli's fingers with each word. "Can I say that? I am so fucking sorry, Eli. I shouldn't have left you."

"But you did. And you know what? I'm still

here." Eli raised one shoulder. "If you want me to go somewhere, Zane, you'll have to make me, and you'll have to try a hell of a lot harder than that. Otherwise you're stuck with me. And a neighborhood clinic. Because I meant what I said. I don't want to go back. You can. If you do, I'll be waiting here for you when you come home."

Zane shook his head, struck as speechless as Eli had been before.

Eli took Zane's face in his hands and made the eye contact he'd wanted since he came to in the hospital. "I love you," he said. "Okay? Everything else in this life can change -- and it probably will -- but that won't. I promise."

Zane's head fit beneath Eli's chin same as it always had. His arms went around Eli as if they'd been made just the right length, for just that purpose. "Don't you do that again," he said, muffled by emotion and Eli's skin. "That's all I'm asking for. Don't you go where I can't follow."

"Try my best not to." Eli's arms weren't so bad at fitting around Zane either. He breathed in the smell of warm skin and Zane's shampoo and hard work and held the man he loved tight enough to hinder his breathing, but he'd bet Zane didn't mind. "I'm gonna lean on you, and you're gonna lean on me, and we're gonna bear each other up."

"I will hold you to that," Zane warned. He thumped Eli's shoulder. "God, I'm a mess."

"Damn right you are. To both. So am I." Eli gave him a little jostle. Just enough to get him looking up. "You really did all this for me? This place?"

Zane's eyelashes were spiked damp, but Eli didn't mind. Better to let it out. "Yes. And I hope you like it. I don't think there's much chance of getting a refund."

"Fortunate that I don't want one. Come here, stand like that. Good." Eli rested his arm atop Zane's strong, warm shoulders and exhaled. He'd been waiting for that far too long. "We'll be okay. I'll make that happen if it's the last thing I do."

"It won't be the last thing," Zane said. He stood straighter, shedding the weight of worry in sheets and layers. A fine sight, to Eli's mind. "Oh, and by the way..."

"Hmm?"

"I haven't forgotten what we talked about before."

Good for him. Eli was drawing a blank.

"You don't remember, do you?"

"Not a bit of it," Eli admitted. "Go on. Give me a clue."

"I'll give you more than that." Inch by inch, and bound by bound, Eli could see the Zane he knew -- and loved -- rising to take the place of a pale, uncertain stranger. Much, much better. They'd be all right. Both of them.

He tweaked Zane's ear. "Good. Get to it."

"Just remember, then, you asked." Zane wound his arms around Eli's neck. "I know it's not going to happen now. Nor anytime soon. Not until you're better, and I mean business. But when that day comes..." Mischief glinted in his gray eyes. "On that day, I'm going to top the hell out of you. Just saying."

Eli laughed. Too loud in the echoing empty space, but he liked the ringing echoes. "I could do with a sneak preview now."

"Good. So could I," Zane said. He closed the distance between them and touched his mouth to Eli's.

There. Yes. Zane fit against him even better this

way. He parted his lips for Eli without being asked, no hints dropped or needed. He tasted of coffee and mint and *home*. He traded breath for breath, in through his nose and sweet over his tongue. When Eli's hands wandered, Zane's followed suit. Not as much as either of them might have wanted, Eli figured, but by far better than he'd hoped for.

One kiss became two. Smaller each time, but no less sweet. He finished with Zane's hand at the back of his head, holding him up, and his arm around Zane's waist for the same purpose. "Welcome home," Zane murmured. "We've got work to do, don't we?"

"And then some," Eli said. "But... it could wait for one more day, hmm?"

Zane chuckled. "Maybe. Do you have something better in mind? Anything a responsible doctor wouldn't scold you for."

"I'll think of something."

"Mmm," Zane said, reaching up for another kiss. "I bet you will."

And he would. Things were as they should be again, and Eli meant to make sure they stayed that way. Through richer or poorer. Good times, bad times. He and Zane, they'd make it through. Nothing like he'd imagined when he made all his grandiose plans, but far better than he'd dreamed.

Best of all... they would do it together. Forever and ever, in the morning and in the evening.

And no need at all to wait and see.

Epilogue

"You're not leaving already? You're welcome to stay as long as you want."

"I know." Holly tapped Eli's chest -- a kinder way of saying she poked him in the ribs. Diana would have gone for the full fist. Eli considered himself lucky and took his small blessings where he could get them. "But *some* of us have to get up and go to work in the morning."

Eli grinned at her. "Coincidentally, so do I. How about that?"

Holly's hug enveloped Eli in a gentle cloud of perfume and shampoo that smelled of pears. "You've done well here, Eli."

Eli patted her narrow back. Over her shoulder, he took another good long look at the old pharmacy -- now the new clinic -- and drank in the sight. Windows gleamed with cleanness as yet unmarred by city dust and grime. A new awning, navy blue with clear white printing, stretched taut over the sidewalk. His name, and Zane's, marching one right after the other. The Jameson-Novia Health Clinic.

Damn right, they'd done well. Eli picked Holly up off her feet for the hell of it and swung her around once before setting her lightly down on the sidewalk. "It'll do," he said, voice tight. He cleared his throat before adding, "It'll do just fine."

"You'd better believe it." Wherever Holly went, a guy could be assured Diana wasn't far behind. She popped up on Eli's left side to sling one arm around him and jab him gently with the knuckles of one birdlike fist. See? "Taxi should be here any minute, Holly. Say good night to the small business owner before we have to make like Cinderella."

"Cinderella knew how to whistle down a Yellow

Cab?" Eli asked.

"She'd have been better off," Diana replied. She winked at him, patted his hand once, and took Holly by the arm in that odd way women could carry off far better than men. "Good night, Eli. We'll swing by tomorrow to make sure you're not overworking."

Eli thumped his chest. Angioplasty scars were small, but he liked reminding himself they were there -- and so was he. Still on his feet. Still moving. Plenty of life left in the old boy yet. "I feel fine. Better than ever."

"And we're going to make sure you stay that way," Holly said with her sweetest smile. "Taye and Richie called a few minutes ago, by the way. They were sorry to miss the grand opening, but they'll be back in town next month, ready to roll up their sleeves and get busy."

Eli grunted in approval. A month ago, Taye and Richie had taken their new-old car and a leave of absence. Eli wasn't sure where they'd planned to go on their road trip, but now they were coming home together. *Good!* They'd have a happy ending to their story, or he'd know the reason why.

But that would be for another day. Now, he brought his hands together in a brisk clap. "No rush. They'll have work when they want it, and there's plenty to go around."

Diana crinkled up her nose in gamine approval. "You're not such a bad guy, Dr. Jameson."

Eli mussed up her hair in retaliation. "Yeah, yeah, yeah. Save the praise for Zane. Or don't. It'll turn his head."

"That's your job," Holly said. She stood on tiptoe to kiss Eli's cheek. "Diana and I will swing by for lunch tomorrow. There's a new macrobiotic place downtown with a mouthwatering heart-healthy menu. You'll love it."

Eli sincerely doubted *that* -- he'd kill for a cheese steak on a toasted roll -- but sticking to the rabbit food in exchange for a few more years with Zane wasn't such a bad tradeoff. Watching the faces Diana was likely to make over a lunch of cress and sprouts was only a bonus. No matter. When Richie rolled back into a kitchen where he could put down roots, Eli would be confidently assured of a diet that satisfied.

Everything comes around, he thought. *The more things change, the more they stay the same, except when they don't. And then, sometimes, they get better.*

Zane waited for him upstairs in the old apartment, where they'd spent more nights in the past month than their house in the suburbs, but Eli loitered on the curb until the taxi had collected Holly and Diana, sweeping them back into their own lives and the fold at Immaculate Grace. He wouldn't work there again himself. Human Resources had yet to give him a call. Would have crushed him, once upon a time.

But even as the thought crossed his mind, the awning over the new clinic snapped briskly in the evening breeze. Eli tipped it a salute and grinned as broadly as Holly had. As broadly as Diana, even. Tradeoffs. Trade-ups. All worth it.

Worth everything he'd paid to get his hands on them.

He took the stairs one at a time, instead of two or three, but his feet carried him back up to his second home, and Zane, his second chance at the good life.

* * *

Zane had planted himself by the kitchen cabinets, digging through soup cans and frowning at the nutritional information, muttering to himself. "*How much sodium? Good God. No wonder it lasts forever.*"

Eli stood in the doorway for a moment, enjoying the view, before saying, "I'm not sure food preservation works that way anymore."

"Doesn't it? People used to store fish and pork in salt back in the old days. Ah well." Zane swept a handful of cans to the side. "It's all going. Sorry. Farewell, oxtail."

Eli snorted. "No problem. Holly's found us a new hangout. Macrobiotics, yum-yum."

"Something to look forward to." Zane slipped off the pair of reading glasses he'd finally given into getting, and tucked them in his pocket. Gray hair or not, he grinned like a boy when he looked back at Eli. "Hello, you. Everyone get away with no trouble?"

"Safe and sound," Eli murmured, paying less attention to the words emerging from his mouth and far more to the man in front of him. Zane looked better these days too. He had good color in his cheeks and a spring in his step. And, Eli couldn't help but notice, newsprint smeared on his fingertips. Eli took and lifted Zane's hand to be sure of it. "Going through the cabinets, he said. Nothing else, he said."

Zane ducked his head, half-sheepish and half-amused. The classic *okay, you caught me.* "So I was reading it again." He pushed a folded newspaper quarter across the kitchen counter to Eli, who caught the section neatly.

Eli had put those folds in the local business section with his own hands, framing up the article about their new clinic front and center. A wallet-sized photo of himself and Zane took pride of place in his amateur origami. They stood side by side, squinting at the camera in the bright light of early morning dawning over the streets, with the clinic awning in the background.

It was, to be frank, one of the least flattering photos of himself Eli had ever seen. He had a face on him longer than a plank, and one of Zane's eyes was crossed.

The worst picture, and the very best.

"Life partners Dr. Jameson and Dr. Novia," he read out loud, tracing the text beneath the picture. "Clinic for low income... to be listed as a safe haven... gay and lesbian friendly." He gave the paper as crisp a shake as one could after so much handling. It waved rather than crackled. Himself and Zane, in print. Out and proud. The look on Zane's face when he'd first seen it... well. Eli savored the memory as much as the article.

"Not bad, eh?" he asked, sounding gruffer than he'd meant to.

No worries. With Zane back in top form, he could be trusted to interpret the difference between what Eli meant and what Eli said. "Not bad, he asks?" Zane's broad grin lingered as he slipped his arm around Eli's waist. He lifted his head to bump his nose against Eli's chin. Not quite a kiss. More like a promise. "Come here, you. I'll show you 'not bad.'"

Eli would hope that kissing Zane never got old, but honestly, he didn't think it ever could. Zane hummed softly as Eli brought their mouths together, soft and hard, sweet and firm, giving and taking and getting in return. Zane slipped both hands beneath Eli's shirt at the back to lazily stroke from shoulder blades to small and down to his ass.

He cupped both cheeks and hung on as Eli took charge of the kiss, breaking it into small bites, then taking Zane by the nape and going for a new record. He held Zane loosely, where Zane held him tightly. Their bodies were molded one against the other so that when Eli breathed, Zane's chest moved with his. *In. Out. Again. Good.* Better than good. Eli put both thumbs under Zane's jaw and changed the angle once again, wishing he could stay just there, just like that, all the livelong night.

The shirts, though. Those were getting in the way. They could go. Zane laughed as Eli impatiently tweaked his way through the buttons until he could push the pin-striped cotton off Zane's shoulders, but didn't laugh so hard he couldn't do his share of the lifting. As soon as Eli's brown tee cleared his head, Zane pressed his mouth to Eli's chest, over his heart. Eli hissed between his teeth and shoved his fingers through Zane's hair, to the back of his head, holding it in the cup of his palm.

"Ribs aren't sore, are they?" Zane asked, breath warm on Eli's skin. He blew a cool stream of air over the patch of hair dampened by his lips and tongue.

"Not too bad." Eli stroked the back of Zane's head. "I'll live."

He'd meant that as teasing -- just a throwaway comment -- but when Zane touched the tip of his tongue to one of the scars, he remembered that it wouldn't be a joke to Zane.

"I will live," he promised. "Good luck ever trying to stop me."

Zane's widest smile flashed out, like fireworks in a night sky. Whew. Good. "I'll hold you to that." He leaned back, trusting to the strength of Eli's arms to keep him from falling. As he did, the change in angle brought their hips into tighter alignment.

As Eli felt fairly sure he'd intended. Not much got past that one. And as for the rest of him...

Eli arched an eyebrow at the partly dreamy, partly wicked smile wreathing Zane's face. "Now there's a look I haven't seen in a while," he said through lips pleasantly a-tingle from kissing. Stubble burn warmed his cheeks and chin. "What kind of mischief are you planning?"

"Mischief, me?" Not even Zane could pull off innocence when half-naked and fully hard in Eli's arms. He hummed, eyes partly closed, and lowered his hands to take hold of Eli's hips. "I know what you're thinking. That you'd like to fuck me."

Eli whistled. He didn't think Zane minded being told -- or indeed, shown, with a nudge of the pelvis -- how the idea appealed.

"But," Zane went on, guiding Eli in to an easy sway almost like dancing, "I was thinking we might shake things up a bit, you and me. Thinking maybe tonight I'd be the one who fucked you, like I promised. *If* you're willing, then I'm able. And if you're able, then I'm willing." He kneaded Eli's ass lightly, firmly, the sweep of his hands coaxing and gentle. Good hands for a good man. "Are you?"

Eli could have answered the question with words. He chose instead to give his reply in the form of a kiss. And if his hands shook a little, well, that was fine. Zane understood his personal language.

He might be scared. He might be fucking terrified, in point of fact. *But,* he wasn't saying no, and he wasn't looking back. He'd take this last step, as long as it was Zane tied to him all the way across the finish line.

Zane nearly purred into Eli's mouth. Slowly -- but definitely, so definitely -- he turned the kiss on its head. Now he was the one who stood taller, and he was the one who turned Eli left or right. Whichever way he wanted Eli to go.

He moved them so that Eli's back rested against

the wall, holding him up, and kept Eli there until there was no choice but to stop for breath. Eli drew in a deep, lusty gulp of the cool summer evening and held it in his lungs until he grew dizzy all over again, and went back for more. His hands still jittered on Zane's bare shoulders, but that would pass. "In case you missed it, that was a yes."

Zane took Eli's hand and dropped a kiss on the back. He didn't look his age. He didn't look *any* age, actually. Just like himself, and the way he made Eli feel. Neither young nor old, but ageless. Beautiful.

"I didn't miss it," Zane said. Slowly, slower still, he clicked open the buckle of Eli's belt and drew the length of leather through the loops, and cast it aside. He was the one to step out of his jeans first, and to ease Eli's pressed khakis down his thighs. When he bent to nuzzle beneath Eli's ear, he took Eli's cock in hand, working it from hesitantly aroused to some place higher and better. Neither did he stop, not before he'd gotten Eli to a full stand, and he sighed with regret when he let go. "I won't hurt you."

"I know you won't," Eli replied. His voice was shredded like a guitar riff, rough and raspy and raw, but he kept his chin high. Even found a tilted smile. "And if you do, you'll fix it. So take me to bed, Doctor. Or do I have to write you a prescription?"

Taking Zane to bed, now that was familiar. Being taken *to* bed, a completely different story.

But not a bad one.

Zane lowered himself and Eli to the mattress without breaking stride. Give credit where credit was due -- the man had skills, and he'd tailored them well to fit the size and shape of their bodies together. He guided Eli without one stumble, or at least no stumbles Eli wasn't willing to overlook immediately. When he knocked their knees a touch too sharply together, the warmth of his hand was right there to rub away the sting, and when he pushed Eli onto his back, the weight and heat of his body was there to blanket Eli, to cover and surround him and to kiss him until the lights in the sky traded place with cool darkness.

"What do you want me to do?" he asked, trying and failing to grab hold of his thoughts. They ran away like kites, bright spots of color against the moon. "You've got the wheel. Drive."

Zane dropped his head briefly against Eli's chest. As hard as he'd gotten Eli, Eli thought Zane might just be harder. He remembered that feeling -- the first time -- like it was yesterday. What it was like not knowing if terror or hunger would rule the day.

Couldn't have that. Eli dealt Zane a firm slap to the ass and a shake on the shoulder. "Oh no you don't. You got me here. Drive it, I said. Drive it like you stole it."

"Oh my God, you idiot." Zane kissed Eli once more, as if for luck, but his grin was back to normal, and lights twinkled in his eyes when he came up for air. His hands were strong now. Confident. "On your hands and knees. I'd rather see your face, but --"

"Easier that way," Eli replied, bending his head in acknowledgment. "I remember."

Though he wasn't sure he'd have made the twist on his own. Lucky for him, Zane helped. He could have flopped like a starfish, and Zane would have been there, patient enough to mold and shape him just as he should be. Hands and knees it was, and it wasn't bad once he'd gotten there.

Zane had a deft touch with the slick. Not too much. Not too little. More than usual, for which Eli grunted his thanks. He'd done the fingers before. One at a time. Two. Enough to know the weird inverted tug by heart, and to breathe, and relax the tightening tension in his back and thighs. Zane never stopped stroking him once, hands gentle and quick over his chest and back, and neither did he cease to whisper calming, quieting things.

Eli looked back over his shoulder. Zane, layered on top of him, was close enough to kiss if he strained for it -- and so he did. "Now or never," he said, pushing back as best he could against the hardness of Zane's erect cock. "Go time."

Zane's look was better than a hundred *I love you's*.

At that angle, Eli felt it all. The stretch -- the burn -- natural enough. He breathed through his nose and refused to feel shame at his hard-on losing its edge. That was only natural too. Zane had to love it for a reason. He'd adjust.

Zane stopped when the wiry bush of his pubic hair snugged tight to Eli's ass. "Okay?" he asked, sounding winded. Startled. Deer in the headlights. Eli tried to look back and see but could only rely on his imagination. "God, please tell me you're okay. You feel so fucking good, Eli. God. I'd forgotten."

Eli shivered. He could still feel everything, but not quite as it had been before. Zane knew his trade, and it'd only been a dash of discomfort. Much better than he'd given Zane years before.

Thank God for experience. It changed, moment by moment -- too slowly to track by the second, but before too many of them fleeted past, the difference became appreciable. He breathed in through his nose and out through his mouth and found himself... smiling. Savagely smiling. Feeling like he'd run a race up a mountain.

One last breath, and Eli looked over his shoulder one more time. "You too. Fuck yes, you too. Go, Zane. Come on. Give me what you've got."

He didn't have to tell the man twice. Zane pressed a hot, sharp kiss to the back of Eli's neck and obeyed the orders he'd been given.

And Eli went with it. Adjusted, stroke by stroke. So gradually he wasn't sure when his cock started to show signs of interest again, but was ready to make a good handful for Zane when Zane reached around to take care of him.

He shifted his hips and caught his breath. "Holy --"

Zane laughed. "I know."

When he picked up speed, Eli rolled with him. Why had he waited for this? Such an idiot, but Zane loved him despite that. His cock slid slick and thick through the circle of Zane's fingers, and he was -- he was --

Eli groaned and thudded his head to the bed when he came, stomach drawn up in a spiky knot that shuddered through the rise, rush, and fall of release. Hit him like a baseball bat. *Home run. Good God.*

"*Eli,*" Zane said, out of breath. "If you could see yourself…"

That would have made a hell of a picture, wouldn't it? Eli could bring it to mind just fine. He chortled choppily, under and over the sound of skin slapping against skin, Zane galloping forward in search of his own peak. Though he hadn't thought he'd be capable, hammered as he was and still jolting with aftershocks, Eli did what he could. Gave Zane the hand he needed to cross the finish line and was strong enough for Zane to drop all his weight against in the seconds following.

He winced, but only for a second, when Zane eased himself out. "Okay?" he asked, rubbing his knuckles over Eli's hip.

"Okay, he asks?" Eli pretended disbelief. "Such a question. What do you think? Am I okay?"

Zane's laugh bubbled up. "You look like you've just won the Indy 500. The grin on you would light up Manhattan."

"Funny man." Eli let Zane guide him again, rolling him to his side, and made room for Zane to lie down beside him.

He thumbed Zane's jaw and touched the point of Zane's chin with his fingertips, airy and teasing. He could tease. He *was* okay. Better than. Sore? Yes. Worth it, though, and he'd do it again. Hell, he *would* do it again. Just give him a chance to rest. He knew Zane understood that without being told.

Such things happened when a man fell in love.

Zane's gray eyes shone like stars, and if Eli looked pleased, he knew it was nothing compared to the happiness written across the face of the man he meant to spend the rest of his life with. "Good," Zane said simply. "Then that's all I could have hoped for."

"Maybe an encore…" Eli suggested.

Zane's smile broadened. "Maybe so. Lives are like stories, you know? There's always another page to turn, and a good thing too." He kissed Eli lightly.

Eli returned the kiss with interest. "I'll take you up on that," he said. "Tomorrow."

"It's a date. See you in the morning." Zane found a blanket that'd been kicked to the floor, and drew the comforting knitted cashmere carelessly over them. He yawned and rested his head against Eli's shoulder. "In the morning…"

And all the mornings for the rest of our lives, Eli

thought with satisfaction as he tucked himself down to sleep, mess be damned. *All the mornings. Always. Right and tight and bent* just *so.*

That's the kind of story I like best.

Will Okati

A storyteller and a sewist, Will Okati has lived through a few *Interesting Times* but come out the other side ready to roll. Looking for them? Look for a keyboard or a vintage Singer. They'll be there. They're most often accompanied by their beloved pair of orange-flavored felines: Hobbit (toothless, sweet) and Onion (spicy, known to bounce off the literal ceiling in pursuit of a ladybug).

Will likes to say still waters run deeper than anyone knows, and life -- like storytelling -- is always a work in progress.

Will at Changeling Press: changelingpress.com/will-okati-a-213